BLACK SCORPION

The Tyrant Reborn

A NOVEL OF FABRIZIO BOCCARDI'S
BESTSELLING CHARACTER
THE TYRANT™

JON LAND

A TOM DOHERTY ASSOCIATES BOOK
NEW YORK

This is a work of fiction. All of the characters, organizations, and events portrayed in this novel are either products of the author's imagination or are used fictitiously.

BLACK SCORPION: THE TYRANT REBORN

Copyright © 2015 by King Midas World Entertainment, Inc.

A Forge Book
Published by Tom Doherty Associates, LLC
175 Fifth Avenue
New York, NY 10010

www.tor-forge.com

Forge® is a registered trademark of Tom Doherty Associates, LLC.

ISBN 978-0-7653-7091-4

Our books may be purchased in bulk for promotional, educational, or business use. Please contact your local bookseller or the Macmillan Corporate and Premium Sales Department at (800) 221-7945, extension 5442, or by e-mail at MacmillanSpecialMarkets@macmillan.com.

First Edition: April 2015
First Mass Market Edition: January 2016

Printed in the United States of America

0 9 8 7 6 5 4 3 2 1

OTHER BOOKS BY JON LAND

*Published by Forge Books

For Tom Doherty. Again.

ACKNOWLEDGMENTS

I'm back with you faster this time, as Caitlin Strong takes a break to let Michael Tiranno return to center stage. Before we start, though, I need to give some much-deserved shout-outs to those who make all this possible.

Stop me if you've heard this before, but let's start at the top with my publisher Tom Doherty and Forge's associate publisher Linda Quinton, dear friends who publish books "the way they should be published," to quote my late agent, the legendary Toni Mendez. Paul Stevens, Karen Lovell, Patty Garcia, and especially Natalia Aponte are there for me at every turn. Natalia's a brilliant editor and friend who never ceases to amaze me with her sensitivity and genius. Editing may be a lost art, but not here, and I think you'll enjoy all of my books, including this one, much more as a result.

Some new names to thank this time out, starting with Todd Lyle and Bob Coppedge, tech experts extraordinaire who were able to help me make sense of the villain's typically dastardly plot. It's always a challenge to come up with new means for bad guys to achieve their nefarious ends, but thanks to Todd and Bob, I think we came up with something special, and scary, here. Todd also shared his military special ops expertise with me to help iron out scenes that are so much better thanks to him. Nick Norocea, father of my Brown football mentee Alex, helped me get things right about his native Romania. And I'd be remiss if I didn't salute the creative inspiration and vision of Fabrizio Boccardi, the man who conceived the Tyrant and sweated out each and every page of this one with me to assure you get your money's worth.

Check back at www.jonlandbooks.com for updates or to drop me a line. Always love hearing from you. For those who miss Caitlin, rest assured she'll be back next fall in *Strong Light of Day*. But trust me when I tell you that if you haven't met Michael Tiranno before, you're in for a real treat. Had a blast writing his latest adventure and have a sense you'll have just as much fun reading it. As a matter of fact, let's make that a promise. Hey, would I lie to you? Only one way to find out, and that's to turn the page so we can begin.

Nearly all men can stand adversity,
but if you want to test a man's character,
give him power.

Abraham Lincoln

PART ONE

BEFORE

*Though wisdom cannot be gotten for gold,
still less can it be gotten without it.*

Samuel Butler

ONE

"They come, oh great King."

Solomon, weary and weak from going so long without rest, leaned heavily on the shoulder of his son as he emerged from inside his goat-hair tent. Already he and his private guard had fought off two ambushes. Bandits appeared to be to blame, but Solomon suspected otherwise given their weaponry, skill, and the fact that they hadn't fled when confronted.

Now his heart pounded with anticipation, but also with fear, in the night's heat. He was so close now, so close to fulfilling the destiny shaped by his father, the great King David. And that reality filled him with the awesome scope of the responsibility before him, along with the price of failure.

He could not fail. The fate of his kingdom was at stake.

Solomon cast his gaze down the road to see a single wagon kicking up a dust cloud in its wake. Traveling under cover of darkness greatly lessened the threat of a raid by bandits and, in any event, at first sight the wagon seemed to be carrying nothing more than a farmer's crops being taken to the open market in Jerusalem.

Solomon peeled back his beggar's hood to reveal long locks of shiny brown hair and finely etched features that looked chiseled onto his face. He'd just nodded off, dreaming of Jerusalem, imagining the lanterns lighting the city twinkling in the night, when the captain of his private guard alerted him to the wagon's coming.

Solomon eased his hand from the shoulder of his fifteen-year-old son Rehoboam as the wagon drew closer, so the boy wouldn't feel him stiffen. "Keep a keen eye, my son, for our enemies are everywhere."

"Father?" the boy said, sliding a hand to the knife Solomon had presented him on the occasion of his bar mitzvah. He was small for his age and a bit frail. But, as heir to the kingdom of Israel, he needed to be part of such a vital mission, no matter how perilous.

"They would seek to destroy this symbol of our people and the foundation of our future. With our temple complete, we have safe refuge for it at last."

The Temple of Solomon had taken nearly eight years to build, requiring men and materials the likes of which had never been seen before in the known world. A staggering two hundred thousand workers had ultimately played a part in its construction, milled from vast quantities of local stone and imported cedar wood. It was a sprawling, palatial structure, perhaps the greatest ever erected—and with good reason, since it would be housing the vast stores of priceless treasures amassed by the Jewish people through time. What Solomon had kept secret from all but his most trusted cadre was the construction of a special chamber within the temple called *Kodesh Hakodashim*, or Holy of Holies. This would house the ark of the covenant, containing the remains of the stone tablets that held the actual Ten Commandments, along with the contents carried in the rear of the simple farmer's wagon approaching now.

It drew close enough to reveal the snorting of the horses and pounding of their hooves atop the roadbed that was dry and cracking from the long drought Solomon took for God's impatience. And, as if to reinforce that belief, he felt the first trickle of raindrops and took this as a good omen, until thunder rumbled in the distance and it became something much different.

A warning.

"Benaiah!" he called to his most trusted advisor, the wagon slowing to a halt before his party now. "Deploy the—"

Too late! Solomon realized, as arrows split the night, taking down two of his guards. The cloaked figures, dark everywhere with scarves pulled over their faces, rushed them from both sides of the road at once, shrieking and bellowing with swords drawn. More arrows split the air, scattering Solomon's outnumbered forces.

Until two dozen riders broke from the cover of darkness and surged onto the scene. The attacking forces hesitated just long enough for Solomon, Benaiah, and the members of the king's private guard to whip out their swords, seizing the offensive.

"The tent!" he ordered Rehoboam, shoving the boy that way.

Rehoboam stiffened, hand straying to the hilt of his sheathed knife. "But, Father, I want to fi—"

"Now!"

The boy scampered away through the rain that had begun to tumble from the sky in waves, swiftly turning the ground to mud. Solomon sloshed through it, sweeping his sword toward any enemy target it could reach. He fought to keep his breath as he split one man's thorax with a thrust and cut another's throat with a whistling slice through the air. He saw a few of the enemy, enough, break through the lines and rush the wagon through his troops, lost in the intensity of battle further complicated by the night and the sudden storm.

With only a quartet of his men left to defend the wagon, Solomon slipped through the carnage of flying limbs and blood mixing with the rain, sword whirling like a wheel to clear his path. He caught two of the enemy rushing the wagon and cut them down from behind when they neared the horses. A third turned to confront him and Solomon unleashed a vicious strike from the side that lopped off his head. By then, though, six more of the enemy had reached the wagon, too many for his guards there to put down.

Solomon rushed to save his destiny, his people's destiny, a desperate cry freezing him in his tracks.

"Father!"

He swung to see Rehoboam in the grasp of one of the enemy soldiers, struggling as the man drew him from the tent with one hand, ready to use his sword with the other. If he moved now, he might be able to save the boy. But the wagon was closer, its desperately vital contents in jeopardy as well.

Solomon turned from his son and his cries and, letting out a scream that pierced the night, surged on. Unleashing a fury when he reached the wagon that reddened the rain and soaked the rags he wore for disguise in both blood and entrails. The smell of it remained thick in the air, the guards who'd stayed with the wagon and those who sought to steal its contents all dead by the time Solomon sank to his knees in the mud, feeling Benaiah jerk him back to his feet.

"It's over, my King. We killed most, chased the others off."

"Rehoboam," Solomon remembered, turning toward the tent breathless.

The boy was kneeling over the body of his attacker, as the rain washed the last of the blood off the blade of his knife. Solomon rushed back to the heir to his crown and took the boy in his arms.

"We live, my son," he said over the boy's sobs. "Now, come with me so you may see what nearly cost us our lives."

He wrapped an arm around his son's trembling shoulders and led him toward the wagon. Rehoboam's shaking had stilled a bit by the time they reached it, Solomon easing back the animal skin covering the rear.

"Behold the most divine symbol of our people."

The boy's eyes widened, his face glistening in the glow emanating from the contents. The horses neighed, kicking at the ground as if suddenly agitated and unsettled.

"Father, is it . . ."

"A gift from God Himself, providing we prove ourselves worthy of it."

Rehoboam stretched a hand out into the glow, but the king covered the wagon again before he could get any closer. He eased his son away, surveying the carnage left behind by the battle and laying a hand lightly upon Rehoboam's head.

"Let the blood spilled this night remind you always of the great responsibility you bear for securing the future of the people of Israel, for you are truly a man now worthy of that," Solomon resumed, picturing the wagon's contents once more in his mind. "And whoever holds this treasure in his hand holds the power of God as well."

TWO

ROME, 47 BC

"Hail, Caesar! Hail Caesar! Hail Caesar!"

The chants came from both sides of the streets, Caesar himself acknowledging them with waves from the head of the military procession that seemed to stretch forever, covering the entire length of his vast legions. After a military campaign that lasted nearly ten years in conquering Gaul, he'd then crossed the Rubicon River en route to an even greater triumph in the civil war that propelled him to power.

Now he basked in the glory of that triumph, beloved by his people and destined to achieve even more glory for himself and Rome.

"Hail, Caesar! Hail Caesar! Hail Caesar!"

The streets were a sea of people roaring and cheering, thrusting their own hands into the air to mimic the swords held high overhead by the soldiers who'd delivered an unprecedented string of victories for their leader. Those swords reflected the midday sun in blinding fashion, stretching so far along the streets of Rome that it seemed as if the procession was being smiled upon by the Gods themselves all the way to the Roman senate. The admiration and devotion shown by his people validated the sense of power that filled Caesar and affirmed the destiny he felt was his to achieve, as he squeezed the golden medallion that hung outside his robes. An ancient relic that was more than just a keepsake or talisman.

Much more.

"Greetings, my friends."

Gaius Julius Caesar, his position as dictator recently secured and approaching the height of his power, entered the room through majestic double doors opened by his helmeted centurions. Immediately the dozen men gathered, mostly strangers to each other until that evening, abandoned the wine and fruit they'd been served, and moved to greet the most powerful man in the world with proper reverence.

In an uncharacteristic show of humility, Caesar waved them off and beckoned them back to their seats and refreshments.

"Please," he said, "partake of my hospitality."

Taking a seat so they'd be comfortable doing the same, Caesar addressed the men he'd summoned here. They were not soldiers or senators, but scribes and scholars. Men hardly used to a royal audience, much less one before Caesar himself.

"You've heard the tales of my victories in battle, in Gaul and beyond," he began, rotating his guise from man to man. "You've heard how I refused to accept submission and chose to subject Rome to civil war in order that the empire might be saved. You've seen since I took control how Rome has expanded its power and how its people have never been better served. I've called you here tonight to undertake a mission vital to the Republic, so its future may not just be preserved, but enhanced to a level never seen by the Gods.

"For the mission you are to embark on may bring you face-to-face with those Gods themselves," Caesar finished.

And with that he eased the golden medallion from beneath his robes, displaying it in hand as he moved about the men for all to see.

"I took this relic off Cilician pirates when I was a consul after they kidnapped me a second time. They thought they were saving their lives," he said, smirking, "but they only bought a quicker death." The smirk vanished, replaced by an icy stare he rotated about the room. "The same fate that awaits any of you who betray my confidence and my trust. Speak out of turn of what you are to learn tonight and afterward, and you will pay with your lives as well as the lives of your families. Any man among you unable to accept such conditions and unwilling to swear such an oath should leave now."

Caesar stopped, waiting to see if any the men he'd chosen for this mission rose. They stiffened to a man, but not a single one so much as moved.

"We are honored by your trust in us, sire," one of the men said, and all the others nodded.

"Very well then," he told them, satisfied as he let the relic dangle over his robes again. "Let us continue. I fully believe this medallion begot the victories I've won and achievements I've made, the power I've gained and expanded. I bring you here before me to form a secret order of loyalists that will travel under the royal seal of Caesar. You will leave tonight, under cloak of darkness with my royal guard, without returning to your families or the lives you will be leaving behind. Your mission, to be undertaken at all and any costs including your very lives in service to mighty Rome and the Republic, is to uncover the origins of this relic. And you will not return until your purpose is fulfilled, no matter how long that quest takes, lest you risk my wrath by failing in your mission, equal to treason for which you will suffer the pain all enemies of Rome have known and will know. And your mission shall continue until such time as you find the answers that you are not to return to Rome without."

Caesar stopped and met each and every one of the men's suddenly apprehensive and fearful gazes before resuming.

"For glory, for Rome. *Curate ut valeatis. Di vos incolumes custodiant,*" he finished. "Take care that you fare well and may the Gods guard your safety."

THREE

SIBERIA, FOUR YEARS AGO

The rumbling shook the snow from the trees, the ice of the frozen inlet quaking and then beginning to crack. The waters draining off the Bering Sea had been frozen for months already, which didn't stop the Yupik, as Siberian Eskimos were known, from fishing the inlet through holes carved in the thick ice. With the worst of winter fast approaching, they needed to stockpile as much food as possible, the portent for this winter especially harsh.

This region was no stranger to earthquakes, so the Yupik fishermen thought nothing of the rumbling until the center of the inlet burst open in a hail of frigid froth. The fishermen scattered, leaving their poles and lures behind to watch something crash through the ice. When the cold mist, laden with chunks of shattered ice, cleared, they saw an oblong obelisk that looked otherworldly until the top popped open and the first of the gunmen climbed out.

Standing on the fractured ice alongside the submarine's conning tower, the woman supervised the process of the snowmobiles being off-loaded: A dozen of them, sized to carry two men each. Their fuel tanks, too, needed to be adapted to be able to manage the journey to and from their target. No easy task in the deteriorating conditions, especially when figuring the likelihood of mechanical breakdown.

"There's a storm coming," a native scout who knew this region better than any of them told the woman from alongside her.

"Good."

"Good?"

"Better to disguise our approach to the prison."

The guards at Koryak Prison saw the storm coming as a vast white wall on the horizon. The wind pushed an ice mist forward ahead of it, a crystal-laden fog that sped across the white land like a rolling ball.

"Shit," said one of the guards in the east tower, shivering from the cold. The tower's internal heating system had failed months before and the space heaters allocated to provide heat in its stead kept blowing fuses in the ancient facility.

The world believed this infamous Soviet-era gulag to have been closed a generation before, an obsolete relic of the

Cold War and nothing more. The atrocities that had taken place within these walls were little known beyond them, since so few ever imprisoned here survived to tell of the tale.

"What's that?" the second guard in the east tower raised.

"What's what?"

"There's something moving in the ice mist."

The second guard raised the binoculars in his gloved hands to his eyes, but pulled the frigid plastic from his flesh at first touch. "I'm too cold to care."

Those were his last words before a bullet pierced his forehead dead center. He fell toward the other guard who reached out to grab him when a bullet caught him in the identical spot.

There were only sixty-three forgotten men currently imprisoned at Koryak, a facility capable of handling ten times that number. As a result, security had gone lax and those serving out their enlistments here passed the time struggling to play cards from within bulky gloves while bundled up in three or four layers of clothing. Indeed, there was little to "secure" when the bulk of the sixty-three prisoners were old, infirm, weak, or some combination of the three. Koryak didn't seem a gulag notorious for its brutality any longer, so much as a rest home for the forgotten. And those charged with guarding it believed the facility's secretive nature, along with its distance from anything even approaching civilization, made for the best security of all. No roads whatsoever led to the complex and helicopters had trouble managing the region's winds in the best of conditions, never mind ones like these.

The recreation room overlooked the front of the prison complex awash in a thick ice mist, before bright orange flashes flared amid it. The soldiers saw the flashes an instant before the explosive percussion burned the air and blew out a measure of the room's glass. A brief wave of heat comforted the soldiers before a frigid blast of air surged inward, just ahead of the combination of shrapnel and ruptured glass tearing them apart.

The woman yanked off the full-face Nomex mask that had protected her from the cold as well as from witnesses and security cameras. A shock of jet-black hair tumbled out, making her green eyes look even more vibrant, so piercing and intense in moments as focused as this that it was difficult to meet them. She led the gunmen down the halls streaked with grime and peeling paint, encountering little resistance along the way until they reached the final fortified checkpoint set before the lone cellblock in use.

"RPGs!" the woman ordered.

Three of her men unshouldered and fired the weapons in rapid succession, obliterating the security station in a mass of twisted steel and shattered glass. The woman led her men over that and the bodies of the guards within, surging on toward the wing's command center.

"Pomogite, nas atakuyut!"

She heard the desperate call that the prison was under attack, screamed by one guard into an old-fashioned shortwave radio, as two more braced themselves before a door barricaded with desk, chairs, and filing cabinets. The woman signaled her men to take cover.

"Use your fire to distract them," she ordered, and heard their gunfire ring out immediately, while she looped around to the command center's lone interior window.

"Pomogite, nas—"

The woman shot the guard operating the radio through it first, then the other two men in rapid succession, never once considering how exposed she'd been herself in the process. Once inside the command center, she yanked a heavy lever sideways to mechanically unlock all the doors in the cellblock beyond and shot out the radio, just in case.

From there, the woman headed down a set of rusted steel stairs to the block and straight to the seventh cell down an endless aisle. The first thing she saw was an interconnected series of landscape drawings that made it look as if the blank cell walls actually formed an expansive picture window offering a majestic view of a pristine landscape beyond. The next thing she noticed was an old man with long gray hair and beard adding to them in deliberate, painstaking fashion with what looked like children's crayons.

"Professor Taupmann?"

The old man continued his drawing, either ignoring or not hearing her call.

"Professor Taupmann," she said louder.

He turned finally, regarding her with a start and then squinting. "Did you find my glasses?"

"Come with me, Professor."

The old man smeared the collection of colors staining his hands onto his drab, worn prison uniform. "Because I need my glasses. I can't read without my glasses."

The woman yanked the cell door open. "We need to go."

He narrowed his gaze. "You're a woman," he said, as if realizing it for the first time.

"Please, Professor. Now."

"Oh, I can't leave," he said quite calmly, unmoved by her presence. "I'm a prisoner."

"Not anymore, Professor," Raven Khan told him, moving a pair of glasses resting atop his head to the bridge of his nose. "There's someone who very much wants to meet with you."

FOUR

The young American woman moved about Weavers' Road amid the old shops that filled the landscape. Most knew her as Amanda, but she always thought of herself as "Manda," from her younger sister's inability to pronounce her name properly as a toddler. *Manda* had stuck, inevitably drawing a smile when she thought back to those happy, simple times that had spawned it.

But not today. Today nothing could make Manda smile, as she traced her way amid the shops and kiosks stacked high with fabrics, hand-woven carpets, and leather goods. The awkward route she'd traced through alleys and along less traveled side streets pressed up against the façades of buildings had left her already torn clothes even more tattered. The blood from scrapes on her arms and face was fresh, but not the swollen, yellowing bruises that persisted long after the beatings had ended.

Where am I?

This surely wasn't any city in America and Manda had traveled far too little in her life to recognize it from the geography or architecture. It took a sign over some kind of municipal building to tell her she was in Ankara.

Turkey, then. The men who'd abducted her had taken her all the way to Turkey.

Barely an hour before, she'd managed to escape her captors here—the brutal, foul-smelling men to whom Manda had been turned over. Her last memory of freedom was a champagne toast with the dashing playboy she'd met while performing at the Seven Sins Resort's *Cirque du Soleil* show called Elysium on the Las Vegas Strip. She'd been putting her gymnastic abilities to great use, was actually hanging upside down the first time she spotted him staring and smiling at her from his front row seat. He was there again at the following night's show after which there was a note from him waiting in her dressing room.

He claimed to be from Russia and swept Manda off her feet. The best restaurants, shopping, front row seats at the biggest shows in town. One glorious week later, she put in for her vacation time in order to take a surprise trip he'd planned for them. She remembered toasting their trip with champagne aboard his private jet, vaguely recalled the flute slipping from her hand.

Manda awakened some indistinguishable time later in a windowless suite fit for a queen where a man she bore only vague memories of took her repeatedly. The suite had a view facing a sea, rich with pounding waves, she didn't recognize. During the day she'd listen to those waves and whatever sounds she could hear in search of clues for where she was. She knew they must have continued to drug her, and yet what little she recalled of the man himself was that he always took her by force, brutally from behind so she wouldn't be able to see his face. And the few glimpses she caught revealed a figure shrouded in darkness everywhere.

"What do you want from me?" Manda had wailed him at one point, finally finding her voice.

The man started away from her and kept walking, didn't even give her the courtesy of looking back before he shut the door behind him, leaving her to the darkness.

That very morning, following the first night in many the man didn't visit her, she managed to hold a noxiously sweet drink in her mouth long enough to spit it out without any of her captors noticing. They packed her into the back of a windowless van where she pretended to be as dazed as the preceding days that had stretched into weeks. And when the van door was thrust open, she burst out and bolted. Manda had barely stopped since fleeing an area close enough to the city's docks to smell the salty sea air.

Now that air was rich instead with the scents rising from the handbags, jackets, belts, and satchels that cluttered the scene. She slid through thin smoke wafting off grills that featured cooked meats, fish, and chicken, some already skewered and roasting on kabob spits. Antiques were featured among the quaint shops as well, along with all manner of jewelry, embroidered artwork, and flatware fashioned by coppersmiths who practiced their craft just as it had been done centuries before in old-fashioned fire-baked kilns.

Manda cocked a gaze to the rear again, conscious of any ripples in the crowd that might indicate the men after her were closing. No sign yet, but she couldn't let herself expect them to give themselves away.

"American Embassy," she said to a few passersby who looked friendly. "Can you tell me where I can find the American Embassy?"

A local man who spoke English finally noted her efforts and approached from the other side of the street.

"Atatürk Boulevard," he said, indicating the direction in which the embassy was located.

It turned out to be in another section of the city entirely, adding to her desperation made even worse by the need to constantly check around her on the chance she'd been followed or spotted. With no money for a cab, no money at all, Manda's best hope of reaching the embassy was the subway, where she could either sneak on or appeal to the mercy of another friendly stranger. Having no mastery or even familiarity with the language, she didn't dare try for a police station or even approach an officer if she spotted one. A few cruised by in boxy sedans with lights on top, and Manda resisted her initial instinct to flag one down.

The stranger who'd finally helped her also pointed her in the direction of the nearest station for the Ankara subway, known as the Ankaray. It was located not far from this ring of old shops, just up the road from a gate before which rested rolling carts selling figs, dried fruits, and spices, their fresh scents already replacing those of grilling meats and leather goods she'd left behind her.

Manda stopped, swung to check the street again.

Still nothing.

She picked up her pace slightly, passing through the assemblage of rolling pushcarts and stationary kiosks. The Ankaray stop seemed so far away, but then it was upon her, and Manda descended into the cool darkness down stone stairs toward the platform below. Clinging to the hope she had made it, believing her escape to be all but complete with the rest just a formality.

Almost to the bottom, though, she saw the gate was chained shut, the station beyond unexpectedly closed.

Manda rattled the chain and kicked at the fence in frustration, feeling trapped again, frightened that all the efforts that had led to escape from her own de facto prison had gone for naught. But she wasn't about to give up after coming so far, with so much at stake. Instead, she swung to remount the stairs and find an alternate route to the U.S. Embassy.

And saw a dark figure looming at the top, staring down at her.

Manda felt her insides gnarl and knot up. She tried to swallow but couldn't find enough breath to manage the effort. She was left with nothing, no way to leave even a signal of the truth, of what the world needed to hear, to know.

Unless . . .

Above her, the dark figure started down the stairs, his heavy boots clacking against the concrete. Manda needed a way, any way, to leave some hint, some clue that could alert someone to her plight, her identity. As the large figure dipped into the shadows, she tore the gold pendant—her lucky charm—from its chain. She had to do anything she could to prevent others from ending up as she had. With any luck, it would be enough to help catch the men behind this.

Manda stole one last look at the beautiful raised design finely emblazoned onto a subtle ridge in the pendant's center. Then she slipped it onto her tongue and found the breath she needed to swallow hard enough to push it down. The pendant scratched at her throat, almost forcing her to gag, but she resisted the reflex long enough for it to slide on and imagined she could feel the pendant plop into her stomach as the figure reached the bottom.

A sliver of sunlight revealed him, thankfully, to be a policeman. Dressed in a navy blue uniform, he eyed her coldly, suspiciously. Probably thought she was a prostitute about to turn a trick.

Manda was reaching out to touch the officer's shoulder, ready to plead with him in English, when he rammed a knife into her gut, twisting first to the side and then up. Amanda felt herself crumpling, felt her insides spilling. She was almost dead by the time she hit the cold concrete, lying at the police officer's feet. The last thing she felt was him ruffling through her pockets to make sure there was nothing on her person that might give away her identity.

Manda pictured the pendant she'd swallowed sitting in her stomach in the final moment before her eyes locked open.

PART TWO

NOW

I am not afraid of an army of lions led by a sheep;
I am afraid of an army of sheep led by a lion.

Alexander the Great

FIVE

LAS VEGAS, NEVADA

"If you could all come forward," began the auctioneer from beneath the covered porch, "we'll begin. I see a lot of familiar faces and the handout describes the procedure," he added, clearly impatient to get to his next location, "so I'm going to assume there are no questions. The starting bid is ten thousand dollars."

A bevy of hands, from virtually all of those gathered, shot up in the air, drawing catcalls from the protestors clustered on the sidewalk. All victims of the spate of foreclosures that had descended upon Las Vegas the last five years, a process further slowed by a severe backlog in the courts. A few of those protests at auctions like these had turned violent recently, leading to a police presence at all of them.

"Do I hear twenty thousand?" the auctioneer, a tall, thin man with dyed black hair matted to his scalp, continued.

A Hispanic couple stood off to the side. The man looking stiff and angry, his expression bent in a bitter scowl, seeming not to feel his wife pressed close against him fighting back tears.

The hands of about half those gathered before the modest sixteen-hundred-square-foot home on Pinecliff Drive eased upward. The home was well maintained but lacked landscaping atop its tiny yard. No garage, but there was a paved driveway where an overhang used to be until the owners removed it to make room for a basketball hoop for their sons. They'd bought at the peak of the housing boom, exceeding their means to make sure each of their boys had a bedroom to himself in a decent neighborhood, something they saw as crucial to the American Dream to which they were committed. They'd emigrated from Guatemala legally, became citizens, and found jobs in the hospitality industry that allowed them to make ends meet.

But only just.

So when the recession cost Imelda Marquez her job and her husband Juan his overtime, the struggles began. They cut back, found a way to survive until Juan was laid off, too. Odd jobs only carried so far and after countless rounds with the bank, loan modification specialists, and anyone else who'd speak to them, foreclosure had proven impossible to forestall and the auction had been scheduled for today.

"Do I hear sixty-five thousand?" the auctioneer announced, after checking his watch.

More of the crowd had peeled away at each ten thousand dollar increment until at sixty-five thousand only two active bidders remained. A pair of men sweating in their suits who represented a real estate investment trust, and a woman wearing a stylish Nicole Miller linen pants suit with white blouse and vest. The woman's dark Dior sunglasses covered part of her brow beneath a bird's nest of thick black hair and makeup so perfectly applied as to seem part of her skin. The woman stood with her back to the men from the trust that operated under several names to avoid scrutiny from local consumer groups and the kind of bad publicity its practices attracted. They had shaken their heads, faces wrinkling in displeasure when she strode onto the scene like it was some kind of red carpet event, paying them no heed whatsoever.

"Eighty thousand," the woman called out before the auctioneer could continue, turning toward the men representing the real estate trust for the first time. "We both know you're not authorized to go above seventy-five, so let's cut to the chase. See you soon."

"How many times does your boss plan on doing this?" one of them asked, brushing past her.

"As many times as you."

Once she'd initialed the preliminary paperwork and handed over a cashier's check in the amount of twenty thousand dollars, the woman walked right past the protestors, ignoring their heckles and taunts. She rounded the corner and veered toward a Lamborghini idling beneath the only trees on the street thick enough to offer any shade.

Naomi Burns made straight for the passenger side door and climbed inside the Tyrant Class model soon to go into production worldwide, already stripping off her wig.

"Another for your collection, Michael," she said to the man in the air-conditioned cool of the driver's seat, listening to the deceptively quiet purr of its V-12, seven hundred horsepower engine.

"You're getting very good at this, Naomi," Michael Tiranno said, grinning.

The economic downturn had hit Las Vegas especially hard, but he took great pride in the fact that he hadn't laid off a single worker at his Seven Sins Resort and Casino, not one. The accountants had been fond of telling him how much he was losing as a result. He countered by telling them how much he'd gain in the long run and, true to his prophecy, the Seven Sins was now the highest grossing property on the Strip. Everyone wanted to know how he'd managed it, against all odds, coming out of the worst economic times imaginable.

"Vision," Michael told them, not bothering to add how he thrived on adversity, able to win a hand against even a stacked deck.

"How much this time?" he asked Naomi, now CEO of King Midas World, parent company of the Seven Sins and all his gaming interests.

"Eighty thousand."

"A worthwhile investment."

"That's what you always say."

"Some things you can't put a price tag on."

"Does that include all forty-two homes you've purchased at auction?"

"It includes the forty-two families that still have a place to live," Michael reminded her, "forty-three now."

"One might say being a knight in Armani armor is bad for business."

"God works in mysterious ways and so do I," Michael said, smiling.

"Well, one might also say it's interesting that all the neighborhoods you're buying up are zoned for commercial as well as residential."

"It always pays to hedge our bets. You never know, Naomi." Michael threw open the Lamborghini's door and started to climb out. "Be right back."

"Better hurry, Michael," she said back to him, checking her Tyrant Class Samsung Note. "The press is already swarming back at the Seven Sins."

"That's right. The fight's tonight. I just remembered."

"I was hoping you'd forget," Naomi told him.

The protesters were already dispersing when Michael rounded the corner and headed toward an ancient pickup truck painted with dust, its cargo bed overflowing with the displaced family's possessions. A stubborn wheel kept spinning on a child's bicycle wedged over one side, and the rest of the contents had been hastily tied down by what looked like a clothesline straining to hold it all in place.

Inside the truck's cab, the Marquezes followed the man's approach with a mix of confusion and fear, figuring him for the person here to make sure they'd removed all their possessions from their former home.

"You can move back in tomorrow," Michael told them instead, taking off his TAG Heuer sunglasses.

Juan and Imelda could only look at each other, wondering if they'd heard him correctly. Their five-year-old son, seated in the middle, started tugging excitedly at them.

"I've also paid your storage bill, so they're ready to release the rest of your things," Michael continued. "Someone will be in touch with you about the details. I hold your mortgage now. You'll be making your payments to me."

The Marquezes swallowed hard, fearing what was coming next.

"Four hundred and fifty dollars a month," Michael said, quoting a price less than half of what they'd been paying before, "no money down. Does that work for you?"

The Marquezes couldn't stop nodding.

"Why do you do this, *señor*?" Juan asked him.

Michael reached inside, smiling reflectively as he patted the boy's head and then winked at him. "Because I know what it's like to lose a home."

SIX

LAS VEGAS, NEVADA

"Tyrant, Tyrant, Tyrant!"

The crowd's chant echoed in his head as Michael Tiranno strode up the aisle of the Seven Sins Casino's Magnum Arena. He gazed ahead at the steel cage in the center of the arena where a giant of a man was currently slapping himself in the chest. His thin gloves, standard issue for Mixed Martial Arts, or MMA, fighters made a hollow whapping sound, getting louder as the slaps became pounds beneath the bright lighting spilling down over the otherwise dark arena.

Durado Segura, better known as "the Executioner," was the reigning heavyweight champion who would be defending his title tomorrow night right here against the undefeated number one contender. Tonight was reserved for a charity "bout" between Michael and Segura with two thousand in attendance at a thousand dollars per head, the money going to one of the numerous efforts supported by Tyrant Entertainment, Tyrant Global, and King Midas World.

"You don't have to do this, Michael," Alexander Koursaris, his personal bodyguard and protector, had said as they made their way through an underwater tunnel that linked the arena to the hotel and casino via the resort's Daring Sea. A few of the marine environment's more curious deadly residents pressed up against the glass, seeming to study him. "You *shouldn't* do it."

"I feel like a clown in this outfit," Michael said, straightening his trunks. "But it's for charity, Alexander. And what's the harm?"

"Harm? Let's start with the risk you're taking by getting in the ring with this monster."

Alexander was every bit the match for Segura in a fair fight and then some. In fact, Michael reasoned, the Executioner would never have stood a chance against this man who'd survived the slums of Athens as a boy only because of his fists, further refining his trade in years of service with the French Foreign Legion where he became a legend.

"Anything for the right cause," Michael said, shrugging. "And this is the right cause."

"So long as your ticket to heaven doesn't come with a stop in the intensive care ward," Alexander warned. "Do I need to remind you that Segura once put a car lot owner through a windshield while filming a public service commercial?"

"Twice already was enough."

"Then what am I missing here? Please, tell me."

Michael thought back to his first meeting as a small boy in Sicily with Luciano Scaglione, the mafia don who'd raised him as his own son after the murder of his parents. How Don Luciano had knelt down before him and eased a notebook from one of his pants pockets. The notebook was covered in well-worn brown leather faded in patches. Inside, the edges of the pages had yellowed with age and featured tabs separating equal-size clumps into sections, seven of them.

"Do you know what sin is, Michele?"

"Something bad," Michael replied.

Don Luciano regarded Michael warmly, making him feel safe for the first time since the shots had rang out. "There are seven deadly sins and all men have committed more than their share of them, me more than most," he said, with some regret in his voice. Don Luciano fanned through the pages with a single hand, skirting over a number of entries to reveal plenty of blank pages waiting for more. "I keep a record of all my sins in this book—in my own special code, of course, that no one else can read. I file my sins away in the appropriate place, careful to note when and where each occurred and, on occasion, to whom. Do you know why I do this, *picciriddu*?"

Michael noticed there was writing on all seven of the tabs, dull and faded now, one for each of the seven sins.

"No, sir," he said.

"To remind myself of how many acts of goodness I must perform to atone for them. A man must achieve his own balance in life. This is how I keep mine."

———

Michael wanted to explain to Alexander how this exhibition bout was mostly about keeping his. Mostly. The rest was about truly wanting to face a man feared through the world of Mixed Martial Arts as a test of his own mettle. The cage was just another metaphorical ring in which to prove himself. But he had no intention of trying to articulate that to Alexander.

"Tell me again why Segura threw that car dealer through a windshield," he said to him instead.

"He said he didn't like the way the man was smiling at him." Alexander shook his head, gazed toward the caged ring. "Just know one thing, Michael: At the first sign of trouble, I'm going to intervene."

"You won't have to."

"Tyrant, Tyrant, Tyrant!"

The chanting grew even louder, as a "Tyrant Girl" named Kim, one of the resort's personal concierges, held the cage's door open so Michael could enter. He moved to his corner and found himself standing directly across from the undefeated champion, conscious of the flashes flaring in the murky half light beyond. He'd never been in any kind of ring before and was amazed at the sensory enhancement and deprivation it created at the same time. On the one hand, Michael was acutely aware of every stitch in the canvas fabric of the thinly padded ring beneath his bare feet, a bright shaft of light all that separated him from the man known as the Executioner sneering from the other side. On the other hand, the world seemed to end at the cage's perimeter, as if it were enclosed by one-way glass that allowed the crowd gathered at ringside to see in while Michael could not see out. The sense of isolation, the insular nature of the sport, gave Michael a fresh appreciation for the fighters who made their living being bloodied and battered by men like Segura.

It shouldn't have bothered him, given that his office in the Seven Sins was a bubble glass structure at the bottom of the Daring Sea, the world's largest self-contained marine environment and one of the resort's most popular attractions. Built at a cost of four hundred million dollars, the Daring Sea featured a trio of great white sharks prowling about. The largest of these, a thirty-footer named Assassino, had grown especially interested as of late in Michael's office, poking his nose against the thick glass and seeming to peer inward. Assassino meant "assassin" in Italian, Michael having named the creature in the wake of the deadly expedition to capture him that cost a trio of sailors their lives.

But Assassino had nothing on Durado Segura's glare from across the ring. Tomorrow night he would fight the challenger for the heavyweight crown in the most highly publicized MMA fight in the sport's history. An expected record number of five million fans watching on Pay-Per-View on top of a sold-out crowd of near twenty thousand here in the Seven Sins's Magnum Arena that would be transformed into a modern equivalent of the Roman Coliseum. For tonight's exhibition the two thousand attendees at ringside stood on their feet, ready to watch Michael spar with the champion and then attend a reception afterward featuring the two of them, along with a host of other celebrities and dignitaries.

Michael was still eyeing Segura warily, when the cage door opened and Kim and a second Tyrant Girl named Tess escorted famed ring announcer Michael Duffer inside, microphone in hand.

"Ladies and gentlemen," Duffer said, moving to center ring. "For the thousands in attendance tonight and the millions who'll be watching tomorrow . . . let's get ready to *raise moneeeeeeeeeyyyyyyyyyy!*"

The crowd went crazy, bobbing up and down on their feet, nothing more than dark opaque shapes to Michael.

From here, the script was clear. Segura was to chase Duffer from the cage, slam the door closed, and grab either Tyrant girl, Kim or Tess. Hoist her overhead, while he paraded around the ring accepting the cheers and accolades fitting for a world champion. Michael would make a show of pulling the woman away, usher her to safety and then engage in a one-round spirited exhibition with only light blows exchanged by the combatants.

"In the black corner, our challenger, with as much money as muscle and a mean streak that ensures what happens in Vegas, stays in Vegas. Ladies and gentlemen, Michael 'the Tyrant' Tirannnnnnnnnnnnnnnnnnnno!"

Michael was conscious of the roaring applause, but even more conscious of the Executioner's stare from across the ring.

"And in the red corner, weighing in at two hundred and sixty pounds of rock-hard muscle, standing all of six feet six inches tall. He is known and feared as the most dangerous man in the world. The undefeated and untied MMA champion of the world, Dorado 'the Executioner' Segurrr-rrrrrrrrra!"

Across the ring, Segura began parading about with hands raised triumphantly in the air, intense gaze rooted on Michael as he chased Duffer from the cage and slammed the door just as planned. Then, also as planned, he chased down the Tyrant girl named Kim and hoisted her effortlessly over his head. For some reason, the sight made Michael think of King Kong clutching the actress Fay Wray atop the Empire State Building, Kim looking like a toy in his grasp.

Until Segura threw her headlong through the air. Kim crashed hard into the steel cage directly over the entry door and fell hard to the canvas. She was bleeding from the nose, her eyes dimming as she clung to consciousness, pinning the sole access point to the ring closed.

Michael glimpsed Seven Sins security, led by Alexander,

charge the ring. Saw Segura's entourage moving to intercept them. Saw the Executioner himself moving to corner Tess, the second Tyrant girl, who hadn't followed Duffer from the ring as she was supposed to.

Michael felt something snap inside him. His focus intensified, his vision sharpened. The awareness that this had stopped being a game in that single, violent instant struck him hard and fast. He didn't welcome or not welcome it, didn't really think anything in that moment that seemed to freeze in time. There was only the hulking Segura moving toward Tess who was trapped in the cage.

Trapped . . .

It's just him and me, Michael thought.

His ears hummed with the assortment of crowd sounds, those gathered at ringside roaring and cheering Michael on in the belief this was all part of the show, the staging. The chants of *"Tyrant, Tyrant, Tyrant!"* resumed amid a sea of bright cell phone screens recording the scene and dotting the darkness with light, as Michael lurched into motion.

SEVEN

LAS VEGAS, NEVADA

"Sir? Your passport. Mr. Devereaux?"

Edward Devereaux finally swung back toward the polished mahogany desk inside the private VIP check-in lounge at the Seven Sins Resort and Casino, forgetting for a moment the guise he had taken for this trip.

"Merci," he said, taking his passport in hand.

"Would you like me to show you to your suite now, sir, or escort you to the casino?"

"Pardonne moi?"

"Due to a problem with your reservation, you've been upgraded to a Daring Sea suite. We're fully booked, but you'll be charged only the price of the posted rate of the room you reserved. And a Daring Sea suite entitles you to a personal concierge to handle every need of your trip from check-in to check-out."

Devereaux forced a smile, hating this chit-chat for the time wasted with distraction. At least inside this well-appointed VIP lounge he was out of view from the many roaming the lobby beyond. Lingering in one place too long left him open to scrutiny, the chance that someone might notice him, warned to expect his presence. He had taken a great risk by coming here. But the stakes called for it.

Justice called for it.

Devereaux had crossed through the sprawling lobby, mentally cataloguing the number and placement of hotel security personnel, each with a cord rising out of their suit collars connecting to a tiny bud in their ears. Security at the Seven Sins was legendarily tight and Devereaux had only recently begun to suspect why.

He'd read that every inch of the hotel had been designed to provide the desired effect for guests of moving from the mundane present into a majestic and ancient past offering the spirit of adventure, right from the moment they passed through the entrance. A forest of golden ionic columns greeted them, stretching upward from the black marble lobby floor adorned with live exotic flowers from the radiant golden iris to rare red poppies. The effect left Devereaux feeling he was standing not so much in a place, as a state of mind. And the state of mind of the Seven Sins conjured visions of glamour and dreams, where opulence and decadence somehow co-existed.

Devereaux had shaken himself from the trance and continued his scrutiny of the setting, forcing himself to view his surroundings in much more of a detached manner, not a typical guest. Because he was here on business, vital business. Not pleasure, not even close. Indeed, it was the pain suffered by others that had drawn him here.

As luck would have it, he'd now be staying in one of the Daring Sea suites erected on ten floors beneath ground level with one entire wall offering view into a massive underwater environment prowled by the only great white sharks to ever survive in captivity. One section of the lobby floor was glass as well, allowing strollers a clear view of marine life captured in a perfectly re-created ocean habitat. Those wishing a longer and better view of the great whites themselves need only wait in line to view "Red Water," an elegant and, for some, wicked spectacle of nature that encompassed the creatures' feeding time.

Devereaux found that to be an apt metaphor for what had drawn him here. Because he'd come to Las Vegas on the trail of a monster.

And he believed that trail led to the Seven Sins.

"One more thing, Mr. Devereaux," the concierge, Melissa, was saying from behind the desk.

"Yes?" he responded, trying not to sound nervous.

She slid a piece of paper toward him. "Here at the Seven Sins, five percent of the proceeds from your stay will be donated to charity. You can check one of those on this form or write a charity of your own choice below."

Devereaux took the page and grabbed a pen from a nearby resting place. "A wonderful gesture."

"Just the way we do business here. Mr. Tiranno believes everything is possible, including helping those in need dream as well."

"I couldn't agree more," Devereaux told her

Only my dream, he thought, *is to catch a monster.*

EIGHT

Michael's thoughts became a blur, swirling about, past and present becoming one. He felt detached from his body, as if he were standing outside himself viewing his own motions.

Tess, the second Tyrant Girl, had shrunk back against the rear of the cage, cowering when Segura reached out and grabbed her by the hair. The Executioner was grinning, as if he intended to make the second Tyrant Girl an offering to a crowd just starting to realize that things had veered off-script.

Segura yanked Tess toward him, twisting his hand to aim her face upward for the lights. He paid Michael no heed whatsoever, so his attack caught the giant utterly by surprise.

Holding the Tyrant girl by the hair had left Segura's arm bent awkwardly at the elbow, a weakness Michael exploited by looping in and around him. He clamped his right hand on the giant's wrist while jamming his left hand directly under Segura's elbow.

Then pushed down with his right.

And up with his left.

Segura's arm snapping at the elbow was as loud as a gunshot. His fingers jerked open, and Michael seized the opportunity to shove Tess protectively behind him.

The crowd roared its appreciation, loving the show, the spectacle.

Segura's eyes had filled with uncertainty, trepidation even, sweat coiling across his upper lip. The sensation of potential defeat, of being hurt the way he had hurt so many others, unsettled him to the point where Michael thought for a moment he might yield, give up the effort, then and there.

But just a moment.

Because the giant's eyes found Michael in their grasp and bulged with rage. The pain in his shattered elbow joint must've struck him in that very moment because he uttered an inhuman wail as he lurched across the ring. Michael left himself positioned to shield the second Tyrant girl, placing him at an odd angle to mount a defense. Still, he was able to deftly duck under a blow from Segura's good arm, never anticipating the blow from the giant's injured arm that followed immediately. It smashed Michael in the right shoulder, stunning him as he whirled away.

The crowd uttered a collective gasp, more murmurs rising through the clutter of faces continuing to grasp this wasn't a show at all.

Michael felt a stinging burst of pain and then a stiff numbness that made his arm drop like a lead weight hanging from his shoulder. The sense of it being detached from his body was no more than an illusion he fought through, aware that Segura was stalking him across the ring. Bouncing up and down on bare feet with both good arm and bad, incredibly, held up in a punching position. Rage filled his eyes and in that instant Michael understood all too well how Segura had managed to remain undefeated through so many bouts. There was something feral in his gaze that unleashed itself in the ring. Segura couldn't bear not to emerge the clear and dominant victor, even in a charity exhibition, unable to separate that out in the part of his brain that rendered him invincible in a title contest.

Michael moved about the ring in rhythm with the giant, shadowing his motions, dimly aware of the frames of Segura's entourage crumpling in Alexander's wake. Alexander now fighting to open the cage door still pinned by Kim's unconscious form. Beyond that, the dim lighting in the arena beyond turned the sea of faces into an endless mishmash of indiscernible features lost in a swirl of emotions.

Michael twisted away from a high snap kick that managed to clip his ear, stinging him with pain anew. A kick for the knee from the giant's other leg followed which Michael deflected. Segura followed up with a wild series of roundhouse blows Michael first parried, then countered with a quick flurry of strikes among feigned kicks to lure the giant to defend his lower half, shrinking his size in the process. The next moment found Michael behind the giant, lashing a kick to the back of his right knee, buckling it and then missing with a follow-up blow when Segura leaped into the air, spinning round to face him anew when he landed. He carried his broken arm stiff by his side, flexing the fingers to keep the blood flowing, and ready somehow to use it again if necessary.

Michael was not a mixed martial artist, nor a cage fighter. The self-defense techniques he'd learned in secret, being revealed to the world beyond Alexander for the first time, were bred for outlasting an opponent in the streets. Fights to the death inevitably about survival, not title belts. He knew success was not about thought, but instinct. Think and you're dead.

Feel, react, respond . . .

And that's what Michael did. He *felt* Segura launch himself into a bull rush a split instant before the giant dropped down. So, as Segura's huge arms moved to wrap Michael up, Michael had already clamped his hands over the giant's bald skull, fingers lacing together to bring his face down as Michael's knee came up.

Impact was stunning. Michael felt Segura's nose compress, bone shattering and cartilage cracking, behind a burst of blood that sprayed downward. Then, as Segura's head whiplashed back upward, Michael rode the momentum by taking hold of his already damaged arm and angling himself to cut the giant's legs out from under him. Michael had never practiced the move before, had never even seen the precise movement to mimic. Instinct had taken over, Michael reacting to a weakness gleaned from some primordial sense of thought normally foreign to civilized man. The world around him had slowed, everything crawling except his own motions. Sight sharpened. Sound vanished. Life unfolded in snippets held in memory as still shots.

One final knee launched upward against the side of the Executioner's skull.

Segura hitting the mat with enough force to rattle the cage.

The crowd going crazy, erupting in cheers and applause so loud Michael's ears bubbled.

"Tyrant, Tyrant, Tyrant!"

The chant resumed as Seven Sins security finally got the cage door open enough for Alexander to push himself through over the Tyrant Girl Kim's unconscious frame. He reached Michael just as he sank to his knees and the cheers hit a new crescendo.

"Tyrant, Tyrant, Tyrant!"

The crowd had leaped to its collective feet, especially the women rooting him on, a hero who'd vanquished a villain intending to do harm to innocents. The simplest of all stories, but also the most complex in his case for the pain that it carried and scars it had left inside him. Scars on the outside, the kind with which Dorado Segura was riddled, were nothing compared to those on the soul. Don Luciano had needed a notebook to remind him of his sins, but Michael needed no such ledger to remind him of his pain.

"Tyrant, Tyrant, Tyrant!"

NINE

Las Vegas, Nevada

Melissa escorted Devereaux toward the private bank of glass elevators reserved only for the underwater suites and extending ten levels down into the resort's Daring Sea.

"No other luggage?" she asked him.

"I travel light," he said, wheeling his two carry-ons with one attached to the top of the other.

They reached the three elevators serving the Daring Sea suites and Melissa pressed the single button, lighting it up.

"You're not claustrophobic, are you, sir?"

"Not at all. Is there something I should be concerned about?"

Melissa smiled. "Just a question we're required to ask. Here at the Seven Sins even an elevator ride is an experience."

It was indeed, Devereaux thought after the glass elevator began its slow descent into the Daring Sea. He might not have been claustrophobic, but there was something initially disconcerting about descending through water on all sides with tropical fish curving agilely around the glass. Imagine all this, in the middle of a *desert* yet! What kind of man could not only dream up such a thing, but also have the persistence and resources to make it a reality?

The kind of man I came here to find, Devereaux thought. And he found himself staring up through the compartment's glass ceiling, noticing a frothy red film descending beyond, that sent the fish fleeing.

"A unique view of Red Water, Mr. Devereaux," Melissa said, following his gaze.

"Red Water?"

"What we call feeding time for the resort's great white

sharks. The fish scattered because sometimes the refuse of the feeding means Assassino and his friends aren't far behind."

Suddenly the giant great white that drew tens of thousands of visitors to the Seven Sins on his own sped toward the elevator. Devereaux's breath bottlenecked in his throat, as the huge man-eater carved a thick swath through the water, coming straight for him and the glass before veering off at the very moment he was about to crash into it.

"Some of us actually believe Assassino has a sense of humor," Melissa told him, smiling, "that he likes playing with people, despite the three sailors who fell overboard during his capture and were killed. Mr. Tiranno spent a fortune on the expedition that took six weeks to catch him and destroyed two boats in the process."

Devereaux didn't ask her to elaborate further. He noticed the pendant, featuring the trademark crest of King Midas World and the Seven Sins, dangling from a chain around Melissa's neck.

"Lovely piece of jewelry," he raised, when she caught him staring at it.

"And part of the uniform," she said, forcing a smile that told Devereaux his gaze had lingered a bit too long.

He felt a *thunk* as the elevator stopped on the fourth underwater level. The elevator's glass door slid open and Melissa stood aside to allow Devereaux to pass.

"Right this way, sir."

Devereaux's Daring Sea suite was beyond anything he could imagine, and he counted himself fortunate that his original reservation had been lost.

Melissa held the door open for him as he entered the suite toting his carry-on bags. It was like stepping into a submarine, albeit an ultra-luxurious one, behind a heavy bulkhead-like door. The far wall was composed entirely of glass that, according to the Web site, comprised three separate layers joined by a special polymer.

The world beyond in the Daring Sea was rich in all manner of marine life, much of it swimming past for him to view. He'd read about guests lucky enough to win a free stay in one of these suites as part of the casino's "Spend a weekend with a great white" promotion. The lights in Devereaux's suite automatically snapped on when he entered. Melissa propped the door open and followed him inside.

"Is this really safe?" Devereaux asked, feeling weak over the need to pose such a question.

"Entirely, sir. And if you ever have a problem . . ."

Melissa waved a hand before an invisible sensor and, suddenly, one of the side walls brightened to life, much of it filled out by a wide screen television that was more like something from a movie theater.

"Hello, Melissa," a softly pleasant, female voice greeted.

"Hello, Angel. I'd like you to meet our guest Mr. Devereaux."

"Hello, Mr. Devereaux. How may I help make your stay an enjoyable one?"

Devereaux came up alongside Melissa, fascinated by the rainbow-like prism swirling around the Seven Sins's famed logo, the computer-generated voice seeming to emanate from within it.

"Angel serves as the resort's virtual concierge," Melissa explained.

"Thank you, Melissa. Mr. Devereaux, may I call you Edward?"

Devereaux found himself nodding at the wall. "Yes, Angel."

"Would you like a reservation in one of our restaurants or a show perhaps, Edward?"

Melissa looked toward Devereaux, beckoning for him to answer.

"No thank you, Angel."

"How about a seat at one of the gaming tables? You can even play from your room."

With that, the screen filled out with a shot of the casino floor, each table having been assigned a superimposed number. The screen rotated from the no-limit blackjack area to craps, roulette, baccarat, and the seemingly endless array of slot machines including those designed by Tyrant Gaming Technologies.

"Edward, just say the number of the table you wish to play at and I can either reserve you a seat or you can play right here from your room. The amount you wish to draw will be charged to your account and I can place all bets for you. Your room also comes with a Tyrant Class Samsung tablet, should you prefer to play that way, located on the desk. You'll find the casino level visible as your home screen as soon as you switch it on. Meanwhile, here are some chips to get you started."

The right-hand side of the screen flashed several fresh stacks of chips.

"Merely an example," Melissa explained. "Move your hand in front of them."

Devereaux did, curious and amazed at the same time, and watched one of the stacks topple.

"Here at the Seven Sins, a guest need not even leave his room, can actually be anywhere at all to enjoy the best gaming experience money can buy. Is there anything else I can assist you with?" Melissa asked him, but for a moment Devereaux thought it was still the virtual concierge talking.

"No, not right now."

"Well, if you need anything, you can either ask Angel or call me," she said, handing him a card. "That's my private number. Or just say my name and Angel will connect you to me directly. I'm available to assist you twenty-four hours a day."

"Thank you," Devereaux said, leading Melissa back to the door, eager for her to be gone.

Once he closed the door behind her, Devereaux found himself alone in the eerie translucence shed by the Daring Sea's underwater lanterns. He could actually imagine a guest entering such a suite and becoming so entrenched with the crystal clear view of marine life that he might barely leave it through his stay. But in Devereaux's mind, at least his imagination, it was the fish who were watching *him*, more curious about his presence than he was about theirs.

Maybe they sensed he hadn't come to Las Vegas to gamble, or see the shows, or enjoy the restaurants. He was not here for the glamour or the glitzy spectacle that had taken over the city, especially the Strip. He was not here for a giant killer shark or a ridiculously over-the-top resort casino. And the only dreaming and daring he'd done lately had been regarding his career, betting everything he had on a quest that had brought him here to Las Vegas on the trail of a monster.

His associates thought him mad for chasing a specter, a phantom, a ghost. A figure of myth and legend, known everywhere and nowhere at the same time. All-powerful and yet nonexistent, the stretch of his invisible web reaching across the world with no corner spared.

Devereaux unpacked his carry-on first, removing a laptop from a padded insert and then a larger black-handled case, the contents of which were more expensive than any car he'd ever owned. He switched on his laptop, entered his password, and opened the file he'd only recently titled "Tyrant."

Then he settled back and eased from his pocket a pendant that was identical to the one Melissa wore, the pendant all Tyrant Girls and other featured employees of the Seven Sins were given.

By Michael Tiranno himself, complete with his personal motto: *Somnia, Aude, Vince . . .*

Dream, Dare, Win.

If Devereaux's suspicions were correct, though, Michael Tiranno would not be doing any of those before too much longer.

TEN

RETEZAT MOUNTAINS, TRANSYLVANIA

Scarlett Swan was used to living in the dark, had come to embrace it for the mysteries it tried to hide in its grasp until she dug them out.

"I'm an archaeologist," she was fond of explaining. "What do you expect?"

Scarlett loved working alone, had always been pretty much a loner, just as her mother, a leftover hippie from the 1960s who'd had her at the age of forty-two, was. Hence, the name Scarlett, chosen because of her mother's obsession with the film *Gone with the Wind*. But none of that mattered while on a dig where Scarlett was concerned only with the mysteries she was unearthing. This dig in the Retezat Mountains of Romania's Transylvania region showed some promise, the region no stranger to discoveries dating back to the Roman Empire, like the one she'd come in search of.

Late that afternoon she'd busied herself with an initial inspection of the ground layered beneath the freshly excavated remains of an ancient Roman temple that was the site's principal find. Swiping a whisk broom across the flat ground revealed a slight depression, and further clearing revealed a limestone plate laid over what Scarlett assumed was a secret underground passageway, leading to and from the temple. Students rolled the mini-crane apparatus over to hoist the plate from its two-thousand-year-old perch, beneath which lay what she recognized as not a passageway at all, but a secret chamber. She could also tell that the chamber was positioned purposefully beneath the temple, making her think it had never been meant to be found.

Archaeologists digging here had been systematically uncovering an ancient Roman center that, during its heyday in the second century AD, commanded the countryside as the capital of the conquered Dacian provinces. After the Dacians were defeated in 106 AD by the forces of Trajan's legions, a city had been built upon the very location where a major battle between the Roman legions and the Dacian troops had taken place. And within that city, this temple and its surrounding monuments had risen, constructed of high quality limestone and marble, no expanse spared as testament to the ever-expanding Roman Empire.

Archaeological teams had been mining this site for finds for nearly a century now, starting in 1924 and continuing through today. Scarlett arrived on the scene with the full backing of her primary benefactor to find the site barely twenty percent exposed even after such a long period. Yet that in itself wasn't nearly as surprising as the secret chamber she'd uncovered beneath the ruins of the temple floor.

"We need to call in some experts," the project manager, Henri Bernard, said as they stood side by side looking down into the exposed chamber.

"I *am* an expert, Henri."

"I mean with real experience in such matters. Until then, I want nothing disturbed. The find is not to be touched at all. Is that clear?"

"You mean, *my* find?"

"No, I mean the *team*'s, the team I'm in charge of," Bernard reminded her.

Scarlett had never worked with Bernard before, had never

even met him until he was assigned to oversee this dig at the last minute as a condition set by Romania's Ministry of Culture. Having yet to publish a thesis to enable her to join the Register of Professional Archaeologists left Scarlett playing second fiddle to men like Bernard with considerably less experience in the field than she. Bureaucrats who often had their own ulterior motives, interested in claiming the credit more than anything else. Bernard, a professor of Archaeology at the Sorbonne in Paris, was well known to her by reputation, but he'd been dropped here out of nowhere. Enough alone to make her suspicious, even without considering his lack of field experience.

"You haven't answered my question yet," Bernard was saying.

"Which question is that?"

"Are my instructions clear enough?"

"Plenty. It's what's best for the dig, right? You'd never do anything that wasn't in the dig's best interests, would you, Henri?"

He checked his watch, suddenly reluctant to meet her gaze. "I've got some calls to make. Where's Francis? I want him to take charge in my absence."

"It's *Franklin*," Scarlett said, pointing over Bernard's shoulder, "and he's standing right behind you."

Late that night, with the camp utterly quiet and still, she slid out from her tent and took the darkest path to the chamber. There, Scarlett eased the tarpaulin covering the opening aside and climbed down the ladder already lowered into place under the light spilled from the dome lamp built into her dig helmet.

Once inside the chamber, she did her best to restrain her excitement to make sure she didn't make an amateurish mistake by rushing. Instead, she worked collapsed sections of the wall deliberately and painstakingly, using a simple trowel and an object not unlike an everyday dustpan and brush to clear the debris without missing a potential find. That process unearthed stones inlaid over the mortar forged from baked mud in a process the Romans were known to have mastered. Scarlett chipped away lightly with a hammer and chisel until she was able to pry the mortar away with her gloved hands to reveal what could only be a secret storage compartment measuring approximately two feet wide and a foot tall.

It had been beveled into the flat rock wall, perfectly symmetrical although she couldn't tell yet how deep into the stone it penetrated—what would have passed for a wall safe circa one hundred AD. The work was painstaking, methodical, and she loved it. There remained such a fine distinction between uncovering a find that could define her career and potentially damaging a fragile artifact buried here for nearly two thousand years. The work was that exacting and challenging.

Scarlett continued chipping away gingerly at the limestone façade inlaid with what looked gold dust for both appearance and structural integrity. Whoever had built this hold of sorts, judging by its layering, had intended its contents be concealed down here forever. That was what had her so excited. The vast bulk of finds recovered from archaeological digs were not hidden or squirreled away at all, but recovered from the ordinary nature of everyday life. Rarely did an archaeologist find something no one was ever meant to, and Scarlett had the very strong sense that was exactly what lay before her now.

It was pleasantly cool down here ten feet below ground level. Scarlett continued chipping, careful to use both her brush and small air gun to clear the dust and debris aside. Her helmet's dome lamp pushed out a focused beam on anything at which she aimed it.

Her toils finally revealed the rectangular chamber in its

entirety, stretching inward between eighteen inches and two feet to fill out the approximate dimensions of a modern-day safety deposit box. Then her dome light illuminated an object her efforts had just revealed. Scarlett eased a hand, cloaked in a plastic glove to keep skin oils from damaging potential finds, inside and closed it around what felt like a stitched leather pouch or sack of some kind. She drew it toward her gently, careful not to let it snare on any debris that might've been left by her toils. Her dome light illuminated the pouch gradually as it emerged, looking to be the kind that scribes of the time used to store or transport their writings, either on papyrus or parchment.

The entire pouch came free, enough weight to indicate a decent number of pages inside. Likely folded over in the codex form that was the forerunner of the book, as opposed to a scroll more common prior to the close of the first century AD and far less likely to avoid degradation through the centuries.

In the night and belowground chill, the pouch suddenly felt warm in her grasp, the heat pulsing through her clear plastic gloves. At first Scarlett thought it was an illusion, a trick of the mind under conditions known for causing such things. But the next moment found the air around her heating up, too, swallowing the cold the narrow confines had maintained. She felt it through her clothes, penetrating her skin, reminding her of a sunburn coming on. Her helmet's dome light flickered, plunging her into intermittent splotches of utter blackness.

Then, as quickly as it had gone, the night's chill returned, and her dome light held its beam straight and steady. Scarlett eased the proper brush from her tool kit and ran it over the pouch in gentle strokes to see if that might reveal anything of note. She found the remnants of a wax seal, much of it having decayed through the years but enough present for her to recognize it as one with the distinctive signature of ancient Rome. And that served only to increase her anticipation and excitement over whatever the pouch contained, to be examined only with the proper equipment and protocols in place.

Scarlett tucked the pouch carefully into her shoulder bag and eased her camera out in its place. She aimed the lens to record the entire find, and touched the button on the right-hand side.

A *poooofffffff* sounded as the flash mechanism exploded.

Shaken, Scarlett started up the ladder, heart thudding against her ribs. At the top of the ladder, she eased the tarpaulin up enough to slither out back into the night and then replaced it when the darkness greeted her anew.

It was, of course, too early to get her hopes up over what the pages might contain. But they clearly told some tale no man, or woman, was ever meant to hear. Otherwise, why would someone have gone through so much trouble to hide them here beneath a holy site? Or, as she'd thought initially, perhaps that holy site had been erected in this spot to conceal the pouch's contents forever as much as anything.

Could it be, could it actually be what I've been searching for?

Scarlett resisted temptation to slip into the command tent and inspect the contents of the pouch for herself. For now.

ELEVEN

CARSON CITY, NEVADA

"State your name for the record, please," the clerk asked, the morning after Michael's battle with Durado Segura.

"Michael Tiranno."

"And Mr. Tiranno, for the purpose of this hearing, do you

swear to tell the truth, the whole truth, and nothing but the truth?"

"I do," said Michael, straightening the sleeves of his suit and fighting the desire to return the glare of the Gaming Control Board hearing's chairman, Robert Kern. Naomi Burns, stepping back into her role as his legal counsel today from corporate CEO of King Midas World, had advised him to avoid making this personal, something that Kern had been doing for years now.

"Could you raise your right hand and repeat that?" the clerk requested.

"No."

"Sir?"

"I can't raise my right hand. I suffered a shoulder injury last night."

"Very well," said the clerk. "You may be seated."

Michael sat down next to Naomi. The Gaming Control Board hearing chamber was laid out on an upward grade like a theater with the witness table on a figurative island between the crowd packed in behind it and the hearing bench placed on a raised dais before it. Kern was currently seated between the other two hearing commissioners who mostly never had anything to say, letting the chairman do all the talking and occasionally passing him a written question as if that were the prescribed protocol.

The main offices of the Nevada Gaming Control Board were located not in Las Vegas, but an office park on College Parkway in Carson City. A seven-hour drive or, in Michael's case, a one-hour flight on board his Tyrant Class Gulfstream into the local airport just a few miles from the building. He was no stranger to this chamber or to Robert Kern, who'd questioned Michael's motives and efforts in building the Seven Sins Casino, as well as anytime he wished to expand his interests.

Most recently, that had involved rumors of a proposed

buyout of MGM Grand's gaming interests across the board. Michael did not lack for enemies in Vegas, given the fact that his greatest adversary Max Price, the mogul who'd once kept men like Kern in his pocket like yesterday's lint, was long missing and presumed buried under the rubble of his Maximus Casino from which the Seven Sins had risen. But this hearing should've been nothing more than routine, given Michael's commitment to expanding his gaming interests along with increasing his investments in a myriad of other areas as well.

"Thank you for coming, Mr. Tiranno," Kern began, careful to speak into the microphone before him. "We appreciate your time."

"As I appreciate yours, Mr. Kern," Michael said, moving his gaze from Kern to the other two board members seated on either side of him, "along with the opportunity to work with the Gaming Control Board in pursuit of what's best for my interests as well as those of Las Vegas."

"You seem in a cooperative mood today."

"I'm always in a cooperative mood when I know what I'm doing will serve the interests of all parties involved."

"Then I'm sure you understand the concern expressed by some about your intent to expand your holdings in Las Vegas and gaming in general."

"*Some*, Mr. Kern? And may I ask who might they be exactly? I ask because perhaps I should be answering their questions instead of yours."

"By answering my questions, Mr. Tiranno, you *are* answering theirs, and I'm sure we can put all matters of concern to rest. As you suggested, we are in this together."

As Kern was speaking, Michael felt his Tyrant Class Samsung Galaxy vibrate with an incoming text. He slid it from his pocket, glancing down to find a message from a woman he'd be meeting in Paris in ten days' time.

MISS YOU

Michael noticed beads of moisture starting to collect on Kern's brow. "For the record, Mr. Tiranno, where are you from?"

"I'm an American, just like you, Mr. Kern. A naturalized citizen of native Italian heritage," Michael added. "And, as you well know, I pay my taxes, more than my share of taxes just like everyone else in this room," Michael said, drawing soft murmurs of assent from the crowd squeezed into every available chair behind him.

"I object to this entire line of questioning," said Naomi, sliding the microphone toward her.

Michael used the opportunity to reply to the text he'd just received: I MISS YOU MORE.

The response from halfway across the world came almost immediately: CAN'T WAIT TO SEE YOU IN PARIS. MAY HAVE A SURPRISE!

"This is not a legal proceeding, Ms. Burns," Kern told her, taking his glasses off. "There is no presumption of innocence, no standard of proof beyond a reasonable doubt. Holding a gaming license in the great state of Nevada is a privilege and not a right. If this committee finds credible new evidence that your client has associated with organized crime figures or is involved in any unsavory activities toward recklessly expanding his interests and holdings in Las Vegas, or is deemed unfit for any other legitimate cause, we will permanently revoke his license to operate a gaming establishment in the state."

"Allow me to reiterate, Mr. Kern," Michael said, leaning back toward the microphone, "I have never had any associations with figures in organized crime, unless you include stock brokers and investment bankers."

Kern waited for the ripple of laughter to dissipate in the chamber before responding. He took off his glasses and laid them down on the raised desk before him. Suddenly his eyes looked too small for his head, the size of dimes when nickels would've been more fitting.

"And do you believe, sir," he resumed, "that casino owners should routinely expand those interests into energy, telecom, and speculative technology in addition to other assorted so-called high risk venture capital bets?"

Naomi Burns eased herself in front of Michael before he could respond. "And how does that lie within the purview of this commission, Mr. Kern?"

"Because, Ms. Burns, this board is well aware of the fact that Tyrant Global Ltd., Mr. Tiranno's holding company, is heavily in debt, continuously seeking capital to expand its business interests and by so doing disproportionately leveraging its assets in Las Vegas that include the Seven Sins Resort. That means any misjudgment or poor decision making at this stage could cost the city of Las Vegas and state of Nevada dearly in loss of revenue and jobs. I speak specifically of a part of the Seven Sins Resort shrouded in mystery far too long, known as the Forbidden City. You're familiar with that, aren't you?"

"I am."

"And would I be correct in stating that this secret project has a price tag of one billion dollars and is now one year overdue, having endured constant delays and cost overruns estimated to be several hundred million dollars?"

"Not entirely, no."

"Would you care to elaborate, Ms. Burns?"

This time it was Michael who seized the microphone before Naomi had the chance. "It's difficult to put a price tag on vision, Mr. Kern. And I would think that an attraction capable of luring hundreds of thousands, if not millions, more visitors to Las Vegas would be in this committee's, and the city's, best interests."

"Perhaps, Mr. Tiranno, providing the developer didn't

find himself overextended and undercapitalized due to such pursuits, since his casino could fall beneath the proper reserve threshold to retain its gaming license. And this commission has reason to believe that is indeed the case with Tyrant Global."

"Since when is debt a crime?" Michael asked him, fighting to remain calm. *Didn't this man understand the fundamentals of how business gets done?*

"It isn't, of course. But the level of your leveraged holdings is a bit disconcerting to us, specifically your bond debt. At such a high interest rate, this commission is concerned it will be very difficult to pay it off in a timely manner, turning your debt into veritable junk bonds which is never good for the image of the gaming industry. As I'm sure you agree, that's a very dangerous situation not only for your holdings, but the many Nevada families that rely on the Seven Sins Resort and Casino to make a living, the state of Nevada included which counts on its taxes. Not to mention the fact that even after all these years of construction there remains a veil of secrecy around this Forbidden City of yours that this commission finds extremely worrisome. We respectfully request the actual architectural plans in contrast to the ones filed to receive the necessary construction permits, since the original plans do not include the numerous changes and reconfigurations made by your own admission."

"All new plans and upgrades have been regularly filed and updated with the proper city officials. And, of course, it would be my pleasure to provide them to you regardless, Mr. Kern. I'd just like to ask you while we're on the record to maintain confidentiality to ensure no information is shared or leaked to the press. I don't need any more publicity."

Michael's remark drew instant laughter and applause from those squeezed into the gallery, leading Kern to rap his gavel atop the table.

"And, for the record, I do indeed agree with you about

the nature of my bond holdings," Michael continued, not giving Kern the chance to jump in. "But I would respectfully remind this commission that every casino, and their respective holding companies, are or have been dependent on those kind of bonds, Mr. Kern. We plan to refinance our debt soon enough."

"The level of such dependence by Tyrant Global exceeds any previous precedents, Mr. Tiranno, and our concern is that your plans for expansion, and cost overruns at this Forbidden City of yours, are at the root of that."

Michael reached over for a number of file folders Naomi had placed on the table from her briefcase. "My financial team has compiled ten analyses of other gaming entities that have pursued interests in expansion comparable to Tyrant Global. You'll note upon review that in all of them the debt levels and ratios approximate my holdings' current standing, in large part because interest rates are far more favorable today. The bottom line is the numbers simply don't back up your claims as to the state of my company and its current liquidity."

Kern smirked again, relishing the opportunity to look down upon Michael. "You speak like a man who's guilty of something, Mr. Tiranno."

"I suppose I am," Michael said, pausing to let a tense murmur flow though the crowd. "Guilty of building the greatest casino this state and the world have ever seen. Guilty of giving my guests the best time and experience, gaming and otherwise, that money can buy. Guilty of building a name in a town operated for years by a private exclusionary boys' club. Guilty of wishing to expand my interests."

"Are you finished, Mr. Tiranno?"

"No, Mr. Kern," Michael told the chairman. "Not even close."

TWELVE

THE BLACK SEA

The *Lucretia Maru* sliced through the calm waters, blaring its horn repeatedly to alert any vessels waylaid by the fog-drenched air of its presence.

"Captain," the executive officer called to the freighter's commander, "a Coast Command patrol boat coming up on our starboard side is hailing us."

"Put it on speaker," Tarek Marmara ordered. "Let's hear what they have to say."

"Lucretia Maru," a male voice announced scratchily, "this is Turkish Coast Command, please identify yourself."

"Tarek Marmara. Captain."

"State your designation."

"Alpha-Niner-Six-Gamma-Xray-four-three-one," Marmara intoned, repeating the freighter's call signal for this voyage. "Now, please identify *your*self."

"Lieutenant Commander Soptir. Captain Marmara, we have a report that your ship has been boarded by pirates."

"Negative, Coast Command. We are under no duress. Repeat, no duress."

"Roger that, Captain. But procedure dictates we must board to confirm. Please acknowledge."

"Procedure be damned," Marmara said, a bit of unease creeping into his voice. "We were late leaving Ankara because of the storm and must make time. Please divert. We are under no danger. Repeat, no danger." The captain only wished he could have explained the protected nature of his cargo, rendering his the safest ship currently at sea, from pirates and anyone else. "Please acknowledge."

"Negative, *Lucretia Maru*. Please stop engines and prepare for boarding."

"Affirmative, Coast Command."

Captain Marmara watched the six Coast Command personnel, including a female crewmember, climb the boarding ladder from the deck of their patrol boat. He recognized it as one of the older, hundred-and-fifty ton models of German origin that were nearing obsolescence twenty years earlier, but somehow still remained in service.

It left him shaking his head.

As a law-enforcing armed unit of the military, Turkish Coast Command was responsible to the Ministry of Internal Affairs in terms of assigned duties and operations along the Turkish coastline. Formed in 1982 as the maritime wing of the gendarmerie, the Coast Command enjoyed a personnel strength of about eleven hundred and over sixty boats and ships, one of which was now going to put the *Lucretia Maru* even more behind schedule.

Marmara watched as his crewmembers helped the Coast Command personnel over the rail. He exchanged a salute with Lieutenant Commander Soptir, not bothering to hide his displeasure.

"This was wholly unnecessary, Commander. You must be new at your job."

"How's that, Captain?"

Marmara couldn't help but smirk. "Some things are better left unsaid."

Then he spotted the female crewmember sliding up from his right. "Yes, Captain Marmara," she said, "they are."

And that's when he felt the pistol pressed into his ribs.

Rifles unshouldered with the *Lucretia Maru* now stalled at sea, the five other fake Coast Command personnel rounded up the remainder of the crew, who now sat with arms draped behind their heads on the foredeck. The operation had been carried out with military swiftness and proficiency, not a single shot fired and the ship's crew knowing better than to resist.

"I believe we're ready for our tour," the woman told Captain Marmara, her face still draped in the shadows cast by her oversize cap.

Stray strands of black hair protruded from the bun contained beneath it. And yet that and the dark blue uniform could not contain her steely sultriness. Her green eyes were empty and ageless, her skin flawless save for a dimple-size scar on her forehead and a larger depression of one that ran diagonally across her right cheek. To the captain of the *Lucretia Maru*, it looked like residue from a knife wound.

One of her men jerked Marmara to his feet. "You have no idea what you're doing," the captain sneered.

"I'm robbing your ship, Captain," she told him, "of the copper piping you're carrying in your holds."

Marmara's sneer became a smirk. "That's what you think?"

"Why don't you show me?"

"As you wish," the captain said.

Just the woman and one of her men accompanied Marmara three levels down to the cargo holds. Believing he could overpower both, he made a fitful launch for a fire ax hanging from a hull perch only to feel himself twisted around in blinding fashion and slammed against the bulkhead. He felt certain it must've been the man who'd overpowered him, but turning he saw it was the woman squeezing his breath off with one hand while the other pressed the pistol against his forehead.

"Don't test me again, Captain."

"You've already failed, pirate," he managed, as they resumed their descent. "Miserably. You just don't know it yet."

Down on the freighter's cargo level, Marmara stopped just short of a bulkhead door. "Last chance, pirate. Once I open this door, there's no going back."

The woman flashed the pistol again. "Do I need to count to three for you?"

He smirked again. "Suit yourself."

And with that Marmara keyed in the proper code, twisting the hatch wheel when the pad's light glowed green. "Like I said, there's no going back now. . . ."

He jerked the door open, allowing the dull light of the grated steel passageway to sift through, illuminating the hold's contents.

Not copper piping at all, Raven Khan realized immediately, feeling her chest tighten as the stench assaulted her. She took a few steps inside, the horrible sounds every bit a match for the smell, even before her eyes adjusted enough to the darkness to see what lay before her. She focused on one section in particular, blinking to make sure the sight, in all its ugliness, was real.

Raven doubled over, feeling suddenly sick and sure she was going to vomit until she composed herself with several deep breaths and stood back up. The floor seemed to wobble beneath her, but she clung to her balance and stiffened her spine.

"You see what I mean?" the captain continued. "Run now, pirate, and you just may live another week. You picked the absolute worst ship on the sea to hijack."

Raven jammed him up against the wall, pistol pressed against his forehead. "I'm going to kill you."

Emotionless, Marmara glanced up at the barrel. "That

would change nothing. You think I have a choice? I don't do what they say, they kill my family."

"What *who* says?"

"I answer that, my family dies, too. So, pirate, make my day and pull the trigger."

THIRTEEN

CARSON CITY, NEVADA

"And do you consider staging exhibition fights against mixed martial arts champions proper behavior for a Las Vegas casino owner?" Kern resumed, after clearing his throat.

"Durado Segura took exception to being asked to turn his title into what he perceived to be a joke. It was supposed to be a simple event carried out for charity, but Mr. Segura overreacted. Perhaps you should ask the two women trapped in the cage whether my intervention was warranted or not. And, if you don't mind me asking, Mr. Chairman, what does such a thing have to do with my gaming license in the state of Nevada?"

Kern leaned forward, as if provided with the opening he'd been waiting for. "Everything, Mr. Tiranno, it has everything to do with that, since it indicates you're no stranger to violence, does it not, sir?"

CALTAGIRONE, SICILY 1975

Riding atop his tractor, Attilio, more grandfather to Michael than farmhand, was still smiling when his face exploded, the old man's teeth vanishing in a burst of gore from his ruptured skull. The tractor continued forward on its own, the hands of its faceless driver still clinging to the wheel.

pffffft . . . pffffft . . . pffffft . . .

From where Michael was standing in the barn, the clacking sounded like sodden firecrackers, the bullets that spawned them taking the farmhands Ercole and Stefano down in their tracks in the middle of the grazing field. The sight of them falling drew his father's attention. Michael saw Vito Nunziato lurch up from the table set upon the house's screen porch and lunge for the lupara *shotgun he had propped up in the corner where screen and wall met.*

pffffft . . . pffffft . . . pffffft . . .

The bullets ripped through the screen, spun his father around before he could reach the shotgun, and slammed him backward against the wall. Michael's mother reappeared in the doorway in that moment, dropping to the porch's plank floor the pair of plates she was carrying. Michael thought she may have screamed, but the sound of the plates shattering drowned everything else out.

"I suppose I'm not," Michael said finally. "Everybody knows my casino was one of those struck in the terrorist attack on Las Vegas a few years ago. But that's not why I'm here today, is it?"

"No, Mr. Tiranno, it's not. That attack is not the subject of today's hearing. Since you brought up the past, though, did you enter into a partnership agreement with a man named Max Price upon coming to Las Vegas?"

"Briefly."

"What happened?"

"He bought out my interests."

"You mean, forced you to sell."

Michael managed a smile. "If you consider making a five million dollar profit on a five hundred thousand dollar investment to imply force to then, yes, Mr. Price forced me to sell."

"He built the Maximus Casino on land you had secured, and then that casino exploded."

"I believe *imploded* is the proper term. You can find all the details in the FBI's report exonerating me from any culpability. The same report blamed a gas leak."

"Then it's a good thing this board is not bound by that conclusion. You were investigated, were you not?"

"No," Naomi corrected before Michael had a chance to. "Mr. Tiranno was only questioned. He was never considered a suspect. I believe other casino owners were questioned as well. None of them were considered suspects either."

"But no other casino owner purchased Price's company for pennies on the dollar after shorting his stock, and then built the Seven Sins on the refuse of the Maximus."

"And, five years ago, no other casino owner saved the city of Las Vegas from destruction at the hands of terrorists."

"Some of the facts surrounding that incident remain a mystery and a matter of dispute," Kern noted tersely.

"But not the fact that a new road in Las Vegas has been named after my client to recognize his heroism and contribution to the city," Naomi reminded. "This commission's proclivity to continually ignore that fact doesn't change its reality. And it's not too much of a stretch to say, Mr. Kern, that without my client's intervention, the aftermath of the attack would've provided a much different economic landscape in the city of Las Vegas and the State of Nevada as a whole, both of which you purport to be guardians for. With all due respect, sir, you should be thanking my client instead of badgering him."

Kern leaned forward over the raised bench, addressing his remarks directly at Michael. "*Thank you*, Mr. Tiranno. And, by the same token, most men would have run last night. Most men would never have picked a fight with a mixed martial arts champion. But you're not most men, are you, Mr. Tiranno?"

CALTAGIRONE, SICILY, 1975

Michael saw his mother jerked backward by the spray of bullets as his father, dragging blood across the old paint, threw himself futilely sideways to shield her.

The guns blared again, shredding the screen, pocking even the mended spots with fresh holes. Vito Nunziato disappeared in the torrent of fire. Michael heard high-pitched screams, as the three men swarmed toward the house, leveled rifles silenced but smoking.

pffffft . . . pffffft . . . pff—

Out in the barn Michael covered his ears, reached the haystack and started to grab for the pitchfork. He wanted to save his family, rush to their rescue. But he got only as far as the door before his fingers slid off the wooden handle as quickly as they'd found it, and he burrowed himself into the hay pile instead.

"I guess I'm not like most men, Mr. Kern," Michael conceded. "Most men never would've built a resort with the scope and grandeur of the Seven Sins, would they?"

"Precisely what this committee is charged with determining. And toward that end, we will reconvene one week from now."

Kern rapped his gavel down on the table and took his leave instantly without answering any questions shouted at him by the press. For his part, Michael rose and checked his cell phone again to see if he'd missed any more text messages. Looking up from the blank screen, he met the gaze of an innocuous-looking man in the rearmost row of the chamber with a bad comb-over and a cheap suit, twirling a Mont Blanc pen about in his hand.

"Michael?" Naomi prodded.

"Sorry," he said, turning toward her. "What were you saying?"

"That we need to get all financial records in order by next week's hearing."

"Sure, of course," Michael told her, gazing again toward the back row.

But the man in the cheap suit who was twirling a Mont Blanc pen was gone.

FOURTEEN

Retezat Mountains, Transylvania

Professor Henri Bernard emerged from the underground chamber unearthed the day before.

"You look as disappointed as I feel," Scarlett said to him.

He looked at her, not bothering to hide his suspicion. "Strange that someone in ancient times would go through so much trouble to hide something that isn't there."

"Unless another team uncovered and removed it ahead of us," Scarlett said, offering a hand to help him off the ladder.

Bernard refused to take it. "There's no mention of that in any of the records I examined."

"You mean the ones that can be accessed, Henri. There are plenty of expeditions known to have explored this area not prone to leaving notes. The Nazis, for example."

"Nazis, Scarlett? Really?"

"It's the truth," she said, shrugging. "What can I say?"

"Maybe you can explain how some of the stone shavings I found on the chamber floor had hardened into clumps."

"Excuse me?"

"The effect of exposure to moist air," Bernard told her, brushing the dust and gravel from his pants. "But the effect takes hours to become this pronounced, not minutes."

"Maybe the air's moister than you think, Henri."

He shook his head, clearly not convinced.

Unable to restrain her curiosity any longer, late that night Scarlett sneaked into the command tent where all the field equipment was located. An impressive array common to all high-end archaeological dig sites, this one included.

She took a stool at the high table containing the various tools and equipment, and laid the pouch down before her. Then she gingerly unfastened the straw ties binding it closed and peeled back the top edge, humbled by the fact she was the first person to do so in two thousand years.

Next came the most painstaking and crucial part. Scarlett opened the top of a clear plastic rectangular box that once sealed would mechanically flush out all air to prevent the ancient contents from being ravaged by the elements. Precious little exposure time was all it took to contaminate writings this ancient, turning them to dust sometimes right before the watcher's eyes.

Scarlett eased the matted contents of the pouch out slowly, again wearing plastic gloves to protect them from the oils of her skin. The pages that emerged were folded over into a book style, formed of parchment as opposed to papyrus. But something else claimed her eye: the worn, otherwise blank cover page was marked by a seal formed of red wax she recognized immediately as the royal seal of Julius Caesar himself. A complete version of the decayed seal she'd spotted upon the pouch itself.

Enough to set her heart fluttering.

Wasting no time at all, Scarlett placed the pages within the clear plastic, resealed the top, and touched a button. She heard a mechanical whir followed by a dull whooshing sound and adjusted the cool light and magnifying glass to inspect the now protected contents by using easily manipulated tools, built into the protective shell with the controls on the outside, to turn and examine the pages.

As civilization turned from BC to AD, parchment emerged as a more practical alternative to papyrus, making the written word far more accessible to the general public and far longer-lasting given parchment's ability to better withstand the elements. The animal skins were soaked in lime and scraped, stretched, and dried, rubbed smooth with pumice, and cut into sheets then sewn together. Eventually, the Romans also substituted parchment for the wooden leaves of the *tabula* to form a kind of notebook, like the one revealed now, that became the prototype of the modern book. Parchment was folded in half, stitched together and then finished in a cover to protect the accounts, notes, drafts, or letters contained inside.

But the contents of these parchment pages were none of those. The layout of the cursive text made it look more like a journal, a recounting of something in the ancient Latin dialect favored by the most noted scribes of the time. Scarlett had become expert with Latin linguistics from the time of the ancient Romans, but was still under no illusions she'd be able to translate the entire contents of the journal in a single night. That would take days, weeks, or months, even for the most adept in the field given that no writings this aged would be totally intact, requiring sophisticated extrapolation to fill in the gaps. But what looked to be the journal's title, printed boldly on the top of page one, was something else again. And Scarlett positioned both the cool light and the magnifying glass over the clear plastic protecting it for closer inspection.

She felt her heart skip a beat, holding her breath as she checked the titled words, the name of the author beneath them lost to the ages, again to make sure she'd read them right.

The figure laid low on a ridge of the Retezat Mountains that overlooked the archaeological dig site. He held the Brunton Eterna ELO Highpower binoculars to his eyes, marveling at how they provided a sharp view over such a long distance, enhanced further by night-vision capabilities. At just thirty-two ounces they delivered a crisp, clear image thanks to a bright fifty-one-millimeter objective and BaK-4 prism glass with fully multicoated lenses. Right now those lenses could make out nothing of the woman who'd sneaked into the tent toting a leather bag around her shoulder. But he kept them pressed against his eyes anyway, waiting for her to reemerge.

The first inside page indicated that the journal contained the results of an expedition indeed ordered by Julius Caesar himself. From what she could glean from the dates provided, the expedition had begun during the height of Caesar's power, undertaken by a loyalist order handpicked for the task, an expedition of an unprecedented elaborate nature for the time.

She couldn't stop now. It was a tedious process. Translating the ancient Latin text but hearing the words as English in her mind, even imagining she could hear the unnamed author's voice, the cadence and rhythm of the words familiar to her as if she'd somehow encountered this particular scribe's writings before. The process went much better than expected, despite the fact that many of the letters had faded over the thousands of years since they'd been scrawled. Scarlett found herself unable to lift her eyes from the fragile parchment pages, falling into a rhythm that saw her make far more progress through the early sections than she'd ever imagined.

She came to a section where the scribe finally identified himself, having to reread that portion three times to be convinced she had it right. And if she did . . .

Scarlett heard a shuffling behind her, a cool breeze entering the tent through a parted flap.

"I thought so," said Henri Bernard.

FIFTEEN

Las Vegas, Nevada

"The Tyrant Global bonds we issued are trading at their lowest level yet," Naomi said, checking the numbers on her Tyrant Class Samsung Galaxy Note as they drove back to the airport outside of Carson City. "And the reporting that will come tomorrow on the hearing is almost certain to depress their value even further."

"I think that's what the hearing was all about," Michael said.

"We need to consider that the value of those bonds makes Tyrant Global a target for a takeover. On top of that, if one party came in and bought up enough of the debt . . ."

"Aldridge Sterling maybe?"

Sterling Capital Partners managed the largest hedge fund in North America and one of the largest in the world, boasting an AUM, or assets under management, of more than five hundred billion dollars. After long professing to have no interest in the gaming industry, Sterling had reportedly changed his mind and was rumored to be seriously pursuing a significant position in Las Vegas and beyond.

"Maybe he does have his sights fixed on MGM Holdings,"

Michael theorized, with that in mind. "Diluting the value of Tyrant Global would make an acquisition of that size impossible for us, clearing the field for him."

"Then we've got to consider what would ordinarily seem ridiculous."

"Like what?"

"Like the possibility that Sterling has the head of the Gaming Control Board in his pocket," Naomi followed.

Michael looked up again from scanning the volume of e-mails that had built up over the course of the hearing. "He's one of the richest men in America. He can put lots of people in his pocket, but he can't put me there and maybe that's the point."

"Aldridge Sterling is gobbling up more of our bonds on the cheap, hoping we default." Naomi studied him. "Sterling and Wall Street both think you're vulnerable, Michael, and that makes you weak. They're hurting our capital position and our ability to borrow."

"Then they're in for a big surprise when I fight to the death to protect what I've built. If Aldridge Sterling is trying to destroy me, I'll find a way to destroy him first."

"Any other news on your end?" Michael asked her.

"On what?" Naomi asked him.

"You know what."

She smiled tightly. "Because you always ask me the same question that way, you mean? And the answer's the same, too: No, nothing new on the search for Raven Khan, in spite of the fact that we've hired the best investigators money can buy. She's a ghost."

"For what we're paying these investigators, they should be able to find a ghost, Naomi."

"Unless she's dead, a possibility you refuse to consider when it comes to Raven."

"Because I know she isn't."

"How?"

"Because I'm not. And she's my sister."

"But she doesn't know that. And maybe she's not as indestructible as you are."

"It runs in the family," Michael said, smiling.

"Apparently, so does disappearing from one's past," Naomi said, more pointedly. "Becoming another person entirely."

"Raven was already that person. We can't find her because she doesn't want us to, anymore than she wants to use the private number we've left with all the contacts we've been able to identify. We'll only find her if she lets us, which means we've got to keep trying. Hire new investigators."

"I told you, these firms are the best."

"Then find better."

Michael busied himself on the brief flight back to Las Vegas with the range of motion exercises the physical therapist had shown him on the mini-gym installed in the Gulfstream. He was lucky, went the prevailing medical opinion, not to have suffered any structural damage to the joint. A few more days and it would be virtually as good as new, although the swelling and purplish bruising made the injury seem much more serious than it actually was.

The hearing, and all the unanswered questions it raised, continued to plague him through the remainder of the flight that ended, as always, by flying as low and close to the Strip as FAA regulations allowed for their flight plan. The Seven Sins never looked so grand as when its palatial scope and shape was contrasted against the rest of the Vegas skyline. Gazing at it from the plane somehow made him feel closer to the resort as a symbol of his life and all his accomplishments, as well as all that remained to be achieved. Because the Seven Sins, and Las Vegas, didn't represent ends so much as beginnings. Once his dreams had involved only owning a casino. Now those dreams, realized more and more with each passing day, had expanded into other arenas, his appetite for expansion insatiable. From software, to telecom, to oil and gas, and to real estate and the entertainment industry as well as gaming, Michael Tiranno continued to expand his interests and his footprint as relentlessly as he had built the Seven Sins from no more than a vision.

Michael felt the medallion, the relic that had come to symbolize his success and perhaps much more, against his skin. Traced its outline through his shirt as he was jolted slightly forward with a thud, the Gulfstream having just touched down at McCarran Airport.

"We're home, Michael," said Naomi.

SIXTEEN

NEW YORK CITY

"How are you feeling tonight, Dad?" Aldridge Sterling said to the figure in the wheelchair at the other end of the dining room table. "I'm waiting for an important call, so I hope you don't mind if I have to interrupt our usual dinner conversation."

Sterling sat at the dining room table in his fifty-million-dollar penthouse inside the towering 15 Central Park West building, the entire floor offering a panoramic view of the city skyline from every room. But right now all Sterling was looking at were the cell phones on either side of him, waiting for either to ring while also waiting for his staff to finish preparing his dinner.

"Urrrrrrrrrrrrr," came a gurgling rasp from the other end

of the table, where his father sat motionless and unblinking in his wheelchair.

"What was that, Dad?"

"Urrrrrrrrrrrr," his father uttered, although not necessarily in response to his son, since the great Harold Sterling had stopped responding to stimuli years before, after his third stroke confined him to his wheelchair for good.

"Remember what it was like to be a rich and powerful man? How's it feel to be helpless, useless, to have to wear diapers?"

No response at all this time, except for some drool that Aldridge Sterling watched trickle down his father's chin. The great Harold Sterling was an immigrant Jew who had managed to survive the Holocaust to become one of the most esteemed United States senators of his generation, respected by his allies and feared by his enemies toward whom his animus knew no bounds. He had blazed a trail to leadership of the Senate based on compassion and good will that cloaked the ruthless cunning that emerged in stories and magazine articles about him later. His father was, by all indications, two entirely different men, and Aldridge might've felt closer to him had he known the ruthless side of Harold Sterling better.

Harold Sterling had hoped for similarly great things from his lone son, but Aldridge had found the life of a playboy much more to his liking. Any number of failed business deals had depleted enough of the family fortune for his father to threaten cutting him off on numerous occasions. And when he finally followed through on those threats, it was the greatest thing he ever did for his son; in fact, the very thing that had led to Aldridge Sterling becoming one of the most successful hedge fund managers of all time. At present, he directed a fund that was growing at a marginal rate of an astounding 25 percent annually.

Sterling specialized in betting on failure, leading a recent cover story in a financial magazine to proclaim him "King of the Short." Making hundreds of millions, even billions, when stocks went down instead of up. Not that his father cared, past ninety now and forever bound to a wheelchair. This hero of the Holocaust, who survived a concentration camp to become the conscience of the senate and the entire United States, kept from the presidency only by the fact he was born a German.

"How will it feel witnessing me become the richest man in the world?" Sterling asked from his side of the table.

The old man finally turned his way, toward a voice instead of a face, no sign of recognition flashing at all. Sterling looked at his father and still saw flickers of his own reflection. Though everything else had given out, the old man's features had somehow remained strong. Same high cheekbones, same deep-set eyes that looked too small for his face. Identical furrows carved across his tanned brow beneath the same thick shock of hair, white in his case but salt and pepper for Aldridge, that had stubbornly refused to fall out. Same piercing eyes that clung to life even after all else had failed him. He'd ground his once perfect set of teeth down to mere nubs and hated more than anything when one of the attendants tried to brush them.

Hard to believe this was the same man who'd built a fortune that had formed the foundation for the Sterling legacy of power. No longer the man who'd gone from Holocaust survivor to American citizen and, finally, legendary and beloved United States senator. No longer any man at all, really.

"How does it feel, Dad?" Aldridge Sterling asked, knowing there could be no response. "How does it feel to be dependent on the son you so despised, to have your life in my hands? I hope somewhere deep inside a part of you can still realize that and it makes your suffering even worse. That's why I cater to your every need, refuse to allow you a merciful death. Because as long as you're still alive, it means you're suffering and nothing pleases me more than to see that."

One of Sterling's cell phones rang. Hong Kong, right on schedule.

"Good morning, Jin," he said to his top trader there, where the market was about to open. "I have new instructions for you. Short every gaming stock you can, even in Macau, and keep scooping up every Tyrant Global bond you can get your hands on. Is that clear? . . . Jin, are you there?"

"I'm here," the man said in perfect English. "But your insistence on this position sounds risky. Everyone else is in a stock buying mode."

"Because they're fucking wrong. And don't ever question me again."

"Apologies, Boss, apologies. I meant no offense. Consider it done. The trading floor opens in five minutes."

"Good," Sterling said, continuing while looking across the table at his father and hoping against hope the old man could understand what he was about to say. "And when you're done with that, review our position on the American dollar. Continue shorting that too. Then put the word out to the other Asian market traders we discussed to do the same and keep it under the radar. Use our funds in Luxembourg, Singapore, and Panama to avoid the prying eyes of the Securities and Exchange Commission."

"Boss?" Jin posed tentatively.

"What?"

"Isn't such leveraging dangerous, given that the dollar has never been stronger against the rest of world currencies?"

"A fair question, Jin," Sterling said, surprising the trader with his conciliatory tone. "But sometimes when you swim upstream, you catch the biggest fish."

SEVENTEEN

Bernard noted the light and let his gaze linger on the magnifying glass. "You'll need one of those to spot what's left of your career."

"Fuck you, Henri."

"Do you always speak to your superiors that way, Ms. Swan?" he asked, barely suppressing a smirk as he glimpsed the contents of the hermetically sealed case.

"Only the ones I don't trust. Why don't you tell me what you're really doing here, why it was so important for the Romanian government to have you placed in charge?"

"To keep you under control, perhaps, since they don't trust Americans to do right by their own country. More than one precious find has found its way out of Romania onto the shelves of American and British museums." Bernard's eyes fell on the case again. "This constitutes theft of intellectual property, Ms. Swan. I could have you arrested by the Romanian authorities now."

"I didn't steal anything."

"No. What would you call it then?"

"My job."

"According to who?"

"The person paying for this dig," she said, lowering herself from the stool stiffly to face him.

"Why don't you tell me what it is you think you've found there?"

"Why don't you tell me why the Romanian government would put someone like you, with minimal field experience, and none when comes to ancient Rome, in charge of this

dig? We both know you haven't even been on one in over
five years. So what's so important about this one?"

"You're digging your grave even deeper, Ms. Swan."

"Digging's my specialty, unlike you apparently."

Bernard glared at her. "Consider yourself suspended. If
I see you anywhere near the site of the find or this tent, I'll
have you arrested and deported. Give you more time to
spend with those wretched gypsies."

Some of those gypsies helped supply the team with food
and had taken to providing laundry services. One teenage
boy spent every afternoon selling water out of his over-
stuffed backpack, actually bottled from a mountain stream
located somewhere nearby. The boy, whose name was Ilie,
had been born deaf but was fluent in ASL, American Sign
Language, in the most widely accepted version across the
globe. Ilie had been taught to sign by missionaries, but
Scarlett proved the only member of the archaeological team
able to communicate with him, since her grandmother was
deaf and she'd learned to sign practically before she learned
to talk. She welcomed the opportunity to use the skill again,
as much for the practice as the fond memories it brought to
mind. And Ilie delighted in signing the Romanian word
lebădă, which meant "swan," when addressing her.

"Have I made myself clear?" Bernard resumed.

"Better make sure nothing happens to the remains of that
manuscript, Henri."

Bernard smirked again. "Of course, Scarlett." His eyes
seemed to twinkle. "I'll guard it with my life, while you're
gone with the wind."

She could only shake her head. "Like I've never heard
that before."

EIGHTEEN

Ismael Saltuk, bodyguard on either side of him, slid past the ancient remains of a Byzantine triumph arch and down a set of stone stairs leading to Istanbul's underground network of cisterns used centuries before to supply the city with water.

Flanked by his bodyguards, Saltuk entered the largest of these, known as the *Yerebatan Sarayi* or, more simply, the Basilika Cistern, although locals preferred to call it the "Sunken Palace," and for good reason. Built in the fourth century, the Sunken Palace was a massive structure that had withstood the ages thanks to 336 marble columns arranged in a dozen neat rows from floor to ceiling. A convenient pathway allowed tourists to stroll past fish that dotted the dark waters.

Saltuk waited until no one else was around before ducking down a narrow, dark alcove with his bodyguards until he came to a section of wall outfitted with a latch he jerked one way, then the other, then back again.

Click.

The door to his secret domain opened and Saltuk entered, leaving his bodyguards on watch and closing the door behind him.

"Hello, Ismael," a female voice called to him, as he threw the locks from the inside.

Saltuk looked at Raven Khan standing in the atmospheric half light of his beloved gallery, his unconscious guards slumped in the chairs on either side of her.

"I'm here to talk about the *Lucretia Maru*," she told him.

"Was there a problem with the cargo?"

"The ship wasn't carrying copper piping, Ismael. It was carrying *people*, mostly women but children, too," Raven said, not bothering to disguise the disgust in her voice. "A few stood out, a toddler hugging her mother most notably. Because she was dead. The little girl was hugging her and crying because she was dead."

Saltuk's mouth dropped. He looked honestly shocked.

"They'd been at sea for several days, in port likely for several more," Raven continued. "Enough time for some awful disease to begin spreading. In such tight confines . . ." She stopped there, not wishing to relive those images. "I think you get the idea."

"Oh, I get that idea, repulsive as it is, just not why it has affected you so much."

Raven glanced about the fully restored, palatial great room dressed with ancient furniture and priceless paintings hanging from walls covered in dark ironwood. The dull lighting came courtesy of sconces placed discriminately about the walls. They could have been fueled by kerosene, although Raven thought she detected the quiet hum of generators pulsing from somewhere beyond, likely powered by propane instead.

Ismael Saltuk's lair was just as she remembered when brought here by her own late mentor, Adnan Talu, various times when he had dealings with the man. It was one thing to be a high-end thief, quite another to be able to successfully move the most rare and priceless of stolen merchandise, given the limitations and peculiarities of that market.

Saltuk was also an established collector in his own right. His appreciation for the finer things in life allowed him to furnish his private hideaway with priceless treasures that added life and color to its otherwise dark, somber confines. He had more than his share of enemies in both the criminal underground and among various agencies of law enforcement from dozens of countries. As a result, he seldom ventured out of Istanbul, or even from his lair for that matter.

Saltuk's eyes flitted to the slumped forms of his guards, both veterans of the Egyptian secret service, who'd managed to keep Mubarak alive for decades in large part by assassinating his potential foes. And this woman had felled them, by all indications, without even raising a sweat.

"Human trafficking, Ismael. You sent me to a slave ship."

"My intelligence was accurate as always, I'm sure of it," he insisted to her.

He was a tall man, thin, with long legs that made him appear more than his inch over six feet. His face was gaunt and angular, featuring a protruding jaw and cheekbones that were a fine match for his overly broad shoulders which peaked on both sides. The darkness of his eyes and hair was further exaggerated by olive skin laced with a sickly pallor from lack of sunlight.

"The copper was a cover," he resumed.

"Obviously.

"That both of us fell for."

"Also obvious."

"And if everything is so obvious, what brought you here?"

"I was raised in an orphanage, Ismael, an orphanage where older children disappeared from time to time. Do I need to draw you a picture?"

"I was about to ask you the same question, Raven, in view of the man who rescued you from that squalor: Adnan Talu, a man I hold in as high a regard as you do. A man both of us are indebted to for our very lives."

Raven remained expressionless, her gaze noncommittal, but she couldn't deny Saltuk's assertion. Talu was the closest thing to a parent Raven had, and she still remembered the day he'd plucked her from the orphanage to be raised as his daughter. He sent her off first to a boarding school in England and then a college where she studied fine arts and antiquities. That in preparation for her following in his footsteps as a leader of the modern-day criminal organization that had grown out of the Cilician pirates whose legacy dated back over two thousand years.

After Talu's death, Raven had expanded the organization's interests. In her mind, the pirates of today controlled cyberspace the way their forebears once controlled the seas, the Internet rapidly becoming the greatest ocean of all and ripe for the picking. But the organization still shipped more stolen cars to the Middle East than new Mercedes and BMWs combined and continued to supply small propeller planes to the drug lords in South America, equipped with the top technology in radar interdiction. And, of course, cargo ships inevitably made for enticing and normally easy prey.

"Make believe I'm Talu and tell me what you're hiding, Raven. What is it about that toddler hugging her dead mother that moved that cold heart of yours?"

"Where can I find the man behind that cargo, Ismael?"

"I have no idea."

"Yes, you do—I saw it in your eyes when I told you what the ship contained. If I didn't know better, I'd say you set me up. Wanted me to find exactly what I did."

Saltuk looked away, speaking with his eyes fixed on one of his treasured paintings. "So many of these are fakes. Would you like to know why?" He turned back toward her, expression bent in bitterness. "Because the man responsible for that slave ship learned I had the originals and insisted I turn them over to him. They weren't even by famous artists, were hardly well known outside of select circles. But they were among my favorites and I did as I was told, Raven, because this is not a man you want to cross under any circumstances. We are his proxy because we have no choice—no one who works for him does."

"A client of yours, then."

Saltuk frowned. "One whose wrath and ruthless methods are what defines his power. And, by the way, you worked for him once, too."

"What arc you talking about?"

"The operation in Siberia you were paid handsomely for four years ago."

"The old man, the professor I rescued from the gulag," Raven reflected.

"The man behind that freighter's cargo? You were working for his organization without even realizing it."

"What organization is that?"

"Black Scorpion."

"I never believed they really existed, at least not to the degree rumor would have us believe."

Saltuk nodded. "The greatest protection for truths desired to be kept secret lies in letting the world believe them to be legends. Black Scorpion is more powerful than most governments. Their reach is immeasurable, way beyond human trafficking alone which they control on a global scale. If there's money to be made from any crime anywhere, chances are Black Scorpion is either behind it or backing whoever is."

Raven moved to the dark nightscape adorning the near wall. "This one looks real."

"One of the few that has escaped Black Scorpion's attention."

She drew a lighter from her pocket and flicked the flame to life, easing it close enough to the painting to lose the smoke in its vibrant colors. "Tell me where to find this man, Ismael."

Saltuk's eyes bulged. He began to shake. "No, please!"

"Tell me where to find him, or see it burn."

"Talu gave me that painting," Saltuk pleaded.

"Then don't make me burn it."

"All right, all right! Just move the flame away. I'm begging you, Raven, begging you!"

Raven released her finger, letting the flame die.

Saltuk moved his gaze from Raven to the painting and then back again. "You know what they say about the devil, that if you see him it means you're already dead? You've never met the man who runs Black Scorpion—no one still alive ever has. Trust me on that, Raven, for your own sake."

"Oh, I trust you, but this man's never met me either."

NINETEEN

LAS VEGAS, NEVADA

Edward Devereaux watched Michael Tiranno enter the lobby, gaze following his stroll across the floor as he was greeted by all manner of guests and employees. On his left, Devereaux recognized Naomi Burns, Tiranno's former corporate counsel who now also served as chief executive officer of the corporate entity behind the Seven Sins and all of his gaming holdings. Hanging back, like a shadow, he noticed Alexander Koursaris, Tiranno's loyal private bodyguard, reputed to be one of the most dangerous men in the world, a warrior of such prowess that he had been compared to a modern-day Achilles who would make even Homer proud.

To the casual follower, both Burns and Koursaris were no more than hired guns, filling roles that would otherwise be taken by others. But Devereaux's exhaustive and painstaking research had revealed them to be much more than that. Naomi Burns, for example, had been instrumental in helping Tiranno realize his purported dream of building the Seven Sins, while Koursaris's formidable reputation and mere presence kept Michael Tiranno's most committed and threatening enemies at bay. It was all part of the mystery, the enigma, that Devereaux now had centered in his cross-hairs.

Given time, though, the kind of criminals and madmen he'd spent his life chasing always made a mistake, and that was what had brought him here to the Seven Sins. Seeing Michael Tiranno crossing the lobby, Devereaux lit out into motion, following the man known as the Tyrant when he veered toward the casino.

TWENTY

Las Vegas, Nevada

Michael moved about the Seven Sins's casino floor, losing himself in the sounds and sights behind which MMA fights and Gaming Control Board hearings vanished, at least for the moment.

No matter what else might be going on in his life, perspective could always be found by trolling the casino. To witness firsthand the vision his original dream had created. A few minutes were often all it took to restore his sense of purpose. Though Michael shunned the limelight, his celebrity often led to him being recognized and approached. He welcomed such encounters for the feedback they provided that was often infinitely more informative and rewarding than hotel surveys and consultants' reports. For no survey or report could capture what a person felt in the deepest part of their being, the part of them the Seven Sins experience endeavored to reach.

Along the way, any number of guests approached to meet him, just as he stopped to greet guests randomly to get a sense of their experience. Perhaps, in a strange way, he was living vicariously through them, back to the days where so often he'd gambled everything he had on anything but sure things. Those days were far more pleasant in memory than the actual experiences he'd buried as deep as he could in his consciousness, sometimes wondering himself if it had all really happened. The Seven Sins defined everything Michael was and ever aspired to be. The constant sense of energy and excitement never failed to draw him back to the crowds seeking action as well as the kind of opportunity they could get only here. It helped him remember the struggles that had led to it coming to be, lest he never take anything for granted. He never moved with an entourage, though he knew Alexander lurked nearby, out of sight but never so distant he couldn't intervene in an instant, on the chance Michael encountered a guest less than hospitable to him.

Occasionally, the spectacle grew greater still, when actual tigers and lions rose out of the casino floor from chambers layered beneath it, built in that respect to resemble the Roman Coliseum, but with tubes made of reinforced space age polymer. Payouts in whatever part of the casino the animals ended up would double for a brief time, while carefully orchestrated circles of fire ringed the area. Michael loved the concept that the whim of fate could change a man's or woman's life, at any time, forever. So much of his vision was about changing the very nature of the gaming experience by making it more entertaining and engaging—interactive as well as, in many respects, a lifestyle. That lifestyle was based on a simple but clear motto inspired by the message immortalized on his relic, applying a "Dream, Dare, Win" philosophy to everyday existence as personified by every roll of the dice or flip of the cards.

And, true to that form, the expressions on the faces of those packed in tight were full of hope and expectation, a sense of the unknown that awaited them, the possibility that they could leave in a substantially different standing in life than when they arrived. The risk posed was minimal in the face of the payoff they could gain. They had positioned themselves for great things to happen and, even if that didn't come to pass, they would depart rejoicing in the notion of the opportunities afforded them.

Michael had just emerged from the casino area when a man appeared before him with a glossy picture-dominated book charting the construction of the Seven Sins titled *The Eighth Wonder of the World.*

"I'm so sorry to bother you," the man apologized, in a vaguely European accent. *French,* Michael thought. "But could you sign this for me?"

"Of course," Michael said, taking the book and readying his pen. "Should I make it out to anyone in particular?"

"Yes, it's my birthday! How about, 'Happy Birthday to my friend Paul.' That would be wonderful!"

Michael scrawled the note and handed the book back to the man.

"Thank you," the man said humbly, letting his gaze sweep about. "I've never seen anything like this place before."

"Thank *you,*" Michael said, smiling, and started away, realizing the man had been wearing thin, designer gloves. European, indeed.

Edward Devereaux held the book extended before him, careful not to come into contact with the part of its glossy cover Michael Tiranno had touched. Then he turned and started toward the elevators that serviced the Daring Sea suites.

TWENTY-ONE

LAS VEGAS, NEVADA

"Hello, Edward," Angel greeted, as he closed the door behind him. *"Is there anything I can assist you with?"*

Devereaux searched around the wall for a curtain to draw before the screen or a switch to shut Angel off altogether, failing to find either. He was convinced the virtual concierge was watching him, following his every motion and action.

"No, I don't . . ." He stopped, having to remind himself he was talking to a machine. "I don't need anything, Angel."

"Just let me know if you change your mind. I have some excellent dinner recommendations for you."

"Maybe later."

"Of course."

Unable to escape Angel, Edward Devereaux carried his black case into the sprawling bathroom complete with both marble bath and shower, its back glass wall offering a view out into the Daring Sea but no view in. After closing the door behind him, he removed a large cotton swab from a pocket on the case, tore away the plastic, and carefully swiped it across the cover of the book Michael Tiranno had signed for him to harvest some DNA. Then he opened the black-handled case atop the bathroom's granite counter to reveal what looked to be a medical kit of some kind on one side and a high-tech machine complete with LED readouts and display screen on the other.

The machine was a portable DNA tester that allowed for the kind of analysis normally performed in a lab to be done in much more expeditious fashion, within minutes actually. The margin for error was understandably higher and the degree of match probability considerably lower. While certainly fallible, the portable testers were still accurate within a range of five hundred to a thousand to one. Significant developments and progress with polymerase chain reaction, the technology used to perform DNA testing, had made this possible, and there was even a handheld PCR amplification device available. But Devereaux still preferred this model, which could provide reasonably reliable results within fifteen minutes.

He popped the cotton swab off from the stem and fitted it into a slot tailored for its precise specifications in the machine. Eased the slot back into place and then touched the button marked RUN. A soft whirring sound, not unlike that of a standard computer hard drive, emanated from the machine's guts as it began its analysis and comparison with the DNA report already entered into its memory. Nothing, under the circumstances, that would stand up in court. But that was of no concern to Devereaux at this point. All he needed was proof that there was merit to his theory, enough to force those who'd shunned him to listen.

The machine would do its work. And then he would know for sure, Deveraux thought, as he fingered the pendant that was a miniature reproduction of the medallion adorning the Seven Sins everywhere, testament to Michael Tiranno's power and prestige.

And soon, perhaps, his undoing.

TWENTY-TWO

LAS VEGAS, NEVADA

"I thought you could use this," one of the Tyrant Girls serving guests in the lobby said, handing Michael a tall glass of fresh-squeezed orange juice mixed with a slight jigger of Tyrant brand vodka.

She wore a shapely designer suit that fit her lines elegantly, waves of shaggy auburn hair tumbling past her shoulders. In the lobby light, the auburn looked speckled with black, adding to her radiance.

Michael took the glass and smiled, letting his gaze drift across the lobby past a check-in line set before the eighteen-station marble reception counter that wound through an elaborate maze of stanchions strung together by velvet rope. He fixed his stare on the entrance to the Gold Medallion VIP room, marked by an elegant replica of his medallion featuring the words, "Dream, Dare, Win."

The Tyrant Girl who had brought him the drink smiled back at him. "The girl you saved last night was my best friend."

"I didn't save anyone. It was just an exhibition."

The Tyrant Girl grinned again. "Is that what you call it? Sure, whatever you say . . . Mr. Tyrant," she said playfully, as she started to slide away.

"Wait. Do you like working at the Seven Sins, Catherine?" he asked, after letting his eyes cheat to her nametag.

She flashed the chained pendant worn by all women selected to become Tyrant Girls. Michael saw the miniature reproduction of his medallion emblazoned on the pendant's center shining in the lobby's naked light.

"The day you gave me this was the happiest day in my life, Mr. Tiranno."

"Call me Michael."

Michael spotted Alexander approaching across the lobby, as Catherine took her leave.

"You've been watching me," Michael said to him.

"I thought Durado Segura might still be on the premises."

"Believe he's out looking for a surgeon. And a new career."

"Thanks to you."

"Did you see another choice?"

"Yes, not to get in the ring with him in the first place."

Only Michael knew Alexander's true heritage and history. That he was Greek by birth, born in the city of Sparta. Poverty had led him to join gangs practicing petty street crime on the streets of Athens, and within just a few years Alexander was running those gangs. His meteoric rise through the underworld ended in the service to the Camorra crime family when he was arrested by French authorities for smuggling. He was sentenced to ten years in prison, until a shadowy intelligence service offered him a way out: His freedom after the same ten years in service to the French Foreign Legion's elite Rapid Insertion Force, the *Force D'Intervention Rapide*, if he managed to survive that long.

"I should have listened to you," Michael admitted.

"Easy to say now."

"Uh-oh, I feel a lecture coming . . ."

"Spare me the trouble, Michael, and tell me what I'm going to say."

"That I knew what might happen when I stepped into the ring with that animal, that part of me *wanted* it to happen."

"And am I right?" Alexander asked him.

"The event was about raising money for charity and nothing more. You think any different?"

"I think you wanted to face Segura in the ring."

"Face, yes; fight, no."

"You wanted to test yourself. You welcomed the opportunity. You knew Segura couldn't be trusted or controlled."

"Plenty say the same thing about me. And it was supposed to be a show, all for—"

"Charity, I know," Alexander completed. "And for everyone in the audience, and watching on television, that was exactly the case. But it was a never a show for you, Michael. It was a test and it worked out exactly as you wanted."

"You really believe that?"

Alexander's steely eyes narrowed on him. "The Seven Sins is your territory and Segura broke one of your prime rules by hurting a woman. But you're also a tycoon responsible for providing jobs and livelihoods for thousands of families. Warriors, even me, are replaceable. You're not."

And that's when all the power in the Seven Sins died.

TWENTY-THREE

LAS VEGAS, NEVADA

Edward Devereaux was standing at the glass wall of his Daring Sea suite, staring at the spectacle beyond and imagining himself living in some hybrid ocean environment as one of the sharks cruised by. He heard his DNA analyzer beep to signal the completion of its work and moved back toward the bathroom.

"Don't forget to try one of our shows, Edward, or our spa, nominated as one of the five best in North America," said Angel. *"Are you sure there's nothing I can do for you?"*

"Not yet, Angel, but thank you."

"Sure thing, sir."

Devereaux had just caught his own reflection in the thick

glass on the suite's Daring Sea side when the lights died, the suite lit suddenly only by the eerie translucent glow emanating from the Daring Sea beyond the glass. No emergency light snapped on. No preprogrammed voice came on to issue a warning, even Angel silent on the matter.

But there was enough light for Devereaux to trace his way to the steel, bulkhead-like door and find the handle. He pulled and twisted to no result. Checked the security bolt and found it unfastened, then tried the door again.

It didn't budge. He was locked in.

Figuring it must be a glitch in the system triggered by the blackout, Devereaux moved cautiously to the nearest phone to ring the front desk.

Nothing. The phone was dead.

"Angel," he called, suddenly longing for the virtual concierge's voice. "Angel?"

But her screen had gone dark, too, lost with the power.

"Angel!" he called out again anyway.

Devereaux was headed back to the desk to retrieve his cell phone when he heard a hum-like buzzing; not so much as heard it really, as *felt* it at the very core of his eardrums. His head began to ring, then pound, feeling like the pressure of a deep underwater dive. Since he was only forty or so feet below the surface and the atmospheric pressure inside all the Daring Sea suites was constantly normalized, he blamed this too on the blackout, feeling the grasp of panic begin to tighten on him.

Devereaux flailed for the souvenir book off which he'd lifted Michael Tiranno's DNA, but it slipped off the desk and rattled to the carpeting. Instead of trying to retrieve it, he stumbled his way to the door and began banging on it, hoping someone might hear his pounds even as the pressure in his head intensified. Then he heard a strange crackling sound, something like popcorn popping in a microwave, and swung back toward his suite's wall looking out into the Daring Sea.

"Angel! . . . Angel!"

But the virtual concierge remained silent, and now the glass was starting to crack, the fissures spreading outward both left and right from the center. Ripples forming into what quickly took on the impression of a vast impressionist design stitched across the thick glass. Devereaux swung back to the door and pounded its steel even harder.

"Help me! Somebody, help me!"

His head throbbed.

"Help me!"

His head felt ready to explode.

"I'm trapped!"

He knew he'd screamed the words, but the pressure building in his head kept him from hearing them. He turned back toward the glass wall to see the ripples joining up and widening. The last sight he ever recorded was that of the center portion of the glass wall caving inward, allowing the first torrents of water from the Daring Sea to crash through and slam into him.

TWENTY-FOUR

LAS VEGAS, NEVADA

The world seemed to freeze, the blackness everywhere within the Seven Sins, and beyond its glass façade.

"Emergency lighting should be coming on now," Michael said to Alexander, after ten seconds had passed.

But it didn't. The two men looked at each other, conscious of the slightest ripple of panic around them.

Alexander raised his backup walkie-talkie to his lips, then lowered it just as fast. "It's dead."

"What the hell is this?"

"It's not just us," Alexander said, gazing outside. "Looks like the whole Strip has been hit."

Those manning the floors and games of the casino initially could have no idea how long the blackness would remain and would thus have immediately instituted their own emergency procedures. First sweeping toward their respective tables from the outside in to keep all wagers in place. Traditionally dealers would literally lay over their chip trays with their arms and elbows pulled up to safeguard the sides of the tray. And they'd remain in this position until such time that either the lighting returned and the games resumed, or closed off with all chips collected. Dealers, boxmen, and floor supervisors would similarly move to secure all monies, chips, markers, cards, and dice from within the betting area from possible theft, bet capping, or pinching. The round in progress when the power died would be called dead with the game, hand, or roll picked up once it returned.

A steady flood of guests began hurrying toward the emergency exits, shoving the doors open and creating a logjam further intensified by a rush of patrons from the casino area with chips they'd managed to pilfer held in their grasps. Michael could feel the chaos around him, a mob mentality setting in with nothing he could do to forestall it. He lost track of time and place, conscious only of Alexander dragging him forward under a protective shield with his pistol drawn.

"Stay alert, Michael."

His enemies had gone through far greater lengths than this to get him. But the unfathomable depths they would've had to manage to achieve a total shutdown of anything electronic was just starting to occur to him, when the lights and power suddenly snapped back on.

And screams erupted from the viewing area of the Daring Sea.

Alexander and Michael sprinted across the lobby, followed by a phalanx of security guards. They slipped through cracks in the mass of humanity still trapped between intentions and pushed their way past those guests heading toward the screams too. They reached the Daring Sea viewing area to find spectators screaming in disbelief, parents covering the eyes of their children so they couldn't see Assassino himself cresting over the surface to snatch what at first glance appeared to be a jagged side of beef in his jaws, but at second look was something else entirely.

A man's upper body, bitten off at the waist.

TWENTY-FIVE

RETEZAT MOUNTAINS, TRANSYLVANIA

"I thought I told you to keep yourself scarce," Henri Bernard sneered when he saw Scarlett standing at the entrance of the command tent.

Scarlett watched him turn all the way around on the stool placed before the sealed case that still contained the ancient journal she'd lifted from the ground.

"You're no linguist, Henri. Why don't you let me have another go at those pages?"

"Because you've proven you can neither be trusted nor relied upon."

"You're overreacting."

"No, I'm just managing the site."

"My actions were wrong. I admit that. But I had my reasons."

She stepped inside the tent and let the flap close behind her. The strong scent of coffee grounds proved overpowering in the tent's tight confines, as Scarlett drew close enough to Bernard to see the coal black brew that looked thick as tar atop the makeshift stove. She could also see he'd set up the portable electron microscope on the simple work table that was coated in a layer of dust.

Bernard shook his head. "You're even a bigger fool than I thought. So much time spent looking at the past that you can no longer see the present clearly."

"What does that mean?"

"That you're hopelessly naive. I'm sorry it's come to this, I truly am."

Something in his eyes scared her.

"A few pages of parchment, Scarlett," Bernard said, following her eyes. "Tell me, were they truly worth your career?"

"I was just about to ask you the same question."

Outside the tent, Scarlett stood in the morning air under the warm sun, perspiration starting to soak through her thick shirt as she tried to steady herself with several deep breaths. Anything to fight off the impulse to storm back inside the command tent.

She'd just started to head toward the area of the dig itself when she spotted a pair of villagers from nearby Vadja approaching with shotguns slung from their shoulders. The dig paid them, rather handsomely, to provide security, thinly veiled tribute to keep local trouble away. It was the way things were done here in Romania and not unlike the way they were done in a multitude of other countries where she'd worked, particularly in Ephesus (Turkey) and

Petra (Jordan). Even Israel wasn't immune to such practices, especially those digs based in the West Bank.

She wondered if Henri had ordered the security guards
to keep an eye on her. But then she saw them veer slightly
in the boy Ilie's direction to get some water, his first customers of the day.

Scarlett crossed the area where a bevy of college archaeology majors were standing around the remains of the vast
Roman temple, wondering when they'd be allowed to get
back to work. She passed behind the ruins and rested her
shoulders against an outgrowth of rock, craving a cigarette
even though she'd quit smoking upon earning her Masters
degree. Quite an accomplishment, considering that—

Rat-tat-tat . . . Rat-tat-tat . . .

Scarlett's thinking was interrupted by the blare of what
sounded like firecrackers, taking her back to Fourth of July
celebrations spent at the family's lakeside home.

But this wasn't the Fourth of July.

And that's when the screams started.

TWENTY-SIX

RETEZAT MOUNTAINS, TRANSYLVANIA

Scarlett poked her head out from behind the excavated
temple ruins long enough to see black-clad gunmen with
what looked like scarves disguising their faces rushing
about everywhere. Opening fire on her friends and associates
wildly and indiscriminately. Mowing down whoever crossed
their paths or had the sense to try to hide or flee.

She ducked back behind cover, breathing turned shallow,
shoulders pressed against jagged rock so hard it bit into
her skin through the fabric of her shirt. More gunfire and

screams, pleas of mercy and cries for help, sounded beyond. A young college student, a beautiful coed who'd borrowed Scarlett's shampoo just yesterday, surged by only to be cut down by bullets that stitched up her spine and sprayed a cloud of frothy blood into the air, as she fell forward. She landed with her face angled on Scarlett, dead eyes seeming to lock upon her.

More booms resounded from the gypsy guards' shotguns, followed by a concentrated automatic fire loud enough to bubble Scarlett's ears. She peeked out again, following another pair of the guards hired to protect the site charging forward with guns spitting fire until they were cut down by a blaze of bullets. Then she spotted the boy Ilie running toward the area of the temple, bullets tearing through his backpack and sending bursts of water flying in his wake.

"Ilie!" she yelled, forgetting in that moment he was deaf. "Il—"

She remembered when he changed direction suddenly. Shedding the backpack as he darted away from one gunman who'd snared him in his line of sight and then another.

He'll never make it. He'll be killed like the others.

Scarlett burst out from behind the heavy stone remains of the excavated ruins of the temple, cut a diagonal path straight to Ilie and dragged him down to the ground just ahead of a fresh staccato burst. Impact with the gravel and stone shattered the cell phone in her front pants pocket and she felt it break apart as she rolled atop the boy to shield him. He was sobbing, the first sounds she'd ever heard him make, save for an occasional laugh. She turned his face so he could read her lips, hoping his English had gotten good enough.

"We're going to be okay, but we've got to get away from here!"

Tears rolled down from his moist eyes, dragging streaks of grime across his cheeks. She'd just helped the boy back to his feet when one of the phantom-like gunman ground to a halt directly before them, ready to shoot in the same moment a huge blast sounded and he went flying backward with his chest erupting blood, gristle, and gore. Scarlett whirled, shoving Ilie behind her, to find one of the gypsy guards on his knees, reloading his shotgun while bleeding badly from the shoulder and side. A fresh hail of fire seemed to lift him almost upright before dropping him back to the ground in a cluttered heap.

By then, Scarlett had taken Ilie in tow and was darting through the obstacle course–like layers of the unearthed temple. She'd had guns pointed at her before in less than friendly countries and settings, but until now had never experienced one fired her way, never mind from a veritable army. She felt the heat of the bullets whizzing past her, or imagined she did, hearing the distinctive thwacks of rounds cracking into unearthed fragments of the ancient Roman temple scattered around her.

Since he couldn't hear the gunfire, those impacts that sprayed flecks of limestone into the air froze Ilie each time, forcing Scarlett to tug him even harder. She heard him whimpering, knew she needed to stay strong if she wanted to save the boy as well as herself.

They reached the foot of the mountains as more gunfire concentrated their way, disappearing into the brush to leave the bullets and gunmen behind them.

But not the last of the screams. Scarlett pictured the faces of her fellow workers and team members, friends now. Thirty-five of them, mostly college age. Wide-eyed and bright, but no more.

Their screams curdled Scarlett's blood. She grabbed tighter hold of the boy so as not to lose track of him in the cover of the brush and woods, finding renewed purpose in saving him, as if saving herself was not enough. She waited for the sounds of pursuit and more gunfire trained their way, certain they'd be coming before too very much longer.

And they did.

Just a single set of steps, though. Scarlett and Ilie rounded a bend leading up a hillside that formed the lowestmost reaches of the mountains that ringed the area like vast stone sentinels. She yanked the boy to a halt, pushed him away from her and signed for him to stay still and quiet. She'd hoped to find a severed branch to slam like a baseball bat into the gunman's face when he rounded the bend. But finding none, she opted for the biggest rock she could hold comfortably, lurching back upright just as their pursuer drew close enough for her to hear his boots thrashing through the ground thickets.

Scarlett lunged out when she first glimpsed him in a hazy blur. She'd planned to crash the rock into his face, but he sped past her, already grinding to a stop when she pounced. Hitting him once in the back of the skull and then again, again, and again as he dropped to his knees and fell over face-first.

Scarlett grabbed Ilie by the hand and led him on an erratic path through the thick and gnarled brush. Finally the boy tugged at her sharply and collapsed to the ground in exhaustion, eyes still wide with terror. Scarlett crouched even with him, hoping she didn't look as scared as she felt.

"The village!" she said, making the sign for that as well. "We need to get to the village!"

Ilie nodded, slowly recovering his breath.

This way, he signed, grabbing hold of her to pull himself back to his feet.

TWENTY-SEVEN

Las Vegas, Nevada

There was no way at that point to either retrieve the body or to determine its identity. Michael initially figured someone must have slipped, or been jostled, into the Daring Sea when the power went out. Then Alexander pulled him aside, the night continuing to grow worse by the moment.

"There's been a breach in the Daring Sea," he reported, adding, "one of the suites."

Those dark five minutes had plunged the entire city of Las Vegas, the Strip in particular, into utter chaos. Traffic remained gridlocked and dozens of accidents had been reported after the traffic signals went down. The Strip itself remained a parking lot, a scene turned all the more frantic and bizarre by tourists spilling into the streets in search of answers. A fair number, fearing terrorism, rushed to pack their bags and flee the city. What they didn't know was that McCarran Airport had been shut down in the wake of the now confirmed crash of a commuter jet coming in for a landing just as the power died on the runways. The commuter plane slid onto the equally darkened tarmac where it collided with a cargo jet and burst into flames on impact. There were some survivors among the eighty-five passengers but the exact number kept changing.

At first Michael rode Alexander's shadow through the clutter, trying to reassure the guests and stem the panic. But he quickly gave up when his efforts proved fruitless.

"They need us in the control room, Michael," Alexander

told him, after listening to a hushed message from a security guard.

The Seven Sins had been built with virtually every eventuality in mind, but there was no precise procedure to follow
for something like this. The authorities had been alerted
as soon as the return of power allowed, and the next step
was to retrieve whatever was left of the victim's remains
via robotic submersible. Eventually, a diver would need to be
sent into the waters, but that required the great whites to
be herded into the holding area, where they were regularly
vaccinated to protect against bacterial infections, no small
chore.

Meanwhile, Michael and Alexander joined Naomi Burns
in the mega-resort's surveillance room, a highly equipped
center dominated by the latest in security technology located directly over the casino floor. The command center
featured dozens and dozens of closed-circuit monitoring
screens showing every inch of the complex thanks to over
two thousand cameras stretched across the property. The
pictures they provided were watched over by hundreds of
personnel also responsible for issues pertaining to climate
control, traffic, and surveillance of suspicious persons. An
endless sea of smaller screens were layered amid larger ones
featuring the most heavily trafficked portions of the property, lighting the otherwise dim confines in a wash of color,
a prism-like kaleidoscope that splashed over the faces of the
monitors, whose eyes never left the screens for which they
were responsible.

"This is what we know, Michael," Naomi Burns reported
as soon as she spotted him enter, having distilled the most
vital information from the constant flow of reports coming
in. "All of Las Vegas was affected, including the control
tower at McCarran. There were reports of a crash that was

just confirmed, but details remain sketchy. This blackout took out cellular service as well and even our security guards' backup walkie-talkies stopped working, along with the backup power system."

"What do we know about the breach?"

"The Daring Sea suite where it occurred," she informed him, "was registered to a man named Edward Devereaux. He checked in last night while you were getting acquainted with Durado Segura. Nothing stands out as irregular in his registration information at this point, other than the fact that he paid with a cash deposit of five thousand dollars."

Meanwhile, emergency procedure was to immediately evacuate all levels of the Daring Sea suites until such time it could be confirmed the breach was contained and no further danger existed. Michael couldn't count the number of people who'd told him he was crazy for even considering the construction of underwater lodging within a marine environment. As a result, those Daring Sea suites were built with so many redundant protocols and safeguards as to be as safe, if not safer, than ordinary aboveground rooms. Among these protocols was the fact that each suite was sealed as tight as a submarine, so if the glass did somehow crack or rupture the entire underwater structure wouldn't flood, and any damage could be contained to that single suite. The glass itself was eleven inches thick; three even, separate layers finished on both sides with a special clear polymer. Michael had ordered his engineers to go beyond even what was required of him by state and city building officials who had advanced their own stringent demands to discourage him from the effort in the first place.

The glass walls of the Daring Sea suites had endured every test imaginable from high-powered bullets to explosions mimicking a terrorist attack. Understandably, that left Michael uneasy over what could have possibly caused an actual breach in a facility that had suffered not so much as a crack or fissure in any of its glass in its entire history of operation.

The investigation into the source had already begun by the time he and Alexander reached the control room, with the lowering of a small robotic submersible into the Daring Sea to provide a firsthand view of the suite in question.

"The breach occurred on sub-level four, suite number forty-one." Naomi turned back toward the wide screen monitor following the submersible's descent. "Robbie should be coming up on it now."

"Robbie" was the resort's pet name for the submersible, after the famed robot from old movies and television shows.

"Here we go," said Naomi, as Robbie approached what looked like an empty chasm amid an otherwise intact bank of individual glass walls so wondrously constructed as to appear to be a single sheet.

"Do we have an exact time for the breach?"

"No, Michael," Naomi told him, "but it was shortly after the blackout struck, almost immediately, that we know for sure."

Michael looked toward Alexander, the two of them sharing the same thought.

The pressure resulting from even a minor breach in the glass on its own would be enough to rupture the entire wall, but not right away. It would take time, certainly enough time for Edward Devereaux to safely flee and return to the surface either by elevator, if they were still working, or up one of the myriad of emergency stairwells. That indicated the breach might have been caused by a catastrophic event that had ruptured all the glass in a single moment, something that seemed unlikely at best.

"No evidence of a blast or explosion?" Michael said, wondering, when Robbie came up on the missing glass wall.

"No signature I can see, whatsoever," Alexander told him. "This was no bomb, Michael, no terrorist attack."

They all continued to watch as Robbie steered toward the breach and entered the Daring Sea suite to a surreal scene of chairs, pillows, magazines, clothes, luggage, a Bose Wave radio, lamps with their cords still connected to the wall sockets, and a laptop all floating in the water.

"Indications are," said a technician viewing the screen with them, "that the victim either swam or floated into the Daring Sea where the sharks found him. But that doesn't explain their erratic behavior." He turned to look toward Michael. "I watch them every day and I've never seen them act this frenzied, not even close."

"Do we know anything else about the victim, Naomi?" Michael asked.

"Just the usual stuff on the registration form. He listed his occupation as sales and left an address in France."

"Sounds routine."

"Maybe not," Naomi told him. "In addition to Devereaux paying in cash, the clerk at the VIP desk remembers him writing down an address, then tearing up the form and requesting a new one."

"As if, what, he'd forgotten it?"

"I don't know, Michael. It just struck her as strange. We just learned that the business number he left in Paris doesn't exist. And the residential address he gave us on the replacement form turned out to be a water treatment facility."

"Normally that would be funny," Alexander noted.

Michael shot him a look. "Not tonight."

"There's something else interesting," Naomi noted. "As his preferred charity, Devereaux chose the International Center of Missing Persons and Exploited Children."

"Do we have a picture?"

Naomi touched a button on the keyboard before her and a grainy shot captured of Edward Devereaux at the VIP registration desk upon check-in filled the screen.

"Wait, I recognize that man," Michael said. "I signed a Seven Sins souvenir book for him just before the blackout."

Michael felt Alexander grasp his arm firmly. "The Las Vegas police want to see you."

"Anything else?"

"Yes, the FBI is on the way."

TWENTY-EIGHT

RETEZAT MOUNTAINS, TRANSYLVANIA

Ilie led Scarlett along the lower line of mountains, clinging to the protective shroud of the woods at their base while never letting go of her hand. The clamminess of the late morning had given way to a day warm and breezy beneath a sun rising high in a clear sky. Its warmth baked the sweat soaking through Scarlett's shirt, gluing it to her flesh. Her cargo pants were even worse, sodden with so much perspiration the heavy cotton and polyester material seemed to squish as she moved.

It felt surreal, *unreal.* Her mouth was bone dry but felt coppery. And she *smelled* blood, too, as if residue of the massacre were somehow clinging to her nostrils. She chased the memory of the awful screams from her ears, knowing she was lucky to be alive. The boy, too.

Could it be the remains of the ancient manuscript the gunmen were after?

The possibility alone left Scarlett trembling. She never should've inspected it on site, should've kept its existence an utter secret and smuggled it out of the country somehow. That meant the responsibility for the deaths of her entire team may have rested, partially at least, with her.

Oh God . . .

Right now Scarlett could only focus on reaching the town of Vadja to call for help. Justice had to be done. Rampant corruption or not, even Romanian officials would respond appropriately to a mass murder.

Faster, she signed to Ilie, *faster.*

TWENTY-NINE

LAS VEGAS, NEVADA

Needing to recharge his mind after his lengthy interview with the police, Michael headed for his private dojo next to the bubble glass office from which he worked at the bottom of the Daring Sea. He loved training with Alexander in hand-to-hand combat and all manner of weaponry, especially knives, while completely surrounded by sharks. His favorite moments were when one of his sharks seemed to hover outside the thick glass enclosing the five-thousand-foot glass-enclosed space watching. Occasionally the shark would veer and shoot away as if shot by a cannon, only for Michael to see Assassino prowling around the glass in its place, sometimes nuzzling it with his snout. Michael enjoyed nothing more than meeting Assassino's eyes, the big fish in those moments seeming to grasp what he was doing.

Today a fight between one of his other great whites and a tiger shark over the remnants of a side of beef dominated the action beyond the glass. The two monsters moving with a grace and agility developed over millions of years of evolution that itself looked terrifying and natural at the same time. Everything fluid, no wasted motion whatsoever. Man could learn a lot from them.

After completing his hand-to-hand and knife combat

training with Alexander, Michael paused atop the straw tatami mats.

"This is just the beginning," he said, after Alexander tossed him a towel. Directly to his rear stood a canvas-covered *makiwara* board that looked like an archery target from his knife throwing practice. "But you know that already, don't you, Alexander?"

His interview with the police had been detailed, but ultimately unproductive. It was clear they had no idea what had shut off all the power for those five minutes. The entire Strip and surrounding area had gone dark. They had no suspects. They probed Michael for some connection to the death of Edward Devereaux which, in itself, was hardly surprising given that Michael's seemed to be the first name that came to mind whenever something unusual happened anywhere in the city. This time the difference lay in the detectives' probative questions about the hotel itself and how a death like this could possibly have happened. Any connection to the greater blackout suggested possible murder, while a mere random occurrence suggested a tragic event linked to some structural flaw in the design of the Daring Sea suites. And, as a precaution, the FBI had ordered all those suites closed until further notice, although Michael had steadfastly refused their overtures to shutter the entire hotel.

None of which boded well for Michael, the Seven Sins Resort and Casino, or Tyrant Global. The FBI decided not to interview him until tomorrow, when Michael's old friend Special Agent Del Slocumb promised to handle the chore himself.

He continued to look toward Alexander, as a huge chunk of meat descended from the Red Water feeding time for the sharks above. Snatched up by Assassino, himself, in a wild flurry that scattered the rest of the sharks.

"There's a predator out there," Michael told Alexander, "and we're the prey."

PART THREE

THE DEVIL

*If you had not committed great sins,
God would not have sent a punishment like
me upon you.*

Genghis Khan

THIRTY

VADJA, ROMANIA

The convoy of massive black Range Rover SUVs, their windows blackened, thumped down the flattened earth road like steel monsters from a far-off future. It seemed to stretch forever, a dust storm kicked up in the convoy's wake. A road that could for days be traveled only by single flatbed trucks lugging loads from farm to market seemed to rebel against their presence, slowing their approach to the town center with pits and potholes forged by the last storm and the one before that.

At the first sign of their presence, Scarlett and Ilie had veered farther up through the hillside that steepened appreciably as they drew closer to the actual mountain range itself. Scarlett assumed the vehicles had taken one of several major spurs that ran off the Transfagarasan Highway to reach such an out-of-the-way spot settled by gypsies years before, atop land to which no one else had laid claim.

She had mixed a bit with the villagers and enjoyed hearing tales of their rich history that had been waylaid in large part by the efforts of former communist dictator Nicolae Ceauşescu to end the roaming that had for so long defined their lifestyle. So the gypsies who'd managed to survive the Nazi onslaught had become virtual prisoners placed, for no better alternative, in fixed locations that could be best described as internment camps that replaced their traditions with strict rules and regulations often brutally enforced.

While things had greatly improved for their people after communism's fall, many of the residents of Vadja complained to Scarlett about the loss of the true old ways. Roaming the countryside had become akin to homelessness and poverty, leading many of what had once been called tribes to settle in villages like this where they could keep their memories and live as they saw fit.

As a result, to the occupants of those Range Rovers, the village of Vadja in Romania's Transylvanian region must have looked plucked from another time. The central square was little more than a tight cluster of clapboard buildings with peaked roofs, comprising both homes and small businesses that served as a gathering point for the once migratory residents. They walked around socializing, enjoying a monthly community lunch, a long tradition kept up now to keep hold of as many of the old ways and spirit amid modern times as possible. Even the larger homes dotting the landscape were uniform in design, square with central chimneys and simple entryways fronted by heavy wooden porticos layered with straw matting to catch the dirt and manure laden within the grooves of the men's work boots. Besides the farm store, combination restaurant and market, old church building, and modest town hall, no structure stood out amid the barns and storage sheds that froze the village in time.

From her perch with Ilie just short of the start of the steep mountain grade, Scarlett saw a dust cloud announce the convoy's presence well before it entered the central square. At the final curve, the ten black Range Rovers seemed to emerge out of nowhere, as if conjured by some mystic or magician, looking as foreign here as spaceships in a modern city. Even more anomalous was the presence of an old blue bus at the convoy's rear.

A pair of Romanian national police officers armed only with pistols, the detail assigned to Vadja, emerged from a small shack and approached the vehicles as they ground to a halt in eerie synchronicity. A small crowd of residents had gathered and the officers sifted their way through them, stopping just short of drawing their weapons when the doors to the Range Rovers flew open.

Scarlett stood alongside Ilie in a shroud of brush, watching from the hillside as upward of sixty men spilled out fast and hard from behind the Range Rovers' blackened windows, brandishing a mix of submachine guns and assault rifles either slung from their shoulders or clutched in their grasp. All wore tight black, form-fitting masks, stitched with thick weaves of white in the pattern of a skull to make them appear like an army of the walking dead. The police officers held their hands forward in a conciliatory fashion, addressing the first gunmen to emerge when the set immediately behind those viciously gunned the officers down. Their bodies crumpled to the dusty town square paved with thin gravel, and the gunmen stepped over them as they advanced into the gathering crowd that collectively shrank back in fear.

Those who turned to flee were swiftly caught, the gunmen sweeping their legs out with blows from the butts of their assault rifles. Others who'd emerged from the Range Rovers paid the gathered townspeople no heed at all, fanning out to search the nearest of the buildings and surrounding homes, while the next wave out did their part to herd the curious and frightened townspeople into a tight cluster in the center of the square.

A third phalanx of gunmen rushed for the homes that dotted the village's perimeter and outskirts. This while a dozen men kept their weapons trained on the increasing numbers being gathered in the town square itself, a number of the villagers not shy about voicing their protests. For the oldest among them, this brought back memories of the persecution they'd suffered under the communists, their reaction understandably indignant, while whatever urge to resist they might have felt was tempered by the bodies of the two police officers now lying atop widening pools of blood.

Though it was daytime, the sky had turned unusually dark, filled with thick black clouds that had begun to sprinkle raindrops instead of unleashing torrents of water from the sky. As if the convoy had somehow dragged the darkness here with them and would take it away again once they departed.

Some of the men who'd dispersed from the vehicles returned to the square shoving stray residents, including the elderly and infirm, ahead of them. Another group continued the process of going door-to-door and breaking into any building that was locked, collecting those residents by any means necessary to shepherd them into the square. Others returned with several dozen grade-school-age children in tow. They ranged from six or seven years old to several boys and girls in their mid-teens.

With the village deemed "cleared," four of the gunmen took up posts on either side of the SUV centered in the ten-vehicle convoy. Then more armed men fanned out through the crowd, their positions chosen strategically to keep all the villagers in their sights and to avoid catching each other in a cross fire should the need arise to let loose with their weapons.

The rain picked up slightly, the sky seeming to darken even more, while the villagers watched a rear door of the center SUV opening to allow a figure to emerge. He was garbed entirely in black, from his gloved hands to his shoes and long coat that scraped across the ground. But what the residents of Vadja noticed more anything else was a dangling, shroud-like black veil draped over the figure's head to conceal his face.

A second figure trailed him out the open door, the SUV rocking on its springs as if grateful to be relieved of his vast bulk. Virtually all of that bulk was muscle, showcased by a military-style jacket that fit his massive frame like a glove, only half of his face covered by a mask. The massive figure had blond hair slicked back to ride his scalp tightly. Standing as close to seven feet as six made his frame seem even more laden with rippling muscle. All told, a terrifying and impossible sight that left the villagers gawking.

The veiled figure, meanwhile, stepped over one of the police officers' bodies and kicked at the next as if to make sure he, too, was dead.

"I wear this veil for your own good," the man began, his voice measured and even, almost mechanically calm. "Because if you saw my face, I'd have no choice but to leave all of you dead. I believe you've heard of me. I believe all of you know who I am."

A few of the old women crossed themselves, muttering words indistinguishable to those even next to them who were mumbling the same thing.

"Now," he continued, rotating his eyes about the crowd, "there's something your village has that I want. Where is the archaeologist you have become familiar with?"

The villagers exchanged blank stares, none offering a response.

"A woman in her late twenties," he added. "An American familiar with your ways and language."

More silence.

"Please don't make me repeat myself," he addressed them, in the same measured tone. "If you know who I am, you know what I'm capable of."

"Diavol," a villager uttered in little more than a whisper.

"Close enough," said the dark man.

THIRTY-ONE

"Black Scorpion," someone in the crowd muttered.

The villagers closest to the dark man caught a flash of white behind the front portion of his veil, a hint of a smile.

"I see you are acquainted with the name both myself and my organization are known by. So it would seem no further introductions are necessary, and we may attend to the business that has brought me here so you may return to your normal lives."

Standing before those cowering in fear, Vladimir Dracu seemed not to blink, his gloved hands clasped before him. Some days he had to remind himself of his own name, since he was almost never addressed by it, and could count on a single hand the number who knew him by any name at all. And Dracu was glad for that, since the years in which he'd gone by his real name were riddled with nothing but misery and memories better forgotten.

But Dracu couldn't forget; not everything, not even most. The tortured experience of those times had forged the essence of the man who became Black Scorpion and one could not exist without the other. The bridge between who he'd been and who he was was soaked in blood, lots of it, shed by those both powerful and weak, the latter not unlike the hopeless lot gathered in the square before him now.

Dracu walked into the cluster of villagers, his huge body-guard following at a discreet distance behind him. Dracu circled amid them, feeling their fear and hearing their sobs at the realization that a dark legend had come to their town. The rain stopped, the clouds moved on, and the sun's rays hit him like a spotlight, turning his black garb and veil shiny, more like a sheen of paint slathered over his skin than clothing. Parents drew their children in closer, clutching them as if that might provide some protection.

"Yes, I am real," Dracu continued. "Not a legend, or a nightmare, or some phantom conjured by the organization to which your village has been paying tribute for so many years now. But I will be here only as long as it takes someone among you to tell me where I can find this American female archaeologist, where she might be hiding."

No one spoke. A few of the villagers exchanged taut glances.

Dracu shook his head again, expression tightening, angered now instead of regretful. "Who speaks for you?" he asked the villagers clustered before him.

There was no response.

"I ask again, who speaks for you?"

Hesitation followed once more, before a big bearded man wearing an old black hat faded to gray in places raised his hand.

"Me, sir," he said, voice muffled by his hood. "I am Arek, chief elder of the village."

Dracu moved to him, close enough to feel the heat and fear on his breath. He stretched a hand outward and laid it atop Arek's shoulder, feeling the man stiffen fearfully.

"Can you feel my touch? Because it's the touch of a man. See, I'm not a monster, am I?" He turned toward the massive figure behind him. "Armura isn't a monster either, in spite of his appearance. Show him, my friend."

With that, Armura tore off his sleeveless military-style jacket to reveal one side of his chest and neck to be horribly scarred by what looked like crisscrossing claw marks.

"Appearances, you see, can be deceiving. Armura means *armor* in Romanian because as a young man growing up in Siberia, his face was mauled by a tiger he ended up killing with his bare hands. He paid for that with the loss of his senses. Armura cannot touch, taste, or smell. He sees and he hears, and that is all he needs. But I call him Armura because he has felt no pain since that fateful day and is physically incapable of ever feeling it again. Some days I envy him for being shielded from the painful world in which we live."

Dracu turned back toward Arek. "But this doesn't have to be painful for you. The real monsters are the outsiders I've already rid you of like a plague. And now I'm going to give you the chance to make things right, Arek. I'm going to give you a chance to tell me where I can find the young American woman I came here for."

"I cannot do this."

"Why?"

"Because I do not know."

"But you know her."

"That I have not denied."

Dracu eased himself closer to the chief elder. "Tell me what you've heard, these stories and legends that make you fear me so, while embracing those who would do your people and your ways such harm."

Arek's face tightened into a scowl, showing no fear. "I've heard how you burned villages, sold young women and children into slavery, left those who crossed you impaled on stakes by the roadside, even stole infants from their cribs." That final line spoken while he cast a tentative gaze toward the blue bus at the back of the parked vehicles.

"All lies, but all true at the same time," Dracu told him with a smirk. "Because I've never done anything of the kind to those who support my efforts. Such acts are aimed solely at my enemies, not my friends. Yes, I have burned villages that betrayed the old ways, taken the women and children of those in my land who have crossed me as retribution, and made examples of those who foolishly opposed me. It is a terrible thing to be misled. So I don't blame you fully for this transgression, I blame the Romanian government that sees fit to welcome foreigners to our land to take what's rightfully ours in pursuit of their own ambitions. All you need do to set things right, Arek, is tell me where I can find this young woman."

Arek swallowed hard and straightened his spine, revealing the true breadth of his shoulders forged by forty years of hard work in the fields. "I already told you I do not know."

"So what are we to do, Arek?" Dracu asked, sounding genuinely mournful. "What choices are we left with? Only one, I'm afraid," he said, drawing a blade from inside his jacket. "A gypsy knifemaker forged this for me out of the finest Damascus steel," Dracu continued, holding the blade so the sun shined upon its perfect shape. "The leather sheath is hand sewn and includes his signature. Perhaps the two of you are acquainted."

"We have no loyalty to the government, no loyalty to anyone other than ourselves and our own ways. We want no trouble, from you or anyone else. We can't help you."

With that, an old gypsy woman next to Arek dropped to her knees, hands flailing at the air. "He speaks the truth! Please, *please*, believe me! I beg you to spare us!"

Dracu looked toward the old woman, passing the knife from his left hand to his right. "You know this archaeologist?"

"I have seen her. She has been here. But she is not here now."

Dracu turned his gaze up toward those hills, squinting into the sun through his veil. He felt, sensed, someone watching him from there.

"I'd tell you more, if there was any more to tell," the old woman was saying. "But there isn't. Arek speaks the truth."

"You agree with the old woman, Arek?"

Arek stiffened even more. "She speaks the truth, just as I did."

"And would you have her die in your place, too?"

"No," the big man said rigidly.

"Then I applaud you for that much, anyway," Dracu said. And, with that, he gently helped the old woman back to her feet and looked her straight in the eyes. "I believe you." He stepped back toward Arek. "Which makes you useless to me."

Dracu's right hand, the one now holding the knife, shot up from its dangling position, the motion so fast as to be little more than a blur. Arek was still staring at him defiantly when the slit in his throat opened and blood began to cascade out. His hands clutched instinctively for the wound. Arek's eyes bulged, looking both shocked and puzzled, before he sank to his knees, then keeled over face-first into a widening pool of his own blood, writhing toward death.

THIRTY-TWO

VADJA, ROMANIA

Ilie tried to bolt down the hill, but Scarlett latched onto the boy and pulled him back behind their meager cover, holding tight while making sure he could see her lips.

"No! There's nothing we can do!"

But that's my grandfather, the boy signed. *My grandfather!*

Scarlett pulled the boy in close, hugging him to spare him further sight of what was transpiring below. He'd witnessed the dark man murder his grandfather, just as she had watched the gunmen murder her entire dig team.

Scarlett had hoped the village would have provided respite, sanctuary and, ultimately, salvation in the form of the Romanian police. At the very least, she wanted to get the boy home and herself to the safety of the nearest American consulate. But now Ilie's grandfather was dead, and Vadja had become a place to run from instead of to.

Scarlett crouched slightly and took Ilie by his bony shoulders. "We have to go," she said, making sure he could see her lips. She had to get to a phone and call for help, with her cell having been smashed when she dove to the hard ground back at the dig site to save the boy. "Do you understand?"

He nodded stiffly, then signed, *Yes.*

Through the woods, she signed this time, to make sure he grasped her whole meaning. *To that bigger village.*

Bună Ziua, he signed.

Yes. Can you get us there?

Ilie nodded just once. *This way,* he signed, and tugged her toward the rise leading deeper into the mountains.

Wait, Scarlett signed back, resisting his effort as her gaze returned to the village below. *Something's happening.*

THIRTY-THREE

VADJA, ROMANIA

Dracu waited until Arek's body had stilled before running his gaze back over the residents of the village. "See what happens to those who defy me? How many more must I kill before you tell me what I want to know? Who among you is brave and loyal enough to prevent that from happening, who will speak the truth before more die needlessly?"

"Please spare our lives!" the old woman pleaded from nearby, hands held up and out in a position of prayer "I beg of you to leave us in peace, in the name of God!"

"Don't you know the old Romanian saying?" Dracu

grinned. "*Până ajungi la Dumnezeu, te mănâncă sfinţii.*
'Before you reach God, the saints will eat you.' I'm not going to eat you, though. My punishment for your insolence
and silence will be much worse."

He ran his eyes around the children standing close to
or pressed against their parents, believing the adults could
protect them.

"This is your final chance," he said. "Tell me where I can
find the archaeologist or I will take that which you love most
in her place."

Dracu walked among the villagers, watching them cower
before his step, waiting for a response.

"Very well," he said, looking toward the nearest of his
men when none came. "Round up the children. And every
young woman you can find."

Dracu watched the last of the children and young women
being loaded onto the blue bus from the backseat of his SUV
through its windows tinted black to prevent anyone from
seeing in. Amazing how clear, though, the view was looking
out. An apt metaphor for life, he supposed, which so often
worked only in one direction.

Watching the last of the young women climbing onto
the bus, he couldn't help but remember being herded into
the back of a truck himself as a frightened little boy. He remembered the pleas and cries for help once its rear door was
hoisted open, how they'd quickly faded out once he was
tossed on board and the truck began rumbling forward.
Those sounds were replaced a few miles down the road by the
retching of kids vomiting from fear, the claustrophobic confines, the darkness, and the bumpy ride. The process fed
off itself until all the other children became sickened by the
awful smell.

All but one.

The people of Romania genuinely believed in the stories, that he was the devil. The truth was they weren't far off, because he knew the devil's ways so well. He knew what evil was and he knew only evil had enabled him to survive when none of the other children from that truck had. All dead within a few years, while Dracu endured, focusing not on where he was, but where he'd be someday.

To seek his revenge.

To become the man he was now.

To distract himself from the memories, he focused on a beautiful blond girl, sixteen or seventeen maybe, who'd squeezed her face out an open window of the bus. Dracu slid down his window and smiled at her through his veil. Their eyes seemed to meet and Dracu cast a wave she, of course, did not return.

Her beauty was rare for its depth, stretching all the way to the purity of her very soul. The sight of her left a lump in his throat and he slid the window back upward to deny himself anything further. Having been reared in squalor and depravity, ugliness had been so long and so much a part of his life that he appreciated beauty more than anything. Beauty made for the greatest distraction. In beauty there was hope.

The girl seemed to stare at him straight through the dark glass of the SUV. She held her green eyes, wet with tears, on him even after the bus started rumbling forward, Dracu finally able to breathe freely when it at last slipped from view.

THIRTY-FOUR

"Tell me what you've learned about the blackout," Michael said to Alexander while standing at the rail of his third-floor balcony, from which he tossed his big cats their evening meal. They circled beneath him, growling with impatience and standing on their hind legs to better reach the food.

"Nevada Power, AT&T, and Verizon can't offer any explanation for it at all."

"Including how it could have possibly affected cell service?"

"Apparently every cell tower serving the city was taken off-line, along with everything else."

"I thought they operated on an entirely separate independent grid."

"They do," Alexander told him.

Michael dropped two more roast-size hunks of beef down to his waiting cats. "And what about the walkie-talkies that don't operate on any grid at all?" he asked Alexander. "What about our backup generators?"

"Not just our walkie-talkies and generators, Michael; every casino was affected the same way. But no transformer blew or overloaded and the readouts at the main distribution and transmission facility never even approached the red. What took place during those five or so minutes is entirely inexplicable."

The cats that had snared their meals pranced off with the meat clamped within their jaws, while the rest snapped at each other while waiting their turn. Michael dropped two more chunks down to them.

"Computer hackers?" he resumed to Alexander.

"Not if the system safeguards and backups are to be believed. This was a hostile action, Michael. We just don't know who pulled it off, how, or why. Not yet. It's as if those five minutes never happened at all."

"Tell that to Edward Devereaux, Alexander."

Removing his remains from the Daring Sea had proved a difficult, close to impossible, task. A larger robotic submersible, complete with hand-like pincers, had to be lowered to collect them after Robbie proved not to be up to that task. Once the larger submersible recovered what little was left of Edward Devereaux, Michael ordered a second feeding time be added for his sharks in the crowd-driven Red Water spectacle to keep them away during its return trip to the holding area where the medical examiner and Las Vegas police were waiting.

"Why only this one room?" Michael said, down to his last three cats now. He emptied the rest of the tray for them and peeled off his gloves as they charged off already munching. "How could it possibly have been targeted by itself, with no collateral effects on any of the neighboring glass walls?"

"I've looked at the video footage taken of the suite a dozen times now. There's no blast residue, no evidence whatsoever of even an extremely limited and focused explosion."

"Something blew out a wall twelve inches thick with triple-layered safety glass, Alexander."

"I know, Michael. But it wasn't caused by anything conventional, anything we can identify. According to the access log," Alexander continued, "Devereaux entered his room twenty-one minutes before the blackout struck."

"We need to find out who he really is, what he was doing at the Seven Sins."

"Ahem," Naomi said from the doorway leading onto the balcony that overlooked his painstaking re-creation of the great beasts' native habitats.

Michael held up the empty tray, still swimming with juice. "You missed all the fun."

"Good, since they don't need to be fed again until morning," she continued, "and we need to talk now."

THIRTY-FIVE

ISTANBUL, TURKEY

"I shouldn't be here," Ismael Saltuk said to Raven Khan as he took a seat next to her on the park bench.

"Sit and enjoy the sun for a few moments. You should get out more often."

Music, Tchaikovsky's First, which was among the most famous and greatest piano concertos ever composed, emanated in barely audible strands from inside the nearby Halic Congress Center. Located along the shores of the Golden Horn in the middle of Istanbul, the concert hall was surrounded by parks and promenades on its other three sides. The paying customers, of course, were able to enjoy the concerto much more inside, but Raven didn't expect to be here long enough to hear the famed crescendo.

"There's nothing I can do to change your mind, is there?" Saltuk said, his thin, knobby shoulders framed by the golden rays of the sun. "You are determined to do this."

They made for a strange pair seated together, thanks in large part to Saltuk's frail appearance contrasted against Raven's vital one. She never wore, nor needed, makeup, preferring the perpetually tanned look her dark shading created. Her unique combination of grace, strength, and beauty led to the stares of men being constantly cast her way. Raven always pretended she didn't notice, never meeting their gazes with her emerald-green eyes she had once been told could pierce any man's very soul.

"Yes," she said to Saltuk, "I am."

"Even if I were to evoke Adnan Talu's name, what he might think of this fool's errand you're about to embark on?"

"I wish I could let it go, I truly do."

"We all have choices, Raven."

"Not this time."

It had been Talu who'd rescued her from the orphanage after she'd given up hope anyone would ever come for her. She remembered his limp, born of a shattered leg in a boyhood accident at sea, that noticeably worsened with the years. As a young girl, Raven had little recollection of him even using a cane and it saddened her to see how badly his infirmity came to hobble him as he aged. Talu was the closest thing to a parent Raven ever had, and she still remembered the day he plucked her from the orphanage to be raised as his daughter.

Raven had virtually no memory of all of the time before she came to the orphanage, as if that's where life had begun for her. She did recall strange dreams that would haunt her sleep and rouse her screaming to awaken the other children in the crowded dormitory. The dream always began with the sound of firecrackers and finished with her feeling the warm soak of blood over her clothes as she struggled to breathe. She hadn't thought much about those dreams in a very long time.

Until sight of the little girl hugging her mother's corpse in the cargo hold of the *Lucretia Maru* brought them all back to her.

"What can you tell me about the organization behind that slave ship and its leader, Ismael?" she asked Saltuk.

"I am doing you no favors by telling you anything. This is bad for business, very bad."

"Some things are more important."

"*Nothing* is more important than business. Beyond that, fighting battles that can't be won risks squandering all we've achieved. Talu taught you that from the first moment he brought you into the organization."

"Talu is dead. So were half the people in that cargo hold. You call *that* good business?"

"No, I don't. But it's also none of *our* business."

"Yours maybe."

"And why do you care so much all of a sudden?"

"Because even a pirate has a code, a sense of honor, lines that are not to be crossed. Because if I do nothing, I'm as bad as the monster responsible for what I saw."

"An excellent explanation. Now, tell me the truth."

Raven thought again of the crying child calling to her dead mother while trying to rouse her. "I don't know, I truly don't. What I saw on that ship triggered something inside me. I haven't been able to think of anything else since, except the man behind the human trafficking that filled that cargo hold with people. Tell me how I can find him, Ismael."

"This man you seek has unfathomable power and an army to protect him."

"Don't make me ask you again."

"You can't get to him; no one can. Even I've never met this man; our business is always conducted through intermediaries who insulate his very existence. In Eastern Europe, where he's reputedly from, they call him the devil. And I've heard nothing to make me dispute that point."

"You wouldn't be here now, if you had nothing for me. You came because you found what I asked for and you want to talk me out of using the information."

Saltuk sighed deeply and shrugged. "Guilty as charged. But I don't have much. Just rumors of Black Scorpion's interest in an archaeological dig."

"Where?"

"Romania. The region of Transylvania."

THIRTY-SIX

LAKE LAS VEGAS, NEVADA

"We're salvaging the contents of Edward Devereaux's room from the Daring Sea," Naomi Burns said back inside, keeping her distance as Michael sprawled on the floor playing with his house-trained pet black panther, Nero. "In cooperation with the police, of course."

In the ten years they had known each other, Michael had never seen Naomi dressed in anything approaching casual. All business, all the time; first as a lawyer with a prestigious New York law firm and then King Midas World's and Tyrant Entertainment's corporate counsel after Michael had intervened during a nasty, and unfounded, fraud investigation. Like everything else, Naomi took her attire seriously, preferring Chanel and Nicole Miller as well as Armani. A mix of colors chosen to accentuate her olive skin and perfectly coiffed auburn hair that was the longest Michael had ever seen it.

She'd been at his side through all his interaction with police earlier in the evening, including an interview with the two LVPD detectives he recognized as frequent patrons of Cobra, one of the Seven Sins nightspots that had become the most popular club in Las Vegas. Their questions at this point were cursory at best, merely preliminary since they knew no more about the victim, or his true purpose in coming to the city in general and the Seven Sins in particular, than Michael did.

Michael continued tussling with Nero, as he weighed the update Naomi had just provided. "Why don't you come closer?"

"Because that thing scares me."

"Nero's tamer than a house cat. Why don't you tell me what's really bothering you?"

"It's about Devereaux," Naomi told him. "He originally reserved a regular room, but his reservation was lost."

"Explaining how he ended up with the upgrade to a Daring Sea suite."

"Could be his killer created the whole scenario to enable the murder. Our upgrade policy in such cases is fairly common knowledge."

"Sure, and there were a thousand easier ways to kill him. But they chose this one because it would do the most damage to the Seven Sins. My gut says somebody wanted to send me a message, Naomi."

Naomi checked an incoming text and said, "Get ready for another bad one."

"One of Devereaux's possessions bears special attention," she continued.

"Besides his laptop?" Alexander posed.

"In addition to: a portable DNA analyzer."

Michael's eyebrows flickered. "I didn't know such a thing existed."

"It does and Devereaux had one at the Seven Sins. The submersible also located one of his hands. It's been turned over to the police, so if there's a match to his fingerprints on any international database, we'll know who he really is soon enough."

"What else, Naomi?"

"That's enough for now."

"Then let me add something," Michael told both her and Alexander. "Remember what that technician in the control room said about the sharks? Well, I've never seen them behave as aggressively as they did last night either. Never. Something set them off."

"Besides blood, you mean," Naomi raised.

"The behavior started before there was any blood. This was something else, something we've never encountered before. We find out what that is and we'll have a much better idea of what we're facing." Michael moved his gaze to a trio of wall-mounted monitors broadcasting a rotation of scenes from inside the Seven Sins property. "If only he could tell us," he added, focusing on the one now picturing Assassino in the Daring Sea.

THIRTY-SEVEN

Bună Ziua, Romania

Scarlett and Ilie had fled after watching two dozen or so young women and children being herded onto the blue bus that had come as part of the convoy. They'd clung to the cover of the trees and brush that dominated the lower reaches of the mountain range that was centered among a host of towns of varying sizes. They'd emerged finally on a narrow, gravelly road with a thin canal dug to siphon off the water from spring storms on the side opposite this part of the range.

Scarlett crouched and again laid her hands on the boy's shoulders. If not for being with her, he'd be on that bus too.

"You must go now," she said and signed at the same time.

No, he signed, shaking his head. *I stay with you.*

You can't. Your family needs you.

She waited for him to nod, then watched the breath catching in his throat, the boy starting to choke up.

My grandfather, he signed.

Scarlett hugged him tight to her as he broke down, and Ilie's sobs finally receded.

You'll be safe, she signed and spoke, easing him away. *I promise.*

The boy nodded resolutely. Scarlett hugged him one more time and then pressed on, looking back only once.

The road signs said Bună Ziua was five kilometers away, but it felt closer to ten by the time she finally got there at dusk. An actual bustling town in comparison to the much smaller Vadja with shops, stores, restaurants, and bars. It was located along a commercial route used by trucks ferrying goods throughout the countryside, a kind of stopover way station.

She walked along the town's main drag, convinced all eyes were turned her way. Had the perpetrators of the massacre and the dark figure in the black veil put out the word to watch out for her? Probably not. After all, how often did the villagers see a grimy and disheveled Western woman wearing torn and tattered clothes ambling along their streets? But the looks those passing closest to her cast left Scarlett checking her reflection in a storefront window lit by a street lamp to find parts of her hair and face still splattered with dried flecks of blood sprayed from the bodies of friends killed close to her back at the dig.

She shuddered again at the thought of them being gunned down at the site and felt herself seized by a fresh wave of terror and panic. Having worked in some of the most dangerous and precarious areas of the world, she was no stranger to risk, to danger. But this kind of experience stretched far, far beyond anything she'd contemplated within the realm of possibility.

Then again, what she'd uncovered in that hidden chamber was far beyond anything history had offered to her before. The means to prove one of the greatest legends science and superstition had ever conspired to create was, in fact, true. But her surviving the massacre at the dig site would mean nothing, if she didn't live to tell of it.

Her clothes had been soiled and shredded by the long trek through the woods. Branches had scratched at her face and scalp, left her wavy hair a matted mess amid scratches and scabs. She'd perspired through her shirt and miles back had come to loathe the stink of herself, embarrassed to enter a public place looking and smelling like this. The last of the day's sun had burned her face, leaving it hot to the touch and stinging incessantly.

Walking along the central square of Bună Ziua, Scarlett was keenly aware of uneasy and curious stares cast her way. Attention was the last thing she needed right now and she crossed the street, since the opposite side seemed less traveled. She took to aiming her eyes downward and quickened her pace, hoping to draw as few stares as possible and focusing on the street as she walked. It was reasonably well paved to a stone-like finish and lined with vehicles. She seemed to recall a nearby mill employed much of the town's people, distinguishing this village from those of the farming variety that enclosed it, the old and the modern mixing well. It even boasted the one movie theater for many miles, but no police station she could see anywhere in evidence.

Not that it mattered. If the dark figure, this devil who'd come to Vadja, was as powerful as she sensed, there was no telling who he held in his pocket, starting with the very authorities charged with protecting the people from him.

So she stopped looking for the local *policia* station and headed toward the first bar she spotted instead.

THIRTY-EIGHT

While they waited for the next series of reports, Michael returned his gaze to the twinkling lights of boats drifting about Lake Las Vegas beyond his property. He had christened his gated seventeen-acre estate *Roma Vetus*, Latin for "Life of Rome." His ten-thousand-square-foot home sat in a modest three-acre section, beyond which lay an additional fourteen acres patrolled by Michael's collection of big cats. His several tigers and five lions had free rein on those fourteen acres Michael had named the Serengeti, adjacent to *Roma Vetus*. He'd hired a caretaker as handler of his animals, amazed at the man's ability to walk safely among them, to supervise their care and feeding along with a veterinarian who was on call twenty-four hours a day.

The rickety cobblestone drive forced those entering to keep their pace slow on the chance that one of the big cats strayed into their path. His house was accessible by a second gate opening into a valet area and enclosed with an electronic fence to keep the big cats from wandering inside.

Roma Vetus, with its marble floors, authentic moldings, and archways constructed in Italy, had long been his sanctuary away from the hurriedness and energy of the Seven Sins. A welcome respite of solitude and peace where he could enjoy all the keepsakes of his various accomplishments. But that wasn't the case tonight.

Michael reclined in a chair hoping he might be able to steal some sleep. But the day's events—first the hearing before the Gaming Control Board, then the inexplicable blackout, and finally the guest's death—all continued to gnaw at him and conspired to keep Michael from holding his eyes closed for more than a moment.

Dawn wasn't that far off when he heard Naomi in the midst of a phone conversation in an adjoining room, her Samsung Galaxy still clutched in hand when she returned to the great room.

"That was the FBI," she told him. "Our old friend Del Slocumb wants to have a chat with you tomorrow."

"You mean today," Michael said, climbing back to his feet.

"I think he'd prefer now."

"Of course. He's been after me for years. You think sharks are the only things that can smell blood in the water?"

THIRTY-NINE

Bună Ziua, Romania

A bar, Scarlett figured, was the place most likely to have a pay phone and the place where her presence would draw the least attention. Entering also reminded her how thirsty she was, and she dragged herself across the plank floor beneath the spill of lights from ancient iron fixtures suspended from the ceiling. Her swollen feet throbbed inside work boots she'd been afraid to remove for fear she'd be unable to squeeze them back on.

The bar served soda and Scarlett had guzzled three down before she checked her pockets to find just enough cash with which to pay. The bartender was a tall man with leathery skin that looked stitched to his face, except for a jagged pale patch where part of his upper lip looked to have been torn off and then sewn back on with a knitting needle. His hands were callused, his hair an unwashed oily mesh of curls and tangles everywhere but an unlikely bald crown.

"Thank you," Scarlett managed, after he poured her a fresh glass, gulping the soda down before the foamy head had settled all the way.

"Is s*h*omething wrong?" The bartender's mangled upper lip left him with a peculiar lisp that accounted for his mispronunciation. She realized when he tried for a smile, it didn't move at all. "You s*h*eem ups*h*et."

"No, I'm fine."

The man regarded Scarlett's torn, soiled clothes and shrugged. "Are you s*h*ure?" he asked, his dull gray eyes looking as if the color, and the life, had been bleached out of them.

Scarlett heard the door open and watched a pair of dark-suited men enter. She looked up and followed their slow scrutiny of the bar in the mirror glass directly before her. They were the only ones so dressed and she could see their eyes scanning about casually, as if pretending not to be searching for someone. A man in a police uniform followed them inside, but Scarlett couldn't tell if he was with the men in suits or not.

"Do you have a pay phone?" she asked the bartender.

"Over there," he said, pointing to an alcove opposite the bar's single rest room.

She made her way toward the alcove and risked a glance back to see if the dark-suited men or the man in the police uniform had followed her. So far, nothing. They were nowhere in sight from this angle and she had the alcove all to herself. For now.

Scarlett reached for the phone in a trembling hand and pressed out the long series of numbers to place a collect call. She fought to still her finger, thoughts of what the man in the black veil intended to do with the young women and children of Vadja cascading through her mind, when the phone was answered.

"International operator."

"Yes," Scarlett said. "Collect from Scarlett Swan. . . . Scar-lett Swan," she added slower.

She heard ringing again, the tone different. She pressed the pay phone's receiver tight against her ear.

Answer, answer! she willed, squeezing the receiver tighter, *please answer!*

The phone, though, continued to ring. Scarlett gave up counting how many times, when suddenly a click sounded. And then she heard the familiar voice, the most welcome sound she could ever remember.

"Yes," said Michael Tiranno, "I'll accept the charges."

FORTY

Bună Ziua, Romania

"Michael, thank God!" Scarlett managed.

"Hey, baby," Michael said, "do you miss me?"

"Please, you need to listen. I don't know how much time I've got," she said, thinking of the men in suits and the police officer.

"What's wrong?" Michael followed, his tone changing instantly.

"Something terrible has happened. My team, they're all—"

Before Scarlett could continue, she felt a grasp like iron fasten on her shoulder, easing her around.

"Are you s*h*ure you're okay?" the bartender asked her, his gray eyes seeming almost translucent.

She wanted to pull away, but his grasp was too strong. "Scarlett, who else is there?" she heard Michael ask. "I heard another voice."

"Would you like me to get you s*h*ome help?" the man was saying. "S*h*ome medical attention perhaps*h*."

"No. I told you I'm fine. Please," Scarlett said, cursing herself for letting the man sneak up on her this way.

"Scarlett, whose voice is that? Where are you?" Michael's voice was louder now, more assertive. "Are you still in Romania? Tell me exactly."

"Yes, the village of Bună Ziua. That's where I'm calling from. I found *something*, Michael, something incredible. I think it's what we've been looking for. I can't believe it myself. If I'm right—"

"You mus*h*t let me help you," the bartender interrupted.

"Please, not now."

"It would be my pleas*h*ure," he continued.

Scarlett felt his grasp tighten, saw something change in his eyes.

"Michael," she managed.

FORTY-ONE

LAKE LAS VEGAS, NEVADA

Michael felt himself stiffen, the hairs prickling the back of his neck. "What's happening, Scarlett? Tell me exactly where you are."

"It would be my pleas*h*ure," Michael heard the other voice say faintly.

"Scarlett, who's with you? Who is that man?"

"Michael—"

A thump sounded, silencing her words.

"Scarlett, what's happening? Talk to me!"

A thud, followed by more silence.

"Scarlett?"

And Michael heard the distinctive click of the phone being hung up an instant before the dial tone returned.

"The archaeologist's call was indeed placed from a bar in the Romanian town of Bună Ziua, population twelve thousand," Alexander told Michael an hour later, as he jogged one of the wall-mounted fifty-inch monitors to a map of Romania, then narrowed in on a mountainous corner of Transylvania.

"That's close to the location of Scarlett's dig." Michael had found the number for the bar from which she'd called and dialed it a dozen times, but the phone rang unanswered on each occasion. "I can tell from the mountains," he added, ready to try dialing again.

Alexander clicked on the Image icon and Google Maps brought up a shot of the actual establishment and the town square around it. "But the local authorities found no trace of her there and insist there are no witnesses willing to say she was ever on the premises."

Something terrible's happened. . . .

Michael's next call was to Romania's Ministry of Culture, the government entity that had signed off on the permits for the dig in Transylvania and arranged for the necessary variances, and facilitated the site logistics—all in return for a sizable cash stipend. Initially, Michael failed to get anyone on the phone, finally managing to reach an underling who professed to have no knowledge of any tragedy befalling Scarlett's team in the field. Nonetheless, the man promised to contact the proper authorities to investigate further and get back to him once he heard something.

Michael wasn't holding his breath in that regard. He knew

corruption in the Romanian government ran rampant and, if some terrible tragedy had indeed befallen the archaeological team under his sponsorship, it stood to reason that at least some elements of the government were involved. Perhaps the stipend his company paid hadn't been large enough. Perhaps this was a not so gentle exercise in extortion to get more money out of him.

But Michael doubted that. Gravely.

"Something terrible has happened. My team, they're all . . ."

They were all *what*? The dig was at this site in Romania thanks to his financial support, Scarlett continuing the quest on which he had set her. He had to find her, had to save her. Fast. She was, she was . . .

Images flooded his mind of the times they'd shared, interludes in cities like London and Florence and a few times at dig sites themselves where she endeavored to teach him things in which he pretended to be interested. Smiling was easy when picturing spending the night with her in a tent or a primitive lodge room. She was so different than all the other women he'd been with, often so enamored with themselves as to not fully appreciate the world around them. Scarlett was different; the world was *everything* to her, its intellectual origins explaining the very existence of civilization. Questions Michael found himself pondering so often now validated and enhanced by this woman who never stopped looking for the answers.

"I can't believe it myself. If I'm right . . ."

Scarlett Swan's final words to him about whatever it was she'd uncovered, cut off in midstream.

"I have to find her," Michael heard himself saying, watching Alexander's expression tighten. "What is it, Alexander?"

"The dig's location."

"What about it?"

"Nothing," he said, his eyes no longer meeting Michael's.

Michael moved back to the glass wall overlooking the rear of his property, Naomi and Alexander following his reflection in the glass, as Nero uttered a low, guttural growl, sensing something awry. Finally he turned slowly, looking toward Alexander.

"Good. Then call McCarran Airport. Tell them to have the Boeing fueled and ready."

Naomi came toward him before Alexander could respond, shaking her head. "We're in the midst of a crisis here, Michael. A public relations nightmare that will have the sharks who walk on land snapping at our asses. There's blood in the water and we're looking at a feeding frenzy if we don't get a handle on all this fast."

"And you can handle things just fine on your own."

"Handle things? Listen to yourself, Michael. You're not thinking straight."

"Yes, Naomi, I am."

"By later today, the authorities will be lined up ten deep to talk to you. That's not something I can just *handle*. The Daring Sea suites are going to be closed for God knows how long, and we're trying to find lodging for all the high-roller guests evicted from their rooms who haven't fled Vegas already. What happened is all over the news, nationally, and our reservation operators can't keep up with all the cancellations—at last check, wait times on the phone are stretching to nearly an hour. We're sixty percent empty, which means we're going to be hemorrhaging three million dollars a day. And beyond that we've got a guest who wasn't who he claimed to be being lifted in pieces from the water."

"And I thought we had *real* problems," Michael said, trying for a wry smile he failed to muster.

Naomi ignored his attempt at humor. "You mean, like the fact that our bonds are likely to trade further down when the markets open, by ten percent at the very least? Aldridge Sterling makes Max Price look like a schoolboy, Michael.

And if he really is involved and keeps pressing, we're look-ing at a massive short sale that could substantially dilute Tyrant Global's value and our ability to borrow."

"There are very few people in the world I trust with my life. Two of them are standing with me in this room right now. Scarlett Swan is another, for different reasons entirely." Michael stopped without elaborating further. "I have a phone, Naomi. I can deal with all this from where Alexan-der and I are headed."

"And where's that?"

Michael looked toward Alexander. "Transylvania."

FORTY-TWO

LAS VEGAS, NEVADA

Naomi Burns was hardly surprised when FBI agent Del Slocumb showed up right on time at the Seven Sins's first-floor corporate offices later that morning. She was waiting for an update from Michael and Alexander when informed he was in the reception area. Naomi briefly flirted with the idea of making this man, who'd turned his various pursuits of Michael Tiranno into an Ahab-like quest, wait for a time, but then thought better of it.

"Ms. Burns," he greeted, rising stiffly from his chair, wincing from knee pain in what she had learned stemmed from an old football injury. "I told your boss to expect me this morning, but I understand he's not available."

"Where'd you hear that?"

"Well, according to officials at McCarran, he left last night on Tyrant Global's seven-thirty-seven. Not like Mr. Tiranno to run from a crisis, is it?"

"I wasn't aware even federal agents were able to obtain such information without cause."

"National security was the cause."

"And how does that concern Mr. Tiranno?"

"Many view him as a threat."

"Many?"

"After last night's blackout, I should think so."

"Oh, so you believe Mr. Tiranno was behind that, along with all the other baseless charges you've leveled against him. All the casinos were blacked out, Agent, and much of the entire city."

Slocumb smirked, clearly enjoying himself. "I wouldn't put it past him; I wouldn't put anything past him."

This cat-and-mouse game had been going for years now, ever since the FBI's investigation into the implosion of the Maximus Casino on the current site of the Seven Sins, for which Michael had been fully exonerated. In everyone's mind, that is, except Del Slocumb's.

"And only one casino was the site of an inexplicable death at the same time," Slocumb continued, leaving the thought dangling.

"So now you suspect Mr. Tiranno of concocting the blackout to draw attention away from killing a man he didn't know and met only in the course of signing an autograph. Can you at least listen to yourself, Agent?"

"I'd rather listen to Mr. Tiranno explain *him*self."

"He's otherwise detained."

"Where?"

"None of your business."

"Would he rather face inquiries from the State Department?"

"Is this a national security interest, too?" Naomi asked him.

"The victim was a foreign national. You tell me."

"I can tell you Mr. Tiranno will be available to meet with you just as soon as he handles some other matters requiring his immediate attention."

"A strange time to leave the city, don't you think, Counselor?"

"Why don't we continue this in my office, Agent Slocumb?"

"What Mr. Tiranno does and why he does it is none of *your* business," Naomi said, taking the matching fabric chair next to Slocumb's set before her desk.

Slocumb smirked. "I thought Durado Segura might be chasing him."

"Durado Segura is in no condition to chase anyone."

"Yes," the FBI agent agreed. "Interesting skills your boss has acquired. And always running to the rescue of pretty women in distress. I wonder if a career in politics might be in his future."

"I was just wondering the same thing about you."

Slocumb gazed around at the elegant furnishings that adorned Naomi's office. She had chosen the pastel wall shades, subtly colorful tapestries, and warm, milky lighting personally, creating a work environment that best exemplified her choice in wardrobe as well, color-keyed to form a perfect match with the office's light tones.

"And I know the first place I'd come for a donation," Slocumb told her.

He hesitated to let his point sink in, his cocoa-shaded features growing tight enough to exaggerate the patchwork of wrinkles forming around his eyes and the furrows lining his brow. A marine who'd served in Desert Storm, Slocumb had a protruding chin at the bottom of a square, angular face and still wore his now graying hair in a close-cropped military style. Naomi remembered him as a smoker, but he carried no smell of that with him today and she noticed his teeth looked freshly bleached.

She made sure Slocumb could see her stiffen in response to his last remark. "I'm not sure how to take that."

"We're just having a nice friendly chat here. There's no reason to get testy."

"Remember, Agent, I'm still a lawyer."

As chief executive officer and corporate counsel of Tyrant Global and King Midas World, Naomi's office was fittingly the largest on the floor, offering a view of the hotel's lavish pool and faux beach area through its one-way windows. The floors were bamboo, the furniture fitting a modern Oriental motif that Naomi found both soothing and functional, an elegant match to the office's light shading. Her favorite piece was a beautiful indoor fountain given to her as a gift by Michael's investors in the Seven Sins Macau, a nearly identical property currently under construction in that booming city. Strange how it had been so much easier to arrange the variances and building permits there than it had been for Michael originally in Vegas. Partly because of a past that was the subject of much scrutiny and legend, some of which had left Michael and King Midas World perpetual targets. The FBI's Del Slocumb was hardly the only official who'd focused his sights here, just the most stubborn and relentless, given that he blamed his lack of advancement in the Bureau on his failure to ever deliver anything of substance on Michael Tiranno.

"Did I mention Tyrant Global's seven-thirty-seven had filed a flight plan for London, Ms. Burns? Could you tell me what was so urgent there that your boss had to leave Las Vegas in the midst of such a crisis?"

"Business."

"You said that already."

"Then why did you ask me again?"

"Let's discuss Edward Devereaux, who was killed here last night."

"A tragic accident," Naomi said, nodding, probing Slocumb's knowledge of the death as well as his intentions.

"That wasn't his real name, you know. We identified him from fingerprints lifted from the hand found in the Daring Sea. His real name was Pierre Faustin. He's a French national."

"That much I was aware of."

"Did you know he worked for Interpol?"

FORTY-THREE

SARDINIA

Aldridge Sterling sat at his desk within the nine-thousand-square-foot, seventy-five-meter yacht, watching the sun shine over Porto Cervo in the distance.

"I'm glad you're pleased," Sterling said from his grand office on the upper deck of his yacht, looking out over a spectacular 360-degree view of the surrounding ocean. This while he engaged in a call over his Polycom speakerphone, simultaneously checking a screen displaying the Hong Kong markets. Yesterday, one of his wealth management funds made fifty million in the first hour of trading there, his fee thirty percent of all profits generated on behalf of his clients.

"How could I not be?" a thick, deep voice responded. "Please transfer all these funds into my offshore accounts. I will have my finance minister contact you for all the necessary paperwork."

Sterling's primary clients, the ones who'd made Sterling

Capital Partners the most successful hedge fund in the world, were primarily the heads of rogue states and nations. They came to him because he was expert in hiding their vast wealth and resources from prying eyes in their own countries as well as internationally, especially now that the American Department of Justice had become increasingly vigilant and aggressive in such pursuits. Legally established accounts in places like Panama, the Cayman Islands, and Luxembourg built up over more than a decade afforded Sterling this luxury. And his own genius at manipulating his AUM funds through shell entities that existed only on paper of his own making kept the authorities none the wiser of his efforts.

"By the way, thank you for the excellent referral last week," Sterling said. "You may have opened up a whole new market for me."

"Just remember that when it comes to taking out your commission."

"Of course," Sterling grinned. "After all, it's the people's money, isn't it?"

Sterling had had his yacht custom-made in Italy by the luxury manufacturer Benetti. *Big Whale* had been outfitted with a sprawling, view-rich master suite, and twenty staterooms that allowed it to sleep upward of forty guests. It was decorated in dark cherrywood and beige marble with leather-upholstered furniture, white carpeting, and walls covered in mauve silk. It featured a fifty-seat theater, two swimming pools, an eight-person whirlpool tub, a boardroom, a gymnasium, four Riva speedboats, a helipad on the flybridge, and an impressive array of diving gear Sterling wanted to pretend he used. The yacht's massive twin-diesel engines and twenty-five-thousand-gallon gas tanks were capable of putting out twenty-eight knots even in rough seas.

Gazing back toward Porto Cervo, though, Sterling could see any number of yachts that were even bigger than the *Big*

Whale at a price tag that made his eyes bulge. Mostly they belonged to Arabs, illiterate mongrels made billionaires without ever working a day in their lives. If not for the oil over which they were lucky enough to live, they'd be dirt. He'd made many of them an even greater fortune over the years but, then, they'd made him a fortune, too.

And someday, very soon, Sterling would own a bigger yacht than theirs anyway. So big he'd turn the *Big Whale* into a dinghy for it.

"Mr. Sterling?" a male voice called tentatively from the door leading to the twenty-five hundred square feet of office space. "I'm sorry to bother you, sir," continued the man dressed in the white uniform not of a sailor, but a nurse. "It's your father. The senator's having one of his spells."

Barely acknowledging the man, Sterling climbed the outdoor spiral staircase up to the top deck where Senator Harold Sterling spent his days when they were here instead of New York, Palm Springs, or his estate in the Florida Keys. It was a laborious chore to have his father moved from place to place, but one Aldridge Sterling found well worth it since there was no better motivator for his relentless pursuit of ultimate success than the senator's presence.

Sterling reached the top deck to find his feeble father thrashing against two attendants struggling to keep him in his chair. He got that way once in a while, a brief moment of lucidity giving way to a violent fit that left him trying to escape the bonds of his chair to chase down some memory captured as a snapshot by his brain, which had pretty much turned to Jell-O. Doctors were able to slow the progressive effects left by his third stroke just enough to let Sterling keep him alive.

"Dad!" Sterling called, as he approached. "Dad!"

The old man's eyes showed no sign of recognition when he grasped his father at the shoulders, the attendants backing off to let Sterling restrain him alone.

"Dad," he said, softer.

The old man finally looked his way, toward a voice instead of a face, still showing no sign he knew it was his son standing before him.

"Calm down, Dad, calm down."

Sterling wondered what the old man might've been thinking during these fits. Perhaps reliving a moment from the war, or an especially important speech on the Senate floor, or just some simple task left undone from a decade before marking the last time he'd been lucid.

"How's it feel to be totally dependent on me?" Sterling asked, crouching before his father.

Harold Sterling thrashed in his chair some more, what might have been a brief blip of recognition flashing in his gaze as drool flecked out both sides of his mouth.

"I'm glad that you're here, because I can show you how wrong you were about me. I was the black sheep, the pariah, the bane of your existence not worthy of the Sterling legacy. You disowned me, but now I own *you*. Everything that happens in your life is at my behest. And here's the kicker."

One of the white-jacketed attendants returned just long enough to hand Sterling a child's sippy cup full of water, and Sterling eased the straw against his father's lips. The old man opened his mouth and sucked it in, slurping up the contents so fast that water began to dribble down his chin to mix with the drool.

"I know I'm not in your will. I know how much you would've enjoyed sticking that in my face. How pawning off the family fortune to charities would be the ultimate fuck you. But it isn't. The ultimate fuck you is me keeping you alive as long as I can to deny you that satisfaction, while all your care eats up the money. I hope somewhere inside you that makes you suffer even more."

Sterling watched his assistant approaching, extending a satellite phone toward him.

"It's him," the assistant said, a tremor of fear clear in his voice.

Sterling took the phone in his grasp and moved to the rail, gazing up into the beautiful Mediterranean sun.

"Hello, my friend."

FORTY-FOUR

LAS VEGAS, NEVADA

Naomi tried not to look taken aback. Instead, she rose and walked around her desk, taking the chair behind it.

"I'm guessing you must enjoy your current posting, rank, and pay grade, Agent," she told Slocumb.

"Excuse me?"

Naomi held his stare. "I understand this quest of yours has attracted plenty of attention here in Vegas, at the supervisory office in Los Angeles, and even in Washington."

"Really? And how would you know that?"

"I guess you can call it common knowledge. So is the fact that you call Mr. Tiranno your 'Wop' Whale, an allusion to Moby Dick, I imagine. I suppose that makes you Ahab, Agent."

"Pierre Faustin was assigned to Interpol's Violent Crimes Division," he said, sounding a bit more defensive. "You've heard of that, I assume."

Naomi had, of course, but couldn't figure out where Slocumb was going with this. "They specialize in international criminal apprehension, drug interdiction, and human trafficking—anything that moves across international borders with relative impunity."

"So what do you think brought a man like Faustin to Las Vegas and the Seven Sins?"

"Maybe he was on vacation. Try the tables, maybe take in a show. Hopefully, he wasn't a fan of Durado Segura."

"Or of Michael Tiranno, Ms. Burns. When I discussed Faustin's career, notice I used the past tense. That's because Pierre Faustin, the man who registered here two nights ago as Edward Devereaux, was suspended from duty six months back and later resigned."

"Interesting."

Slocumb crossed his legs. "What's really interesting is he was fired for cause."

"What cause might that be?"

"I'm afraid I'm not authorized to reveal the specifics, Ms. Burns, other than to say his termination was due to an investigation he insisted on continuing to follow up against the orders of his superiors."

"And this was for the Violent Crimes Division."

"Presumably."

Naomi hesitated, trying to find her bearings in Slocumb's barrage of innuendo. "Am I to presume that it's your belief Michael Tiranno is somehow a part of this investigation Pierre Faustin, aka Edward Devereaux, couldn't let go of?"

"You sound like a lawyer now, Ms. Burns."

"It's how I respond when baseless allegations are lodged against my employer."

"You're the one who suggested the connection, not me."

"It was a question, Mr. Slocumb, and I'm still waiting for an answer."

Slocumb took a deep breath. Naomi had long been familiar with how lawyers reacted in court when they needed to buy a few moments to collect their thoughts and prepare their next line of attack. Obviously Slocumb was, too.

"A lot of beautiful women work at the Seven Sins, Ms. Burns," he said suddenly, "don't they?"

"We're hardly alone in Vegas in that respect."

"They come and go, yes? A great deal of turnover."

"The Seven Sins enjoys the least of any resort and casino on the Strip."

"I commend you and Mr. Tiranno for that," Slocumb told her. "But, tell me, have any of the girls employed here gone missing recently, say in the past few months?"

"I'm not sure I understand your question."

"Then let me be more specific. Have any participants in your Elysium *Cirque du Soleil* show suddenly needed to be replaced without explanation in that time frame?"

"I really couldn't say."

"But you could find out. And if I'd posed the same question to him, would Michael Tiranno's answer have been the same as yours?"

"What are you alleging here exactly, Agent Slocumb? And what does any of this have to do with Pierre Faustin's presence at the Seven Sins?"

"We could assume the connection lies in an international investigation Faustin was supervising under the radar."

"Then you choose to dismiss the fact that Faustin was fired for cause, that he wasn't working in any capacity for Interpol when he came here, that he registered under an assumed name. I'd say that throws his credibility into serious question."

"Challenging an investigator's credibility is a defensive reaction, wouldn't you say?"

"Yes, if this Faustin, or Devereaux, was still an investigator. We're dealing in supposition here, not facts."

Slocumb appeared to be beaming, enjoying a rare moment of seeming to hold the upper hand. "Well, Faustin's dying inside the Seven Sins, and the bizarre circumstances surrounding his murder, aren't supposition at all."

"*Murder*, Agent?"

"Did I say 'murder'? My apologies, Ms. Burns. I meant to say 'death.' Surely you acknowledge a man dying in a hotel owned by the man he came here to investigate is beyond coincidence."

"Can you definitively confirm that this investigation Faustin was conducting even involved Mr. Tiranno?"

"Like I said, I'm not—"

"—authorized to reveal the specifics. Yes, I remember, Agent Slocumb."

Slocumb leaned forward to shrink the distance between them. "Look, Counselor, we both know Michael Tiranno blew up the former Maximus Casino on the eve of its opening and built the Seven Sins atop its ashes. Oh, and did I forget to mention he also buried his archenemy, the casino mogul Max Price, in those millions of tons of debris?"

"You never forget to mention that, Agent."

"Now let me tell you something else. I think your boss is frustrated by the old boys' club colluding to make sure he can't expand his brand in Vegas. I think the Gaming Control Board sniffing around his financial difficulties and irregularities is really pissing him off. I think the cost overruns related to Mr. Tiranno's obsession with completing this Forbidden City of his on the top floors of this monstrosity you call a hotel is driving him toward bankruptcy. And if he happened to find out an Interpol agent had information that could complicate things even further . . ."

"Former Interpol agent," Naomi corrected quickly.

". . . I think he may have reacted preemptively."

"Preemptively?"

"Let me put this another way, Ms. Burns. To your knowledge, did Mr. Tiranno have any contact with the man registered here as Edward Devereaux?"

"As I've already said, not besides signing an autograph for the man in our souvenir book. Mr. Tiranno probably signs more than a dozen of those a day."

"But yesterday eleven of those who got his autograph

managed to stay alive, didn't they?" Slocumb's expression remained flat and intense at the same time, a man playing with the house's money. "Does the name Amanda Johansen ring any bells?"

"Not to me."

"She was the player in your Elysium show I just mentioned. She disappeared six weeks ago, last seen here at the end of her shift. A missing persons report was filed by her roommate after she never returned from a sudden vacation she took with a very wealthy man she told the roommate she was having an affair with, and her cell phone went unanswered."

Naomi continued to hold Slocumb's gaze when he paused, hating the fact he'd caught her off guard.

"Amanda Johansen was found murdered in Ankara, Turkey two weeks ago," Slocumb resumed, when Naomi remained silent. "She was only recently identified with the help of DNA samples, thanks to a certain former Interpol agent who was following up another investigation."

Naomi rose from her chair. "Anything else, Agent?"

"Oh, yes. Did I forget to mention Amanda was pregnant?"

FORTY-FIVE

RETEZAT MOUNTAINS, TRANSYLVANIA

Raven Khan walked around the grounds at the foot of the Retezat Mountains that alternated between tall grass colored a vibrant green and rock-strewn gravel. The bulk of the gravel was packed down in the area around the unearthed remains of some archaeological find now left, along with everything else, abandoned to the wind.

She knew a sanitized scene when she saw one, mostly because she had been party to sanitizing plenty herself. And this reeked of just that.

There were no tents, no trash bins or bags, not even any darker, flatter patches of ground indicative of a standard-size archaeological dig team settling down for a while. There was nothing, but in nothing there were indications of plenty.

According to the intelligence she'd gathered, the archaeological dig that had attracted the interest of the same shadowy figure behind the human cargo of the *Lucretia Maru* had been fully operational just two days ago. While it was certainly possible they'd pulled up stakes in the forty-eight hours since, it seemed inconceivable they wouldn't have left some trace of their presence behind. More likely somebody had cleaned up after them.

Further scrutiny of the grounds in what she estimated would have been closer to the center of their camp revealed a few stray expended bullet shells cloaked by stones and ground debris. That area must've been washed of blood and swept of such shells, but a few had clearly escaped the sweep. And she found additional evidence of gunfire, lots of it, in chipped portions of tree bark that bore the distinctive signature of bullets of a caliber normally associated with assault weapons.

Raven felt she was standing on the scene of a massacre. She couldn't say how she knew this; perhaps it was true that so much violence leaves its own imprint on the air, like at the sites of famous historical battles. She'd felt something amiss even before she uncovered the shells or noticed the unfinished condition of the uncovered dig. She'd felt it as soon as she approached the area after making sure her Land Rover was hidden from view under the cover of the trees at the foot of the mountain range.

Suddenly she saw a cloud of dust lifting into the air ahead of a sedan speeding down the same hard-packed dirt road she'd taken to get here. A driver and two passengers, Raven noted, the man in charge likely to be the one in the back. After their car ground to a dust-churning stop, the three men emerged, all wearing the uniform of the Romanian police, or *Poliţia Română*, the country's central unit of law enforcement. The driver and passenger remained by the car while the third, a captain judging by the bars on his uniform, headed off to inspect the grounds by himself. Hands clasped behind his back, wearing shoes ill-suited for this purpose, and carrying no weapon she could see.

Raven settled back behind the cover of some brush and waited for him to draw farther away from his two guards.

Raven noticed the young Romanian police captain's uniform was untouched by the swirling dirt when she came at him from the rear, hand looped around his neck as she pressed her pistol into his spine. Raven felt him stiffen, eyes lurching back toward the men who'd accompanied him.

"You can't see them because they're in the trunk," she told the man in English. "You understand me?"

"I speak English," the captain said, nodding fearfully.

"Don't worry, they're still alive. Now turn around."

The captain did.

"I'm not going to ask your name or tell you mine. You want to report the fact that a woman incapacitated your guards and snuck up on you, be my guest. You see what I'm getting at?"

The man nodded, relaxing slightly.

"I'm not going to kill you or your men, unless you leave me no choice. Just answer my questions, starting with what you're doing here."

"A report was filed," the captain said. He looked young,

still in his twenties with rosy cheeks and hair that rode his scalp like a bowl.

"By who? About what?"

"By the owners of the dig claiming they'd lost contact with their archaeological team. About the fact they'd received a report that made them fear something very bad had happened."

"Then you'll want to bring these back to your superiors," Raven said, extending the trio of spent shells she'd found. "Who sent you here?"

"A request from the Ministry of Culture."

Raven gazed about the empty expanse of land. "And does the Ministry of Culture always dispatch the *Poliţia Română* for such things?"

"The dig was funded by a powerful American foundation," the captain said, by way of explanation.

"Then you can let this foundation know that its dig team is dead or taken, every one of them probably."

The young man looked down at the shells he was now holding, and let them rattle about in his hand. He seemed to quiver in the breeze, looking as if it might spill him over. Started to take a deep breath, then abandoned the effort halfway through.

"I found two sets of tracks leading off toward the edge of the mountains," Raven continued, "heading west. Is there a town or village in that direction?"

"Yes," the captain nodded. "Vadja. Gypsies mostly, the kind of folk who keep to themselves. We maintain a police post there. It's where I'm headed next."

"Why?"

"Because the post hasn't reported in for two days."

"One more question before you can be on your way. What was the name of this American foundation that was responsible for the dig?"

He pulled a piece of paper with some notes hastily scrawled

on it from his pocket, squinting as if having trouble reading his own writing.

"T-G-H-F," the captain said, finally. "Tyrant Global
Historical Foundation."

Now it was Raven Khan who quivered.

FORTY-SIX

THE BOEING 737

"It's not like you to leave something unfinished, Alexander,"
Michael said, as the Boeing descended for London's Heathrow Airport.

"Michael?"

"Transylvania. I saw the look on your face back in Vegas
when we were discussing the bar where Scarlett called
from."

Alexander continued to stare into the emptiness beyond.
"I've heard things," he said finally.

"Things? Could you be a bit more explicit?"

"Rumors, legends, about an all-powerful criminal organization that holds much of Romania, much of Eastern
Europe, in the grip of fear. It's run by a man who's never
been identified, never named, never even been seen."

"Does this man have a name?" Michael asked.

"The same one his organization is known by," Alexander told him, turning from the window. "Black Scorpion."

The Boeing landed at Heathrow, where they were to board
a smaller jet arranged by one of Alexander's most trusted
contacts that would keep the remainder of their journey as
cloaked as possible.

While waiting for the smaller jet to be prepped, Michael climbed into a waiting limousine which took him and Alexander, as planned, to the Baglioni Hotel thirty minutes from Heathrow. He registered for three nights in a suite that had been booked for him. Then, after lingering in the lobby just long enough to make sure the security cameras caught him, he and Alexander used a side exit where a rental sedan was parked with the keys on the visor. Alexander drove them back to the airport, keeping to the speed limit to avoid any police interference. Once back at Heathrow they boarded not the Boeing, but a much smaller Cessna Citation jet.

A tall, broad-shouldered man was sitting with his back to them, rising when they entered with a grin stretched across his face.

"Hello, mate," he greeted Michael.

FORTY-SEVEN

FRENCH GUIANA, FIVE YEARS AGO

"Hello, mate."

That was the first thing the man Michael knew only as "Paddy" said to him when they first met.

Paddy . . .

Michael knew the man only by his first name; that was part of the deal struck by Alexander with him five years before, when Michael found himself strangely melancholy after almost single-handedly saving the city of Las Vegas from destruction. An experience that should have left him feeling triumphant and vindicated in every respect instead, in his mind, highlighted his lack of the skill sets required to survive the kind of threats he was almost certain to face again. In essence, he was still very much the frightened boy in the barn unable to defend his own family from their killers; he was just older now.

Never again, Michael promised himself, *never again*.

Strangely and inexplicably, he knew in his heart that battles like this and the challenges they bred would continue to define him. Who knew what the next ordeal might bear. He needed the kind of training that could prepare him for whatever it might entail.

Otherwise, the world he loved so much, the world constructed from his vision and passion, could be torn from his grasp. It wasn't enough to rely strictly on Alexander and the forces his money could employ. If the ruthless cunning that had helped Michael thrive in the world of money and power had taught him nothing else, it had taught him that the first and most important person any man could rely on was himself. All that money and power wouldn't be able to save him from a bullet or a blade.

"What else is it you want?" Alexander had asked him, after Michael had done his best to explain. "I've taught you weapons training, hand-to-hand combat—everything I know."

"But not what you've experienced. And you haven't been tough enough on me. I need to know I can do it for real. I need to be trained by someone who doesn't give a shit who I am or whether I live or die."

"You want the best. But the best is also the most dangerous."

"Good. That's what we need."

They flew to São Paulo, Brazil, aboard King Midas World's elegantly appointed Boeing, normally reserved for high rollers from all over the world. From there, they drove straight from the airport to an outdoor café in the center of the city, waiting two hours in the heat beneath a table shrouded by a canopy that didn't open all the way.

"What did you say this man's name is?" Michael asked, impatience starting to get the better of him.

"Paddy," Alexander replied.

"Paddy *what*?"

"Just Paddy."

"British SAS—you did say that."

"You better fucking believe it," a man said in a thick brogue, as he rose from the table immediately behind theirs, seeming to have appeared out of nowhere.

Michael stood, looking up at the strapping figure the man cut. Massive shoulders, rough-hewn skin darkened and leathery in patches. A thick handlebar mustache rose over his gleaming smile, and a scar sliced down the length of his left cheek all the way to his chin.

"Michael Tiranno," Michael said, extending his hand.

The big man didn't take it. "Paddy. But you can call me Sergeant-Major."

Michael looked on, waiting for him to continue.

"Hope that doesn't bother you, mate."

"Not at all."

"I don't give a shit whether it does or not anyway." The big man cocked his gaze toward Alexander, the tilt of his eyes entirely different when regarding a perceived equal. "He know the rules?"

"I thought you'd prefer to tell him."

Paddy looked back at Michael. "My rules, mate, each and every one. First time you break one, you get on home or I leave you for dead."

"Leave me for dead where?"

"Did he just ask me a question?" Paddy posed to Alexander.

"He doesn't get the rules."

"You don't get to ask any questions," Paddy told Michael.

"That's rule number one. Rule number two is it's just us from this point on. Rule number three is you do exactly what I say when I say it. You don't do that, I leave and you're on your own. You read me, mate?"

The Boeing was already warming on the tarmac at Guarulhos International Airport's private terminal when they arrived in an ancient Jeep. Michael watched as the big man carried three packs on board, two that matched. Plenty of supplies, at the very least.

"You ready, mate?" Paddy asked, as they strapped themselves into the plane's luxurious confines.

"Ready for what?"

Paddy smiled and looked around him, shaking his head. "To leave all this for bloody French Guiana."

"Nobody'll bother us there" was all Paddy offered for an explanation once they were airborne, "that's for sure." Then he slapped Michael's shoulder with a hand that felt like pressed steel. "Plenty of places for me to tuck your body, if you die when we drop. Trained there myself in my early days with the SAS, and your friend Alexander's Foreign Legion uses it to train their pups as well."

"Hold on, you mean 'drop' as in *parachute*?"

"You know another kind?"

"I've never *dropped* before."

Ninety minutes into the flight, the sky dark now, Paddy stripped open two of the three packs he'd brought on board and yanked parachutes out from each of them. "So you'll learn. You don't learn, you die. That's what this is all about, teaching you how to die so you can live safer. Get it, mate?"

"No."

Paddy grinned. "You will."

Michael knew French Guiana was a territory of France located on the North Atlantic Coast of South America, bordering Brazil to the east and south and Suriname to the west. He also knew it was one of the least densely populated areas on the continent, with only three inhabitants per kilometer with the bulk of these living in the city of Cayenne.

Known for its rain forests, French Guiana remained truly pristine, even primitive, in its flora-rich appearance that was home to thousands of species of plants, mammals, amphibians, and fish. Some of these could be found nowhere else on Earth, rendering them severely endangered, rare to the point where the region in recent years had become popular for poachers, as well as kidnappers who victimized environmentalists prone to worrying about wildlife more than their own safety.

"We go in five," Paddy said.

"I can't see a damn thing. It's dark."

"That's what happens at night, mate."

"What about supplies?"

"We eat what we hunt or we bloody starve. How's that sit with you?"

"Just remember that I've never jumped in my life."

Paddy slapped him on the back again. "Gonna be a lot of firsts on this trip, mate," he continued, wedging an earpiece into and over Michael's left ear. "Stay close and follow me. I'll talk you through everything you need to know. Now, let's get you strapped in. . . ."

The parachute worn tight over his shoulders was surprisingly light, but bulky. The Boeing had been outfitted with a rear cargo door, useful for jumping out since it allowed for a clear field beneath them.

"See you on the ground," Paddy told him, five thousand feet over splotches of land and water below. "You don't follow me out, this ends here, and we'll never see each other again. So what say we find out how serious you really are?"

FORTY-EIGHT

FRENCH GUIANA, FIVE YEARS AGO

Michael did follow him outside into the air of the dark sky, waiting the instructed five-count after Paddy had dropped, and following a very brief tutorial on the perils of landing wrong or ending up in a tree. Paddy told Michael all the things he shouldn't do, but none of the things he should.

Survival. That's what this was about now.

Paddy had actually guided Michael down in the direction of a clearing that he overshot slightly, dropping into the shallows of a lake and ending up drenched in cool waters pumped from underground streams. His first thought was how badly he needed to change his clothes, his second that he wasn't alone. The water rippled, the currents bobbing up against him just after he heard one *plop* and then another. He turned toward the shoreline just in time to glimpse a third crocodile lurch into the water, and scrambled to shore before any of them could reach him.

"Get yourself dry, mate," Paddy said, folded-up parachute tucked under his arm, as he checked the night sky. "Let's make camp. We get started in the morning."

Michael would be wearing these same clothes for the next six weeks. His work started with what Paddy called "agility" training. Michael hoisted a severed log over his shoulders and ran along a path carved ages before through the forest.

"Where do I go?" Michael asked him.

"Just follow the path."

"But to where?"

"Same answer."

And he did, never daring to shed the log no matter how much his shoulders ached, and never stopping no matter how much his lungs burned. The trek brought him, surprisingly, through a camp of archaeologists nestled in the thickest part of the jungle where a young woman was lecturing even younger college-age students on the process of recognizing and identifying various sediments in the ground down here. Their eyes met, their gazes lingering, nearly tripping Michael up.

"You'd already be dead if that was combat, mate," Paddy warned when Michael reached him at the point where the path ended in a steep drop-off toward rushing rapids below. "Bet you didn't even see the bloody snake you almost stepped on while you were eyeing that piece of arse. Don't know how you missed it, given the thing's the size of a fire hose."

"I get the point."

"Missing the point means getting yourself killed. You get that?"

"It won't happen again," Michael managed, shedding the log and finding himself unable to lift his arms even to his waist.

"Don't apologize to me 'cause I don't give a shit."

"I didn't apologize. I said it won't happen again and I meant it."

"Good, because you die down here, I won't give it as much as a second thought. But there is a bright side to the story."

"What's that?"

Paddy yanked a twelve-inch hunting knife from the

sheath on his belt and handed it to Michael. "You get to catch dinner tonight."

"How about a gun instead?"

"Now there's a good idea, mate. Except I didn't bring any along, not a one. Just blades on this trip to make things more interesting. Now, let's go catch us a wild boar. Real tasty pork, take it from me."

Paddy must've already spotted the animal's trail, and used the opportunity to teach Michael how to track. Hunched low while smoothing the ground, finding the impressions of hoof prints and learning how to discern their freshness from feel.

Hunting through the brush, listening to Paddy expound on the most vital elements of tracking, reminded Michael of the expedition that had caught Assassino for the Daring Sea. How he'd jumped into the water to save a sailor who'd been washed overboard and for a moment, just a moment, was eye-to-eye with the great white in his own element. Assassino seemed to look at him differently that day, though he couldn't say exactly how.

"Now," Paddy said, as they crouched together over what Michael had already identified as fresh prints, "that's interesting."

"What?"

"Trail stops here. Whatcha make of that, mate?"

"I have no idea, Sergeant-Major."

"Well, I do. Wild boars are about the only creatures on the planet that'll hunt a man, sometimes even doubling back on him. I'd check behind you, if I were you."

Michael canted his head around and saw a pair of huge hooded eyes and big tusks poking out from the brush back along the trail.

"Have at it, mate," Paddy said, grinning.

He stood up and backpedaled, then slipped into the brush for cover, leaving Michael alone with his knife. And the boar that charged at him as soon as Paddy was gone.

Michael had no time to react, had time only to turn sideways to reduce his target and ready his knife before him. He was bending his knees to better balance his weight when the boar leaped headlong through the air, its massive rear legs extended straight out behind him. Michael heard its roar, smelled its musky stench, then felt its hot breath when the animal was over him, its battle-marred tusks coming up just short of impaling him with their broken tips.

He remembered jerking his twelve-inch killing knife forward and up, felt the blade tear into something first hard, then soft. Warm blood that felt like bathwater drenched him, as he went down beneath the still snarling, snapping animal. But Michael maintained the presence of mind to keep stabbing at it, more flesh and fur torn with each thrust and more warm, thick blood splashing against him.

"Easy there," Paddy cautioned, as he emerged from the brush to get a closer look at Michael's handiwork. "There's a lot of meals in that meat, unless you go shredding it all."

Michael shoved the creature off him, its tusks close enough to tear his shirt in the process.

The next morning found him in waist-deep black water, slogging through the mud-rich bottom and weed-encrusted shallows.

"Watch out for the crocs, mate," Paddy warned him from shore.

"How am I supposed to watch for them when I can't see shit through all this muck?"

"Like this, mate," Paddy said, and proceeded to smack a croc Michael hadn't even noticed on the snout, startling the creature enough to make it swing back toward shore. "Look for motion. Follow the ripples in the water. If they see you before you see those, start reading yourself last rites, because down here nobody's gonna do that for you."

Or anything else for that matter.

They ate only what Michael caught, first under Paddy's tutelage and then, after a few days, on his own. Utilizing a makeshift fishing line with worms dug from the ground as bait. Or laying in wait for small rodent-like game to happen past and be speared by a tightly layered branch filed to a tip.

Conditioning drills, building up both his upper and lower body, took place during the day. By night they trained with the assortment of knives Paddy had brought along.

"Did you know most firefights happen at night, mate?"

"Then why aren't we practicing with guns instead?"

"Because I don't want you getting dependent on bullets. You want a shooter's mindset, join a gun club; you want a soldier's, you listen up to me. I don't teach people how to shoot, I teach 'em how to survive."

"And if I can survive your teachings, I guess I can survive anything," Michael said, more sarcastically than he'd meant.

"Keep taking that tone with me, and I just might forget to be as nice as I've been."

A few days later, Paddy set up yet another of his target-laden courses for Michael through the jungle. Always a new one, the same course and targets never repeated. Some he was meant to stab or lash. Others he was meant to kill by throwing this knife. Just a flick of the wrist was all it took, a deceptively simple motion to send death winging in blinding fashion through the air. Each night, the targets got smaller and harder to spot. If he missed any, and was thus killed, Paddy wouldn't let him eat his next meal, because dead men didn't need to eat.

"I'm not eating either, mate, so if you don't want me pissed at you, I suggest you make it through the night intact."

One night, when Michael's path took him close once more to the archaeological camp, the brush rustled at his rear. Michael spun, ducking to avoid a branch swung his way that shattered on impact with the tree behind which he'd taken cover. Not to be denied, the woman he recognized as the young archaeologist struck at him with what little of the branch she still held, managing to smack him a few times before Michael seized control of the branch and used it to pin her against the same tree.

"If you're a poacher," she snapped, "you better kill me now or I'll shove whatever you're carrying in that pouch down your throat."

"I'm not a poacher," Michael said, still holding her.

"Oh, yeah? Then what are you—Tarzan?"

"Nobody—that's who I am."

Because out here in the middle of nowhere, that's exactly what he felt like.

"I'm guessing you're far from that. Since 'nobodies' don't normally last long in this jungle."

"I'm different."

"I guess so." Her eyes left his for her own arms he was still holding in place. "You going to let go of me?"

Michael did. "Sorry."

And she immediately socked him in the face with a fist, stinging his cheek.

"Makes us even for you slamming my skull against the tree," she told him.

"You attacked me, remember?"

"You're lucky I missed."

"What's your name?" Michael asked her.

"Fuck you."

"Scarlett Swan," she followed with, a moment later.

"No, really."

"That's my name."

"As in *Gone with—*"

"Yes, goddamnit. And, if it matters, I love my name."

"I love it, too."

"Frankly, my dear—"

"You don't give a damn," Michael completed.

"And my brother's name is Rhett."

"You're kidding."

"Nope. Blame my mother."

Scarlett went on to explain she was down here on a dig funded by the French government in conjunction with Brown University, where she was working on her masters degree in Archaeology and Anthropology.

"I didn't know there was anything valuable in these parts," Michael said.

"There isn't," Scarlett told him, looking away and sounding evasive. "It's historical value I'm after. Money isn't everything."

"But it's plenty important if you want your digs funded."

"Carrying the money for my next one in your pants?"

Michael looked down at his ripped pockets. "Not anymore."

It turned out her archaeological team was here under the auspices of INRAP, or *Institut National de Recherches Archéologiques Préventives* of France. Comprising twenty or so college students, accompanied by six professional archaeologists and two armed guards supplied by French Guiana. They were here studying tribes indigenous to this rain forest thousands of years ago and had unearthed a wealth of pottery, funeral "boxes," and other evidence of how their civilization had functioned.

"They should've learned from what happened to the other bloody teams that came down here," Paddy lamented.

"What's that?" Michael asked him.

"None of our concern, mate. Back to work now."

Learning skill sets was one thing; the real purpose of the training he was about to endure was to survive by making them instinctive. True to Paddy's teachings Michael began to feel things before he could see or hear them. Paddy made him strip to his boxers one night to make him especially vulnerable to insect bites that first stung, then itched, then stung again.

"You been too comfortable for too long, mate," Paddy explained disdainfully. "I want you to be uncomfortable and learn how to fight while you are."

Spoken just as a mosquito the size of a dragonfly bit him on the back of the neck, Michael's hand coming away streaked with blood when he crushed it.

"Men die just as easy when you know how to kill them," Paddy winked.

During this kind of hand-to-hand practice, Paddy was fond of going all out and pummeling Michael to submission, until one morning Michael thought he'd finally bested the bloke. Turning from a beaten Paddy and walking away, only to drop straight into a trap hole Paddy had dug.

"Means no breakfast for you, mate."

Instead, Michael was down at the river when the gunmen came.

FORTY-NINE

And, true to form, Michael hadn't seen or heard from Paddy ever since.

Until now, five years later. According to plan, they'd be transferring onto this much smaller Citation jet arranged by Paddy that Alexander and Michael would pilot themselves for the remainder of the trip to hide any connection to Michael, Tyrant Global, or King Midas World once they left London. And that precaution would be supplemented by the fake IDs, passports, and visas Paddy had brought along for them to use once in Romania. The last five years had seen him become associated with GS-Ultra, the world's largest private security company, further enhancing his ability to produce trained personnel for private high-level security needs, weaponry, and documents—all strictly first rate and at first-rate prices.

"You look good, mate," Paddy said, taking the seat on the Citation across the aisle from Michael, after tucking an envelope stuffed with large bills given to him by Alexander into his pocket. He drew a finger along the scar that ran down his left cheek as if it were the blade that had left the wound originally. "Been keeping up with your lessons, I take it."

"What have you got for us?"

"My man found no trace anywhere of your archaeological team. Scene had been sanitized."

"Sanitized?"

"I don't suspect any of those folks'll be home for the holidays. Let's leave it there."

"One of them got away and contacted me."

"I bet it's a woman."

"Nice guess."

Paddy grinned. "You taking your arse halfway across the world about her?"

"In part."

Paddy smiled broadly at that, coming up just short of a laugh. "When it comes to bloody women, there's no such thing." He thought for a moment. "And another archaeologist yet."

"Not another."

The big man narrowed his gaze, features tightening to make his scar look more pronounced. "I don't like what I see in your eyes, mate."

"You put some of it there, Sergeant-Major."

"Not what I'm looking at right now, I didn't. Kind of look you got right now belongs to a man who could let things get away from him. That's the opposite of what I taught you."

"I've got Alexander with me this time," Michael said, glancing his way.

"Even he's not enough for what you're going up against, mate. What little is known about Black Scorpion is all in here," Paddy said, handing Michael a thin manila envelope. "Let me give you the quick version: Drugs, gambling, murder, blackmail, gunrunning, prostitution, loan sharking, street crime, and they've cornered the market on human trafficking all over the world, including the United States. Black Scorpion has its bloody fucking hand in everything the underworld has to offer. Might even say, they've *become* the underworld."

"If you know that, it stands to reason law enforcement worldwide does as well."

"Most law enforcement entities worldwide, according to this report, don't believe Black Scorpion even exists, the man or the organization. They believe they're both legends, myths. After all, you can't arrest what you can't identify or even find. This is an organization that has insulated itself on all levels, clinging to the dark and avoiding the light at all costs. Those who go looking don't normally come back."

"In countries like Romania," Michael said, nodding, understanding, "where the authorities can be easily bought or persuaded to look the other way."

"According to my sources, Black Scorpion is thought to have powerful friends in legitimate branches of government all across the world, many of which were bought and paid for from the time they were candidates. Forget bullets. The greatest weapon wielded by an organization like this is corruption. They know to exploit that. And any official they can't bribe they extort, often going as far as to manufacture the very incident that becomes the source of their blackmail."

Paddy's assertions left Michael shaking his head. "And you're telling me the authorities worldwide, including Interpol, have done nothing to stop them?"

"Stop *who* exactly? That's the blasted problem, mate. In spite of everything I just told you, authorities internationally can't point to a single person and tell you he's part of Black Scorpion. And its leader is a shadow, protected by the Romanian government and the country's military officials because he keeps them and their families very well fed. No one knows his name, his nationality. What he looks like or how he takes his tea. There's nothing about him in these pages at all," Paddy said, flapping the file's contents lightly. "The man's a bloody ghost."

"There's not a single photo of him *anywhere*?"

"Google *Black Scorpion* and all you get is the insect. My sources say this is an organization with a reach that stretches across the globe to groups with similar interests on every continent, in every country."

"And we're talking about *criminal* interests."

Paddy nodded. "With huge resources and manpower scat-

tered all over the world and with good reason. Human trafficking alone is a forty-two-billion-dollar-a-year industry
and Black Scorpion has basically cornered the market on
it. I've seen a lot of bloody *shite* in the world, mate, so much
that I've learned not to use the word *evil* lightly. But I make
an exception in the case of Black Scorpion."

"Your sources have any idea what their interest could
possibly be in an archaeological dig?"

"Not a clue. I'd say because nothing happens in the Transylvanian region without their knowledge and approval, so
maybe they were pissed at you for something, like not paying them off. Of course . . ."

"Of course *what*?"

Paddy tightened his gaze even more. "Maybe there's
something about that dig site that's important to them,
maybe they're sending some kind of message. All the more
reason, if you don't mind me saying, why you got no business going up against them."

"This isn't about *business*."

"Take such things seriously now, do you?"

"When it involves somebody I care about, you're damn
right, Paddy."

"Tell you what else is right: That it's for real this time.
That you should leave such things to the experts like Alexander and me," Paddy finished. "Say the word, put up the
cash, a lot of it, and I'll make it happen."

"There's no time."

Paddy snickered. "Oh, nearly forgot. This blasted
woman . . . Smart man'd walk away while he's still got his
legs under him."

"Is that what you trained me for? To walk away from
someone I care about very much, leave her in the hands of
these fucking slave traders?"

"I get it, mate, but I trained you to survive, not die. You
getting killed's not about to free her."

"And I get that, Paddy, but there are lines that can't be crossed. I can't help the code I live by."

"Bollocks, mate. Right now the only code that matters is the one that gives you maybe another twenty-four to forty-eight hours before this woman is off the map for good, something you'd best keep in mind. Remember, I trained you to know where the snakes were so they couldn't kill you, not so they could. Black Scorpion's like the snakes that pop down out of the trees. You can't see 'em until they've already bit you."

The small man in the rumpled suit watched the Citation arch toward the sky from behind the terminal window, twirling his Mont Blanc pen. He wedged the pen back in his pocket and pressed a preprogrammed number on his phone.

PART FOUR

BLACK
SCORPION

It is not because things are difficult that
we do not dare;
it is because we do not dare that they are difficult.

Seneca

FIFTY

Vladimir Dracu's convoy headed along the narrow road through the Hoia-Baciu Forest. He felt the brush, extra thick in the warmer months, whipping against the Range Rover in which he rode. Occasionally a stray branch thwacked against the windshield, though at this low speed no damage resulted.

Dracu kept looking out through the SUV's tinted rear window, checking to make sure the bus was able to negotiate the difficult terrain of this route that had been literally carved out of the forest. And with each glance back, he thought of the blond girl with the green eyes.

Such beauty . . .

The same could not be said for the view around him, explaining why Dracu had opted to base his headquarters here. The fact that the "Black Forest" was rumored to be the most haunted wooded area in the world kept locals and tourists alike far away. And for the few that ventured or strayed too close to these woods laden with warped, dense trees that resembled gnarled arthritis-riddled fingers, well, their "disappearances" served to further fuel the legend that left this part of Transylvania the private domain of Black Scorpion.

Even those, in law enforcement and otherwise, who came looking would find their quests fruitless for good reason, one that revealed itself moments later when the road approached the Apuseni Mountains. This particular range was riddled with massive caves carved out of the rock and flora, most notably the Coiba Mare and Coiba Mica systems. These were well known, far more so than the Coiba Moarte system that Dracu had christened himself, fittingly since *moarte* meant "death" in Romanian.

The convoy rolled on, heading straight for a waterfall spiraling down the dark lower ledges of the Apuseni range. Beyond it was more of the dark sheen indicative of the unbroken jagged sprawl of the mountain, but this was an illusion, a trick of reflection off the cascading waters. The convoy slid to a halt at the shore of the shallow lake into which the waterfall spilled, apparently reaching a dead end.

Then a transmitted signal from the lead vehicle in the convoy lowered a bridge fashioned to look like a huge section of the mountain face, spanning the entire width of the lake to the shore on which the vehicles waited. The convoy eased forward, passing directly under the waterfall and into the fortress that Dracu had built from the remnants of a nuclear command and control bunker the Soviets had constructed within Coiba Moarte. It was connected to a network of silos constructed during the height of the Cold War, strategically placed beneath the ideal cover of the manmade lake that enclosed the mountain. Black Scorpion had added ten levels to the original structure and gutted the existing interior, rebuilding it from scratch.

The result was a marvel of construction in all respects, completed against impossible logistics and in half the time anticipated. A true miracle when the challenges posed by turning a long abandoned compound mired within a massive internal cave structure into a habitable and defensible fortress were considered, even with cost being no object. Each task proved more daunting than the last. Installing appropriate plumbing and wiring, for example, or a newly expanded air filtration and circulation system.

The one feature Vladimir Dracu barely touched at all was the command center itself, erected by the Soviets in a single underground layer protected by thousands of tons of steel, concrete, and natural stone fortifications. From here he intended to stage his greatest operation, one that would allow him to claim what was rightfully his.

The massive construction project also required Black Scorpion to spend vast resources on forging roads through a veritable wilderness to allow for proper passage of vehicles. This even though much of the bulkiest materials were ferried in by freight helicopter after being trucked to the nearest city. Some of those roads had been destroyed, overgrown by vegetation again in practically no time inside the Hoia-Baciu Forest. The single access route the convoy had just traversed was camouflaged and could be best negotiated by powerful SUVs with off-road capabilities.

One thing that had proven no problem at all was manpower. Black Scorpion's structural engineers were culled from the best minds the former Soviet-bloc nations had to offer, then unemployed and just glad to have a job to feed their families no matter how challenging or dangerous. Dracu had also found an endless source of labor from the human trafficking network that he'd built, teenagers mostly taken from a host of isolated, surrounding villages on the false promise that hard work was their ticket back home. Hundreds of virtual slaves entrusted with backbreaking work on ground that would eventually hold their graves.

Dracu had long lost count of the dollars the process had expended, nor did it matter to him; the mountain fortress was now an unprecedented, secured residence, one with a bevy of propane-fueled generators buried within rock. Deep within the bowels of the fortress lay stores of emergency rations, enough to feed his entire complement of men for a full year. The bridge rose after the last vehicle in the convoy had swung into a sprawling internal courtyard within the monolithic fortress built to conform to the cave's shape.

He rode the private elevator down to his suite of rooms. Once there, he left Armura posted at the door and entered his study, dominated by his art collection consisting of items stolen or taken from by force from Romania's National Museum of Art or Bulgaria's National Art Gallery. Chosen not for their notoriety, but the design and vision of the artists in crafting a world that appealed to him, the way they used light to illuminate the worlds they had fashioned. He could gaze at them for hours, always finding something new to see in each and glad for the beauty they brought to the fortress's chilly, dark confines, replacing both windows and something else.

Mirrors.

Dracu had no desire to look at himself, even in the reflection of glass, to which he avoid turning at all costs. He had learned to shave and perform other menial tasks without the benefit of viewing his reflection, hiding the view from himself just as the veil he wore whenever in the company of others hid it from the rest of the world.

His collection of paintings made for a striking contrast with the contents of a side room just off his study, housing the only reason he was still alive today. He entered it through an inner door, struck as always by the humid blast of heat in stark contrast to the ever-present chill in the rooms beyond.

The terrarium was kept always at ninety degrees to mimic the climate best tolerated by his collection of deathstalker and black scorpions. So they might thrive even more, Dracu had had the terrarium constructed to take on as much of the creatures' native semiarid environment as possible. They crawled in and under the thick sand layered with patches of recirculated water to maintain the proper levels of humidity, though most of the scorpions seemed to prefer the branches of the brush and shrub growth that thrived in the indoor climate. That climate was made remarkably hospitable for them by a combination of sprayers and incandescent sun-like lighting that burned in the very same degree and hours as the sun in their natural habitats. Within it, though, Dracu felt the makeup he wore over the thinning flesh of his face beginning to recede, thanks to the perspiration soaking through it in the terrarium's fetid atmosphere. He welcomed that heat, though, since it was one of the few times he ever felt warm.

As a result, Dracu's scorpions were able to thrive beyond his greatest expectations, even mimicking the creatures' battle for survival with endless fights for supremacy that occurred in the wild. Dracu was convinced such a practice enhanced the creatures' ability to manufacture vast amounts of the venom that was responsible for his continued survival.

He rolled up his right sleeve to reveal a host of ugly purplish bruising and extended his gloved right hand into the bramble and thickets to snare one of the creatures in his grasp. His treatment required only a single sting per day, sometimes every other, to flush their venom through his diseased blood and hold the pestilence inside him at bay.

Dracu eased the scorpion he'd snatched from the terrarium into place on his forearm and watched its stinger snap downward in an arching motion, felt the needle-like prick as is it pierced his skin and a flush of heat as its venom joined his blood. Then the pain started, an awful, wrenching agony that struck him everywhere at once, briefly freezing his breath. It had been like that the first time he'd been stung and had never abated; if anything, growing more intense over time, even as his veins blued and seemed to expand before slowly returning to normal after the agony peaked.

Dracu closed his eyes, letting the pain of the sting consume him. As a boy, from the day he'd been herded with the others into the back of that box truck, he'd learned all about pain. Sometimes when he closed his eyes, feeling his body racked by spasms as the venom spread its magic treatment through him, he was struck by visions of a past he kept both close and faraway at the same time. Close because he needed to remember. Faraway because those years had stolen everything from him.

"Domnule," a voice called over the intercom, shocking Dracu back to the present, his eyes jerking open. The pain had receded, replaced with the strangely soothing warmth of the venom spreading through his veins so he might continue to cheat death, just as life had cheated him. "The man has arrived and has been properly searched. He would not open the satchel he is carrying."

"With good reason, I suspect," Dracu said toward the terrarium's wall-mounted speaker, feeling the equally familiar rush of euphoric pleasure spreading through him in the agony's wake. "Bring him up."

After returning the scorpion to its home and rolling his sleeve back down, Dracu moved back into his elegantly furnished study. He made sure his veil was in place and was waiting at the door when the heavy knock fell upon it. He touched the open button on the interior keypad and backed up so his guest could enter, accompanied by Armura.

"I trust you have it," Dracu said to him.

"Right here," said Henri Bernard.

FIFTY-ONE

"Does he have to stay?" Bernard asked, eyeing Armura as he closed the door behind him.

"Why, is that a problem?"

Bernard seemed to have trouble taking his eyes off Armura's massive frame and the mask covering the ravaged portion of his face.

"I suppose not."

"Good." Dracu caught Bernard's gaze lingering too long on him. "Now, let's get down to business."

Bernard held up the thickly padded satchel for Dracu to see. "The pages are inside a specially sealed chamber. Most are in relatively good condition, given their age, but they're still degraded overall and very sensitive to the elements and touch."

"Any luck with the translation?"

"The woman was the ancient languages expert, not me. But I'm sure you'll have no problem securing someone to handle that task."

"That was your responsibility, Henri."

"All men have their limitations."

"Not all men," Dracu noted. "And my orders were to provide a manuscript *with* translation. What good is it to me otherwise? Are we certain the manuscript is authentic, at the very least?"

"Scarlett Swan believed it was, and she's the expert."

"Then I'll have my linguistics expert soon."

Bernard's brow rose and fell again. "You found her?"

"It wasn't hard. I'm having her brought in at first light."

"Then you won't be needing me anymore."

"You want to leave already?" With that, Dracu led Bernard across the floor to the terrarium. "Come," he said, "don't be afraid."

Once inside, Bernard was transfixed by the various cages housing expertly re-created environments for the scorpions dwelling within them, his attention so focused that he failed to notice Armura join them.

"Beautiful, aren't they, Henri?"

Bernard shrugged, stiffening when he glimpsed Armura standing just behind him. "I suppose that's in the eye of the beholder."

"True enough. You know what else is true? That these creatures have the ability to instill life as well as death. Call it a cruel irony of nature. Trust me, I know of this firsthand." Dracu removed one of the lids and pointed to a scorpion nesting all by itself on a branch. "This is the deathstalker, the most deadly of any scorpion. Its stinger releases a neurotoxin that paralyzes the muscles, while it inflames the nerve endings. The result is unspeakable pain, while the victim is rendered utterly helpless prior to death. In the insect world, this allows the deathstalker to feast on his prey over the course of several days, even weeks."

With that, Armura grabbed one of Bernard's arms in his powerful grasp and jerked the other one inside the cage, straight for the deathstalker scorpion. The scorpion twisted toward the back of his hand, raising its deadly tail stinger into position before lashing it downward, digging the sharp tip in and clinging long enough to inject its deadly venom. Armura waited until the scorpion had retracted its stinger before jerking Bernard's arm back out of the cage.

He was already shaking, his knees wobbling so much they banged into each other.

"It's easier if you don't struggle, Henri. Struggling only increases the pain and the time it takes to die."

Henri Bernard's eyes bulged. His mouth dropped. He

started to scream but the sound dissolved into a horrible airless rasp. His knees locked. Agony stretched across his features, drawing a stream of tears from both eyes, as he collapsed to the floor.

"The scorpion didn't kill you," Dracu told him, "your greed did. You betrayed your own people. This is what you deserved. You didn't really think I could let you walk out of here, did you? This is what happens when you make a deal with the devil."

Bernard was making shallow, rasping noises now, struggling for every breath as his throat began to close, his face starting to darken to a purplish shade. The writhing turned to spasms that stilled slowly until he lay motionless on the floor for Armura to effortlessly scoop up.

"Too bad you weren't a better linguist, Henri," Dracu said over his corpse. "It would have kept you alive a bit longer."

Then he moved to the intercom. The euphoria was just starting to peak, the scorpion venom pulsing through his veins and feeding the nutrients to his blood that were responsible for his very survival. The rush leaving the world before him awash in color suddenly brighter and sharper, the air itself turned thick enough to grasp in his hand. His senses enhanced to the point where he imagined he could feel the wind whistling through the mountain beyond and hear the lapping of the lake waters surrounding it.

"Alert the professor that I'm coming to see him," he said toward the speaker.

FIFTY-TWO

The Citation

"I have your passport and other documents from Paddy here," Alexander told Michael, handing them over while flying the Citation on autopilot the last stretch over Europe, approaching Romanian airspace.

"Pablo Garcia of Panama," Michael said, after opening the passport. "Good thing I speak fluent Spanish."

"You'll need to change your hairstyle, and I have contact lenses with me, a beard, too."

"I hope Scarlett gets the chance to see me wearing them."

Paddy had also arranged for a vehicle, an Alfa Romeo sedan, to be left for them at Napoca Airport in the small city of Cluj-Napoca, a ninety-minute drive from the town of Bună Ziua. Hidden in a secret compartment in the trunk was a heavily stuffed duffel bag that Alexander unzipped and checked carefully, cataloguing its contents before returning the bag to its hiding place.

"For emergencies," Alexander explained. "Our ticket home, if the shit hits the fan."

They followed the directions already programmed into the car's navigation system to Bună Ziua from which Scarlett Swan had placed her desperate call, the route dissolving into an endless series of side roads with Michael playing copilot. Alexander's past had taken him all over Europe, but never to Romania, a fact that seemed to increase his discomfort even more.

They finally reached the village at dusk. Quaint would have been a polite way to describe the surroundings dominated by buildings laid out along and around a central square. But those buildings were refugees from another age and, by all appearances, little had been done to update them with the times. They were drab and dreary, finished in brown tones that looked even darker in the fading light. A few were clustered practically atop one another, while others seemed to have entire sections of blocks to themselves, although Michael thought he detected the remnants of foundations and even some crumpled husks of buildings that had been razed or simply collapsed over time.

The bar matching the address Alexander had written down wouldn't open for another hour and sat directly across from a bank, post office, and what looked like a municipal building. The village's lone hotel, meanwhile, turned out to be located on its outskirts with a fine view of the surrounding mountains currently shrouded in fog. A stately building Michael took for a former residence of a local dignitary and easily the best maintained structure that they'd seen.

Bells jangled as Alexander and Michael entered, each toting a single light bag.

"Do you speak English?" Michael asked an older man standing behind a simple counter.

"*Da.* Yes. English. I am the hotel manager, Arsen Norocea," the man said, stretching a hand out and shaking Michael's enthusiastically when he took it. "You wish to stay with us? You wish a room?"

"Something with a view of the hotel's front," Alexander requested.

Alexander was adjusting the blinds of the simple, clean, and well-maintained room to make sure the positioning of the slats allowed a view out but not in. Michael mimicked his motions at a second window kitty-corner to that one, noticing a flower-rich memorial in a large plot of land across the road from the hotel. It looked like a war memorial of some kind, right down to the marble plaque Michael glimpsed just inside its grounds.

Michael was still staring when a knock fell on the door. Alexander moved to answer it, cracking it open to see who was there since the door wasn't outfitted with a peephole.

"I just wanted to make sure you like the room," Arsen Norocea said, through the crack, "and if you needed anything."

Alexander was ready to close the door when Michael drew even with him and eased it all the way open. "As a matter of fact, there is. I have a question for you. What's that garden across the street?"

"It used to be a *crisma*, a local eating and drinking establishment that wasn't worth the communists bothering with. It burned to the ground many years ago. That's a memorial to the victims."

"Strange to memorialize such a tragedy," Michael said, still gazing at the beautifully tended garden.

"This one had quite a story behind it, a virtual legend in these parts. About a hero who saved many lives. This would've been, let's see, the late nineteen-fifties. The man wasn't from around here."

"It's time, Michael," Alexander said from the window, before Michael could question the hotel manager further.

FIFTY-THREE

VADJA, ROMANIA

Raven Khan watched the town nearest to the dig site for hours, until dusk had fallen, before driving in along the hard-packed dirt roads turned soggy by a recent rainstorm. Her scrutiny had revealed shops open for business with barely any customers, all of which closed hastily in advance of nightfall. A small police post was shuttered, and no one lingered in the streets any longer than was absolutely necessary. The same police detachment she'd run into at the dig site had come and gone, clearly dissatisfied with the level of cooperation. Raven would've bet that no one in the village had told them anything, perhaps not even opened their doors when they saw uniforms lurking outside.

But the oddest thing of all wasn't what Raven saw, so much as what she didn't see.

Children.

In the hours she stood or sat watching the town, she saw not a single boy or girl.

At dusk's fall, she parked her SUV on the outskirts and walked into the center of town. She raised her hands into the air, making no effort to disguise her presence. Suddenly, doors were thrown open and windows jacked up, rifle barrels aimed at her from seemingly everywhere at once.

Raven stopped and left her hands in the air, rotating her frame about the square so everyone aiming at her could see she wasn't armed. This as men toting hunting rifles and shotguns poured out, doors slamming in their wake. Seconds later, she was surrounded, the hammers of the guns pulled back with fingers coiled over two dozen triggers.

"I've come here in peace because we have the same enemy," she said, loud enough for all to hear. "Black Scorpion, and I can help you."

She listened to the tale of what had happened from several of the town leaders inside what she took to be the square's lone municipal building. The terror evoked by the masked man, calling himself Black Scorpion, who came in search of the dig site massacre's lone survivor, a female archaeologist. How he had killed the town elder and then, when the townspeople proved unable to give up his quarry, how he had collected the children and young women into a bus and driven off.

Raven felt suddenly chilled, thoughts of the unthinkable scene inside the cargo hold of the *Lucretia Maru* returning, along with the deeper-seated memories that haunted her dreams. She stopped the narrative not once for questions, soaking it in and trying to process it all at once.

"You said a boy was with this woman in the mountains, a boy who escaped the dig site with her."

The men nodded sullenly. "His grandfather was the elder killed by this devil."

"I'd like to speak to this boy," Raven continued.

"That will be difficult."

Ilie's mother spoke enough English to serve as interpreter for Raven so she might learn everything she could. Initially, though, the boy refused to cooperate, shaking his head adamantly and signing something just as forcefully when his mother pressed him.

"He says he does not trust you," Ilie's mother interpreted. "He says you could be one of them, a spy."

"The killers of his grandfather."

The woman nodded.

"Ask him if he saw any women with them."

Ilie's mother did just that and the boy replied rapidly, his gaze softening a bit, enough.

"The woman you helped was important to you."

The boy read her lips and nodded.

"I want to help her, too. But before I can do that, you need to help me."

Ilie nodded again. Then, signing rapidly, the boy provided a chilling depiction of the massacre of the dig team, the power of his gestures seeming to increase the impact of the horrible event he'd witnessed. He explained, through his mother, how the woman saved his life in the camp and then how they fled into the mountains together. He smashed his fist into his hand repeatedly when he got to the part about the veiled man dressed all in black killing his grandfather, tears welling in his eyes.

Raven was already back on her feet, looking at the boy and wishing there was something she could say that might comfort him. She moved her eyes from him to the four men, meeting their taut, bitter stares one at a time. She imagined each had watched their children stolen right out from under them, some perhaps no older than the little girl hugging her mother's corpse aboard the freighter.

"I'm going to get your children back for you," Raven promised, as if reading their minds. "I'm going to bring them home. Just tell me where to find them."

The villagers looked at each other. "Nobody knows."

"But you must have thoughts, suspicions."

"We have stories of an area in the Black Forest where people have ventured, but never returned. Maybe it was Black Scorpion and maybe it wasn't. We'll never know what they found, because nobody ever saw them again."

"Just tell me where they went, and I promise you'll see me again."

Raven was still trembling when she returned to her SUV. She was dizzy, sweating, felt her heart hammering against her chest and held her eyes closed in an attempt to compose herself. She thought she'd managed that task and drove off, only to find herself both weak and dizzy another twenty miles down the road. A wave of fatigue swept over her so strong and sudden that she started nodding off at the wheel and found a place to pull off the road in the night to rest for a time.

Sleep, though, claimed her as soon as she closed her eyes,

a deep restless sleep dominated by the most vivid dream she'd ever had. First the villagers she'd just left were surrounding her in a circle, staring at her in silence. Then the deaf boy began speaking, warning her, she thought, but she couldn't be sure because his words didn't register and he was talking out loud, not signing.

Then the villagers were gone and she heard a woman screaming, a toddler crying, the cries morphing into her own within the dream. The village gone now, the cargo hold of the *Lucretia Maru* replacing it. Then there was blood soaking her, drenching her, drowning her.

Raven snapped alert with a start, breathing heavily and tasting the same blood she'd smelled because she had bitten her own lip. Felt her heart begin to settle and a clammy chill replace the heat rush that had soaked her shirt with sweat. She cleared her throat and forced herself to take several deep breaths with the window slid down to compose herself, then gulped down one of the bottles of water she'd brought along.

Raven tucked it back into the cup holder in the console when she spotted her cell phone lying on the passenger seat, somehow shed during the dream that must've left her shifting wildly about. She groped for it and pressed out a number with a finger that was still shaking.

"Ismael," she said simply, after Saltuk picked up.

"Where are you, Raven?" he asked, voice piqued with concern.

"Where I am doesn't matter," she told him. "*Who* I am and where I came from matters. That's why I'm calling. I think I'm going crazy, losing my mind. It's time for you to tell me the truth Talu never did about how I ended up in that orphanage."

"Let it go, Raven."

"The truth, Ismael," she said, feeling herself begin to tremble anew. "Now."

FIFTY-FOUR

Bună Ziua, Romania

Alexander and Michael waited until several patrons were already inside the bar before entering. It had a simple wood-carved sign over the front door that read *Vremuri Bune*, or "Good Times" in Romanian.

"Let me help you, shister."

That was the line that stuck most in Michael's mind from his desperate exchange with Scarlett, uttered in passable English by someone affected by a speech impediment. A modest number of Romanians spoke English, but only a few could be afflicted by such a clear malady. Of course, that didn't mean the same person would be in this bar tonight, in which case they'd have to uncover a lead to his identity elsewhere.

Michael and Alexander entered to find *Vremuri Bune* in surprisingly good condition. The bar was either elegantly maintained or restored to provide a portrait of traditional Transylvania that included plank flooring just slightly more weathered than at the hotel. Iron light fixtures were suspended from the ceiling and faux lanterns of the same black steel composite were strung from hooks. Some sort of ceremonial crossed swords hung on the wall behind the bar itself. The dozen patrons inside already seemed an even mix of locals and tourists.

Transylvania in recent years, after all, had become a rising tourist attraction, its appeal stretching far beyond interest in the fifteenth-century Walachian prince Vlad Tepes, the inspiration for Bram Stoker's *Dracula*. While that obsession remained to some degree, the world had discovered the sprawling region with a population of almost five million to also be home to some of Europe's best-preserved medieval towns, most notably Brasov, featuring Old Saxon architecture and citadel ruins, and Sibiu with its cobblestone streets and pastel-colored houses.

The bar continued to fill up with a blend of locals and tourists alike who seemed to mix easily. But that did little to keep Michael and Alexander from standing out inside *Vremuri Bune*. The longer they sat nursing their drinks, the more stares were cast their way as they watched and listened.

"Too bad Paddy couldn't teach me how to become invisible," Michael lamented.

"That would've been your next lesson," Alexander said, never taking his eyes off the various scenes unfolding before them.

"Let me help you, shister."

The passage of each minute decreased the odds further that the man behind the voice over the phone would magically appear, especially if his presence here yesterday was owed strictly to his pursuit of Scarlett.

"Hey," a young woman said, approaching their table with her eyes fixed on Michael as if Alexander wasn't even there. "Hey, mister. You American, right?"

She stopped at the table, smelling of too much perfume. Attractive in an earthy sort of way.

"I'm guessing you're Romanian," Michael said, without saying whether he was American or not.

"You want a date, a good time?"

"I'm a little busy right now."

"You don't look busy."

"Appearances can be deceiving."

She seemed not to grasp his meaning. "I don't charge you because you so . . . handsome," she said, as if searching for a different word. "Come on, what you say?" Her gaze finally fixed on Alexander. Briefly. "I even get your big friend a date, but not free for him."

"Thank you," Michael said. "But not tonight."

"Tomorrow maybe?"

"Maybe."

"I be here. Same time. I look for you. You look for me, yes?"

Michael nodded, the woman holding her gaze on him as she backpedaled, turning only when she was sucked back into the crowd gathered before the bar.

"Handsome?" Alexander said, shaking his head.

"Don't be jealous."

Alexander noticed the commotion at the bar first, a clutter of German tourists lined up to take shots of *țuică,* a Romanian spirit milled from plums. The beefy, bearded bartender was pouring up a storm, adding a hefty glass for himself and proposing a toast loud enough for everyone in the bar to hear.

"To Germany!"

The tourists drank.

"To Romania!"

The tourists drank again.

The bartender came out from behind his station to join the tourists with one of the ceremonial swords in one hand and bottle of *țuică* in the other, refilling as he moved among them. Light from one of the steel fixtures overhead caught him in its spill, showcasing an upper lip marred by scar tissue that made it look as if a seamstress instead of a doctor had done the stitching.

"To *Vremuri Bune!*" he said, thrusting the curved sword's tip into the air. "Good times*h* . . . and my big dick!"

Laughter preceded the drinking this time.

"And to my hometown of S*h*ibiu!"

Michael's breath caught in his throat.

"Let me help you, shister."

The bartender was toasting again, flirting with a pair of attractive German women, both blonds.

"To all my new brothers*h* . . ." Then, with a squeeze of one woman's cheek and then the other, ". . . and s*h*isters!"

The bartender was drunkenly mumbling through a song in Romanian while cleaning the bar after closing time:

> *Bun îi vinul ghiurghiuliu*
> *Cules toamna prin târziu*
> *Mai pe brumă, mai pe-omăt*
> *Mult mai beu şi nu mă-mbăt*

He felt a cool breeze he recognized from the door opening, but was certain he'd thrown the lock. He moved to check it, passing through the shadows in that section of the bar when he felt an arm close around his throat from behind. His hands flailed desperately, groping for purchase on his assailant, when his air was choked off and the darkness swallowed him.

FIFTY-FIVE

Bună Ziua, Romania

"Who are you?"

The bartender came awake to the awareness that his bound hands were suspended above him, strung by electrical cord that had been looped through the iron casing of an overhead light fixture in the dingy basement of the bar. His ankles were bound by an identical cord, the angle on which he was perched forcing him to crouch in midair over a heavy wooden desk chair. And he was facing a tall figure cloaked in a mask.

"What do you want?" the bartender resumed.

"Neither of those questions are important," the hooded Alexander said from the shadows cast by the single bulb that spilled mostly downward, capturing his prisoner in the haze of a dull spotlight. Only Alexander's eyes were visible and the dull light played tricks with them, shifting their shade from piercing blue to aquamarine depending on how he was positioned in relation to the dangling bulb. "The important questions are the ones I'm going to ask and you're going to answer. Is that clear?"

"You want to rob me, I have nothing."

"I'm after answers."

"About what?"

Instead of responding, Alexander lifted a blade with a sharply curved tip from a nearby table in a gloved hand. "This isn't a toy, though you wouldn't know that from the way you were playing with it. It's called a *rhomphaia*, a sword native to the ancient Thracians. The warriors wielding it were reputed to have impeded the Roman conquest of your country. Its power was such that it could split Roman helmets and shields, leading Emperor Trajan to order extensive modifications to Roman equipment. Its hilt and blade were of equal length, as long as three feet combined. Its uses varied from a slashing motion to hooking shields and opponents."

From a darkened corner that smelled of must, mold, and rat turds, hidden from view of the bartender, Michael watched Alexander agilely provide a demonstration of the sword, from which he'd removed the handle.

"You know why I'm telling you this?" he continued to the bartender, the sword back at his side.

The bartender shook his head.

"Let me show you."

Alexander took a single step forward and jammed the sword's exposed tang into the wood of the chair seat so the blade was standing straight up, its tip just below the bartender's buttocks. Then he grabbed hold of the electrical cord strung through the overhead light fixture dangling nearby. Yanked tightly to unlash a simple tie, so his hold was now all that supported the bartender's weight. Then Alexander let out a slight bit of cord, until the tip of the sword blade grazed the bartender's trousers even with his sphincter, drawing a wince from him and then a smirk.

"So you're going to torture me?"

"What's your name?"

"It'sh been tried before. You shee my face? Shomeone cut my upper lip off onche to get me to talk. Promished he'd do the shame with my lower one and then move on to my tongue. I told him nothing."

"What's your name?" Alexander repeated.

"Andrei."

"I have no interest in your tongue or your lips." Alexander gave the cord more slack, forcing the bartender upon his toes with a grimace this time. "How long do you think you can stay on your toes, Andrei? Because you'll be on them for as long as it takes to tell me what I want to know. Is my English clear enough for you?"

"Go to fucking hell!"

"I'll take that as a yesh," Alexander said, mimicking the bartender's lisp as he took a step closer to him, still holding the electrical cord. "It will start with your toes cramping, making it impossible to keep balanced on them. The sword will pierce your flesh and you'll start to bleed; just a little at first, but much faster very quickly as the blade enters your insides. I've seen this before, Andrei. It isn't pretty." Now he took the same step backward. "But cooperate and I'll take up some of the slack. For each question you answer acceptably, there will be less pain. For each one you don't, there will be more blood. Your choice."

"You're an animal!"

"Who do you work for?"

"I work for no one," Andrei insisted, lower lip trembling as a sign he was already weakening.

"Black Scorpion," Alexander said, as if in answer to his own question.

Andrei's eyes started to widen, then stopped suddenly. "What does a bug have to do with anything?"

Alexander sat down in a chair directly in front of the bartender and crossed his legs casually, still holding fast to the cord. "A woman came into your bar yesterday, yes?"

Andrei forced a smile. "Women come into my bar every day."

"I'm talking about an *American* woman."

"Fuck you."

"An American woman came into your bar yesterday, *yes*?"

Silence this time.

"I have all night, Andrei, while you only have a few more minutes before you'll be begging to tell me anything I want to know. Don't wait for the inevitable. Tell me now."

"Tell you what?"

"About the young woman."

"Fuck you."

"You said that already."

"Fuck you, *asshhole*."

Alexander weighed the bartender's words calmly. "You know what people do when they're terrified? They act tough, even when they're not. Even when they're cowards. But I don't think you're a coward, Andrei, I just think you're scared."

"Not of you, shit head!"

"I don't care. Because if you don't tell me what I want to know, you'll die the rat you are, right at home with the others nesting down here. If you talk, you get out of this alive and nobody finds out where I got the answers to my questions."

The bartender lapsed into silence, seeming to consider Alexander's offer.

"There's no third option, Andrei," Alexander continued. "You need to choose from those two."

Andrei swallowed hard, seemed to nod. "I received a call before she arrived."

"From who?"

The bartender's legs had started to shake. "Pleas*h*e."

"Answer the question."

"From s*h*omeone in the s*h*ecret police telling me to watch for s*h*uch a young woman."

"Secret police."

"The *Shecuritate*."

"You're lying. There's no such thing anymore."

The bartender started to smile, but stopped. "Really? A man can hope I s*h*uppose."

From his darkened corner, Michael watched Alexander take up some of the slack on the electrical cord strung overhead, the bartender's twisted features relaxing slightly.

"Then we're making progress. This man from the *Securitate* who called you, does he work for Black Scorpion?"

Tears had begun rolling down Andrei's cheeks. "S*h*top, pleas*h*e. They won't just kill me. They'll kill my family, my *children*!" He was choking up now, struggling to speak through the sobs. "You don't know thes*h*e people!"

Alexander rose from his chair and moved closer to the bartender, his black hood swallowing the spill of light that reached it. "You think you're the first man I've tortured? You think I haven't heard all this before? Believe me when

I tell you it's going to get worse, much worse. Talk. Tell me everything or you'll wish you were only crying."

"I can't!"

"Yes, you can. What happened when the young woman came into the bar?"

The bartender was wailing horribly now, struggling to catch his breath and failing miserably.

"Look at me, Andrei. *Look at me!*"

Andrei looked up at that, snot leaking from his nose now.

"Do I look like a man who gives a shit?" Alexander asked him from inside his hood. "Do I look like a man who cares about anything but what I want to find out? *Answer me!*"

Andrei just stared at him.

"Your family's not safe from me either. Neither are your friends, your customers, the accountant who does your taxes, and the man who shines your shoes. You hear me? You tell me everything now or you die and then they die. Nod if you understand."

Andrei nodded again.

"The woman came into the bar."

Nod.

"You recognized her."

Nod.

"She went to make a phone call and you followed her."

A nod so demonstrative this time it shook off some of the tears streaming down the bartender's cheeks.

"Then what?"

"I . . . took her."

"Where?"

"To the s*h*tock room here in the bas*h*ement and tied her up. Then I called the colonel from the *Shecuritate*. He mus*h*t have come for her or s*h*ent his men. I never even s*h*aw him. She was there and then she wasn't. That's*h* all."

Alexander shook his head, slowly. "No, it isn't, because you haven't told us where we can find her now."

"Becaus*h*e I don't know, *you fuck*!" He was spitting saliva, continuing to drool more out between labored breaths.

Alexander let some of the slack back out of the electrical cord and the bartender's spine snapped erect, his knees quaking horribly now.

"Yes, Andrei, you do."

"They'll kill me if I tell you!"

"You're trying my patience. We've already been over this. And they're not going to kill you."

"How can you know that?"

"Because I'm going to kill them, after you tell me where to find the young woman."

The bartender shook his head slowly, beads of sweat starting to dapple his brow and cheeks. "It'*sh* too late. You have no idea what the*sh*e people are like, how far they'll go. They'll kill *you* and feed your *sh*kin to their dogs*h*."

Alexander took a larger step forward, sharing the light now with the bartender, making sure the man met his icy, unblinking stare. "Look into my eyes, Andrei, and tell me if you think anyone will be feeding my skin to their dogs." He stepped back again, making sure Andrei could see that he held the electrical cord, and the man's life, in his grasp. "Now, one more time, where is the young woman?"

"Clos*h*e by."

"Where?"

Andrei took as deep a breath as he could manage.

"Where?"

Andrei began to speak again.

FIFTY-SIX

HOIA-BACIU FOREST, ROMANIA

Dracu entered another code into the keypad set before the entrance to a suite of rooms in the fortress reserved for the man most vital to his coming plans. Niels Taupmann, the German genius Dracu called "Professor," was under video surveillance within these walls and anywhere else in the fortress. No real concern he'd try to escape and he wasn't exactly a prisoner per se, except of his own mind and the eccentricities that had helped him survive his years in a Russian gulag when he refused to give that government what he was giving to Black Scorpion.

Because Dracu had asked him nothing, said please, gave him a choice as well as a purpose. Sometimes things really were that simple, especially to a man who despised modern Russia as much as he did the communist regime of the old Soviet Union above all else. Taupmann's father, also a scientist, had traveled there during the Cold War from East Germany and died in a freakish accident that was never fully explained. When his mother insisted on investigating, she disappeared too, around Moscow. Taupmann was a young man then, a boy really, and was forced to fend for himself as a result. He lived in a communist-backed orphanage for similarly displaced youngsters while devoting himself passionately to his studies. He evolved into one of the greatest minds of his time, at the forefront of building the stratagems meant to secure the original information superhighway. His focus then and in later years was to develop the means to best safeguard the transmission of data across cyberspace.

So nothing could have pleased him more than to be

invited to participate in a 2008 Moscow symposium at which he and other scientists would expound on their theories on the future of information technology. Taupmman arrived in Moscow on schedule and was met by a reception committee of prominent officials most interested in his work.

"We would like to retain your services," the leader, a man wearing the uniform of a general, told him.

"I'm not interested."

"We are willing to make you a very wealthy man in return for your cooperation."

"I'm still not interested."

The three men exchanged glances. "What can we do to attract your interest, Professor?" asked another one of them.

"You know what you can do? Go to hell."

Two nights later, Taupmann went to sleep in his hotel only to wake up in a windowless room facing a pair of big, menacing guards. Then the original trio of men entered the room and the guards left.

"You will provide us with the information we want," the general said.

"No, I won't."

"You will. You just don't know it yet."

"Who are you? Why do you do this to me?"

The speaker had smiled. "We are either your best friends or worst enemies. The choice is yours. You either can resume your life, Professor, or you have no life."

"I'm an important man," Taupmann insisted indignantly. "I can't just disappear. People will look for me, people will come for me."

The general looked him in the eye, smiling again. "This is Russia, Professor. Nobody finds anything here we don't want found."

When Taupmann still refused to talk, he was transferred to a military prison, not to be released until such time that he cooperated. His continued silence led to Taupmann's transfer to the gulag from which Black Scorpion had liberated him after he'd been forgotten there and left to rot. And the old man had embraced the opportunity he believed Dracu was providing to achieve something he wanted more than anything in the world: The destruction of Russia.

The door opened with a click, allowing the noxious scent of marijuana to flood the hall in a haze of smoke. Dracu entered the sprawling confines of what Professor Niels Taupmann referred to as his workshop, but looked more like an art studio. Original paintings of all sizes, exclusively landscapes, filled out the walls while canvases in various stages of development sat on easels scattered along the spacious floor. Dracu knew there was some sense to the placement, some balance, but he didn't dare ask what, reluctant to do anything that might upset the even more delicate balance that defined the old man's mind. The art studio, workshop, or whatever it was reeked even more pungently of the pot stench.

The landscapes were wondrously realistic, looking not so much like art as windows offering various views of the world as the old man must've imagined it to be.

"You should try it," Taupmann said to him, without looking up from the canvas he was working on. "Creating beauty soothes the soul. The world can never have too much beauty."

"No, Professor, it can't."

"So grab a brush and join me. The world needs all the light it can get."

"I'm not much good at art . . . or light."

Taumpann chided him with his eyes. "A man with your vision? You are a great artist, my friend, on a different canvas of your own choosing." The old man held up a brush. "Why not let me teach you the basics? I used to be a teacher, you know; at least, I think I was."

"You were," Dracu confirmed. "And a very good one, until the Russians made you their prisoner."

Taupmann's expression tightened, seeming to forget all

about the paintbrush he was holding. "Did my students miss me?"

"I'm sure they did."

His expression began to darken, progressing through various shades he'd used in any number of paintings to craft the sky at sunset. "I hate Russia."

"I know."

"Ugly country."

Taupmann laid his paintbrush down and stepped out from behind the canvas, stuffing his hands in the pockets of his bathrobe worn over a pair of pajamas. Dracu couldn't remember the last time he'd seen the professor dressed in anything else.

The old man stopped at a long table cluttered with any number of jerry-rigged inventions he'd concocted either on his own or on Dracu's coaxing. Several of these were identical Bose clock radios common to high-end luxury hotels and resorts, a facsimile of which had already provided another centerpiece of Black Scorpion's plan. Taupmann lifted a marijuana blunt rolled in a flavored cigar wrapper from the sill of an ashtray. He touched a lighter to its end and inhaled deeply, the odor of grape-scented weed swallowing the harsh scent of oil paint that would've otherwise dominated the room.

Taupmann coughed out a thick curtain of smoke that seemed to hang in the air. "If you haven't come to paint, what have you come for?"

"I just wanted to check in on you. See how your final set of calculations and estimates were coming."

The old man smoothed one side of the wild hair growing like weeds from his scalp down, leaving the other to skew in all directions. "Wonderfully. Everything checks out. We're ready. Just one problem, though. A big one."

"What is it?" Dracu asked, feeling the annoying tug of trepidation.

Taupmann shook a nearly empty plastic bag down to pot stems and seeds. "My supply is drained. Need more, need much, much more!"

To help blur the truth behind the professor's presence here, Dracu had also come to offer something that quickly became as important to Taupmann as his paintings and desire for vengeance against Russia:

Marijuana.

"I'll have it sent up immediately," he promised.

"Good, good, good! Helps me think, keeps the ghosts away. You believe in ghosts?"

"I've never seen one. But I believe in plenty I've never seen."

"They're real, all fellow residents of the gulag. I watched so many die. They went, others came, then they died, too. Vicious cycle, vicious!"

"I understand."

"My parents stop by sometimes, too. We watch television together," Taupmann said, pointing toward a big widescreen mounted on the wall. He lifted the blunt back to his mouth and sucked in another deep drag. "Join me?" he said, offering it to Dracu.

"Not today."

"Come, then, I have something to show you."

Taupmann took the ashtray in hand and led Dracu to a beautifully drawn painting of Russia, complete with literally thousands of tiny, pin-size dots marring the landscape, often in large clusters.

"What do you think? The red is for our primary targets. Blue represents the more outlying, secondary ones. Green represents the densest areas of population, yellow the next level, and white the sparsest. The red and green pins are in perfect combination. Looks like Christmas."

"Yes," Dracu agreed, "it does indeed. I'm counting on you, Professor. I've waited a very long time for this."

"So have I," Taupmann said, through the haze of smoke that had settled between them. "But we must take care, my friend, because almost invariably it's in the eleventh hour when failure occurs, always unexpected and always preventable had all appropriate measures been taken." He shook his nearly empty plastic bag. "That's why you'd best replenish my supply."

Dracu found a subordinate waiting for him outside the professor's suite of rooms, along with Armura.

"We're ready to pick up the woman in Bună Ziua."

"I'm glad you waited, because I've decided to join you," Dracu said, recalling Niels Taupmann's cautionary words. "Add some additional vehicles and men. And make sure the *Securitate* station is secure."

"Is there a problem, *domnule*?"

"No, just a feeling."

FIFTY-SEVEN

BUNĂ ZIUA, ROMANIA

Michael and Alexander sat in the darkness of their Alfa Romeo down the street from the wrought-iron fence that enclosed an old building lifted from another century. Very likely some member of the Romanian ruling party, and royal family before him, had resided here at one point. It was an architectural masterpiece, several centuries old at the very least, but beautifully maintained thanks in large part to the detail that went into its construction with wood and glass that were the best of their time. The roof came to a single peak ridden by a weather vane. Steel grating covered the windows and the Romanian flag hung over the front door. The exterior was finished in burnished concrete, polished to be completely smooth.

"You believe the bartender?" Michael asked, referring to the man they'd left bound and gagged back in the basement of the bar.

"Yes," Alexander told him, "because he was scared. More of who's inside that building than us."

"He called them the *Securitate*."

"The predecessor for today's SRI for *Serviciul Român de Informaţii*."

"You're talking about the old Romanian secret police," Michael said, realizing.

He knew that the *Securitate* had been dismantled after the fall of the Berlin Wall ushered in the end of the Cold War, leading to the purported demise of Soviet-style secret police organizations. In Romania, this process was further expedited by the overthrow of the dictator Nicolae Ceausescu, who ruled the country with an iron fist defined by the now defunct *Securitate*.

At least thought to be defunct.

Like its sister organization in Russia, the KGB, though, the members of the *Securitate* never really went away. Instead, they remained still and quiet and sought positions in the rebranded *Serviciul Român de Informaţii,* or SRI, from which they could reclaim the power they believed to be rightfully theirs. And, like Black Scorpion, the revamped *Securitate* knew well enough to remain in the shadows, leaving their ever-increasing measure of control over the country to the subject of innuendo and conspiracy theorists.

Alexander's silence affirmed Michael's conclusion. "This isn't going to be easy."

Michael returned his gaze to the building, picturing Scarlett Swan as a prisoner inside.

"Where do you think they're keeping her?" he asked Alexander.

"The basement would be my first thought, but I noticed staining in the concrete of the foundation."

"Staining?"

Alexander lowered the tiny set of powerful binoculars with night-vision capabilities from his eyes. They'd chosen this spot because a garbage truck parked on an awkward angle perhaps fifty feet before them precluded clear view of their car from the SRI building.

"Indicates flooding, very common in this region," Alexander explained, handing Michael the binoculars. "My guess is it rendered the basement unusable long ago. If it were me, I'd place her on the top floor in the room furthest from the street, looking out over the back."

"So no one would be able to hear her screams." Michael felt his heart skip a beat, as he lowered the binoculars and handed them back.

"You saved this woman once, Michael," said Alexander. "You can do it again."

FIFTY-EIGHT

FRENCH GUIANA, FIVE YEARS AGO

The gunmen had come in canoe-like crafts that were actually hollowed-out logs; six of them packed three in each. Their weapons looked old, dated, but deadly.

"Must be poachers," Michael assumed, after explaining to Paddy what he'd seen.

"Not armed like that, they ain't."

"What then?"

"Let's break camp."

"We're leaving?" Michael raised.

"Moving. Men you spotted are likely kidnappers. We move on, unless you got eyes on killing them, mate."

"They were headed down the path that leads to the camp of those archaeologists."

"Bad day for those diggers, then. Bad day for that bitch you got yourself a hard-on for."

"We've got to do something."

"Then by all means," Paddy told him, sitting down on a rock, "gear up and go do it, mate."

"You're not coming?"

"Rules are rules, mate. You do what I say when I say, and right now I say to take your arse where I tell you. You don't want to do that, you're welcome to all the knives you can carry."

"Where will you be?"

"Fucking gone," Paddy told him.

"Maybe you should practice what you preach."

Michael felt his heart thudding in his chest as he dropped into a facedown body crawl through ground brush the last stretch of the way into the camp. It was hot and steamy, and the moist dirt used his sweat like glue to stick to his clothes and face.

Michael had just reached the rim of the camp and outermost tents when he heard the crackle of gunfire. Training was one thing; putting that training into practice was something else entirely. The truth was he desperately wished Paddy was here, or Alexander, but the greater truth was they weren't and this was up to him alone.

He eased himself along the camp's outskirts, careful to belly crawl through its darkest reaches and prepared to use his knives just the way Paddy had taught him. The gunmen were rousing the twenty-five or so archaeological students and professionals from their tents, ordering them about in a language neither the students nor Michael understood, as he studied their movements, their faces. He recognized the two camp guards and realized they were actually part of the kidnappers, had likely been behind alerting these men to the presence of so many potential victims, each representing a sizeable bounty.

That's when he heard a rustling in the brush behind him and turned to see Scarlett Swan returning from a makeshift bath in a nearby stream, wearing only a towel. Emerging into the clearing twenty feet before him with no idea of what she was walking into.

"Scarlett!" Michael called in a hushed voice too soft for her to hear.

Her sandaled steps froze too late, one of the kidnappers on her before she could retreat. Dragging her all the way into the clearing and stopping only when her towel fell, leaving her naked. The kidnapper gawked at her, eyes bulging at the perfect shape of her body.

Scarlett slapped him across the face, drawing laughter from the other kidnappers standing over their now kneeling hostages. The kidnapper laughed too, was still laughing when he slapped Scarlett back.

And she slapped him.

And he slapped her, each blow harder than the one preceding it, the laughter growing louder as the two of them stood face-to-face exchanging slap after slap and blood started dribbling from Scarlett's mouth.

Another kidnapper, meanwhile, was dragging one of the college-age women by the hair across the rough ground toward a tent. And a third kidnapper stood over a kneeling man, spinning the cylinder of an ancient revolver after filling only a single chamber with a bullet.

By then Michael had started to rise. None of the kidnappers noticed, too busy slapping their knees in rhythm with their laughter. They were nearing hysterics when Michael got to his feet behind the thin cover of the brush, not a single eye turned toward him when he burst into motion, twin knives in either hand.

Michael clung to the shadows, obscuring any view of him for the longest time possible. The first kidnapper to spot him was the one holding the revolver against the kneeling man's head. He jerked the pistol upward in the same moment Michael unleashed his first knife.

The hammer clicked on an empty chamber as Michael's blade thwacked into the man's chest. The man regarded it briefly, looking puzzled, and then keeled over to the jungle floor dead.

Michael's second blade was already in motion by then, taking the kidnapper dragging the girl off toward the tent in the throat and unleashing a fountain of blood that showered her.

Six left, Michael had the sense to register in his mind.

The kidnapper exchanging slaps with Scarlett was twisting to free a submachine gun from his shoulder when Michael twirled toward him and cut his throat. Felt the warm spray of blood as he kept in motion, machete unsheathed now and cutting one way, then the other. It didn't feel real, it didn't feel like *anything* and seemed to unfold in the gap between single breaths.

Michael thought he heard cries of anguish and panic but couldn't be sure. Another gunman opened up with a wild spray that found nothing but brush, before Michael plunged the same hunting knife he'd used on the wild boar in as far as it would go and left it there. Some primal instinct made him duck, and a barrage fired by another kidnapper found the man he'd just stabbed instead.

The dead man's submachine gun hit the ground ahead of him and Michael dove after it, spinning as he took its warm steel in his grasp. He clacked off a barrage that was wild at first, before quickly honing in on the motion of targets darting about the clearing that had turned to utter chaos.

Michael recorded high-pitched screams, the hostages he thought, as he recorded three more kidnappers downed before the weapon clicked empty. He glimpsed Scarlett slamming into the final man just as he was about to fire a clear shot Michael's way. That shot went skyward instead and, enraged, the man cracked the weapon's butt into Scarlett's skull. Should've swung back toward Michael at that point, but moved to finish her instead.

Michael grazed the man's shoulder with his next toss, leaving him only a single knife left. His mind calculated distance and angle, enough to tell him he didn't dare risk his last knife on another errant throw, and surged toward the final gunman instead.

The kidnapper had just started the butt of his rifle down toward Scarlett again, his expression twisted in fury, when Michael jammed the blade into his thorax all the way to the hilt. Feeling it dig through muscle and sinew felt like slicing through thick burlap. The man lashed his rifle around in a slicing motion that caught Michael in the side of the head, turning him wobbly on his feet with his senses gone fuzzy. Saw two of the man, a double image, looming over him when the man re-steadied his submachine gun, just as Michael's hand closed on a rock beneath him on the ground.

But which of the images to aim it at?

He wasn't sure why he chose the one on the right, only that the thud of impact was followed by both of them tumbling over. Michael pounced upon the only one that landed, the same rock pounding the man's face again and again until there was nothing recognizable left and he tossed it aside, his clothes and skin covered in blood.

He might have stayed there forever if he hadn't heard a rhythmic beating he first took to be his own heartbeat until he turned and spotted Paddy standing at the edge of the clearing, applauding him.

"You're ready, mate," he said, grinning.

"I thought you'd be fucking gone."

"Changed my mind," Paddy said.

Michael swung toward Scarlett, who was shaking her head, flabbergasted, unable to believe what she'd just seen him do.

"Who'd you say you were again?" she asked, stepping behind some thick brush to cover her naked form.

"Just a friend," Michael told her.

Paddy sent Michael and Scarlett, dressed in fresh clothes, for help, offering to stay with the others until at least she returned. Their trek through the woods would take them to an international way station from which they could summon the proper authorities. The jungle trails were too narrow to accommodate vehicles and the canopy too thick to allow for helicopters. Supply runs were normally made on the back of donkeys or horses, and they clung to the same path along which those runs were made. Cellular service was nonexistent down here and the kidnappers had destroyed the archaeological team's satellite phone. It would take nearly a day to reach the way station on foot, nothing to do but talk through the long duration of the walk.

"My turn," Michael told her. "What are *you* doing in a place like this?"

"I'm an archaeologist, remember? I go where the dig takes me. In this case, supervising undergraduates as a requirement of my masters degree."

"In pursuit of pots and pans?"

"The native tribes had pots, no pans."

"Why don't you tell me what you're really looking for, Scarlett?"

"Not until you do."

"I asked you first," Michael said, with a smile and a wink.

She looked away, then back again. "There are some well-regarded accounts of the Mayans venturing this far south in search of something."

"What?"

"If it was the Mayans, something powerful or priceless, or both."

"So you came down here, even though you have no idea what that might be?"

"I'll know when I find it," Scarlett told him. "It's what every archaeologist wants more than anything, to make a discovery that changes the way we see the world, something about history no one's ever known before." Her gaze tightened on him. "It's my turn now. What are *you* looking for?"

"The same thing you are, actually," Michael told her.

"Answers. And I think you can help me," he continued, thinking of the mysterious relic medallion he'd left with Alexander for safekeeping, the only thing he had left of his family. "In fact, I think we can help each other."

Scarlett regarded his clothes, his disheveled appearance. *"You?* And how much more can you do than save my life?"

"Plenty," Michael winked. "Trust me. And I only ask one thing in return."

"What's that?"

"You give me your phone number. And we keep what just happened quiet."

"That's two things."

"File any reports you need to but leave me out of it."

"What am I supposed to do, say it was Tarzan and Cheetah who saved me and my team?"

"With a little help from Jane," Michael said, grinning.

Scarlett hugged Michael tight at the way station, her embrace lingering out of something more than just gratitude.

"Give me that number where I can reach you," Michael said, when they finally eased apart. "So we can talk about that next dig."

"All of a sudden you find ancient pots and pans interesting."

"Actually, it's something else I'm after."

"Like what?"

"You'll have to answer my call to find out."

Michael left Scarlett reluctantly, staring at her until she drifted out of sight through the rear window of the SUV that would take him to Felix Eboue Airport in the city of Cayenne. He'd called ahead to make sure the Boeing 737 was waiting for him and, sure enough, it stood prepped and ready on the tarmac.

The door opened as he neared the stairs, a grinning Alexander stepping into the sun.

"Welcome back, Michael."

Michael climbed the steps, suddenly realizing how taxed and worn every muscle in his body was from the exertion of the past six weeks, or maybe it was more; he wasn't sure anymore. All he was thinking about was taking a shower as soon as he was on board.

"Paddy sends his best."

"Who's Paddy?" Alexander smiled.

FIFTY-NINE

After French Guiana, the next time Michael saw Scarlett was three months later when he invited her to meet him in Las Vegas to discuss his offer to fund future digs.

"You're serious."

"I'm going to e-mail you a ticket."

"What about a hotel room?"

"I have a connection at the city's best resort," Michael told her.

He picked her up personally at the airport in his Ferrari Testarossa.

"I googled you," she told him, as she climbed in.

"Happy with what you found?"

"Surprised."

"Why?"

"Because I couldn't figure out for the life of me what someone like you would be doing playing Navy SEAL in French Guiana."

"Can you keep a secret?"

"Like what?"

"Me. No one can ever know of how we met or what happened in that jungle. No one can ever know of my involvement or interest in your activities. Consider me a secret partner, and a friend," Michael said, and pulled into traffic.

"I never expected you to call."

"I have my reasons."

"*Archaeological* reasons?"

"An archaeological and historical mystery. The origins of a relic handed down to me by my family," Michael elaborated, leaving things at that.

"You flew me to Las Vegas and want to fund digs because of a *family heirloom*?"

"Let me explain."

Bună Ziua, Romania, now

The initial digs that followed had yielded little, nothing really until the dig in Transylvania that had gotten Scarlett's entire team murdered and landed her in the custody of the *Securitate*.

"I've seen what I needed to see," Alexander informed Michael. "I count between six and eight men inside, no more. We stick to the plan and get the woman out."

And in that moment a convoy of police cars tore onto the scene, a parade of officers armed with assault rifles spilling out and taking up posts around the building's perimeter or rushing inside.

"Looks like we're going to have to change our plans," said Michael.

SIXTY

Bună Ziua, Romania

Scarlett heard the key turning in the lock, the heavy wood door starting to ease open.

She had awoken initially with her head resting on a heavy plank table. Jolted by the shock of her unfamiliar surroundings, Scarlett jerked her hands upward to find they were bound by chains that ran through dual slots in the table descending all the way to heavy bolts drilled into the floor. Her legs, too, were chained and similarly affixed to another bolt drilled next to the first.

At first glance the room seemed to have no window. Then, on second, Scarlett realized there were actually two equally spaced on the wall to her left. But they were covered by shutters made of the same light wood paneling that adorned the walls. She noticed the fittings had been tied in a sash formed of chain link through which a lock had been bolted, denying her any sense of time's passage since she'd been taken, whether this was day or night.

Scarlett sat up all the way, her stiff spine crackling. Her head was pounding, each breath drawing a throb of its own. Scarlett realized her upper arm was sore in the same place it was after she got her annual flu shot back home.

What had they given her?

Some sort of sedative for sure, denying her any memory beyond being dragged out the rear of the bar that opened onto an alley, and thrust into the back of a waiting van.

They knew I was coming. The bartender was waiting for me. . . .

Scarlett again tried to recall what little exchange there'd been with Michael Tiranno. Had she told him where she was, what had happened? Then the door opened all the way and she stopped trying.

A burly man wearing a dark blue uniform, complete with tassels riding the shoulders, entered. He stood board stiff and had the look of a man who practiced his stance and posture in the mirror. He was flanked on either side by men wearing stiff low-rise jackets with holstered pistols clipped to their belts.

"I am Colonel Gastman," the uniformed figure announced. "I wanted to make sure you are enjoying your stay with us, that you have everything you need."

Scarlett stretched her arms out enough to rattle her chains. "I'm an American citizen."

"We are well aware of that."

"I want to call my embassy. I have nothing to say to you until you let me call my embassy."

"You misunderstand, young lady. You are here for your own safety and protection."

"I don't believe you."

"That does not change the fact that you are in danger and, as commander of this post, it is my duty to protect you."

"Then let me call my embassy."

"In time. For now, you are under our protection."

Scarlett leaned as far forward over the table as her bonds would allow. "You work for the man in the mask."

"What man in a mask?"

"The one who ordered my team killed," she followed, without missing a beat. "The one who kidnapped the young women and children from the village of Vadja. It's him you should be after, those villagers you should be protecting."

"I will see you safely transported in the morning," the colonel said, instead of responding.

"Transported *where*?"

"A place where you will be safe, a place from where you can call anyone you like."

"He's coming for me, isn't he? The man in the mask is coming for me."

"I don't know this masked man. Your safety is my only concern."

He handed a set of keys to the man on his right.

"We are required to perform a search of your person before you are transferred." A hint of a smile crossed Colonel Gastman's face, as he pulled a plastic glove over his right hand. "I promise to make this as painless as possible."

And he was moving toward Scarlett when explosions rattled the building, all the lights dying in the next instant.

SIXTY-ONE

Bună Ziua, Romania

The guards who'd remained posted along the SRI building perimeter paid little heed to the approaching garbage truck until they realized it was angled straight for the iron fence and picking up speed. Its headlights looked dim and cloudy, barely denting the night. Nothing was revealed in its cab when the guards closest to the stairs opened fire, stitching a jagged design across the windshield and hood, which burst upward under the barrage. The engine belched steam as the truck crashed through the fence and slammed into the building façade.

"Now!" Alexander signaled Michael as they jogged in the garbage truck's wake.

In the same moment, Alexander touched a key on his digital detonator rigged to the plastic explosives he'd pulled from the duffel bag that had been waiting for them in the Alfa Romeo, now packed into the stolen garbage truck's cab. Michael felt the explosion suck the air out of him, as deafening as it was blinding, the entire front of the truck turned into a shrapnel bomb that obliterated anyone within twenty feet of the entrance while decimating the building façade.

Alexander tucked a hood over his face and watched Michael do the same. "Your goggles," he reminded, both of them dressed in black military assault uniforms associated with special operations forces.

Michael fit the prototype for the next stage of night-vision goggles being developed by Tyrant Technologies over his eyes. Specially formulated, lightweight lenses coated with a clear resin designed to magnify available light while looking and fitting like ordinary sports goggles. Much less bulky and cumbersome than the current models being employed by the military today.

"Nice to have a chance to test them personally."

"Stay in my shadow until we're inside," Alexander ordered, sliding into motion.

Michael followed, feet rolling over the rubble shed by the blast strewn all the way to the street, straight for the smoke and lingering flames. Stray gunshots rang out and he was conscious of Alexander returning the fire one way and then the other, seeming to hit everything he aimed at. Michael added his own bullets as his senses caught up with his consciousness, the feeling nothing like firing practice rounds at all.

The rubble reminded him of the brushy, hard-packed trails Paddy left him to negotiate in bare feet in the French Guiana jungle. He understood in that moment better than ever how men like Alexander came to be. How much practice was required to survive moments like this where a single misstep could easily mean death.

Michael began clacking off single shots with his submachine gun, a Heckler & Koch MP5, aimed at motion still rendered desperate by the explosion that had laid waste to the building. As Alexander had anticipated, their timing was perfect. Surging up the pile of rocks that had been the front steps and into the building, just as the forces concentrated inside were fighting to recover their bearings from the shock and overcome the debris hurtled inward by the blast. It smelled just as the refuse of Max Price's Maximus Casino had after it imploded, the soot and gravelly grime washing through the air of the Strip like a blanket.

Michael realized he was holding his breath, still firing at anything that moved. He stumbled a few times over a floor littered with wall fragments and seared metal of the garbage truck along with chunks of tire rubber and a wheel somehow spinning on the floor. The interior was dark and smoke-rich, stealing sight of Alexander from him except for the muzzle flash of his sound-suppressed submachine gun firing left and forward, taking out all visible cameras first, while Michael advanced aiming his fire to the right through the haze of the emergency lighting that had kicked on once the explosion had cut the primary power.

They reached a set of stairs covered in bloodred carpeting now streaked with dust and more pieces of the shattered façade, just as four gunmen surged downward shooting blindly. Alexander shoved Michael aside, out of their narrow fire zone, both of them opening up with full automatic sprays that left the four uniformed men tumbling downward to land at the foot of the stairs in a heap.

Alexander was firing at another figure who'd appeared on the next landing up, when Michael heard the clatter of boots clacking over the same rubble they'd just negotiated. He swung and opened up with a fresh spray on the front door where two figures who'd survived the blast had just charged inside. Dropped them both, but felt his submachine gun click empty and cursed himself for not having kept better track of his bullets. He dove to the floor, reloading as he rolled beneath a fresh spray of fire, and glimpsing Alexander twirling to gun down another pair pouring inside after the first.

That exposed him to a concentrated assault from the second-floor landing, forcing him to spin to the cover of the nearest stud-bearing wall. Michael had just lurched back to his feet when he saw Alexander yank the pin from one of his grenades and hurl it upward. It exploded while still in the air, a single bright flash that blinded Michael even as his ears began ringing again, all sound shut out for the moment. He thought he heard Alexander calling to him but wasn't sure until he saw his lithe shape flying up the stairs through a wave of descending smoke that looked like a storm cloud.

Michael started to pull himself back to his feet only to realize, incredibly, that he was already standing. Starting up the stairs as the soft spits of Alexander's silenced submachine gun clacked again and again, conscious for the first time in that moment of the horrible cries of pain that seemed to be coming from everywhere at once.

Alexander was waiting for him on the second-floor landing, Michael reaching it just as fresh fire resounded from an open doorway down the hall. Alexander rolled a fresh grenade along the dark wood floor. It erupted in a blinding flash that rained a shower of dark smoke and shrapnel inward over those inside now covering their ears.

He disappeared into that smoke before Michael found the bearings to follow. Reaching the room to find two dead gunmen and a man wearing a dark blue suit jacket with red tassels on the shoulders and bars identifying him as a colonel in the SRI.

Or *Securitate.*

"*Vă rog!*" he pleaded in Romanian. "Please!"

His shoulders rested against the wall, trembling hands raised in the air. The desk behind which he had hidden was cluttered with files and photos the colonel was in the process of dumping into a flaming trash bin. Smoke, ash, and char from the smoldering refuse thickened the air, coating it with a gray sheen.

Michael watched Alexander jam the taped suppressor on his submachine gun under the man's double chin, finger coiled over the trigger.

"One chance. The girl—where is she?"

One of the colonel's hands flopped back to his side while the other pointed a single finger upward. "Fourth floor. All the way down on right."

"Keys," Alexander demanded. "Keys!"

The colonel's lowered hand moved to a pants pocket. Alexander slammed a booted foot atop it, mashing the fingers, and crouched to retrieve the keys himself. A slim pocketknife followed them out and Alexander pressed harder with his boot until he felt bones crack. Then reared back and slammed the man in the skull with the butt of his rifle. The colonel's eyes rolled back in his head and his face fell forward to his chest, dazed but still conscious.

"Michael," Alexander called, backpedaling while keeping his eyes on the colonel whose expression was now twisted in agony.

Michael watched the smoke from the flaming trash bin waft over the floor, a patch opening to reveal a thick folder waiting to join the others in the fire.

"Now!" Alexander ordered from the doorway.

But Michael had already stooped to retrieve the folder, his senses drifting in dreamlike fashion over the picture clipped to its front of a man he was sure he recognized.

Because it was his father.

SIXTY-TWO

Bună Ziua, Romania

As a much younger man, late twenties or early thirties, probably, some time in the late 1950s.

What was his picture doing on the desk of a colonel in the Romanian Securitate?

Michael peeled the picture back to better read the name scrawled partially beneath it.

Davide Schapira.

He regarded the folder again, the picture and the name, wondering if his vision had been skewed by the goggles and the smoke. But it hadn't. This was definitely Vito Nunziato.

Then who was Davide Schapira?

Michael tucked the thick contents of the folder under his ammo vest. He felt Alexander grasp him hard at the elbow and tug, the sound of wailing sirens clear in his mind now. The two of them surged back into the hallway for the stairs. Michael heard moans of pain and occasional screams from the security forces who'd managed to survive the onslaught. The next thing he knew he was following Alexander down the fourth-floor hall toward a locked door on the right-hand side.

Facing the rear of the building, just as Alexander had surmised.

Michael trained his weapon back toward the stairs, while Alexander fit the key into the lock. The Heckler & Koch submachine gun suddenly felt heavy in his hands, as if its cooling steel made for a heavier tote. He heard Alexander kick the unlocked door all the way open, ready with his submachine gun as well, and rushed to join him in the doorway.

Scarlett Swan sat chained to a wooden plank table, fear and resignation claiming her expression when she saw weapons in the hands of two masked figures, certain she was going to die. Until Michael peeled up his mask and her eyes widened, in shock and then relief.

"Michael," she managed, her emotions choking off most of his name before her senses cleared further. "I knew you'd come, *I knew it*!"

Alexander unlocked the chains binding her in place and she staggered into Michael's arms, kissing him more deeply and passionately than he'd ever been kissed before. She hugged him tight and Michael hugged her back, not wanting the embrace to end.

"Michael," she kept muttering, as they held each other. "Michael . . ."

He eased her away and kissed her again. Emotions swept through him, starting with relief that she was alive, that he'd managed to save her life a second time. His hands swam through her hair that smelled of the same lilac-scented shampoo it had the first time they'd met, felt her hands sliding about the slippery surface of the Nomex hood that still rode his skull. Michael didn't want to let go. He wanted to hold her, and be held, like this forever.

"Time, Michael," he heard Alexander say.

It still took all his resolve to ease Scarlett away. "We have to go," he said, holding her by the shoulders.

"Quickly," Alexander added, the wail of sirens screaming closer now. "This way," he added, pulling back the heavy wood shutters over a window to reveal a fire escape that descended all the way to the ground. "And take off your mask, so we're not spotted."

He went first, followed by Scarlett in the middle and Michael bringing up the rear, grateful this route of escape would keep her from seeing the bodies of all the men he and Alexander had killed to reach her.

Michael shielded her from view of the carnage, when they reached the bottom of the fire escape. His feet suddenly felt slow and heavy, his steps labored as if slowed by the slog of thick air. He had feared the worst. And the worst had happened.

Which didn't explain why the archaeologists had been killed, what all this was about.

Or what a mug shot of his father as a young man under the name Davide Schapira was doing on the desk of a colonel in the Romanian secret police.

Alexander yanked them both forward, on toward their rental car just as a flood of fire, rescue, and police vehicles tore onto the scene from all directions at once. Screeching to halts in whatever space the road before the smoking building allowed.

"Don't look back," Alexander instructed, "and follow me."

He led them to where the Alfa Romeo was parked in a

darkened patch across the street just within the spill of the flames' glow. In that moment Michael realized how all the practice and training in the world was nothing compared to the kind of true experience that defined Alexander's life. Michael had known danger before, had experienced his life threatened before, but never anything like this. And nothing could prepare him, or any man, for the fog it left implanted in his mind hazing over memories of actions completed just moments before. A defense mechanism that cloaked it all with a dreamlike quality that left him wondering if he was about to wake up.

Michael piled into the back of the car with Scarlett in tow, while Alexander climbed behind the wheel and tore off down the street, leaving the flames and chaos in the rearview mirror.

Alexander kept his eyes glued to that mirror until finally satisfied no one was in pursuit. At that point, Michael settled himself with a deep breath, and opened the file folder featuring a picture of his father under the name Davide Schapira.

SIXTY-THREE

BUNĂ ZIUA, ROMANIA, 1958

The man arrived on the noon train, one of the last passengers to step off into a driving rainstorm. He was tall and lean, casually dressed with a single suitcase and no hat or coat to shield him from the torrents. Had there been anyone about to notice, they would've thought the presence of such a man strange here, since it wasn't a place prone to visitors.

The Socialist Republic of Romania, formed just over a

decade earlier, after all, was little more than a Soviet satellite, the country's resources drained at will by one-sided SovRom agreements and the move to collectivization draining morale along with any hope for a better life. Stalin himself saw the country as no more than a "breadbasket," his death five years before the man's arrival ushering in few changes, other than a festering of crime under those bosses with the resources to pay off corrupt local officials who were mere Soviet sycophants.

The past, meanwhile, had proven no friendlier than the present. World War II had ravaged the countryside, stripping the fertile, generous lands of their beauty and innocence. Barely a dent had been made in ridding Romania of the war's residue and, over the years, a general malaise and grim acceptance had set in that the sorry conditions were there to stay under communism.

That made it unusual to say the least to see any stranger, and a foreigner no less, in a remote Transylvanian town like Bună Ziua. Yet the tall man who climbed off the train that day attracted little attention. His dark, rugged features drew not a second look, except from the poor children hoping to fetch a few coins by carrying his bags. But the man carried his single bag himself, his ratty, tattered clothes indicating he was likely as poor as they were.

The man walked the short distance from the train station to a still privately owned and operated type of establishment unique in Eastern Europe known as a *crisma*, a combination restaurant and bar that also offered a few rooms for rent. The man bypassed the small, local hotel on an adjoining street in favor of it and entered to the sight of heavy wooden tables spread about a plank floor. A smell like cabbage wafted out from what must've been the kitchen and the stranger moved toward a smiling, attractive young woman standing behind a counter.

"I understand you have rooms available for rent."

"Just one right now, on the fourth floor," the woman said. She was close to beautiful with flawless skin and a warm smile. "Where are you from?" she asked the man.

"Italy."

"And what brings you to Transylvania?"

The man looked about the restaurant tables that remained empty, leaving them the only two people present.

"I smell food cooking in your kitchen," he told the young woman. "I'd like some lunch. What did you say your name was?"

"Stefania," he repeated after she told him, taking a seat at one of the tables. "Nice. Your last name . . ."

"Tepesche."

"Similar to Vlad Tepes, the monster who terrorized this area back in the fifteenth century."

"Some consider him a hero, actually, for protecting them against the Turks. And my family's original name *was* Tepes, thought to be descended from Vlad himself. They changed it to *Tepesche* for obvious reasons. And what's yours?" she asked, after studying his reaction.

"Davide Schapira."

"Schapira doesn't sound Italian."

"I'm also Jewish. You can't join me?"

"I'm not allowed."

"Please, just for a moment. I don't know anyone here."

"I can't sit."

"But you can talk. We're talking now."

Stefania recommended the *sarmale*, mincemeat wrapped in cabbage leaves.

"Then that's what I'll have. I'm here searching for relatives lost during the war. Perhaps you can help me."

"I don't know anyone by the name Schapira," Stefania told him, still holding her order pad in hand. "And there are few Jews left in this area."

"They wouldn't be using Jewish names—that's one of the reasons why they've been so difficult to track down." Schapira paused, as if gathering his thoughts. "And they may have resettled in different parts of this area, might even still be keeping themselves scarce out of fear of what happened in the war."

"They wouldn't settle here if they wanted jobs. We have more going than coming. Who can blame them with all the poverty around in these parts?"

"Tough for a woman to make a living then."

"Tougher for some than others, like those of us who refuse to sell their bodies."

Schapira looked about again. "Is this a . . ."

"No," she broke in, "not officially. The government looks the other way here in the mountains. As long as the owner keeps making his payments to the local branch of the *Securitate*, the secret police, there are no problems. Just a few women, each with a room to use upstairs. Would you like to meet one?"

"I've enjoyed meeting you."

"I'm just a clerk and housekeeper. Sorry." She hesitated, growing uneasy. "Let me put your order in. I really should get back to—"

"I'm wondering if the Jews I'm searching for might be among these other women's customers."

"I wouldn't know."

Schapira leaned forward. "You know this town well."

Stefania nervously brushed the dark hair that had strayed from her face. She had a luscious mouth and the deepest, most piercing eyes he'd ever seen, almost hypnotic in how they never seemed to leave him.

"I've lived around here all my life. But I really should be getting back to—"

"Then you must know everyone. I'm interested in those who came here after or even during the war. That would've been the case for my relatives who fled Italy after Mussolini let them."

Finally, he had exhausted her patience. "I can't help you."

And then she was gone.

After that day, they crossed paths occasionally in the house when he was coming or going from the fourth-floor room he rented. The rumor was that Davide Schapira might be hiding out in Romania, but no one ever learned for sure. He always carried a notebook with a vinyl cover that grew more tattered by the day, and he was sometimes spotted making a notation inside it.

Then one night Schapira answered a pounding on his fourth-floor room door to find Stefania standing before him.

"Please, Davide, please help!" she managed between sobs, swiping the tears from her eyes. "One of the women . . ."

He grasped her shoulders to help settle her down. "What is it?"

"A man is beating her," Stefania completed through trembling lips.

"Show me," Schapira said, joining her in the hallway.

The second-floor room door was locked when they got there. So Schapira reared back with his work boot and slammed it into the wood frame even with the latch. The door splintered and flew inward, just as a resounding thwack of an open hand striking flesh sounded.

A big, hairy man, much broader than Schapira but not as

tall, lurched away from the pleading woman, snatching a knife from his pants strewn over the back of a nearby chair. He smelled like stale onions and lumbered forward emitting a guttural growl-like sound.

His knife slashed forward, straight for Schapira who'd come dangerously close to the stocky man. In a blur of motion, Schapira twisted to the side and snatched the man's wrist out of the air. Then the knife was gone, clamoring against the floor, and the man's wrist and hand were bent the wrong way. He was screaming horribly until Schapira rammed the heel of his hand into the man's face. Again and again. Until the man's eyes grew glassy and he went limp. Schapira then hoisted the bulky frame over his shoulders and deposited him outside the house in the gutter.

Stefania was waiting for him back on the stoop, wide-eyed with relief and appreciation.

"I'm looking for outsiders," Schapira said, wasting no time, "foreigners like me even, who arrived out of nowhere and would not have advertised their true identities. Maybe they live in town, maybe in the countryside. Would you know such men, because my lost relatives could be among them?"

"We call them the Strangers," she said, when Schapira drew near. "I serve them food. Between me and the women working here, we probably know all of them in these parts."

Schapira's face changed; no, more than *changed*. As if a mask he'd been wearing had fallen off to reveal an entirely different man beneath it. A man with eyes like black ice whose intense stare chilled Stefania to the bone.

"And you can tell me their names, where they live?"

Stefania nodded. "Given time."

"Take all you need. How much do I owe you?"

She looked toward the bloodied body lying in the gutter, his face mashed to pulp. "You've already paid in advance. And he was one of them, one of these Strangers."

Schapira touched her shoulder with a gentleness and compassion that belied the display of violence Stefania had just witnessed. "The women in this house are under my protection now," he told her. "I won't let any harm come to them or to you. Especially to you," he added, before he could think twice about it.

"Thank you, thank you," Stefania said, repeating it two more times before kissing the hand that had just left her shoulder. "Please, if there's ever anything I can do to help you . . ."

"You already have," Schapira said, smiling.

SIXTY-FOUR

CLUJ-NAPOCA, ROMANIA

Michael finished studying the contents of the file folder just as they reached Napoca Airport. He felt numb, on the inside as well as out, the killing he had done tonight transposed over the mystery of what had brought his father to Romania in the guise of a Jew looking for missing relatives.

What had he really been doing here? Who had sent him? And who were these "Strangers" he'd seemed so interested in?

None of it made any sense.

Michael didn't know what to feel, to think. The car's cabin seemed to be closing in on him and only him, leaving Alexander and Scarlett unscathed. He realized only then a storm had swept in, battering the car with torrents of rain. The windshield wipers were fighting a losing battle against the windswept downpour.

Alexander finally screeched to a halt in a parking space out of sight from the private terminal around the corner. The three of them lurched out together and hurried the rest of the way inside.

"She needs to clean up," Alexander told Michael, casting a glance toward Scarlett. "She'll attract too much attention looking like this. And we need to disguise ourselves. Fast."

Michael, his mind still in a fog, looked at Scarlett.

"I heard him," she said, spotting the nearest woman's bathroom. "See if you can find me something to wear."

The best they could do was a souvenir sweatshirt that read I SURVIVED ROMANIA and a New York Yankees baseball cap, of all things. Michael knocked on the lavatory door and handed them to Scarlett as soon as she opened it, her skin smelling of commercial soap and hair sodden and matted from being rinsed in the sink.

"Thanks," she told him, managing a smile. "For everything."

Fortunately, they'd prepared for this eventuality by having Paddy fabricate a British passport with Scarlett's picture for her to use. As he and Alexander used an adjacent men's room to better disguise themselves to resemble the faces in their passports, Michael's mind drifted back to the contents of the file on his father. He continued to struggle with what it all meant, as his turn finally came in the line to pass through Romanian Customs and Immigration.

"I asked you," the clerk repeated in English, his voice growing impatient, "what was your purpose here?"

"I was on vacation," Michael responded in broken English with a thick Spanish accent. His fake beard was itching and he didn't dare scratch it for fear it might come off.

"Did you buy anything while in the country? . . . Sir?"

"What?"

"Did you buy anything while in the country?" the clerk asked, clearly perturbed now.

"I'm sorry. No, I didn't buy anything. I was here to visit Transylvania, the mountains and the countryside. Very beautiful."

Michael realized he'd said too much, the clerk eyeing him suspiciously and letting the passport stamp hang in the air between them. Their eyes met, the clerk's intentions unsure.

Michael's heart was racing. What if a warning had been already been issued to be on the lookout for two men meeting his and Alexander's general descriptions? What if the clerk had already triggered an alarm and was stalling so security could arrive?

Madness!

His heart skipped a beat when he heard a *thump*, realizing in the next breathless moment the sound had come from the clerk smacking the proper immigration stamp down on Michael's fake passport.

"Come back and visit us again. Next, please."

"I need you to copilot for takeoff," Alexander told him, once they were on board the Citation. "I need you, Michael, and you need to focus. I just scheduled the flight plan, but we haven't been cleared for departure."

Michael saw why once he was seated in the cockpit. The storm was pounding the Citation so hard he could barely make out the airport buildings around him. The flashing red beacon atop the air traffic control tower cast an occasional pinkish haze through a narrow break in the relentless rain that the jet's windshield wipers were having even less luck clearing than the Alfa Romeo's.

"Whatever you say. Just get us out of here, Alexander," he called, feeling for his seat belt.

"I'll lay in the course back for London."

"No," Michael told him, "not London. Not yet."

"Where then?"

"Sicily," he told Alexander. "Catania, the nearest airport to Caltagirone."

Alexander had switched on the engines while Michael completed the more mundane preflight protocols. Then Alexander hailed the tower over the radio.

"This is Citation Larry-Delta-Charlie. Again requesting immediate clearance for takeoff."

"Citation Larry-Delta-Charlie," an air traffic controller blurted in heavily accented English, *"you do not have clearance for takeoff. The airport is closed to all departures. Repeat, the airport is closed to all departures due to extreme weather conditions."*

"What do you want me to do, Michael?" Alexander said, as heavy winds shook the Citation in its perch on the tarmac.

"Get us the fuck out of here."

"Just what I was thinking."

And with that Alexander eased the throttle forward and turned the Citation's nose for the nearest runway, the small jet bucking as he pushed it straight into the wind.

"Citation Larry-Delta-Charlie," came the air traffic controller's harried voice again, *"I say again, you do not have clearance."*

"Tower, we have an emergency on board and are contravening your instructions. Please clear approach traffic from our course."

"Negative, Citation Larry-Delta-Charlie. You are not cleared for takeoff."

"The responsibility is ours. Wind speed and the potential for shear are increasing. We have a brief window to takeoff now. Please clear heading . . ."

Alexander completed plugging in their coordinates from memory and eased the Citation into motion without waiting for confirmation. The jet picked up speed in blinding fashion, so quick Michael could feel the G-forces seeming to contract his chest. Crosswinds from the storm caught the Citation in their grasp and shook it about once they were airborne, Alexander struggling to level the jet off. The controls vibrated madly in his grasp, then slowed to a tremble, as the small jet clung to a steady climb through the choppy air and driving rain. Climbing felt like swimming against a riptide to the point where Michael began to wonder if they might stall out or even roll. Suddenly cockpit lights started to flash, warning buzzers sounding as their air speed reached dangerously low levels. The small jet pitched downward suddenly; then, just as suddenly, it managed to regain altitude with the engines still screaming in protest. Finally, it found a gap in the storm, both Michael and Alexander able to breathe again.

"You okay back there?" Michael called to Scarlett in the cabin.

"Oh, just fine," she said to him, her voice broken by fear. "At least you're consistent."

"How's that?"

"You always know how to keep things interesting."

SIXTY-FIVE

Bună Ziua, Romania

Dracu smelled the aftermath of the battle in the first light of dawn blocks from turning onto the street housing the decimated *Securitate* building. He had his convoy park well down from the chaos of rescue and police vehicles surrounding it and sent a pair of his most trusted captains on ahead.

They returned through the haze of smoke and confusion, toting a man with char, ash, and grime all over his face and uniform with an adhesive wrapping fastened over his clearly swollen right hand. His men shoved the colonel into the back of the Range Rover to join Dracu and Armura.

"How many men were there?" Dracu asked, resuming when the man seated next to him remained silent. "I'm giving you a chance to talk and stay alive."

The colonel seemed unable to take his eyes off first Armura, and then Dracu's veil. "I only saw two," he said finally. "Two men."

"Did you recognize them?"

"They wore masks and goggles," the colonel said, passing a hand before his own face. "Spoke English."

"Anything else?"

"One of them took a file."

"What file?"

Dracu handed him his phone after Colonel Gastman explained its contents.

"Call your men at the airport. Find out if any foreigners have made it past security in the past hour."

Gastman did just that as the man in the veil looked on, hoping to learn enough information to stay alive.

"They boarded a Citation," he reported finally. "Its originating point was listed as London. It took off from Napoca despite the storm against the tower's instructions not long ago."

"Bound back for London?"

"Originally. But the flight plan was switched in flight to Catania in Sicily."

"Sicily," Dracu repeated.

"My man at the airport isolated their pictures from Customs. They've been sent to the number you gave me."

Dracu checked his pocket-size tablet and found the pictures waiting. But none of the three faces were recognizable or could be identified, as if all three had been schooled to avoid looking directly at the cameras. Two men and one woman, obviously disguised, was all he could tell.

And that was enough.

"One more thing," he said to Colonel Gastman, still staring at one of the two men pictured. "Tell your man at the airport to have my jet readied for takeoff."

SIXTY-SIX

LAS VEGAS, NEVADA

"It wasn't an explosion that caused the rupture," Gregory John Markham told Naomi, as they viewed the footage picturing the aftermath of the destruction of Edward Devereaux's Daring Sea suite yet again.

The Seven Sins had hired Markham away from Perini Building Company after he proved to be the only engineer neither intimidated nor overwhelmed by the challenges involved in constructing the Daring Sea and its underwater suites. Far from it. Instead, he embraced the project as the challenge of a lifetime and didn't quit even after dozens of failures with models and various composites.

"At least, not the kind of explosion you'd expect," Markham continued.

Markham was all of thirty-four now, but had been barely twenty-six when he was hired during the construction of the Daring Sea environment. It was the crowning achievement of his young career, enhancing his reputation to the point where he had gained more work than he could handle. Not about to forget who'd entrusted him with such an opportunity, Markham dropped everything as soon as Naomi called.

Markham's knowledge and foresight had led him to conclude that glass, no matter how sturdy and stable, was prone to rupture. In fact, the stronger it was, the higher the likelihood of a catastrophic event in what he called an ascending arithmetic scale. The solution was to create "softer," more malleable sections of glass that displaced energy and absorbed a force strong enough to rupture the glass-like polymer before the rapid chain of events, better known as cracking, could even begin.

Not surprisingly, then, Markham looked at investigating the circumstances of Deveraux/Faustin's death as a matter of personal pride. He was convinced from the start what happened was in no way an accident or a random occurrence under any circumstances. Proving that meant not only exonerating himself from some level of responsibility, but also providing further validation of his theories on building large-scale underwater habitats that could potentially house thousands, even tens of thousands.

"What do you mean by not the kind of explosion I'd expect?" Naomi asked him in the sprawling Seven Sins command center that offered every conceivable view of the entire resort, including the Daring Sea.

"Well," Markham started to explain, having to remind himself not to sound too academic, "explosives are normally incendiary, relying on a combination of a blast wave, heat displacement, and shrapnel spread to do their damage. But the fragments of the glass I examined that were recovered from the victim's suite showed no signs whatsoever of any of those, no scoring or searing at all." With that, Markham slid an anomalously smooth fragment of the glass from Devereaux's suite atop a lab tray in front of her. "See, no scorching, no external rupture. The cracking you see exemplified here that ultimately compromised the glass polymer's integrity happened from the inside out, not the outside in."

"How is that possible?" Naomi asked.

"Only one way," Markham told her and proceeded to emit a high-pitched wail that forced Naomi, and any technician on duty around them, to squeeze her hands over her ears.

"There was a point to that, I assume," she said when the sound finally waned.

"You've seen demonstrations of opera singers capable of shattering glass with their voice."

"I never believed they were real."

"Oh, they most certainly are. Not common, mind you, but very much real. Sound travels in waves and when those waves reach a certain pitch or modulation, they have the capacity to damage any object. Glass is far more molecularly fragile than, say, wood or steel, and that makes it much more subject to the effects of these waves that are better described as ultrasonic frequencies."

"Wait a minute, are you saying *sound* is what killed Edward Devereaux?"

"A sonic bomb would be a more apt description," confirmed Gregory John Markham. "But, yes, that's exactly what I'm saying."

SIXTY-SEVEN

LAS VEGAS, NEVADA

"I've reviewed footage of the great whites in the moments during the blackout," Markham continued. "What you need to understand is that sharks use sound to locate food; in fact, it's often the first sense they rely on because sound travels faster and farther underwater than on land. They key on low-frequency pulsed sounds. So the kind of disruption in sonic waves that bomb caused to their scanning field would have thrown all their systems out of whack, essentially driving them crazy. I've isolated the footage of them both before and during the blackout so you can review my findings. The difference is drastic, undeniable."

Naomi nodded, trying to process Markham's conclusions. "I've heard of sonic weapons being deployed before, but never anything like a sonic bomb."

"That's because the research on them is flimsy and unproven at best, purely theoretical but still based on some fairly well-established principles," Markham explained. "Those sonic weapons you just mentioned?"

"Yes."

"Well, extremely high-power sound waves can disrupt and/or destroy the eardrums of a target and cause severe pain or disorientation. This is usually sufficient to incapacitate a person. Less powerful sound waves can cause humans to experience nausea or discomfort. The use of these frequencies to incapacitate persons has occurred both in counterterrorist and crowd control scenarios—in ships at sea seeking to defend themselves against terrorists, for example. Something called a long-range acoustic device was used by a cruise ship to chase off pirates not too long ago. A similar system called a magnetic acoustic device has been used successfully, especially in Europe, to even break up riots. So the technology's definitely there."

"But how did it get *here*?" Naomi asked him.

"The first challenge is size. The kind of long-range acoustic devices being deployed on ships at sea is the size of a small tire."

"Nothing like that was recovered from Edward Devereaux's suite or anywhere else in the Daring Sea."

"You mean, nothing that anyone noticed. That only

means the weapon was likely deployed within something already present inside the suite. But a sonic bomb wouldn't work under the same principles as acoustic weapons do. They deploy ultrasonic waves; a sonic bomb, instead, would utilize something called infrasound."

"Infrasound?"

Markham nodded, clearly enjoying himself. "The low frequency of infrasonic sound and its corresponding long wavelength makes it much more capable of bending around or penetrating your body, creating an oscillating pressure system. Depending on the frequency, different parts of your body will resonate, which can have very unusual non-auditory effects. Almost any part of your body, based on its volume and makeup, will vibrate at specific frequencies with enough power. Human eyeballs are fluid-filled ovoids, lungs are gas-filled membranes, and the human abdomen contains a variety of liquid, solid, and gas-filled pockets. All of these structures have limits to how much they can stretch when subjected to force, so if you provide enough power behind a vibration, they will stretch and shrink in time with the low-frequency vibrations of the air molecules around them."

"Would an autopsy reveal evidence of that?"

"It would reveal evidence of something normal forensics would be unable to explain, that is if the great whites hadn't pretty much ravaged the victim's remains. I'm not sure if there's enough left of our victim to come up with anything definitive. So my conclusions are based on the infrasound's effects on the glass. It wasn't the harder portions of the pane that were struck first, it was the softer layers that ruptured from the inside out, like I said before, creating a chain re-action that destroyed the structural integrity of the glass wall. An infrasound weapon that powerful would have killed the victim, even if the wall hadn't ruptured, as an autopsy on whatever's left of him might yet reveal."

"What about the means of delivery?"

"An infrasound weapon doesn't rely on a focused beam the way an acoustic weapon does. It dispenses waves instead, and the actual device could have been disguised as practically anything."

"Dispensed *how*, Greg?" Naomi asked him.

"I've been reviewing an inventory of all Daring Sea suites, and I'm guessing through something electronic. If it were me, I'd go with this," he said, freezing the screen on a high-end Bose clock radio that was among the objects recovered from Devereaux's suite.

"Why?"

"Because it already has a fairly sophisticated sound system built in. Means less of a chore to modify it into a sonic bomb. And the clock radios in the Daring Sea suites also have automatic battery backup power, meaning—"

"They'd work in the event of a blackout," Naomi interrupted.

Markham nodded. "Unfortunately, the police took the clock radio as evidence, so I can't examine it myself and I can't be absolutely sure until I do. Right now, though, I'm sure enough." He paused. "And I'm also sure you're dealing with one brilliant, and exceptionally dangerous, mind here."

"Brilliant enough to cause the blackout, too?"

"Not in my realm of expertise, I'm afraid."

"Then find me somebody whose realm it is in. How soon can you get him . . . or her on the job?"

"It's a *him*. Give me until tomorrow. He'll want to be paid in cash, quite a bit I should add. He doesn't work cheap."

"Not a problem, so long as you're willing to vouch for him," Naomi said, realizing she sounded like Michael. "My boss isn't the kind of man who takes being betrayed well."

"I wouldn't recommend someone unless I was sure you could trust him. This guy's the best hacker in the business, wanted by companies and countries alike who have absolutely no idea who he is. You want to find out how somebody staged this blackout, he's your man."

Naomi's cell phone rang, her private number known only to a select few.

"I have to take this," she told Markham, turning away to answer.

"Hello, Counselor," greeted the voice of Del Slocumb.

"How'd you get this number, Agent?"

"We're the FBI. You'd be surprised what we can pull off when we put our minds to it," he said, sounding almost jovial.

"You're right, I would."

"Then let me prove it to you another way," Slocumb said. "I've got some more news about your boss I think you'll want to hear."

SIXTY-EIGHT

SICILY

"The truth, Ismael. Now."

And the truth Saltuk shared with her had taken Raven Khan to Sicily where a private jet arranged via her myriad of trusted contacts landed at Vincenzo Bellini Airport. A rental car was waiting for her at the private terminal.

A cloudless sky and full moon as dawn approached made for an easy ride through countryside she had never once traveled, but somehow seemed familiar. The directions took her along the A19 to a destination located at the near halfway point between Catania and Palermo. Even with those directions, she thought she'd missed her target, finding herself in the middle of a town that seemed lifted from another century.

The light wood and stone buildings were uniformly ancient, most dating back hundreds of years and many remaining frozen in time. Like much of Italy, the town claimed churches as its most cherished landmarks along, in this case, with a castle-like town hall in the piazza municipio that, according to a historic plaque aglow in a ground-mounted spotlight, was registered among official Italian landmarks. Soft rolling hills bracketed the town on either side, layered with more graveyards than she'd ever seen in her life, something that seemed oddly appropriate right now.

Raven slid down the window and smelled the air, refreshingly cool for summer and laced with a pleasant aroma of the flora that suddenly seemed strangely familiar.

Oranges, she realized, *I can smell oranges.*

Just then she came to a sign featuring the name of the town in reflective letters that caught the moonlight:

Caltagirone.

For Raven, though, it smelled oddly like something else entirely.

Home.

PART FIVE

HOME

A man's character is his fate.

Heraclitus

SIXTY-NINE

The Citation

"Do you always travel like this?" Scarlett asked Michael in the rear of the cabin.

"No, this is a piece of cake. Usually, it's really challenging," he tried to joke.

She started to smile. Then, just as fast, her features sunk and tears began streaming down her face.

Michael had moved from the cockpit and settled into the seat next to her, just in time for Scarlett to lurch into his arms when a fresh blast of turbulence shook the Citation.

"I'm not a very good flier," she said, breaking the embrace but still clinging to him. "Guess I'm a coward at heart."

"The storm will be behind us soon."

"Which one?" Scarlett asked him, as turbulence rocked the Citation again and sent her back into Michael's arms.

"On second thought, maybe I'll tell Alexander to circle back. I kind of like this."

Scarlett managed a smile that slipped quickly from her face, as she began to sob again. "I'm sorry, Michael, I'm so sorry."

"For what?" he asked, still holding her against him, feeling the Citation leveling off now.

"Making you come all this way, take all this risk."

"You'd only have something to be sorry for if you *hadn't* called me."

She eased herself away from him. "I didn't know what else to do. What happened . . . It was so much worse than anything I could imagine. I thought I'd never experience anything like that again after French Guiana. Guess I was wrong. Remember what I told you when we first met, about uncovering a find that would change how we perceive the world, even history itself?"

"That's when I told you I wanted to fund that effort."

She looked at him plaintively. "To find the truth behind your relic, whether it really does hold some mysterious power dating back to the ancients."

"We don't have to do this now, Scarlett."

She eased away, then was thrown back against him by another blast of turbulence. "Yes, Michael, we do. There's something I never told you about your relic, because I thought the results had to be wrong. Remember when I tried to determine its age?"

"Through carbon dating or something. You told me the results were inconclusive."

"More like impossible, because the readings and analysis were all over the map. They indicated the relic had *no* age, at least none that could be determined within any degree of reasonable certainty. Almost like it had existed forever, since the dawn of time. I've spent the last five years following its trail, spending as much time in libraries as I have in the field. I thought it was a fool's errand at first, I truly did. A wild goose chase with only dead ends."

"But that's not what you found in Romania, is it?" Michael asked, thinking of all the cities where he'd managed to meet Scarlett. He remembered the first time he'd shown her the relic, avoiding an explanation of the circumstances of how he'd come to possess it, while wondering out loud if the legends others had associated with it might be true.

If this is what I think it may be . . .

She'd left things there, never elaborating further on her suspicions. Until now.

"No," Scarlett said finally. "I believe I've found proof, Michael, proof of what I suspected about the origins of your relic all along."

"What origins?"

Turbulence rocked the Citation anew, and Scarlett waited for it to subside before resuming.

"The treasure of the Gods."

SEVENTY

THE CITATION

"The day before the massacre," Scarlett continued, "I uncovered an ancient journal, a manuscript written on parchment at the dig site." She swallowed hard, lips trembling at the memory. "I only got a chance to read a portion of it but the contents were incredible, starting with the author: Josephus."

"Most famous scribe of that era."

"And a vast amount of what we know of those times comes from his writings," Scarlett explained. "In this case, he was chronicling discoveries made by others that somehow ended up with him."

"You're losing me, Scarlett."

"Then let's back up a bit to Caesar," she said, eyes dipping to Michael's chest where his relic was likely held hidden beneath his shirt. "After conquering Gaul, after returning to Rome a hero in the wake of the civil war and becoming dictator, Caesar became obsessed by the power he was convinced the relic had given him, obsessed by its origins.

Where had it come from? What if there were more? What about the gold from which it had been forged? Caesar formed an order of loyalists he instructed to find the answers to those questions for him, no matter how long or exhaustive that quest became. Josephus's journal indicates the loyalists started their research in Rome sometime in forty-five or forty-six BC and didn't complete it until more than a decade later."

"By which time Caesar was long dead."

"You can imagine the loyalists' dilemma when they had no one to whom to report their findings once they finally returned, not that they had any real desire to do so."

"Why?"

"Josephus's report was titled 'The Treasure of the Gods' because the Romans believed in multiple deities back then, a tradition they inherited from the Greeks. But what the loyalists found on this quest that took them far beyond the borders of the Roman Empire contradicted that dogma long before the Romans began worshipping a single God. Judea, for example, where members of Caesar's order of loyalists apparently met with a number of scribes and historians, even rabbis, who filled them in what they believed were the treasure's origins."

A fresh wave of turbulence shook the Citation and Michael finally belted himself in.

"Those origins," Scarlett continued, "went back all the way to the original Temple of Solomon that was built specifically to house the greatest treasures of the Jewish faith, including the Ark of the Covenant. Among the rest were three pieces that included a candelabra, a pair of trumpets, and the Table of Divine Presence."

"Sunday school stuff."

"Maybe, but what's not was the reason for the creation of those objects in the first place. How well do you know the Old Testament?"

"Why?"

"Because it states that God gave the plans for a great temple to David but refused to let him build it."

"So that task ended up falling on his son Solomon. More Sunday school stuff."

"Not according to what I was able to decipher in the early parts of Josephus's writings summarizing the expedition. 'He gave of gold,'" Scarlett quoted. "That's from *Chronicles*. And it implies God didn't just provide detailed plans for the sanctuary he wanted built, He also provided *the gold* that made up at least some of that sanctuary's contents."

"Origins of this treasure of the Gods . . ."

"Josephus's writings suggest that David gave only the plans to the temple to Solomon, but hid the actual treasure until the temple was complete and ready to accept the three objects in question and everything else it was built to safeguard."

"But the temple was destroyed and all its contents looted. By Nebuchadnezzar, I think."

"No," Scarlett corrected. "Nebuchadnezzar sacked and looted the *second* Temple of Solomon. The original temple, built by Solomon with plans passed from David, was destroyed centuries earlier by the Egyptian pharaoh Shishaq, also known as Sheshonk the First, who 'took away the treasures of the house of the Lord.' Quoting *Chronicles* again, as opposed to Josephus."

"Keep going," Michael urged, after another surge of turbulence had subsided.

"Speaking historically, it wasn't long after the Egyptians sacked the temple that the Assyrians sacked the Egyptians—in nine hundred eleven BC, to be specific." Scarlett returned her gaze to Michael's shirt, again picturing the medallion beneath it. "Remember the markings on the relic, what I told you the first time you showed it to me?"

"You said the language was Phrygian," Michael recalled.

"And that the initials stood for King Mita, who ruled Phrygia, what's now Turkey, in the 8th century BC."

"Mita accumulated vast stores of gold and became the wealthiest and most powerful ruler of his time. He also struck a truce with Sargon of Assyria, accepting great riches as a token of Sargon's desire to avoid war. So what if . . ."

"Part of those riches was this treasure of the Gods plundered by the Egyptians," Michael completed.

"King Mita takes the gold and melts it down so he can forge different treasures of his own making, treasures forged from gold provided, according to Josephus's writings, by God Himself."

Michael traced the outline of his medallion beneath his shirt, feeling its warmth against his chest.

"And there's something else you need to hear."

SEVENTY-ONE

The Citation

"Alexander the Great," Scarlett continued. "His travels took him to Phrygia, Gordian specifically, in search of the famed Knot which he ultimately severed. According to Josephus's writings compiled from the reports of that order of loyalists, though, he had come there in search of something else entirely."

"The treasure plundered from the temple of Solomon?"

"No, Michael, because that treasure no longer existed. Mita supposedly melted it down, remember? And Alexander came to Phrygia in search of whatever items Mita had forged from it. Came away empty and died not too long afterward. You realize what all this means, don't you? It's proof that Caesar really did possess your relic, proof that Alexander the Great was after it, too, and at least a suggestion of where it actually comes from. That was as far as I got in the manuscript before the massacre," Scarlett told him, not bothering to elaborate further. "But what if the man in black came looking for what I found? What if he's after the treasure of the Gods? Why, though, why kill all those people for a *manuscript*? . . . Michael?"

He heard her but didn't respond, his mind elsewhere.

It had been the night before another massacre at his own home when his father slipped into his room and took a seat at his bedside while Michael laid in bed reading a book.

"Hello, Papa."

"It's time to show you something special, Michele," Vito Nunziato said, opening his hand to reveal a gold medallion. Even weathered with age, it was the most beautiful thing the boy had ever seen. "I found this medallion one day off Isla de Levanzo when I was little older than you. It is the treasure of kings, Michele. There are men in Sicily, scum really, who steal and murder for money and power. But they will never be kings."

With that, Vito pressed the medallion into his son's hand, Michael taking it as if he never wanted to let it go.

"What are those words, Papa?"

"*Somnia, aude, vince.* Latin. It means, 'Dream, Dare, Win.' Words to live by. Someday the medallion will be yours and will inspire you to become a king, not another mafia pig . . . or farmer. No matter what happens, when that day comes, you must never part with it."

With that, his father had hugged Michael for one of the few times the boy would ever remember.

"Be a king, Michele," he whispered, his voice cracking. "Be a king."

"What are you thinking about, Michael?" he heard Scarlett ask him, but he wasn't ready to return to the present yet.

Had his father somehow sensed what was coming? he wondered, as another wave of turbulence shook the Citation. Could his choosing the very night before the massacre to show his son his cherished medallion been nothing more than coincidence?

Michael remembered his father's hug, the gesture unusual not just for its rarity, but also for something else. He remembered Vito Nunziato trembling through the embrace. As if he sensed, even knew, what was in the offing, just as he knew there was nothing he could do to prevent it, because it was fated just as was Michael's own destiny.

The medallion had not helped Vito Nunziato become anything more than the farmer he was when he died, so poor in the end that he nearly sold his cherished relic to a broker to save the farm he'd built for his family. So why had he been chosen to find it in the first place?

Maybe he was meant to find it to give to me.

If his father had not shown the relic to him that fateful night in the farmhouse, if Michael had not lifted the relic from Vito Nunziato's drawer the next morning, his family's killers would've found it and who knows how different his life would have been.

"My father," Michael answered finally. "I was thinking about my father."

"Your life changed entirely, you became a multimillionaire the moment that relic became yours," Scarlett told him, eyes boring into his. "Because you've been chosen, Michael, chosen by forces we can't even come close to comprehending. I know this all sounds crazy, but it's not, not according to the legacy of your relic. It's invaluable, priceless. And now we've got actual proof of its origins.

And there's something else that separates the treasure of the Gods from other artifacts of lore."

"What's that?"

"Unlike those that rise exclusively from Judeo-Christian teachings, what could very well be the treasure of the Gods is referenced both in Islam and Chinese. The prophet Mohammed writes in the Koran that one day 'the river Euphrates dries up to unveil a mountain of gold.' And the Chinese have a legend about something called the Jade Treasure. During an ancient time when seven Chinese kingdoms battled for supremacy, the king of one received a piece of jade that was different from all others. According to the legend, it shined in the dark and could heat an entire room when it was cold or cool it when it was hot. 'You must always guard it,' the stranger who bequeathed the jade to the king advised, 'because this is a magnificent priceless treasure.' Sound familiar?"

"Talk to me about the dig site," Michael said, still tracing the shape of his medallion and needing to change the subject, at least for the moment. "About what happened to that manuscript."

Scarlett shrugged, shifting uneasily in the confines of her seat belt. "I don't know. It could have been destroyed, along with everything else."

"Not if it's what drew those killers there. If they came for it, it's a safe assumption they left with it. The Romanian authorities reported finding absolutely nothing, as if the camp had never existed at all. The scene had been sanitized."

Scarlett shivered. "I can't get it out of my mind. Every time I close my eyes, I see the gunmen, the bodies, all the blood. They were my friends, Michael, my *friends*! And there's something else. In the village, where I went after, more gunmen came looking for me. They wore masks that looked like skulls, led by a man dressed all in black wearing a veil instead. He called himself—"

"Black Scorpion," Michael finished for her.

SEVENTY-TWO

Las Vegas, Nevada

"Interesting choice for a meeting," Naomi Burns said, approaching FBI special agent Del Slocumb in the lobby of the Mob Museum, one of Vegas's more recent tourist attractions.

"I thought it to be especially fitting," Slocumb returned, smiling tightly. He looked around them. "Familiar territory for you, given your association with Michael Tiranno."

"Some courts would consider that grounds for a harassment suit, Agent, given that your accusations have no foundation in fact."

"They do now, Ms. Burns."

Located in the former and very first federal building in Las Vegas, the building was listed on both the Nevada and National Registers of Historic Places. It contained the very courtroom where one of fourteen national hearings to expose organized crime to America took place in the years 1950 and 1951. The museum's builders were able to maintain the building's original neo-classical architectural style, period perfect for the age it sought to replicate while providing an authentic view of the Mob's impact on Las Vegas history and the imprint left on America. The Mob Museum, also known as the National Museum of Organized Crime and Law Enforcement, prided itself on bringing true stories to life in a bold, contemporary style via engaging exhibits and multisensory experiences with high-tech theater presentations, interactive displays, themed environments, and authentic, iconic artifacts.

"Let's talk as we walk," Slocumb resumed.

The lobby lighting was warm and ambient, the bulk of it inside the main display area beyond trained toward the wall-mounted pictures and exhibits staged inside glass cases with the spray of bulbs focused out instead of in. Naomi walked slightly behind Slocumb, letting the agent dictate the pace and at least their initial destination.

That destination turned out to be an exhibit room marked MOB BUSTERS. Slocumb veered toward it from memory, not needing to read the signs. The interior featured both wall-mounted and floor displays of photographs and artifacts highlighting the war on organized crime undertaken by the likes of J. Edgar Hoover, Estes Kefauver, and Eliot Ness.

"A man can dream, I suppose," Naomi commented, as she surveyed the scenery.

"So can a woman, Counselor. Of not going down when I nail her boss, anyway."

"I appreciate the concern, Agent."

"Then you'll appreciate this even more: We're not here right now and the conversation we're having never took place."

Slocumb spoke from beneath a mural of Estes Kefauver holding one of his many hearings into organized crime, making it seem as if the agent was actually standing even with the dais on which the Kefauver Committee sat. A dull patch of light seemed to shade Slocumb's face in even more shadows than usual, shadows that dug themselves into the furrowed lines marking both his cheeks.

"Okay," Naomi said suspiciously.

"I assume I don't have to review the RICO statutes for you, that once I nail your boss it'll be easy to make a case for you as being connected to a criminal enterprise. This meeting is your one chance to use your get-out-of-jail-for-free card. Cooperate with me and you'll have a life and career after I put Michael Tiranno away."

"Michael Tiranno is *my* career, Agent."

Slocumb shook his head, making a face like he'd swallowed something bitter. "You know what I hate? When innocent people go down with the likes of your boss. They all sound exactly like you at first. Loyal to a fault and convinced we'll never be able to make our case. By the time they realize they've fucked up, the deal's off the table and their get-out-of-jail-for-free card has expired. So we're not here today and I never made this offer to you." Slocumb paused briefly. "But here's what I'm putting on the table: Turn state's evidence, come clean with everything you know about Michael Tiranno's past and illicit dealings, and you walk away from this free and still a member of the bar with a future."

"I appreciate the offer, but I can't tell you about something that doesn't exist. And you seem to forget that we're talking about a man whose heroism resulted in having a street named after him. Or maybe you don't care he saved the city of Las Vegas from terrorists."

"It takes one to know one, Ms. Burns."

"So now Michael Tiranno is a terrorist, on top of everything else you allege?"

"Ever since your client arrived in this city, sand storms have been replaced by shit storms. I don't believe that's a coincidence any more than I believe your client is traveling right now on ordinary business. Michael Tiranno is a cancer that's infected this city. And like all cancers, sometimes the diagnosis comes too late, after the infestation has become so pervasive that there's no treatment."

"So you're the cure, is that it?"

"Where's your boss, Counselor?"

"En route home now."

"That's not what I asked you."

"The question was inevitable. I thought I could save us both some time."

"Like twenty years federal time, maybe. I figure that's what you're looking at just for being Michael Tiranno's CEO."

"His board's, actually. The by-laws of corporate entities in Nevada are very specific when it comes to such things."

"Glad you're keeping to the rules," Slocumb told her, smirking. "This normally goes quicker when the target has a family. But you've given your life to Michael Tiranno instead and he fucked you in return."

"Your information is entirely wrong, Agent. Michael Tiranno has never fucked me."

Slocumb's smirk widened into a tight smile. "As soon as he gets back to Vegas, I'm going to arrest your boss."

Naomi feigned indifference. "Max Price again, Agent? Here's some free *legal* advice: You really should let that go."

"Oh, I assure you I have, Counselor. No, I'm going to arrest your boss for the murder of Amanda Johansen."

"This would be the former Seven Sins Elysium performer who was found dead in Turkey," Naomi said, trying to keep her thoughts straight.

"The very same. And you forgot to mention she was also found pregnant."

"Because it's irrelevant."

"Not to that Interpol agent Pierre Faustin, it wasn't."

"*Former* agent, you mean."

"Faustin came to Las Vegas in the guise of Edward Devereaux to nail a monster. He already had his suspicions, thanks to a pendant found in the victim's stomach."

"Pendant?"

"I thought I told you," Slocumb said, even though it was clear he didn't. "It was found during Amanda Johansen's autopsy, one of those pendants worn by all your boss's female employees."

"You mean, the *casino*'s employees, Agent."

"*His* casino, Counselor. The pendant keyed Faustin to the Seven Sins and the fact that the victim was pregnant told him he had the evidence he needed."

"This would be the same Pierre Faustin, aka Edward Devereaux, who Interpol fired for cause."

Slocumb stepped out of the light splashed by floods against the Kefauver Hearings mural. "That cause was the pursuit of an international criminal no one else believed existed."

"And you believe that criminal to be Michael Tiranno."

"I believe Faustin came to the Seven Sins to nail the murderer of Amanda Johansen." Slocumb gazed fondly up at a portrait of J. Edgar Hoover. "Otherwise, I prefer to reserve judgment and remain objective."

"You—objective about Michael Tiranno? Please spare me the bullshit, Agent." Naomi moved the center of the exhibit hall, finally getting her bearings. "It was from right here in this room that lawyers for a number of alleged mob associates told members of the Kefauver Committee that they didn't have anything. Seems like the perfect spot for me to say you don't have anything either."

"When's your boss due back in Vegas, Ms. Burns?"

"Asked and answered. And, by the way, Kefauver never brought charges against a single individual he paraded through this room. You're finished, Agent, you just don't know it yet."

"It's your boss who's finished, Counselor. See, we've given that portable DNA analyzer Faustin brought with him to the Seven Sins the real once-over. Turns out Faustin left Turkey with a sample of Amanda Johansen's fetus's DNA with him. Turns out that DNA is a match for Michael Tiranno's."

SEVENTY-THREE

Sardinia

Aldridge Sterling stood at the deck of his yacht looking out at the majestic view toward Porto Cervo, waiting for the cell phone clutched in his hand to ring. Better to take the call out here himself than to risk one of his assistants again hearing the voice on the other end of the line, as to leave no trail whatsoever between him and the client who was about to make him the richest man in the world.

The phone rang. Sterling steeled himself with a deep breath and answered.

"Buna pritene," he said in Romanian. "Hello, my friend."

"I've sent you a gift," Dracu said over his satellite phone, from the private section of his jet's cabin. "It should be arriving soon."

"Should I be worried?" Sterling asked, warily.

"Consider it a token of my appreciation for your recent successful maneuverings. And a reminder."

"Of what?"

"That the press is misleading the world by lauding your genius. That the world has no idea of the truth behind your fortune. That everything you possess—from your yacht, to your estates, even the women you sleep with—you owe to me. That I can take it all away and break you as easily as I made you."

"You sound like my father once did."

"You mean the father who disowned, disinherited, and disgraced you? Are we talking about the same man?"

Sterling was glad Dracu couldn't see him turning red

with rage, fighting to retain his composure from being treated so disrespectfully. "We serve each other's needs, Vlad," he started, feeling the need to claim that respect back. "You're hardly the only one of my VIP clients who has special requirements that present unique challenges."

"Really?" Dracu asked him. "And did you meet all these other VIP clients the same way?"

It was fifteen years ago now. A disgraced Aldridge Sterling, scion of a famed family and son of one of modern history's greatest men, was down almost literally to his last dollar. His father, the great hero Harold Sterling, had managed to survive the Holocaust to become one of the most esteemed senators of his generation. He'd hoped for similarly great things from his lone son, but Aldridge had found the life of a playboy much more to his liking. Any number of failed business dealings had damaged the family fortune enough for his father to threaten cutting him off on numerous occasions. But his latest threat had proven real and Aldridge had no idea what the future held in store for him now that his father ordered him off the yacht he intended to put up immediately for sale.

So Aldridge, or "Aldy" to his fawning friends only interested in spending his money on booze, drugs, women, and lavish parties featuring a combination of all three, decided to throw a final bash. They brought a host of beautiful women back with them from the mainland, applauding the soon-to-be-broke Aldy as he paraded around the deck in nothing but boxers and a bathrobe and barely noticing a speedboat approaching his yacht anchored off Monte Carlo Bay.

A few minutes later he was snorting coke off the breasts of three gorgeous women in his stateroom bed when the lights went out. A door burst open and a tall, dark figure entered.

"What the fuck?" Sterling managed, excess cocaine blown from his nose as he jerked upright in bed, squinting to get a better look at a man who clung to the shadows, silhouetted by the light from the hall beyond.

The dark figure ignored him, running his eyes from one girl to the next instead. "Get dressed," he ordered them, as Sterling glimpsed a second man, a massive hulking figure, toss the women the clothes strewn about the floor. "Then get out."

"Who the *hell* are you?" Sterling managed, trying very hard not to sound scared even though this man had scared him enough to utterly break his high.

"A friend."

Sterling stumbled off the bed, as the second figure retreated and the women quickly put their clothes back on. "Do we know each other?"

"No, but we will," the dark man said from the shadows. "Now, put your clothes on and meet me on deck."

By the time, Sterling reached the deck, his party guests had been ushered into waiting launches already en route back to port. Pissed off, Sterling stormed to the gunwale where the stranger was standing but found his bravado gone by the time he got there. All the deck lights had been turned off, leaving them in near darkness. Sterling glimpsed dark hair and skin that looked pasty in the dim glow radiating from the lights of Monte Carlo. He also noticed none of the yacht's crew in evidence, leaving the deck all to themselves.

"Where's the crew?"

"With my men. Still alive. Whether they stay that way, whether *you* stay that way, depends entirely on the next few minutes. Your friends call you Aldy," the stranger continued, not looking directly at Sterling to deny him clear view of his own face. "I'm not your friend so I won't call you that."

"And what should I call you?"

"Your savior."

"That's not a name."

"Then call me daddy," the dark man said, bursting into laughter. "Sorry, couldn't help myself. But that's what I'm going to become for you—everything your real father wasn't."

"And what makes you my savior?"

"Money. I have tons of it, literally, that I'd like you to invest on my behalf, enough so that soon you'll be able to buy a yacht twice the size of this one."

"Okay, you've got my attention."

The dark man explained that he'd already accumulated a vast amount of cash with the likelihood of making far, far more in the future. For that reason, he was in search of someone of Sterling's investment daring and acumen to figure out how to legitimately launder the vast fortune.

"You're describing profits gained from some sort of criminal enterprise, aren't you?" Sterling asked him.

"Do you care?"

"Not particularly, so long as the funds are in no way traceable to me. I don't want to go to jail."

"No, of course not," the stranger said sarcastically. "You'd rather be broke."

No stranger to the fringes of the investment world, and desperately wanting to separate his interests from the father he despised, Sterling embraced the opportunity.

"I do have one question for you, though," Sterling asked, still not having gotten a good look at the man's face. "Why me?"

Dracu flashed a smile that glistened through the night. "Well, you do have excellent taste in women. I should know, since I arranged for the whores you were with tonight."

"You *what*?" Sterling snapped, starting toward the dark figure until the man's stare left him backpedaling. The first close look he got at the figure had left him recalling only eyes so black they seemed to have swallowed the whites.

"I know your weaknesses, but I also know your strengths. And there's something else."

"What?"

"You hate your father as much as I hate mine."

SEVENTY-FOUR

ANKARA, TURKEY, 1964

"Someday your father will come back for us, Vlad," he recalled his mother saying in one of his earliest memories on a frigid night he was shaking so hard he couldn't sleep *"Someday we will be free of all this. He promised."*

Years later, though, when his father had still failed to keep that promise, his mother used every penny she'd ever saved to take Vlad and flee Romania. The plan was to reach Sicily, homeland of his father, through Albania. But they'd never even gotten close, snatched by human traffickers from the Port of Durrës while waiting for a ferry. In the hellish days that followed, they were taken to Turkey where his mother had been forced into the sexual servitude she'd resisted all those years in Romania. The cruelest of ironies. Dracu's memories of those months that stretched into years was hazy at best.

"Someday your father will come back for us, Vlad."

They need only be patient, she insisted, and take solace in the certainty that things could only get better, since it was inconceivable they could get any worse.

But they did.

"Your father loves us very much, Vlad, and he will come for us. I'm sure this time. He's going to find us."

His mother had spoken those words of typically false hope just days before she was murdered by a customer a few weeks past Vlad's sixth birthday. Her body was taken away while he screeched and wailed, trying to tear free of the men holding him. It was his last memory until the jolt of being thrust into the back of the truck that stank of urine, vomit, and fear. The utter darkness hiding sight of the other boys, but not the sound of their plaintive wails and cries. Vlad ended up squeezing himself into a space on the truck floor amid a pool of piss from a boy nearby who was cold and stiff.

Dead.

Vlad would remember that clanking, clamoring ride over rocky, pit-marred roads with crystal clarity no matter how hard he tried to forget it. Sometimes even today he would awaken from a deep sleep drenched in a sweat, and nauseous from the sense of the bouncing journey inside the blackness of a truck riddled with bad shocks and tires that provided no cushion whatsoever. Vlad thought he remembered the dead boy's stiff body rolling up against him and the feel of his dead fingers digging into his arms, trying to drag him along to hell, too.

And if he'd known what awaited him at the end of the truck's journey, he would have gone.

Especially on stormy nights when winds slammed the mountain beyond and the halls of his fortress forged from the former Soviet bunker grew black and frigid, Dracu would feel the agony caused by the men who found pleasure in his pain. He tried to make his mind go somewhere else when they hurt and abused him, but there was nowhere else to go save for the last home he'd known, where his mind could only conjure thoughts of his mother's blood-soaked body and the coppery stench that had clung to his nostrils ever since.

Dracu should have been dead many times over, like the other boys who'd shared the confines of the truck with him, but he endured. With no happy place to go in his mind, he busied himself instead with the face of the man who'd emerged from his mother's room covered in her blood. Instead of joy, he lost himself in hatred, in a rage he was powerless to vent, believing that looking toward a time where he would no longer be powerless was what kept him alive through the unspeakable ordeal.

Even with the disease that was slowly killing him.

Vlad had no conception of who had infected him, or when exactly he realized he was sick. Feeling that way had been the norm for him for as long as he could remember. Trembling in the hall in the cold of winter and barely ever feeling warm, racked by chills even in the height of summer.

He was fifteen when he decided to mount an escape. If the attempt failed, he'd likely face death, but Vlad had come to prefer that over what barely passed as life. He hated waking up in the morning, because it meant the whole day was in front of him. Another day of pain and heartache with nothing to look forward to or look back upon. For years, the only thoughts that took his mind off that pain and heartache were of escape; first fantasizing about it, then planning. To make escape a reality, he needed to be strong. And to be strong he used the hate that had festered inside him for so long.

Hate for his keepers, hate for his abusers, hate for the world that allowed them all to be, but especially hate for the father who'd abandoned him and his mother and left them to this wretched life. And that hate made him more than strong; it spurred a vision of having enough power so no one would ever be able to hurt him again.

So he resolved to eat whatever was shoved in front of him and clean the plates left behind by others, too. His closet-size, windowless room was just long enough to allow him to do push-ups, so many he'd lose count both in the morning upon waking and then again at night before surrendering to blissful sleep in which there were dreams toward which to look forward.

At thirteen, he was still fantasizing. At fourteen, he began to plan. And at fifteen, Vlad celebrated his birthday in the surety that the time had come.

He was cursed by his dark, brooding looks. Vlad had inherited his mother's beauty except for the warm smile he so remembered when she'd assure him things were going to get better. Holding him in her lap while telling him tales of the way their life would be when his father finally came for them. Dracu believed her because that's what children do. Now as a young adult he resolved to make the life his mother envisioned for both of them a reality for at least himself. Sometimes when he looked in the mirror he expected a six-year-old's face to peer back, instead of the shaggy hair and big black eyes that made him the *groapă*'s most treasured commodity.

Groapă was Romanian for "pit."

Men Dracu came to call "Watchers" oversaw life in the *groapă* and transported him to the men all around Ankara who paid for their time with him. Often the men lived in the kind of beautiful homes Dracu dreamed of having someday, the kind of palatial residences his mother had described for him while he snuggled against her in the cold. These Watchers could be alternately kind and cruel on a whim, as prone to offering a comforting touch as unleashing a small whip-like weapon at the slightest provocation.

One of them was coming at him with whip in hand the night Vlad had the chain binding his legs to a heavy wooden post already lashed around his wrist. So when the man drew close enough, Vlad looped it around his throat and pulled tight, strangling the life out of him. He kept pulling even as the man gurgled and thrashed and writhed.

Vlad could never remember a time where he felt more alive, letting the hatred spill out of him at long last. He wasn't powerless; he would never be a victim again. The feeling was almost euphoric, so much so that he longed to kill again almost immediately because nothing had made him feel more vital; he could feel the power it imbued and wanted more. Even as he realized what he'd been thinking of, picturing, as he nearly severed the Watcher's head from his body: His father, the man he'd never met, the man who was no more than a blurry shape in a newspaper photo tacked to a wall that was lost the night they came for him.

After his escape, Vlad walked for what felt like days straight, afraid at every turn others would find and punish him for what he'd done. He found himself in the center of Ankara, begging for food and drinking water out of a hose used to clean the sidewalks.

One night he tucked himself into an alley to sleep only to be awoken with a start by a hand jostling his shoulder.

"Hey, you lost or something?"

Vlad's eyes sharpened to the sight of a ravishingly beautiful Slavic girl, sixteen or maybe seventeen, standing over him wearing ill-fitting clothes that looked like a boy's.

"Something," Vlad told her.

"You a gypsy?"

"No."

"I am a gypsy. You have a place to go?"

She spoke a different dialect of Romanian, but Vlad understood it well enough. Hearing it made him think of home, before he and his mother had embarked on their ill-fated journey through Albania to reach Sicily and somehow find his father.

"No," he told her.

"Then why you come here?"

"Because this is where I ended up."

"Me, too."

Their eyes met and Vlad saw a warmth lurking in hers he hadn't recognized in a very long time. He watched her reaching down to take his hand, almost jerking it away at the last from being detached for so long from anything resembling genuine emotion.

"Come," the girl said, "I show you something."

Her name was Dorina but she asked Vlad to call her Dori. For the next few hours, he watched her flash her smile, looking beautiful and innocent, as she asked a series of men for directions while picking their pockets. Her smile, friendliness, and looks kept the men's eyes upon her, distracting them from the fact that their wallets were now missing. Strength in subtlety, something Vlad had never considered before. It made him smile until he remembered the way other men's eyes had looked upon him.

"How old are you?" he asked her. "I'm fifteen."

"That's what I am."

"And if I'd said sixteen?"

"Then I would've been that instead."

Dori introduced him to a band of lost children like them who'd banded together as a gang that lived out of the shell of an apartment building in a run-down neighborhood. When he looked back on those times, Vlad remembered Dori above all else, including how she had helped him when she caught him trembling with chills one steamy night.

"You are very sick," she said, touching his forehead.

"How did you . . . know?" he asked, not bothering to deny it.

"I have a gift," she said, not quite meeting his eyes anymore. "Or maybe a curse. I can see things, *feel* things. In my village they thought I was a witch and made me leave—that's how I came to be here. But someday I will return and make them pay."

"I'll help you."

Dori met his eyes again. "You have your own problems to deal with. Give me your hand."

But he pulled it away when she tried to reach for it. "Why?"

"So I can read your palm and tell your future."

"I don't believe in such things," Vlad said, giving his hand to her anyway.

"Fortune telling?"

"The future."

She traced it with a finger, the way a blind person reads Braille.

"Much *sânge* has brought you here," Dori told him, still tracing. "Both your blood and the blood you have spilled." Her finger stopped, began to tremble, her eyes filling with fear. "You have killed, haven't you?"

"Is that why you're scared of me all of a sudden?"

"What frightens me is what you may yet do, not what you've already done."

"I killed because I had no choice. But only one man."

"So far," Dori told him. "There has been much death in your past. There will be far more of it in your future."

"Then use your gift. Tell me what you see."

Dori seemed as if she no longer wanted to look, but continued tracing his palm anyway. "They kept you prisoner. They caused you pain—no, they brought you *durere*." Finally her eyes met his again, his hand still locked in her grasp. "This man you killed deserved to die. You should not feel *vinovat*."

"I don't feel guilty at all."

"Yes, Vlad, you do. But not for this—for not being able to save someone close to you. Your mother, wasn't it? You felt she deserved better than the life she had. You hated what she had to become in order to survive." Dori had looked up at him from his palm here. "Your hate dominates you."

"It's the only thing that makes me feel alive," he managed, trying to push back the tears welling in his eyes.

"But it's dangerous to hate so much because you can end up hating yourself."

"Maybe I already do."

Dori went back to studying his palm. "I thought it was the man who killed your mother that you're after. But now I'm not so sure."

"Because it is another man," Vlad said. "A man I hate even more."

Dori kept tracing his palm, then stopped suddenly.

"What is it?" he asked her. "Will I find this man? Tell me what you see."

Dori's eyes had turned suddenly glassy as if seeing nothing at all.

"Your father, Vlad," she said finally.

"What about him?" he said, something icy grabbing his insides. "What do you see?"

"Only that he will yet be a part of your life."

"How? Tell me how! Please!"

"I don't know." Dori's eyes cleared. "The vision is gone. Slipped away because it too is incomplete, unfinished, just like your own life. The path you choose from this point is yours."

"Is it?"

"Nothing is set. But . . ."

"But *what*?"

She let go of his hand and hugged him to her. "You are very sick, Vlad, and now I understand."

He eased her away so he could meet her eyes. "Tell me. Say it."

She swallowed hard. "I was brought to you to save your life."

Dracu fought to stifle another of the coughing fits that had plagued him lately, but failed. "Maybe it's too late."

"It's not."

"You can't know that."

"I can," Dori said, and lifted his palm so it was facing him instead of her. "Your lifeline runs strong, but is broken. The break here," she continued, touching a thin crevice in his flesh, "represents today. I will see that you survive it. See that you live many more years."

"Maybe I'm not worth the effort."

She took him by the shoulders. "You have the potential to be a great man who can do great things . . . or terrible things."

"Are you still telling me my future?"

"I told you, the future's not set. And what I just said is what I feel, not what I saw. But I did see something else. No one is going to be able to stop you. You are going to be a very powerful and dangerous man."

"And that's why you're so scared?"

"I'm scared because of how you are to become that way. There is a . . . monster in your future. But he takes your innocence even now."

"Am I to kill him? Is he going to kill me?"

"Neither," Dori said, looking away as if suddenly frightened by him, "because the monster is in you."

SEVENTY-FIVE

SARDINIA

"Vlad?" Aldridge Sterling prodded from his yacht, when Dracu stopped on the other end of the line.

"I was just thinking," he mused over the phone, jolted from his thoughts back to the present.

"Of what?"

"Dori was the first and only girl I ever cared about. She realized I was sick, so sick that traditional medicine wouldn't be able to save me. So she brought me to a gypsy *drabarni* healer who'd been ostracized because of the communists, too. It was this *drabarni*, an old woman, who introduced me to the scorpions. Years before modern medicine realized their venom had chemotherapeutic capabilities, gypsies had been using scorpions to treat some of the most serious diseases. This *drabarni*, an obese woman who smelled of garlic, warned me the odds were good the first sting would kill me. But if I could survive the pain, then the venom pulsing through my veins would work better than any *drab* or medicine, keeping the *caeninaflipen*, as she called the disease, at bay."

"Is there a point somewhere in this story?"

"Yes, but if you interrupt me again I'll show you pain worse than any I ever felt." Dracu waited for a response, continuing when none came. "Dori was the first girl I ever slept with," Dracu continued. "She's the one I always picture, always remember, when I'm with all the others that have come since. She told my fortune once, told me someday I'd be a very powerful but dangerous man."

"And so you are."

"But she said I have a monster within me I might not be able to control. I've managed to prove her wrong."

"Because you're not a monster?"

"No, because I've managed to control it. That's why I sent you this gift, to remind you how fleeting that control can be should you lose my trust."

And, true to Dracu's word, Sterling noticed a launch approaching. The launch slowed its speed as it neared the *Big Whale*, Sterling spotting a luscious figure clinging to the railing, her blond hair splayed about by the wind.

"Your gift just arrived," he said into the phone.

"A token of appreciation for handling the financial end of things so well," Dracu said, before his tone sharpened again. "Just don't betray me, Aldridge, or the next gift you receive from me won't be nearly as pleasant."

SEVENTY-SIX

CALTAGIRONE, SICILY

Michael walked the grounds of the farm where he'd been born in a state that felt like the first moments of consciousness upon being jarred awake. He had to keep reminding himself where he was, even though it was a place deeply imbedded in his memory. But now all of those memories had turned suspect, thrown into question by the shattering truth about his father, Vito Nunziato.

Or Davide Schapira.

That truth made the entire farm look and feel different to him, as if he could trust nothing his mind conjured of it. He'd purchased the property, and all the land surrounding it, from the bank years before under the name of an untraceable Hong Kong shell company, never with an eye on doing anything with it other than make sure no one else ever owned it. He had come here for the closing, at which point he'd seen his boyhood home for the first time since leaving Sicily fifteen years before, finding it so overgrown as to be barely recognizable.

It was in even worse shape today, the grounds untended and what was left of the buildings ravaged by time and the elements. Both the barn and farmhouse were mostly shells, most of their roofs having collapsed inward and the walls crumbling visibly as well. It was a beautiful sunny day and the breeze blew softly, rustling the leaves of the trees that had managed to survive. Michael gazed toward the fields where the family's crops of oranges and olives had once rustled in the breeze, too. He half expected the old farmhand Attilio to roll by atop the tractor, taking his hat off and grinning in greeting. His mind drew back the sounds of horses and cows, along with the strangely sweet odor of manure Michael had always hated, but now found himself longing for. He took a deep breath and imagined he could smell the fragrant scent of oranges fresh from the vine piled high in baskets upon the bed of the old flatbed truck his father would drive to market, cursing whenever a bump in the road cost him even a single item in his load.

They were just overgrown weeds and dead brush now; but when he first looked that way, for a moment, just a moment, he saw the neat rows of trees whole again in their groves. His father toiling amid them in his old straw hat. He never looked happy with the labor, as if he'd rather be elsewhere doing something else. And now, finally, Michael thought he understood why.

Because his father was not who everyone thought he was, a mere farmer. He was Davide Schapira, a hero who came to Romania on some secret mission. The missing pieces of a story Michael desperately wanted to understand. And if such pieces still existed, they'd be found somewhere here on the grounds where Vito Nunziato had been gunned down and his son Michele had been born.

In spite of everything else confronting him, Michael had to learn the truth, had to *know* how his father could've been hero and farmer at the same time. Who was Davide Schapira?

Or a better question, maybe, who was Vito Nunziato?

Michael walked under the warm sun to the ruins of the barn, the timber having been swallowed up by the earth that had originally given it life. He had left Scarlett and Alexander back with the Citation at the airport in Catania and proceeded here alone against Alexander's heated protestations, because he knew this was a journey he needed to make by himself.

A journey into not just his past, but also, especially, his father's.

Michael turned his gaze toward what little remained of the farmhouse—just the first floor with the clapboard and studding showing—and thought of himself as a little boy again, listening to the gunshots and watching his parents die. He remembered the night before that, when his father had hugged him tight and urged him to be a king and not a peasant.

Something about him had been different that night, something in his eyes and his manner, that made Michael wonder today if he'd actually caught his first and only glimpse of Davide Schapira. If Vito Nunziato had been nothing more than a guise, a mask he wore to disguise his true self. This was the same man, after all, who'd found the relic in the waters off Isla de Levanzo, who almost drowned trying to retrieve it only to come awake miraculously back on shore.

Maybe it was the relic that defined his heroism. Maybe it really had been meant for him. Michael couldn't know for sure, wouldn't know until he found something more to tell him. On these grounds, somewhere on what had once been a farm.

It was here; he could feel it as clearly as the breeze billowing his shirt over skin that felt clammy with sweat. A chronicle, some documentation, of his father's life apart from his family, before his family. But his father had never even had a safety deposit box, hardly a man to trust secrets or personal business to third parties. He was intensely old-fashioned, believing private matters to be just that.

Michael reflected on that with strange fondness, wondering what his life might have been like if the relic had never existed and Michele Nunziato had grown up to be a farmer like his father instead of the man known as the Tyrant. Would he have been happier?

Michael recalled so much gruff coldness, so few smiles or warmth. Perhaps it was hard for his father to settle into such an ordinary life after whatever experiences had defined him during his mission in Romania. And how did Vito Nunziato end up a farmer anyway? What happened in that Transylvanian village that brought him to this land where his previous life became a secret never to be shared? No medals on display, no framed commendations or other memorabilia.

What had happened?

So, too, as a boy, overly curious at times, Michael had explored every nook and cranny of the farmhouse that today looked gobbled up by the ground; it was how he had found the medallion tucked in his father's sock drawer the fateful morning of the massacre. And none of his explorations had ever revealed anything passing for secret documents, pictures, letters, passports—the kind of material a man with dual identities was certain to have. The farmhouse had no secret chambers, loose floorboards, or hollowed walls in which to hide such things; if it had, Michael would've found them.

So what then?

Michael continued to walk the grounds, as if in search of some cosmic inspiration, but his thoughts were consumed by his father. Every memory recaptured and reframed because now he saw the man entirely different from what he ever had before. And suddenly the world morphed around him in a surreal vision that left seeing the past through the prism of the present and all its conflicting emotions. He was a young boy again. His sister Rosina holding his mother's hand as they traipsed through the gardens. Michael busy in the fields and mimicking his father mopping the sweat from

his brow with his kerchief. Working the hoe just as his father had taught him.

"Like this, Papa?"

"Like that, Michele."

Rewinding those memories as if they could be relived.
Searching them as they unfolded before him for some,
any, indication that Vito Nunziato was more than just a
farmer.

But there was nothing. His father was his father, demand-
ing and distant. Worn down by life. Smelling of the fresh
paint staining his fingers and the manure Michael remembered roosting in the grooves of his shoes.

Michael froze halfway between the remains of the farmhouse and the barn, holding onto that memory. Because, he
realized now, those dark stains hadn't been paint at all, but
ink. Even as a boy, Michael had wondered why his father
wanted to paint the root cellar because he always had the
dark stains on his fingers when he emerged from it.

The root cellar, Michael thought, moving fast for the refuse of the farmhouse.

SEVENTY SEVEN

CALTAGIRONE, SICILY

Michael stood outside the shell of the house briefly before
continuing on, long enough to see the inside again as he remembered it. His mother always seemed to be cooking in
the kitchen, his sister Rosina either crying loudly or totally
silent, his father at the kitchen table paying bills and keeping a running tab of the transactions on a piece of loose-
leaf paper with the fringe carefully peeled off.

It was another long-forgotten memory, though, that stirred

him now. Of finding a padlock on a heavy plank door angled over the ground at the farmhouse's rear, the one spot the sun never reached. His father had caught him and slapped him across the face, telling him it was dangerous, that he'd closed up the old root cellar after a particularly wet spring had flooded it and left only mold and mildew behind in place of the ruined crops.

But one night Michael remembered being roused from bed by a strange creaking sound while he sat reading by flashlight under the covers. He'd gone to the window and spotted the last of his father's frame disappearing through the same plank door, leaving it hoisted open behind him. Maybe it had only happened that one time or, perhaps, other memories of it had merged into this one.

Michael pulled more of the thick brush, bramble, weeds that had grown into thickly knotted vines and moss aside to reveal that plank door, now faded to a sickly, washed-out gray color. The lock was still in place, all rusted over, and broke apart as soon as Michael tugged on it.

The doors resisted at first but then gave with a jolt that pushed dust and grime into the air behind a gush of rancid air escaping from below. Dry and spoiled, laced with must and decay, from being trapped for so long.

No food had been stored down here for a very long time. And, even before he shined a flashlight about and descended a set of plank stairs into the darkness, Michael doubted food storage was ever the root cellar's primary purpose. One of the wooden steps gave under his weight and two others cracked audibly before he reached the bottom, sweeping his flashlight around to find piles of petrified refuse that had once been freshly harvested crops. Just enough to throw anyone coming down here in search of something else off the track. The root cellar was cramped and claustrophobic, no more than ten feet square with a ceiling just high enough to accommodate Michael's six-foot frame. He continued to shine his flashlight around the earthen walls and kicked at the petrified remnants of crops that must've been stored down here in the days before the massacre.

Wishing he'd donned gloves first, Michael then began pulling the collection of spoiled rot away to see what the floor and walls might reveal. Something inside him expected to find some secret passage or doorway into the clandestine world his father had forged. He imagined a closet-size chamber full of secrets stacked and catalogued in alphabetical order to ease the sorting process.

What he uncovered in a rear corner beneath the pulpy remains of stench-riddled turnips and radishes was a single metal footlocker covered in a cheap tarpaulin that had weathered the years reasonably well. Michael peeled away the plastic, having to pry some of it from the metal, to reveal a lid which caught stubbornly until Michael wedged a pen into the narrow gap and pried it open.

He saw the weapons first: World War II vintage, a pistol and a rifle. Then cardboard boxes packed with old pictures and letters dating back, it seemed, to his father's own childhood, left hidden down here along with the never-revealed secrets of his life.

Under the spill of his flashlight, an assortment of pictures greeted Michael first, all capturing his father around the same time as the mug shot of Davide Schapira. There were more weapons too—old pistols, rifles manufactured by a long-bankrupt Italian gun manufacturer, even a Thompson machine gun—all sheathed in a coating of dust that hid the rust the moist air had draped over the old weapons.

It was all here, the secret life of Vito Nunziato from tattered birth certificate missing two edges and browned through the middle forward. Pictures of him as a boy, a teenager, one that looked like it had been taken on Isla de Levanzo around the time an ancient gold relic had cried out to him from the shallows.

The last thing Michael spotted was a thick notebook missing its cover to reveal the yellowed pages within. The pages of the notebook were full of notations of addresses, descriptions of places and people coming and going, each entry ending with a bold strike being drawn through a name.

A German name. They were all German names.

All written in Italian in his father's scratchy scrawl. Regarding that handwriting again now, for the first time in so many years, sent a chill up Michael's spine. He hadn't thought about his father very much in a long time. Right now, though, Vito Nunziato was all he was thinking about.

Or Davide Schapira, that is.

The notebook sat upon a stack of larger, ledger-size journals bound in cheap leather or vinyl. He eased the journal from the top of the pile to him and thumbed it open to find the same familiar handwriting, the dark paint-like ink a bit faded by the years but otherwise intact. Michael started to run his flashlight over the contents, then spotted an old oil lantern on a nearby ledge. He pulled his cigar lighter from his pocket and touched it to the wick, then turned the knob to increase the flow of oil.

Surprisingly, the oil still burned. The light came up instantly in surprisingly bright fashion, just as it must have for his father all the times he'd sneaked down here to lose himself in the past. When Michael realized the lantern was dulled by its dust-encrusted glass, he swiped it clean as best he could to let the light better sift through. He imagined his father positioning the lantern to maximize the spill before he started writing, just as Michael did before he started reading.

The journal, all in Italian, looked to begin in a period around 1958 and opened on the first page with a title in capital letters:

OPERATION SLEDGEHAMMER

SEVENTY-EIGHT

From Vito Nunziato's Journal

That's where this all starts, an odd name for a secret operation but they had to call it something.

See, as the war neared its end, and the Nazi war machine fell, an estimated thirty thousand Nazi soldiers and cadre managed to flee Germany ahead of the coming Allied invasion. In the wake of the surrender and ensuing armistice, the United States Department of Justice, working in concert with the Organization of Special Services, OSS (that would soon become the CIA), formed the Office of Special Investigation. Though its existence was not acknowledged until decades later, the OSI joined forces with similarly formed French and British bureaus to bring as many of these Nazi war criminals to justice as possible. In the early years following the war, this mandate was carried out in the spirit of Nuremberg, an overriding obsession to parade as many Nazis before public tribunals as possible.

In later years, beginning in the late 1950s, it became something much different.

The world could stomach and relive only so many atrocities committed at Nazi hands. Ultimately, the public tired of the spectacle and the endless string of trials became redundant. Captures and subsequent incarcerations were paid less and less heed, until some escaped Nazis even dared to live in the open, not bothering to disguise their experiences, if not their very identities. They refused to go away.

So Operation Sledgehammer was born.

With the rest of the world's attention turned to the Cold War, the Office of Special Investigations and its various international partners coordinated a worldwide effort to recruit a team of Nazi hunters dedicated to tracking down and bringing to justice the remaining Nazi fugitives. The focus being on the worst offenders culled from the rolls of extermination camps, the Waffen SS, and the Gestapo.

The problem faced by those doggedly administering Operation Sledgehammer was that the traditional Nazi hunters pulled from the ranks of elite American, French, and British agents could not operate in such closeted regions without arousing a level of suspicion likely to spook their targets into flight. The solution was to expand the ranks of Sledgehammer to include troops previously excluded from serving the former Allied cause due to their Axis leanings. Indeed, Italian, Austrian, and even fellow German operatives would stir far less, if any, attention to their true cause. They would work entirely as individuals instead of teams and be dispatched to regions hardly adverse to their specific nationalities to provoke even less scrutiny.

During the nineteenth and twentieth centuries, for example, many Italians from Western Austria-Hungary settled in Transylvania. During the interwar period, even more Italians took up residence in Dobruja, more than enough to assure that the arrival of an Italian in a small village would draw no notice. That made me the perfect candidate to go to Romania where my arrival in the town of Bună Ziua raised no eyebrows at all. So I was recruited from my position in military intelligence, an opportunity I welcomed greatly for such a noble cause.

My father had fought on the side of the Axis powers in World War II. He'd been involved in Anzio and some of the biggest battles of the war. I was too young to understand that at the time, just as I was too young to understand he fought on the side of Hitler and the Nazis. As I grew older, the mere thought of this revolted me. I know choices must be viewed through the prism of history, but I was disgusted by the thought of my father as a Black Shirt serving the Fascist regime of Italy and wanted more than anything to atone for the blood he had spilled and the lives he had taken for such a wicked and unworthy cause.

Operation Sledgehammer provided me that opportunity. And I became Davide Schapira, an Italian Jew searching for lost relatives in Romania nearly fifteen years after the war's end. It was a solid cover, since Mussolini had merely exiled Italian Jews from the country instead of following the German example. Still, the practice led to a million people displaced and isolated from family members spread through other countries. As Davide Schapira, I wouldn't be the first Jew to go in search of what might remain of his family, and I wouldn't be the last.

The perfect cover, in other words.

Once in Romania, with the help of a beautiful young woman who befriended me almost from the start, I uncovered a hive of Nazi fugitives far larger than had been reported or estimated. But I never expected to fall in love with Stefania Tepesche and I suppose I did from the first time we met, no matter how well I managed to hide it. Loving her, I realize now, gave me hope, reminding me there was beauty amid all the ugliness. A number of very powerful Nazis had not gone away after World War II; instead they had attached themselves to the Romanian countryside like parasites, living off the land they'd ravaged, supported, and protected by any number of organizations like Odessa created to hide them from their crimes under new identities. By the time I arrived in Romania, a large number of them had managed to blend in unobtrusively with the locals and had grown so emboldened as to feel themselves free to enjoy their lives after destroying those of so many.

I welcomed the opportunity to impart justice on them and Stefania became a beacon of light shining through that darkness. She was nineteen, barely more than a child, and I had just turned thirty. Her smile refreshed me, her touch reenergized me, and her mere presence filled me with hope that my actions had relevance. That there was a greater purpose in those actions beyond pinpointing targets who'd managed to escape justice for their own personal judgment day.

Times were difficult under the communists, Romania becoming little more than a bank for Stalin's Soviet Union where only withdrawals were made, no deposits. The only exceptions to this were the older mountain villages, too remote and too small for the Soviet Union to concern itself with. As such, small pockets of private ownership continued to exist, especially in Transylvania and especially in the form of small establishments that were called crismas. Generally, these were combination bar and restaurants known and frequented only by locals. All that was required to stay in business was a relatively modest stipend paid to officials of the local Securitate, the Romanian Secret Police. Though these crismas were in no way brothels, young women were free to take the local men to rooms maintained upstairs for just that purpose. Such a practice was neither advertised nor criminalized.

The closeted natures of these mountain villages and towns had also made them preferred hideouts for the Nazis I was hunting. And several had been identified by Operation Sledgehammer's intelligence in Bună Ziua itself.

Stefania, meanwhile, preferred being poor over prostituting herself in the crisma where we first met. Orphaned by the war herself, it would've been easy to have chosen the path so many other young women did in Romania. Those other women, not nearly as pretty as Stefania, made a decent wage, but it was some of their primary customers that most interested me, men Stefania and the other girls at the crisma called "the Strangers," since none seemed to be natives and yet they were all Romanian citizens and spoke the language perfectly.

So my early days were spent locating and identifying each of them, chronicling their comings and goings from the crisma *and other parts of the town, as well as their places of employment, with notebook in hand. One at a time over the ensuing weeks, I followed them to where they lived, cataloguing everything I learned and saw. I was not a killer, though. My assignment was to conduct reconnaissance and build intelligence, then wire my findings in coded telegrams to a drop that would funnel my reports to the parties overseeing Operation Sledgehammer. My role ended with that. I never met the killers who were dispatched and only occasionally learned of the product of their work. Most of the deaths were made to look like accidents, attesting to their level of expertise.*

That meant exercising patience, something this mission seemed to reject. How long could I remain in place before I too was found out, perhaps by Odessa, which was known to check up on areas where a substantial concentration of former Nazis had been resettled under fake covers and identities? But my task was made possible by the fact that my targets lived in locations that were often isolated and, as near as I can tell, made virtually no contact with each other to avoid drawing suspicion. In fact, very likely the only time they glimpsed one other was in the crisma *where they came to be in each other's company over alcohol and women. So as their number was depleted, they could just as easily believe relocation was to blame instead of foul play.*

I came to learn that the larger than expected number of Nazi fugitives who'd settled in the region was no accident. Hives like the ones I had uncovered in Transylvania were the result of carefully orchestrated planning to resettle as many Nazis as possible in preparation for the expected rise of another Reich. In essence, I'd hit the jackpot.

As I write this I have no idea of Stefania's ultimate fate.

I'm sure I'll learn it someday, but it's not a subject for these pages. Stefania made the success of my mission possible. She and the other young women became my de facto spies, willingly enlisting themselves after I rescued one of their own from a brutal beating.

Stefania, though, was the most beautiful by far. She had come to the crisma *to work for food and lodging from a life on the streets, forced into destitution and poverty as a child after her family's bombed-out apartment building was officially condemned. We went there together one day and I watched her eyes fall on it excitedly, as if just for that moment expecting to see it miraculously restored and her relatives waiting happily to greet her.*

But it was just a pile of wood and rubble, nothing recognizable still standing. In that moment, I wanted so much to tell her who I really was and why I'd really come to Romania. That the people responsible for destroying the country and leaving it for the communists deserved the fates I was helping to dispense. I would probably have lost count of all the men I'd marked for death if I didn't keep meticulous records of all those I identified as were my orders.

It was the longest and most dangerous year of my life, made tolerable only by Stefania and all the hope and good she represented. I let myself believe I had a future with her far away from the darkness and depravity of this place. I let myself believe I could take her with me.

Until the day my life changed forever.

SEVENTY-NINE

Caltagirone, Sicily

A chill breeze interrupted Michael's reading, ruffling the lantern flame. It seemed to come from a back corner of the root cellar, an illusion likely fostered by the depth of his concentration and sudden realization of how cold it was down here below a patch of ground the sun barely reached. But then he felt the breeze again and briefly lifted his gaze from where it seemed to be coming, wanting only to return to his father's journal.

Michael found himself utterly enraptured by its contents. He imagined his father filling the journal's pages down here, under the light of the very same lantern. But it was a different man from the father he thought he'd known.

For the past five years, his ruminations on the medallion had branded his father as perhaps nothing more than the vehicle to deliver the relic unto him. But this journal, written in his own hand, proved otherwise. And yet he had died so violently, in a hail of bullets as if he could not escape the legacy he thought left behind in Romania, as if those acts left their own indelible impressions on a fate that had ultimately chased him down.

And, directly because of that, the relic had ended up with his son. Fate again.

But why had Vito Nunziato buried the truth of his heroism down in a root cellar?

The only way to find the answer to that was to read on.

EIGHTY

That day a former Nazi arrived in Bună Ziua. His real name was Hans Wolff and I recognized him immediately from the scar on his right jaw near his chin. I recalled from my briefings that he was one of Operation Sledgehammer's prime targets. If there was any man I'd been sent into Romania to find, it was him. He had been the youngest SS officer Colonel Himmler had ever made in that loathsome outfit. A sadist and cold-blooded murderer, Wolff oversaw operations at the Nazi concentration camps throughout Eastern Europe and was especially fond of gutting children and making their parents watch them die in slow and agonizing fashion.

Himmler had also been the officer Hitler entrusted with one of his most important pet projects: Scouring the world in pursuit of legendary artifacts that possessed some mystical power. Hitler was obsessed with the occult, but I was never sure in my own mind whether such expeditions really existed until I began following Wolff.

Wolff wasn't like the others I had uncovered for Operation Sledgehammer's kill teams; instead, he had the look of a man on a mission. Arrived in Bună Ziua in the company of three cold-eyed young Romanian men who would've made perfect Nazis if this had been twenty or even fifteen years ago. Just well-paid thugs likely funded by Odessa, since monsters like Hans Wolff needed sycophants to do their bidding.

I followed him and his hired men to any number of stops around the countryside, all of which I catalogued as best I could in my notebook. All these places that interested them

*were archaeological dig sites, most of them long aban-
doned. Wolff had traded his gun for a shovel and, under
his command, his thugs did the same, mining the ground
for something.*

*Yes, Hitler had fallen and the Third Reich with him. But
I came to realize in those moments that Operation Sledgehammer wasn't just about dispensing punishment for the
past; it was also about preserving the future, by making
sure the Nazis never achieved some sort of resurrection that
would bring them to power again.*

Thanks to men like Hans Wolff.

*To this day, I have no idea what he was searching for,
only that he must have continued the work begun under
Himmler's direction, perhaps even in connection to establishing the next Reich. The sites he explored and chose to
dig at mostly contained remnants left behind by the ancient
Romans but I never discerned any more than that, although
I had seen reports of similar expeditions in Greece, Turkey, and even Israel of all places. I cabled headquarters
and waited for the prescribed one hour for a response.
When none came, the next day I cabled again from a different location and waited another hour for instructions.*

*The receiver remained quiet still, as it would for two
more days until I finally received my response, although not
the one I was expecting. I was ordered to stand down
immediately, cease all actions, and return home. Operation Sledgehammer had been summarily shut down. I'd
learn later that some oversight committee in Washington
had caught wind of the operation's existence, necessitating
its shuttering for political reasons. I didn't care one bit
about politics; all I cared about was Hans Wolff, the primary target that had brought me to Romania. A psychopath
and sadist I couldn't simply turn my back to, no matter
what my orders were.*

What, though, was I to do? I was no gunman or killer,

much less the kind of trained assassin who'd used my intelligence to dispatch a host of Nazi targets during my single year in Romania. I never met a single one of those assassins; there was no reason for me to. But now I needed to become one, lest Hans Wolff be allowed to escape justice yet again.

I knew I was violating my orders, knew that if I managed to succeed in the mission I'd assigned myself, I could never return to my life in military intelligence. A price I was more than willing to pay if it meant giving Wolff what he had coming to him.

He and his trio of Romanian thugs had come to the crisma for "entertainment" for three consecutive nights already. I decided I would strike on the fourth. Wolff and his men drank and drank that night, while I lingered over my dinner far longer than I needed to, my back to them so I'd draw no notice. I had interest only in Wolff, not his thugs. I'd already arranged for Stefania to tell me in which room I could find him once the group went upstairs with women in tow. I'd taped my Beretta pistol under the table earlier in the day so as not to arouse any suspicion from Wolff and his thugs if they spotted me toting a weapon.

Twenty minutes after the men disappeared upstairs, Stefania passed me a note indicating Wolff had retired to a room on the third floor, immediately below mine, and asked her to bring a bottle of whiskey up to him. I was concerned about her safety, wanting her nowhere near such a monster. But she assuaged my fears and told me she'd be right back, and I could take that for the signal to move on Wolff while he was busy with drink as well as a woman.

Stefania . . .

She had brought beauty and light into the dark nature of my mission, the ugliness of a cause that marks men for execution, no matter how much they deserve it. In the wake of what I was about to do, this would have to be my last *night in Romania and my thoughts turned to how I might spirit her away with me, then settled on the fact it was too risky for both of us. Better I go alone and come back for her, or send for her, someday.*

I believe she's the reason I'm penning these words today. Not for duty, obligation, or testament, but to remind myself of her so I might feel her close to me again, since we never saw each other again after that night. I think of her every day and dream of her every night, wonder how my life might have turned out if I'd chosen to stay with her in Romania, or to have somehow brought her with me.

My concern became palpable when Stefania still hadn't returned ten minutes after climbing the stairs toting a bottle of whiskey and a single glass on a tray. I reached under my table and pulled the Beretta free. Then I headed upstairs, padding my way toward the third-floor room where Wolff had taken his woman. I hesitated outside the door, composing myself with several deep breaths while trying to still my gun hand that was trembling so badly I could barely maintain my grasp of the Beretta.

Hesitation was one thing, doubt something else again. And before that doubt, and second thoughts, entered into the picture, I felt myself bursting through the door, a shoulder following a kick, before I changed my mind.

"Drop the weapon," Wolff ordered me from the bed, where he was seated with a knife pressed against Stefania's throat.

I had no choice but to comply, and as soon as my gun clamored to the floor Wolff slammed Stefania's head against a nearby wall and let her drop to the floor like a sack of garbage.

Two of his thugs were on me immediately and I realized I'd walked straight into their trap. They tossed my pistol aside and I felt their punches hammer my face and gut. Wolff should've simply killed me, but one of his thugs tied me weakly to a chair instead. Wolff hovered over me, and I watched him slide a black SS death's head ring with the initials "HW" from his pocket and slip it on his finger, as if to remind me of his legacy and the source of his power. I noticed the scar near his chin looked shiny in contrast to the rest of his face, almost seemed to glisten in the room's thin light.

"You think I don't know when someone's hunting me? I've been hunting men all my life."

I remained silent and noticed the third of his thugs had taken up post at the door, as if guarding it.

"You think I was born yesterday?" Wolff said over me. "You think I've managed to remain free all these years by not sniffing the air for the scent of scum like you?"

"Go fuck yourself."

"While you fuck that pretty girl over there who cleans up all the shit in this place?"

I felt my eyes widen, looking toward Stefania still slumped in the corner.

"Who sent you here?"

"No one. I came on my own."

Wolff leaned in close enough for me to smell the dry foul odor of his breath. "I ask you again, who are you working for?"

"No one."

"Who else knows I'm in Romania?"

"No one."

Wolff spit in my face. "You're no Jew. I know a Jew when I see one, when I smell one. Whatever mission you're on, whoever sent you after me, it all ends tonight."

With that, Wolff signaled to one of his thugs who pulled a can of gasoline from the corner and brought it over. I watched him screw off the top.

"You will drink this," he said.

"No."

"You will drink this and I will set your insides on fire so you die slow and horrible," Wolff added, flicking to life a lighter embossed with a skull and crossbones.

"No," I repeated, indignant to the last.

"Then I will carve a hole in your throat and pour the gas down it," he said.

"Fuck you."

"You want to play tough? Fine." He started toward me. *"If you don't swallow the gasoline,"* he resumed, eyeing Stefania with a grinning sneer, *"I'll tape your eyelids to your forehead and make you watch me cut your woman apart one piece at a time."*

"All right," I relented, *"I'll drink it."*

His thug holding the gasoline can came forward, stopped by Wolff.

"Let me," he said, handing the man his lighter and taking the can in its place.

A second thug held my head back and pushed open my mouth. Wolff tilted the can's opening and gasoline splashed across the floor and walls, its rich scent instantly taking control of the room's air. He started pouring and I took as much of the gasoline into my mouth as I could without gagging. But I didn't swallow it, no.

Instead, I spewed it straight into Wolff's thug who'd just flicked his lighter to life.

His face caught with a poooofffffff, flames devouring all of his features, filling the air with the scent of burning skin, hair, and fabric.

At that point, everything became a blur that has yet to sharpen to this day. I remember bounding up out of my chair, tearing free from the knots Wolff's thug had hastily tied. I remember Wolff desperately trying to put out a patch of flames that had splashed with the gasoline to a jacket he struggled to shed. I remember his Romanian thug by the door coming at me with pistol ready to fire, when I rapidly

*jerked it around and added my own finger over his. Pulling
again and again and feeling the thud of each bullet's impact into him.*

*I tried to wrench the pistol from his grasp, but it had
clenched tight reflexively in death, so I gave up and spun toward Wolff instead. His charred shirt was still smoking, as
he worked to free his own pistol. I slammed into him and we
whirled about the room, struggling for control of the weapon.*

*I managed to fight Wolff to a draw but his final surviv-
ing Romanian thug had recovered enough of his bearings
to shoot at me, too. He fired twice, resulting in deafening
percussions that turned my hearing hollow. A series of shots
I recognized as coming from my own Beretta followed and
I glimpsed the thug crumpling to the floor to reveal Stefania kneeling behind him, having recovered my lost pistol
and emptying its magazine into him.*

*I coughed, felt hot, acrid smoke burn my throat, and re-
alized the room had caught fire. All three of Wolff's thugs
were dead, but our struggle had slammed us against the
closed door, blocking the escape route for Stefania.*

The flames were spreading fast by then, the old crisma
*little more than a tinderbox of dried wood and the cheap-
est furnishings, fueling the spread farther until the fire was
climbing the walls and spreading across the ceiling. Wolff
and I continued to struggle, exchanging blows. He tried to
tear his pistol free again, but I managed to latch a hand
onto his wrist as we pirouetted across the room. I saw the
window coming up too fast to avoid it, felt the intense heat
bred by the fire replaced by the chill night air as we crashed
through the glass, still struggling against each other.*

*A first-floor awning slowed our fall enough to save us
from breaking our necks on impact with the ground. Wolff's
pistol was lost somewhere and both our gazes sought it out
while we continued to exchange blows, rolling around the
ground and then the pavement.*

Finally I ended up on top, even as those pouring from the burning building in panic rushed by us like we weren't even there. Each time I managed a glance, more of the building was consumed. I felt my fists pounding Wolff's face, the knuckles spitting blood as his skin split and teeth flew past me through the air. I knew I was killing him and wouldn't stop until the deed was done.

But then I heard Stefania's screams coming from the third floor room where she must still be trapped. I stopped my pounding of Wolff to reveal his battered face and mashed nose, his blood coughed against me. But he still had plenty of life left, and taking the moments needed to finish him would mean Stefania would die a horrible death.

Before I knew it, before I could claim the thought, I had lurched off him and was charging past those still emerging from the building, coughing and retching, some with blankets covering their heads. I rushed up the stairs, the flames growing bigger, stronger, and hotter the more I climbed. I finally reached the third-floor room and kicked in the door warped by the flames and heat. Stefania collapsed into my arms. I scooped her up and carried her back toward the stairs.

She looked more beautiful to me than she ever had before. My love for her had made the last year tolerable, our nights of joyful pleasure together filling me with purpose and her beauty helping to negate the ugliness of my work.

I rushed down the stairs, shielding her as best I could from the spreading flames, feeling their heat as I staggered through them. I rushed toward the feeling of air, nearly overcome by the smoke. I felt my legs weakening at the bottom of the stairs, going soft, then stumbled outside with Stefania still in my grasp as a flashbulb went off, someone from the press snapping a picture.

Some bystanders who'd just reached the scene were there to catch me when I fell. They laid Stefania down and one pressed an ear against her chest, nodding to the man next to him that she was still alive. I collapsed next to her, feeling my breath return and the hot tingly sensation of the skin that had singed beneath my clothes. But then I remembered the other women of the crisma, saw none of them anywhere around, which could only mean they were still trapped inside somehow.

The fire department had just arrived and one of the men in uniform tried to grab hold of me to prevent me from rushing back into the flames. I shook him free, gasping too much myself to argue and charged back up the stairs to the second floor. Sure enough, Wolff's thugs had smashed the door latches of the three rooms on this hall, trapping the women inside them from where I could hear their desperate cries for help.

I kicked those doors in just as I'd kicked in the one on the third floor to rescue Stefania. Two of the women had been incapacitated by smoke and a third was barely mobile. But I managed to get them into the hall and carried the two in the worst condition down the stairs over either shoulder, holding my breath the whole time. Then I rushed back inside a third time and climbed the stairs through flame and smoke for the final woman.

I reached her just in time, tucked her face against my chest and surged down those stairs yet again. I was heaving for breath, feeling my parched throat burning when I laid her down near the others. Swallowing made my throat feel like sandpaper and I pictured it charred black inside.

I started to sink to my knees, before I found Stefania being tended to by a member of the fire brigade and stumbled over to her. I took her head and laid it in my lap. Her eyes opened and she wet her lips, managing a smile. I stroked her hair, hot to the touch of the fingers I could still feel. Some of the strands came away in patches, baked dead by the heat and fire.

"It's going to be okay," I managed. "Everything's going to be okay."

Even as I knew they wouldn't be. My time in Romania was done. I had outstayed my welcome and the truth of my identity and purpose would soon be forfeit, even though my pursuit of Hans Wolff had ended with his escaping yet again. I couldn't both kill him and save Stefania, but have never regretted my decision, not even for a moment.

By the morning I would be gone, never to see Stefania again. I promised her I'd come back someday, maybe soon. I promised her we would be together. I said that because I couldn't bear to tell her the truth that now, like the Nazis I'd hunted, I needed to disappear forever and we would never see each other again. I said it pushing back tears of my own and hating myself for lying, even though I had no choice.

We parted with the promise from my lips that I'd come back for her, that she only needed to be patient. Stefania kissed and hugged me, nodding. I'm glad she couldn't see my eyes because she might have seen the truth, that the nights we'd shared were all we'd ever have to express our love.

And that would have to be enough.

EIGHTY-ONE

CALTAGIRONE, SICILY

The journal ended there. And as Michael turned the page to see if anything more followed, a tattered black-and-white photo fluttered out. He snatched it from the floor to find the face of a Nazi colonel in full uniform with the familiar SS bars on both shoulders and a small jagged scar near his chin.

Hans Wolff.

Michael spotted Wolff's SS ring at the bottom of the crate, embossed with "HW" in black letters. He figured his father must've retrieved it at some point and kept it as a sullen souvenir. He fished it out and stuck its cold shape in his pocket

Then Michael noticed something else was protruding slightly from the back of the journal. A yellowed, faded news clipping that stuck when he tried to remove it. Michael peeled it away gently and turned his flashlight upon it, seeing a big headline in Romanian that he couldn't read, but a picture he identified immediately. A picture of a man rushing out from a burning building with a woman in his grasp. The shot was slightly blurred, grainy even without the clipping's deterioration, an amateur shot likely taken by someone with a camera who just happened to be nearby at the time.

Michael felt his heart slam against his rib cage, realizing he was looking at the soot-covered, grizzled face of his father. Based on the journal's depiction, the woman he was holding could only be Stefania Tepesche, her own face turned away so he couldn't make out any of her features. He looked again at his father captured in the midst of an incredibly heroic act, his passion and strength clear even through the blur and the clipping's degradation through the long years down here in the root cellar. He felt that strange cool breeze from its rear again, passed it off to his own twisted emotions this time.

"Michele," Michael thought he heard a voice call.

It sounded like his father, and Michael shuddered.

Then he heard the wind whistle again and realized it was just his ears playing tricks on him.

Michael tucked the photograph of Hans Wolff and the news clipping back into the journal and closed it, eyes brimming with tears as he struggled to stand after sitting stiff for so long. His father's journal and ledger tucked in his grasp, Michael then climbed back up the stairs, eyes squinting from the sudden wash of early afternoon sunlight at the top. He held a hand up briefly to shield them and pulled it away to the sight of dark blurry blips of shape enclosing him in a semicircle. Just an illusion, Michael thought, until his clearing vision locked on a figure dressed all in black, including a long thin coat riding just above the ground and a veil draped over his face, standing before the blurred shapes Michael now realized were gunmen.

"Welcome home," said Vladimir Dracu.

EIGHTY-TWO

CALTAGIRONE, SICILY

Michael knew he was looking at the man Scarlett had described from the village of Vadja, the same man who'd undoubtedly ordered the massacre at the dig site. A muscular giant stood in his shadow, the biggest man Michael had ever seen, with a mask covering half his face.

"My name is Vladimir Dracu. Call me Vlad," the man said through his black veil. "You may know me better as Black Scorpion. You are one of very few people alive who knows that now." He advanced a single step. "Tell me, does my name mean anything to you?"

"Should it?"

"I suspect so. Your name, after all, means something to me."

"How did you know this was my home?"

"You mean the home of Michele Nunziato?"

Michael stiffened, his eyes darting again to the hulking, masked figure at Dracu's side.

"I see you've noticed Armura. That's Romanian for armor. Do you know why I call him that? Because Armura, like steel, feels nothing. No emotion, no pain." Dracu turned toward the hulking form. "The scars that deface him came from a Siberian tiger he killed to survive before it could kill him. It was the last time he felt pain, the last time he felt anything, because the attack stole his senses from him, damaged his nervous system to a degree that would've killed any other man. It was the last time the tiger felt anything, too. There's a lesson in that for all of us."

"What's wrong with your face?" Michael asked him. "Or is that veil just some kind of fashion statement?"

Dracu angled his frame to keep Michael from glimpsing anything through the mesh. "We all have our crosses to bear. This is mine," he continued, sweeping his gaze about the refuse of the farm, "while this is *yours*, Michele. Of course, this wasn't Michele Nunziato's home for all that long, was it? Seven years or so, yes? That's how old you were when your father was gunned down. Tell me, Michele, how is the woman you and your warrior managed to rescue from the *Securitate* building?"

"Alive and well. She says she feels lucky to have escaped the devil."

"That would be me, of course. Unfortunately, you will not be as lucky. How gracious of you to come here alone. It's perfect, almost as if you wanted this meeting to be just the two of us."

Michael ran his eyes from Armura about Dracu's gunmen. "It's hardly just the two of us."

"I wish you'd brought the woman, Michele. She looks a bit like the first girl I ever loved. I guess you and I must have the same taste in women, so maybe we are not so different. My first love's name was Dorina and she was a gypsy who found me wandering in Ankara after I escaped from my keepers. She was part of a gang of petty thieves and pickpockets. I never knew what love was until I met Dorina. Then a few years later I was forced to kill her when she betrayed me for another man who sought the gang's leadership instead of me. So I killed them both, *Michele*."

"My name is Michael."

"Not to me it isn't. After her death the memories of Dori were too strong, too painful. So I joined a band of cutthroats who fancied themselves modern-day pirates. Their leader was a man named Adnan Talu who sent a team to a simple farm to recover a certain invaluable relic, as priceless as it was potentially powerful. Am I getting through to you yet, Michele?"

Michael's mouth dropped, but no words emerged. The past and present swirled together, clashing as a terrible truth began to dawn.

In that moment Michael became the boy in the barn from 1975 again, recalling the man who'd come looking while he hid in the haystack. Just about to plunge a pitchfork into the stack and twirl it about for good measure, when another of the killers rushed in and dragged him away, saying they had to hurry because the authorities were coming. A young man who was the same size as Vlad Dracu had dropped the pitchfork, coming to meet Michael's gaze briefly through the haystack before leaving the barn reluctantly.

"Ah, I can see from your eyes you remember me now," Dracu resumed. "Vito Nunziato deserved what he got, your mother and sister, too. I violated my orders. Your family wasn't supposed to die; our instructions were only to take the medallion from your father. Some rich and powerful American hired these Turkish pirates to retrieve it for him. I really didn't give a shit. So I disobeyed my orders and came here that day to kill Vito Nunziato, and I'd kill him a hundred more times if I could," Dracu paused, regarding Michael with a strange calm. "I would've killed you too that day, Michele. But you'd taken the relic we'd come for and run off to hide like the coward you are." Dracu rotated his veiled visage about. "This should have been mine, too."

"What are you talking about?"

"My childhood, Michele. Would you like to hear what it's like to be sold like a piece of meat? The other boys never had the chance to grow up. They gave up, while I got stronger, and at fifteen the man assigned to watch me became my first kill. I strangled him with a chain that bound me to a bedpost the night I escaped into the streets of Ankara." Dracu paused and held Michael's stare through the mesh veil. "And after I disobeyed orders and killed your family, I went back to Romania and built Black Scorpion from nothing. Call it my revenge against the world. Fitting, don't you think?"

"Tell me why you followed me here, what it is you want?"

Dracu took another two steps forward, out of the shadows and into the sun, seeming uncomfortable in the light. "It's too late to get everything I want, so I'll have to settle for a certain object that is rightfully mine: The relic we came for the day I murdered your father," he finished, pointing toward Michael's chest.

"Rightfully *yours*?"

"Your father was a brave man, Michele, but also a liar," Dracu said, noticing the ledger and journal in Michael's grasp. "I suppose you've figured out all of the truth by now."

"Except what it has to do with you."

"Your father had fallen in love with one of the women he saved from the fire, a beautiful and kind young woman named Stefania Tepesche." Dracu paused there, as if the words were suddenly coming hard for him. "She was my mother, and Davide Schapira was my father. We're half brothers, Michele."

EIGHTY-THREE

CALTAGIRONE, SICILY

"My full name is Vladimir Tepes Dracu," he continued. "I took my *real* last name and joined it to my new last name because it was especially fitting."

"Because it means devil? Because your mother believed her family was descended from the actual Vlad Tepes?"

Dracu gestured toward the dilapidated remains of the farmhouse. "Let's continue this where I should have grown up, too. Inside."

He took a Beretta pistol from Armura, and they came forward together. Michael felt the hulkish figure frisk him with hands that felt like slabs of steel, leaving his father's journal in Michael's possession. Then Dracu signaled Armura to remain where he was and gestured Michael on ahead of him at gunpoint toward the farmhouse.

Still trying to process Dracu's revelation about them being half brothers, Michael squeezed through a chasm just beyond the entrance to the root cellar into what had been the home's first floor. The walls were all gone now, most of the ceiling too. And what wood framing and stone foundation remained smelled of mold and rot. The ceiling's absence allowed the sun to bore through into what had been the kitchen and living room. But there were no shingles in evidence, as if petty thieves had made off with them. Dust swirled through the air with each breeze, deepening the stench of decay and hopelessness.

Dracu followed him inside, holding the Beretta on Michael from across what had been the living room.

"How's it feel to be home, Michele?"

"This hasn't been my home in a very long time."

"As it was never mine."

Michael watched Dracu slowly lift the mesh mask to reveal a smooth face that might've been handsome, if not for its pasty, milk-colored complexion.

"I was our father's firstborn, Michele. But he never knew I even existed. I remember my mother telling me stories about how brave and strong he was, how handsome. How someday he'd come back and rescue us from all the poverty and despair. I would go to sleep at night staring at a picture from a newspaper of him carrying my mother out of the burning building where she worked. It was the only picture she had of him, because he'd never allow any to be taken.

"So many nights I'd catch her shivering in the cold by the window, looking out as if expecting him to come. But he never did and I grew to hate him more every day, because he was a coward and a liar. How do you feel about our heroic father now? Being a farmer I imagine how he must've stank of cow shit. I would've liked to stuff it down his throat until he choked to death, instead of just shooting him while you hid somewhere, a coward just like he was. I bet you even smell the same."

"Why don't you come closer and find out?" Michael said, feeling his own rage starting to simmer.

"But I haven't finished my story yet, Michele. Finally, my mother and I set out to find the piece of shit and found only hell instead. My mother was forced into the life she'd avoided in Romania at all costs, because our chickenshit father never came for us. I was a little boy, what did I know? I thought he'd come for us someday. I really believed that because I believed my mother. And she wasn't a lying scum like our father—she believed he'd come for us, too." Dracu gazed about the house's crumbling confines and advanced farther forward, into a ray of sunlight where his flesh took on a painted-on, corpse-like quality. "I remember the men who paid her pennies to ravage her body, but not their faces, as if they all had the same face. Most were drunk. Some would beat her and one night one of them beat her so much she died. I dreamed of killing them all, Michele, the same way you probably dreamed of killing me. The difference is I finally got my chance to kill the man I wanted dead more than anything while you never got to kill me."

"Not yet."

Dracu's expression flirted with a smile. "I wouldn't hold your breath, if I was you."

"You're not me."

"Not yet," Dracu said, Michael's own words thrown back at him. His expression had gone stiff as plaster in the sunlight. "My mother died that night when I was six, but her heart had already given out years before when her only true love, our father, never returned. How I came to hate him in the years that followed; it was that hatred more than anything that kept me alive in Turkey. Imagine what it was like when I got my chance to kill him while working for those pirates, when I recognized his face from that newspaper I stared at every night I can remember until they took me to hell. Imagine what it felt like to see this man I'd been told was so brave and strong nothing but an ignorant farmer."

"You blame him for not coming to your rescue, even though he never knew you existed," Michael charged.

"Because he never came back for my mother. He promised and then he didn't, left her waiting by the window, looking for her one true love without realizing he was a peasant and a scum. An ant in the afterbirth whose life amounted to nothing. You know that in your heart as well as I, Michele. You just don't dare admit it for fear you're no different, a coward just like him in the end."

Michael felt the urge to rush Dracu then and there, to risk the hail of bullets on the chance he might be able to kill him before the gunshots took their toll.

"I knew our father, you didn't," he said instead, opting for a different means of attack. "You said it yourself, Vlad, he was a hero. If he'd known you existed, he never would've let you become the monster you are."

Dracu sneered, his eyes holding the glassy look of a man about to be sick. The sun streaming in through the hole where the ceiling had been caught only half of his face now, leaving the rest in shadows and seeming to cut him in half.

"Or maybe he would've just left me as he left my mother," he said. "He didn't care about her, only about the Nazi monsters he was hunting. Like Hans Wolff, the SS legend he let escape."

"In order to save *your* mother."

"And then he abandoned her and broke her heart. He should've just let her die." The sun ducked behind a cloud, placing all of Dracu in the shadows. Contempt had twisted his features into an angry knot, the flat softness of his pale features turning even more hateful, as Michael watched. "You fancy yourself a genius, the billionaire boy wonder of Las Vegas who beat the boys' club. And the name you took, Tiranno, I imagine you fancy yourself a tyrant, too, so perhaps we have more in common than just blood."

"We have *nothing* in common."

"Really? So you've never killed, Michele, never taken a life or ordered one to be taken? Because I seem to recall a freighter called the *Achilles* and its captain who went by the name of Skouros. He worked for me. That ship was mine, along with the twenty crewmembers who died at your hand or the hand of someone you sent, your warrior probably. I should've sent you a bill for sinking it."

"They all deserved what they got."

"But that doesn't change the fact that you think of yourself as a high and mighty hero dispensing justice, when what you really were was a cold-blooded murderer, just like me. You see, it takes one to know one. But imagine my surprise when I put it altogether. Imagine another blessed twist of fate delivered to me when I learned who you were and then followed who you became. I've been watching you since you showed up in Las Vegas as Michael Tiranno, Michele, following your rise to fame and fortune, thinking you had it all without realizing I could strike at any time and take it all away." He shook his head, smugly satisfied by the effect his words were having. "Look at you: A tyrant, a tycoon? Hah! You're nothing but a peasant who happened to find a relic. It was the relic that made you, so I guess you could say that *I* made you, Michele, my coming here and killing the rest of your family. Without me, you might still be planting crops, milking cows, and shoveling shit today. You should be *thanking* me, brother."

"I'll pass on that, if you don't mind. But you do seem to know an awful lot about my medallion."

"Because it's rightfully mine."

"You don't deserve it, Vlad."

Dracu laughed, shaking his head when he finally stopped. "Oh, so you believe yourself less wicked than me? You think I don't know all you've done to get where you are, all the sins you've committed, all the men who paid with their lives for standing in your way? The time has come to make you pay for your sins, Michele. I've watched you long enough."

Michael maintained the stare that held them together. "Watched me through that veil?"

Reflexively, Dracu stepped farther back into the shadows, clinging to them now to avoid the sun altogether. He started to raise a hand to lower his veil again, but stopped in mid-motion.

"What's it for?" Michael continued. "To hide your face or your intentions? You're ashamed of your past, of yourself, of the ugliness that's permeated your entire life. But hiding behind a mask changes nothing. You're still the same person when you take it off. Were you hoping to scare me with it like you scare everyone else? Sorry to disappoint you, Vlad, but I don't scare so easily. And I could see right through that veil to the man you really are even before you raised it for me. I may have hidden in the barn as a boy, but who's the real coward now?"

Dracu started forward once more, getting only as far as the sunlight stretching across the floor. "I've lived in darkness long enough. It's time to try the light, see if it treats me as well as it's treated you. Your relic will be mine, Michele, everything you have will be mine."

"By killing me, taking my medallion? You think it's as simple as that?"

"You're missing the point. But this is a point you can't possibly see. Nobody can, not yet. But soon everyone will, the entire world. That's when what I started the day I killed our father comes full circle. Fitting, don't you think?"

"I think you're a psycho."

"All geniuses are a bit crazy, Michele, even you. The difference is my rise to ultimate power comes without any help from a piece of gold our father gave to you instead of me. And now it's just you and me, Michele."

"Really? Are you sure you got everyone that day?" Michael heard himself say, as if it were someone else talking, the long disparate pieces of his past falling into place. "Are you sure there wasn't a little girl? You said the orders you disobeyed came from a man named Adnan Talu. What you don't know is that Talu adopted the little girl you missed killing and raised her as his heir, probably out of guilt over what you'd done against his orders. Our sister, Vlad."

Dracu's expression tightened, his brow starting to furrow when he seemed to rein his emotions back in. "Then I'll find and kill her too, but not before I kill you, not—"

And that's when the first shots rang out.

EIGHTY-FOUR

The barrage of gunfire into the house was sporadic but precise, a single shooter or maybe two repositioning themselves as they fired. Chips of stone, mortar, and wood flew into the air to mix with the dust, concentrated toward Dracu before he dropped to the remnants of the floor covered by what remained of the walls. Shouts and more gunfire erupted from beyond, Dracu's men obviously as confused by the barrage's origins as Michael was, shooting in what sounded like wild, erratic bursts.

Michael had no idea where the shots crackling through the farmhouse were coming from or who was firing. He'd instructed Alexander to remain at the airport and protect Scarlett no matter what. But if it wasn't Alexander, then *who* was it?

He'd barely formed that question when Armura burst through what remained of a wall and, covered in chips of paint and plaster, rushed to help Dracu. Michael could see the top of his veil popping up behind the jagged remains of a wall and knew this was his chance.

While Armura hoisted Dracu to his feet, shielding him with his own body, Michael risked the bullets still pouring into the house and leaped through a chasm at its rear. Then he dropped down the stairs into the darkness of the root cellar. With gunfire continuing to flare in all directions above him, he felt about the earthen wall. He tapped as he went with the butt of the flashlight he'd recovered until he struck something hard, still with his father's journal tucked under one arm. He threw his shoulder against it, felt something buckle, but not give. On his third thrust a camouflaged wooden door shattered inward, snapping off at its rusted hinges.

Michael charged down a narrow tunnel carved out of the ground beneath the farm. The meager spill from the root cellar lasted only until the first bend, after which he switched on the flashlight to illuminate his path forward.

Michael rushed on, looping through the tunnel's jagged design. He imagined it had been forged this way to avoid the shale and limestone deposits, along with the powerful root structures of the farm's biggest trees. His father must have dug the tunnel with any number of additional hands shortly after settling here. Effectively burying Davide Schapira, a hero of a secret operation launched by the West to hunt down Nazis hiding years after World War II, down in the root cellar along with his journals and memorabilia of that time.

In the end, though, that had had nothing to do with the massacre, the roots of which lay in a trip a desperate Vito Nunziato had made to get his precious relic appraised. Fearful of losing the farm, losing everything that defined the man he became, he'd come very close to selling it. That trip, if Vladimir Dracu was to be believed, had set the wheels in motion for the Turkish pirates to come after the relic at all costs, hired by a mysterious third party, some rich American, to do the deed.

Michael looked ahead into a darkness broken only by the narrow spray of his flashlight beam and saw the final truths of his past revealed at last. His feet thrashed through the soil covering what must've once been a hard-packed floor. The tunnel was barely wide enough to accommodate a single person's width, its claustrophobic confines mirroring the tightly knotted truths that formed Michael's true past.

He trudged on, flabbergasted this tunnel even existed as further proof of his father's secret life. Wondering if it had an end, wondering if he'd been shot back in the gunfight and this was the road to whatever eternity wrought. Not a warm bright light at all, but a darkened labyrinth through which he was doomed to roam forever.

Michael felt his feet pounding now, felt every thud of his heart against his rib cage, as each breath drew in more flecks of soil and dirt kicked upward into the air. He stifled the urge to cough several times, feeling the tunnel path alternately dip and rise, drop off and climb, carved through the old grounds that must have despised its trespass.

Michael ran like he was running from everything left in his wake from the day of the massacre, from the moment he'd lifted the gold relic from his father's sock drawer and claimed it as his own. No matter how fast or far he ran, though, the past felt like a cold hand stretching out to graze his spine. A featureless force refusing to let go of a hold on him that had tightened with Vlad Dracu's revelation.

We're half brothers. I guess I'm home, too.

But this wasn't Michael's home, not anymore. It was a graveyard of memories and pain, a landscape where the world had gone dry and spoiled, no longer able to sprout life. A place where only death resided instead.

It was that place from which Michael was running as much as the gunmen and bullets. A straightaway brought warmer temperatures and drier walls baked by thicker air. Slivers of light appeared outside the range of his beam and, before Michael could judge distance or placement, he found a wooden hatch and shouldered through it back into daylight.

He'd emerged just short of a back road he remembered from his youth. It led to a small stream where his father had taken him fishing. Now, though, Michael wondered if the dirt-paved road was real, if any of this was real. Thought of Scarlett, rescuing her from the *Securitate* so they could be together again.

And only then did he know the road was real, all of this was real.

But Michael wasn't in the clear yet, not by a long shot with Black Scorpion gunmen certain to be giving chase. He tried to run, then jog, but felt cramps seize him on both sides. Still, he rushed on, fighting back the pain. Clinging to the side of the road rimming the woods, when an SUV encased in dirt screeched to a halt before him, sideways across the road.

The passenger door flew open.

"Get in!" Raven Khan yelled to him from the driver's seat.

PART SIX

THE FORBIDDEN CITY

It is not in the stars to hold our destiny but in ourselves.

William Shakespeare

EIGHTY-FIVE

Las Vegas, Nevada

"What am I supposed to call you?" Naomi Burns asked the chubby man with thick glasses, uncomfortable as they walked around the nearly pristine iron and steel husks culled from Las Vegas history to be gathered in this museum formed by neon signs.

"It varies," the man said, winking. "How about Samuel?"

"Closing time was hours ago, Samuel."

"That's why we're here," Samuel said, sweeping a hand through hair that looked overly long for someone in his mid-twenties. "I know who you work for. Last thing I wanna do is take any chances and risk pissing him off."

"You don't need to be frightened."

"Only thing I'm frightened of is not being brilliant enough. We're talking about Michael Tiranno here. Anything that puts me in the dude's good graces, well, let's just say I'd welcome the opportunity. I'm not about to disappoint him, believe me."

According to Gregory John Markham, Samuel was a computer hacker extraordinaire forever on the run from the authorities, a man who lived entirely off the grid. If anyone could solve the mystery of what had turned Vegas dark last week, Markham insisted, it was Samuel. And, toward that end, for the past two days he'd been permitted unfettered access to the Seven Sins and the computer systems controlling its day-to-day operations.

"Hear that?" he asked Naomi suddenly, with hand cupped at his ear.

"Hear what?"

"The old days. If you listen hard enough, you can almost hear the magic from them."

Strange, Naomi thought, coming from a man who'd been born long after Vegas's original golden age. Samuel had his reasons for wanting to meet in a place like this at such an odd hour, and Naomi was in no position to question him.

"The Boneyard is my favorite place in Vegas," he said, as they continued their stroll. "Actual history served up in the form of all these neon signs around us that once lit the city. Makes you wonder, doesn't it, what Bugsy Siegel or Meyer Lansky would make of Vegas today. Michael Tirrano's old school, just like them."

"So you think . . ."

Samuel winked. "You know what they say about walking and talking like a duck. And don't bother denying it either. I'm on your side."

"Oh," Naomi said, thinking on the fly, "I wouldn't dare."

"But something this big, what do you need me for? Why not just call nine-one-one and get the cavalry, better known as the FBI, on the line?"

"Because that door's closed to us," Naomi said, stopping there to let her point sink in.

Samuel slapped the side of his head. "Of course, sure. I get it."

Naomi knew the signs around them had been banished here as massive electronic LED and LCD screens usurped them on the Strip and elsewhere, ambient light replacing the glittery glow that had drenched Vegas in a soft haze. Spared the indignity of the junkyard only by the city's devotion to its own history, to the point where the vintage marquees were dumped downtown on the east side of Las Vegas Boulevard. For convenience and practicality, that land became home to the Neon Museum and official Boneyard laid out over a two-acre spread lined with well over a hundred signs.

"Here's the original from the Oasis Café on Fremont Street," Samuel said to Naomi, beneath the glow of the LED lights spilling light down from overhead. "Erected in 1929 and reputedly the first neon sign ever to go up in Vegas."

The sign rested on its side with a cartoon character–like woman stretching a hand toward the moonlit sky. Ancient bulbs were still screwed into sockets rimmed by rust and peeling paint.

"I do my best thinking here," Samuel told her. "Guess history agrees with me." He walked diagonally across the Boneyard toward the old Sahara Hotel sign, just beyond which lay the original from Binion's Horseshoe. "But the past isn't why we're here," Samuel said, sweeping his gaze toward her suddenly. "The future is. I think I know what caused that blackout and, if I'm right, somebody might be about to change that future as we speak."

EIGHTY-SIX

LAS VEGAS, NEVADA

Naomi hoped Samuel was being melodramatic, but the look on his face lit by the reflection of the pole lighting off the old neon told her otherwise. That reflection made his pudgy cheeks seem as if they'd been pumped full of air.

They stopped before the once glittery, now rusted out, sign for the Moulin Rouge Casino. "First integrated casino in Vegas, you know," Samuel noted to Naomi. "The city's casino owners gathered there in nineteen-sixty to sign the

Moulin Rouge accord that led to the desegregation of all casinos. What do you know about computers, Ms. Burns?" he asked her, abruptly changing the subject.

"I turn mine on and when I'm finished I turn it off."

Naomi's response drew a smile from him. "How about the fact that they control pretty much everything these days, from the power grid, to the banking industry, the gaming industry here in Vegas, to all manner of travel, and pretty much any communication?"

"That's obvious."

"Yes, it is. What isn't nearly as obvious, though, is the vulnerabilities that creates."

"You mean like viruses?"

"What else?"

"Aren't I supposed to be the one asking the questions here?"

"Humor me, Ms. Burns."

"Okay," Naomi said, "hacking. Like the spate of those department stores that had their customer data exposed."

"Indeed," Samuel told her, winking as if all too familiar with the subject she had raised. "On point. And the primary solution to enhance cybersecurity is enhanced data encryption."

"Easier said than done, Samuel."

"Except it's not. Until three years ago, the problem with the computer chips responsible for the process is no matter how well they did their job of encrypting data to render it safe from bad guys, the smartest of those bad guys, like me, always found a workaround. A way in that left the data exposed and vulnerable. Putty in our hands."

"What happened three years ago?"

"Well, Ms. Burns, it turns out that up until that point encryption chips only utilized a small portion of their cores at any time to avoid burning out. But then somebody discovered how to enable those chips to utilize virtually their entire cores at any given time without burning out. Allows them to perform far more functions faster than ever before, reducing network vulnerability in the process. Like to hear the specification details?"

"No."

"It has to do with utilizing—"

"Stick with what's directly relevant to what we're facing *now*, Samuel."

"Okay, these new encryption chips appear and immediately take control of the market. By now as many as three-quarters of the motherboards of the computer systems and networks controlling our lives have either been fitted, or retrofitted, with Guardian."

"Guardian?"

"Name of the chip discovered by a relatively small start-up now worth billions. That explains why, in the wake of the Target and Home Depot fiascos, data breaches have fallen off drastically, especially in areas far more vital to everyday life than retail sales. In many cases, Guardian has made them a thing of the past."

"Where are you going with this?"

Samuel moved to a marquee so old and battered Naomi couldn't even read the words from her vantage point, but she did recognize a cowboy-hatted figure tipping his cap at the top. "In the old days, you flip a switch and these babies would simply turn on. Now when you flip a switch, a relay working off a computer network sends a signal to make that happen. You see the point?"

"Computer networks functioning as middlemen."

"Exactly, and not the average PC or Mac either. *Networks*, just like you said, where everything is processed through a motherboard. Even the things we take most for granted, like traffic lights and sliding doors and elevators and thermostats, are controlled one way or another by computers rigged to these networks. And Guardian has theoretically made them far more secure than they've ever been."

"I hate the word theoretically," Naomi droned.

"Because Guardian created a Janus problem. You know Janus?"

"The Roman God who presided over both war and peace, the best of times and the worst of times."

"Well," Samuel picked up, "Guardian functioned even better than advertised, but opened a new vulnerability while closing an old one: Someone able to control all the chips responsible for securing networks through their mother-boards could, by connection, take over or shut down those same networks."

"How?

"Either through a set of coded instructions programmed to activate at a specific point in time, or through a signal sent to the chips at another point in time. What happened in Las Vegas last week had me opting for the latter. And I was right."

Naomi could see Samuel getting genuinely excited about his findings, ready and eager to please anyone who worked for "old school" Michael Tiranno in the hope word might get back to the man himself.

"You know those vintage slot machines against a lobby wall in the Seven Sins?"

"We retrofitted them to work with our existing payout software."

"But their ancient technology isn't compatible with the system's motherboard on which Guardian is installed. It's the only subsystem in your entire resort that hasn't been up-graded, and know what? They didn't shut down during the blackout. They continued to function. To those machines, no one was playing. For all others, no one *could* play. See the distinction?"

"Sure, but that doesn't seem to be enough to base a conclusion this big on."

"And I'm not, not alone anyway. I can tell you that every system in the Seven Sins and beyond with Guardian installed shut down while every system with motherboards without Guardian remained functional. PCs, Macs, and notebooks, too, except nobody could log on to the Internet because the servers of all the local providers had been disabled."

"That's why the blackout was so pervasive. . . ."

"Right you are, Ms. Burns," Samuel said, starting on through the Boneyard again. "And it even affected the emergency backup systems of yours and the other properties on the Strip because those systems are rigged into a network watched over by Guardian as well. Data transmissions, what powers the world basically, are all about computers communicating with each other. And all incoming data, every single bit of it, goes through these encryption chips installed on the motherboards that run these computers. A single system equipped with Guardian in any network would be enough to put the brakes on any data traveling through that network. So if the estimates of Guardian now being installed in somewhere between half and three-quarters of the country's primary systems responsible for transmitting data across cyberspace are accurate, that would be more than enough to shut the whole country down."

"Did you say *country*?"

"Did I? I didn't mean to but, yes, that's the point here. In fact, you could just as easily substitute *world*. The information super-highway is just that. The data gets on at one point and gets off at another. From the lights going on when you flip the switch, to your cell phone's ability to communicate with the nearest cell tower, to traffic lights, and airplane landings, bank transactions, the checkout lanes at our favorite supermarket—you name it. One way or another it's all controlled by computers talking to each other. That's how data moves along the information superhighway. And if somebody goes national or worldwide with the kind of signal to Guardian that shut down Las Vegas, it's lights out."

"For how long?"

"Good question," Samuel said, shrugging. "And I'd be lying if I told you I had the answer."

"But these encryption chips can be removed and replaced, right?"

"Sure. But it would take awhile and even longer to get all the systems up and running securely again."

"How long?" Naomi asked him.

"I'd guess a week, two weeks, three weeks maybe? Hard to know exactly, given that we're in uncharted territory here. Think how bad those five minutes were in Vegas last week, then multiply by a week or two or three, only on a much larger scale." Samuel had stopped before the Stardust Hotel sign that even today seemed to catch him in its golden glow. "Dismantling and moving this antique cost two hundred thousand dollars, more than three times what it cost to build the sign in the first place."

"How do we stop it?"

Samuel swung from the Stardust sign with a start. "I'm not sure you can. The problem is we're not looking for anything installed on the chip itself, so much as an embedded signal."

"Embedded signal?"

"A preprogrammed sequence of letters and numbers that once recognized would trigger Guardian to shut down the system it's supposed to be protecting. Could be something as simple as, 'Your mother wears army boots.' Flooding the systems with a sequence of characters, a sleeper code, that would not randomly come up otherwise. Whoever's behind this would then send that signal to all the systems Guardian is responsible for monitoring and boom, things go dark."

"A signal to the chip itself?"

"Far more likely a simple message left on a message board asking for feedback from an airline, a bank, an energy supplier—you name it. All of those pass through the encryption system to make sure they don't contain viruses or worms. And once Guardian recognizes the embedded code, it flips the switch it was designed to flip."

"Then lights out."

"Worse," Samuel told her, "because these systems send out code to every device on their network and, in turn, every device on the network would be infected. The message would be replicated and spread by every system it comes into contact along the server path is what I'm saying. And so on, and so on. In other words, you end up with exponential expansion of the embedded code's reach, spreading the shutdown signal far and wide, as in farthest and widest."

Samuel moved on toward the bloodred glow of an ancient sign labeled STARR, the origins of which eluded Naomi. "Your only hope would be to preempt the plot at the source. Stop whoever it is from sending the activation signal in the first place."

"Easier said than done, Samuel. Is there any way to determine exactly how many Guardian chips have actually been installed?"

"All computer networks that transmit data of any kind have encryption technology built in—that's a given. The average system replaces its encryption chips, sometimes their entire motherboards, no more than every three years, or even less. So if you have reason to believe that this plot has been in the works for those three years it's more than conceivable that whoever's behind it can send a signal that can shut down pretty much anything and everything across the country and other parts of the world where Guardian has achieved a comparable degree of saturation. Comparing it to flipping a switch is a nice metaphor, but the effects wouldn't be felt that way. Over the course of a day or two would be my guess for the spread to reach maximum density."

Samuel stopped and ran his gaze about the endless rows of neon signage that was ancient by today's standards.

"Maybe we were better off back in the days these babies lit the strip. The world worked simpler, wasn't subject to such threats."

"And, if you're right, trying to secure all these systems was what created the very vulnerability we're facing today."

"Oh, I'm right, Ms. Burns. I know I am," Samuel said. "And I'm not telling you it's going to happen, only that it damn well can."

Samuel had started toward another display, when Naomi grasped his arm to hold him in place. "I'm assuming this had something to do with the murder of Edward Devereaux by sonic bomb in his Daring Sea suite at the Seven Sins."

"Oh, you bet it did," Samuel told her. "Everything in those suites is controlled by computer. And when Guardian shut down Vegas, the system tripped and locked all the doors."

"Sealing Devereaux inside his room," Naomi picked up, "and trapping him so he couldn't escape once the glass began to rupture. I get that. What I don't get is why go through such lengths to kill one man?"

"That's not the only thing this was about. I think whoever's behind this figured out a way to embed a second signal unique to the motherboards for systems controlling Vegas. Not as hard as it may seem, given that there are motherboards task specific to the gaming industry. I think those few minutes here were a test of the system's functionality, and I think whoever was behind the test used it as an opportunity to dispose of Devereaux."

"I guess we can assume they passed."

"Oh, with flying colors."

"So why not—"

"Just put the word out," Samuel picked up, figuring where Naomi was going, "and have Guardian removed from all these motherboards? First off, you'd have to present a very compelling case that would take a lot of time to build. Remember the whole Y2K fiasco, all the money that got wasted because people hit the panic button? Some in IT, plenty if not most, would see this as a repeat of that."

Naomi nodded, conceding his point. "Just one more question, Samuel. Tell me what you know about this tech start-up that invented the Guardian chip."

EIGHTY-SEVEN

THE CITATION

Michael sat by himself on the Citation after takeoff, across the aisle from Scarlett, who left him to his thoughts. Raven Khan had dropped him at the airport a mere twenty minutes earlier but it felt like so much longer, time slowed to a crawl.

Back on the road that rimmed the farm, she'd torn off in the SUV before Michael could even get his door all the way closed.

"You look like shit."

"Appearances can be deceiving," Michael told her, feeling the heavy force of cool air slamming him from the vents to break the interior's blistering heat.

"Something both of us know intimately."

"It was you, wasn't it, Raven? You were the one who saved me back there at the farm."

She gave the SUV more speed so it thumped over the pitted road, her eyes constantly checking the rearview mirror.

"You came *home*," Michael resumed, when Raven remained silent. "That can only mean you finally figured out the truth."

"Thanks to a nightmare I've been having for as long as I can remember. A part of me recognized that farm as soon as I set foot on the grounds; I wish I could tell you how." She tried for a smile and came away looking only sad. "So what do I call you? Brother?"

Michael nodded, slowly. "Our parents were murdered," he managed, realizing his mouth had gone bone dry. Saying the words made him feel strange, almost like someone else was speaking them. "I witnessed it from the barn. Until five years ago, I thought you were dead, too."

"Then the woman who died protecting me in my dreams . . ."

"Our mother. She was making lunch," Michael added for reasons he didn't understand. "A few minutes more and I would've been killed too."

"But you weren't."

"No."

A pause, dominated by the thickest silence Michael could ever recall, broken only by the steady hum of the SUV's engine.

"Last week, I boarded a ship that had women and children for cargo, Brother," Raven said finally. "It was the worst thing I've ever seen in my life and I've seen a lot of bad things. Some disease had swept through the hold. The sight, the smell . . . There was a child, three or four years old maybe, clutching her dead mother. I haven't been able to close my eyes since without seeing her, and now I understand why."

"The man you shot at, Vladimir Dracu, the one wearing the veil. It was him on the farm that day," Michael told her.

"He's the one who murdered our parents, the monster who's haunted your dreams."

Raven's gaze grew distant. "Returning to that farm triggered something in me. For a few brief moments—the sights, the sounds, the smells—I felt . . . innocent, a little girl again, maybe for the first time. It made me realize that little girl on the ship *was* me, both of our lives destroyed by Black Scorpion. I have to kill him, Michael. I wish I didn't, but I do. This Vladimir Dracu has to die, or there'll be countless more lives ruined, more innocence stolen. He made me a victim, he made *you* a victim. We were there for his beginning. Now we have to be there for his end."

"There's something else, Raven. Adnan Talu, your adopted father."

"What?"

"He was in charge of Vlad Dracu and the other men who came to the farm that day." Michael stopped, heard Raven's breathing and nothing more. "They were after my gold relic, filling an order for some rich American. Dracu was the one who started shooting, acting against orders because he didn't care about the relic. He only wanted Vito Nunziato dead."

"Why?"

Michael told her.

Raven said nothing for what seemed like a very long time. Finally she cracked a slight smile, even as a tear rolled down one side of her face. Michael watched her from across the seat and pictured her processing the truth about their father of whom she held no memory, likely making it even harder for her to accept and reconcile.

She sighed deeply, sniffled. "I guess it figures."

"That our half brother is a monster?"

"That it's up to us to stop him." She wiped the tear from

her cheek. "I've never needed anyone's help, Brother. Just Talu, who put me in that orphanage he ultimately pulled me out of."

"I'm sorry."

"Why?"

"Because I know what you're feeling."

"Walk away, Michael. Leave this to me."

"I can't."

"Then stay out of my way."

"Vlad's out to destroy me, Raven. I need to take him down first."

"Then you need to know I worked for Black Scorpion once—unwittingly. When I rescued some scientific genius from a Russian gulag. The man's name was Taupmann, Niels Taupmann, I think."

"Niels Taupmann," Michael repeated.

"We need to take down all of Black Scorpion, and Michael Tiranno can't help me do that." Her eyes bore into his. "But the Tyrant can. Think you're up to it?"

"Try me."

And now the Citation was streaking toward London with Alexander behind the controls. Michael tried to read his father's journal from scratch again, but his thoughts kept veering back to his sister Rosina, now Raven Khan. As gratified as he was to be reunited with her, he knew it wouldn't last. Knew that when all this was over, like so many other things in his life, she'd be gone. Again.

"You're scaring me, Michael," Scarlett said suddenly.

"Why?"

"Because I've never seen you this quiet."

He rose from his seat to settle into the one next to her. "I'm sorry," he said, and kissed her on the forehead.

"You have nothing to apologize for. I'm the one who should be sorry."

"For what?"

"Making you come halfway around the world to risk your life."

"It wasn't your fault, Scarlett."

"Whose fault was it then?"

Michael felt the outline of the relic beneath his shirt. "No one's."

EIGHTY-EIGHT

HOIA-BACIU FOREST, ROMANIA

Dracu entered the underground lab without fanfare, adjusting his veil as he approached his supervisor, a tall man with pointy, angular features named Bemke.

"Domnule," Bemke greeted, stiffening.

The lab in question had been constructed within the mountain fortress's single underground level, formerly the Soviets' command and control facility for this installation forged out of near solid rock, reinforced by steel at all points, and contained actually beneath the surface of the lake waters beyond. The satellite relays connecting its vast array of machines to the outside world were located in the surrounding forest, camouflaged to the point of being rendered invisible.

The lab itself, a sprawling open floor with walls of natural stone formation that bled moisture sucked up almost immediately by powerful dehumidifiers, contained the most advanced communications and monitoring technology anywhere. Built at incredible cost, though over the course of several years, as Dracu's plan took shape with the rescue of Niels Taupmann from the Russian gulag as its centerpiece. It was lined wall-to-wall with real-time satellite schematics and depictions, so Dracu would be able to follow the results of his plan once it was put into motion. More important, though, were additional screens offering detailed maps of various regions of his target that filled out the entire front wall. Had those screens been fit together, they would've formed a perfect schematic of the United States. Taken individually, they would allow Dracu to similarly gauge the country's plight on a minute-by-minute basis. The many dots lit up across the various maps onto which they'd been squeezed represented power grids, cell phone towers, airports, banking centers, traffic systems, data relays and interchanges, and broadcast transmission sources. Once they started flashing, he'd know another part of his plan had succeeded.

An army of technicians, recruited mostly from among the many engineers and specialists displaced from Eastern Europe after the fall of the Soviet Union, occupied endless rows of individual computer stations, each with its own grid to follow and report on. Checking the system, both practically and in theory, was constant, and Dracu had been down here to personally witness the five minutes Las Vegas had been turned dark as a test of the system's functionality.

Which it had passed with flying colors.

With the moment of activation fast approaching, personnel worked furiously on final preparations that to no small degree included building monitoring networks capable of charting the Guardian chip's effects. Dracu's gaze lingered on the electronic maps covering the walls awash in flashing lights congested in the areas of densest populations. He imagined the hundreds of thousands of people each of those lights represented, all just three days away from being plunged into darkness.

"I wanted to alert you that the professor is coming down for a visit," Dracu told his supervisor. "He's en route now."

"Then let's make sure he sees exactly what he expects to see," Bemke said, grinning, approaching the nearest keyboard.

EIGHTY-NINE

LAS VEGAS, NEVADA

Michael's thoughts were still a jumble when the Boeing 737 touched down back at McCarran. He'd tried to sleep on the flight home from London, but every time he closed his eyes, the ghosts came for him.

There was his father—both his fathers now, the hero Davide Schapira and the farmer Vito Nunziato. He felt them merge in his consciousness, realizing how much he'd loved his father and, more than anything, perhaps resenting how little that affection had been returned. Now Michael understood that the source of Vito Nunziato's detachment lay in his fear of losing what he loved again. His experience in Romania had scarred him in a way both profound and indelible, as if he'd left a piece of himself back there with Stefania Tepesche he knew he'd never be able to recover.

There was Michael's mother, too, old before her time, always smiling and ready with a hug no matter what ills the family was facing. There was his sister Rosina and Raven Khan, the same person separated by the years. Raven a great mystery and puzzle who'd resisted all his overtures until fate had thrust them together once more.

Naomi Burns was waiting outside the terminal when the 737 taxied to a halt, not far from the helicopter affixed with the logo of Tyrant Global. The pilot saw him emerge and started the engine.

"You know, I've never actually ridden in a chopper before," Scarlett told him, as they moved toward it.

"There's a first time for everything," Michael said.

Michael glued his gaze downward as they reached the outskirts of the city, soaring over the Las Vegas Strip. A hefty police presence remained, perhaps even increased since he'd left in the blackout's wake. He noticed occasional checkpoints near the largest of the hotels, including the Seven Sins; even a National Guard presence, its soldiers armed with assault rifles and wearing flak jackets.

His city, his home. Under siege again, this time at the hands of Vladimir Dracu who was determined to destroy everything Michael loved to finish the process he started with the massacre. His half brother having been denied love and now wanting to steal it away from him, so they could truly be the same. And the upshot of his resolve was a city that had already come under attack, with the entire country soon to follow.

Did Michael bear the responsibility simply because Vlad was his blood, or for some greater, more intrinsic reason rooted in a fate he was just beginning to grasp? The prospects of that confused him, left his thoughts a jumble, his own resolve tightened into knots by sight of the city he loved again held hostage by a madman. First Max Price, now a powerful organization called Black Scorpion.

Michael saw the Seven Sins growing majestically before him as the Tyrant Phantom Class, custom-made black helicopter soared straight for the resort's roof atop the Forbidden City. It gleamed beneath the sunlight like a palace of old, an oasis of hope amid a rising tide of decadence and destruction. Saving all he'd built, preserving it, was only part of the greater responsibility he bore, a microcosm rooted in symbol. He had made himself into an American, a businessman, a casino owner, and finally a tycoon. But all of that paled in comparison to what he must accept himself as now and forever if the madness that enveloped the world was to be beaten back:

The Tyrant.

The chopper landed on the roof, Michael and Naomi taking the private glass elevator straight down through the Daring Sea to his bubble glass office at the very bottom, while Alexander remained with Scarlett. Michael brought Naomi up to date on what had transpired in Caltagirone quickly as the cab whirred downward, continuing even after the glass doors had opened again at the entrance to his office.

"I'm speechless," was all Naomi could manage. "Raven Khan, after we tried to find her for so long . . . And what happened at the farm, the *three of you* all in the same place . . ."

"Right. The children of Vito Nunziato together for the first time. Talk about your twisted family reunions," Michael continued, finally stepping out of the elevator.

Naomi followed him past his two assistants who rose respectfully. She moved straight with Michael for his desk, piled high with work that had built up in the three days he'd been gone. Watched him place an old ledger down carefully, separate from the pile.

"My father's journal," Michael explained. "Reading it was like meeting him for the first time. Because that's what it was, at least the man he really was."

"A hero, by the sound of things."

"He was a hero afterward, too, just a different kind. Speaking of which," Michael continued, plucking an old black-and-white photo, tattered at the edges, from the back of the journal and handing it to Naomi.

"Who's this?"

"Hans Wolff, the worst of the Nazis my father was sent to pursue and one of the worst who escaped justice, period. Let's see if we can figure out what became of him after he escaped that village in Romania."

"You're not thinking of going after Wolff, are you?" Naomi said, her voice laced with concern. "Finish the job your father couldn't?"

Michael shook his head. "He'd be in his nineties now. I just, I just need to know what happened to him, where he ended up in life."

Naomi looked at the picture again, then tucked it in against her. "It's that important to you?"

"A missing piece, and I'm tired of having so many missing pieces in my life. Find everything you can about whoever Hans Wolff became after he left Romania in 1959, after my father let him live in order to save the woman he loved."

Naomi studied him briefly. "You take after your father, Michael. You never realized it before because you never realized what kind of man he really was."

"Are you going to ask me how that feels now?"

"I don't have to, because I already know."

"Everything changed the day of the massacre, more so than I ever realized before. I already knew the man I am was born that day, but so was Black Scorpion."

"And if Vladimir Dracu had managed to get his hands on the relic at the farm?"

"I don't know, Naomi, I truly don't."

"You haven't said much about what the girl uncovered."

"The girl?"

"Scarlett Swan, Michael."

"I've got enough on my mind right now without chasing myths."

"But if she's right, and the medallion does exert some incredible power . . ."

Michael let her comment hang, remaining silent.

"At least we now have an explanation for how DNA that was a fifty percent match for yours was found in that girl who was murdered in Turkey," Naomi resumed.

"What was her name?"

"Amanda Johansen."

"She was killed because of me. Dracu impregnated her, because of me. It was all a setup. Black Scorpion's doing."

Michael's phone buzzed.

"Yes," he called toward the speaker.

"The FBI is here, Mr. Tiranno," came the voice of one of his assistants.

"Tell them I'll be right up."

"Er, sir, they're already coming *down*."

Michael stepped back into the reception area just in time to see Del Slocumb emerge from the glass elevator, followed by five men wearing FBI windbreakers with badges dangling from lanyards on their necks.

"Welcome home," Slocumb said, grinning.

NINETY

LAS VEGAS, NEVADA

Slocumb waited until his entourage had escorted Michael up to the lobby, where a bevy of paparazzi stood shouting questions with cameras at the ready, to hand him a triply folded set of pages that Naomi promptly snatched out of the air.

"Michael Tiranno," he said, working to hold back another smile, "I hereby inform you that your license to operate a casino in the State of Nevada has been suspended by the Nevada Gaming Commission, pending a scheduled hearing before the Gaming Control Board. Further, it's my duty to escort you from these premises and ensure that you don't return until that suspension is lifted. Any questions?"

Michael held to his composure, viewing the five agents accompanying Slocumb with a smirk. "Did you really need all this backup, Agent?"

"You're not the only one who plays better for an audience, Mr. Tiranno."

The walk through the lobby continued in a blur, Michael passing into the blistering heat outside to be greeted by even more paparazzi being held back by Seven Sins security personnel. Alexander appeared out of nowhere, suddenly by his side, escorting him to his Lamborghini.

"Get Scarlett and Naomi to my house," Michael instructed, as he climbed behind the wheel, taking one last look at FBI Special Agent Del Slocumb.

"You have no idea how long I've been waiting for this day," Slocumb said.

"The clock's ticking on your fifteen minutes of fame, Agent," Michael told him. "Just remember that small victories often lead to lost wars."

"I'll keep it in mind," Slocumb said, smirking.

"Do that," Michael said, and tore off.

NINETY-ONE

Istanbul, Turkey

Ismael Saltuk feasted on the view from the restaurant in Maiden's Tower at the same time he enjoyed a wonderful meal of karniyarik. The eggplants, his favorite dish, were perfectly fried with a combination of minced meat, onion, parsley, garlic, and tomato filling. Living in the dark confines of his self-imposed prison made forays like this to be cherished, especially when contrasted against the expansive views the tower offered of the city. At night Istanbul's lights twinkled, while during the day the sun shined off the Bosphorus to make the entire city seem hued with gold.

According to Turkish legend, a princess was once locked in the 2,500-year-old tower to protect her from being bitten by a snake. Later it was used as a customs station, converted into a lighthouse, and then became a residence for retired naval officers, before being turned into a prime attraction for locals and tourists alike that inevitably included a stop in its vaunted restaurant. Many patrons came by ferry, but Saltuk preferred to use the underwater Mamaray railway tunnel that ran through the Bosphorus, barely necessitating him to risk traveling above ground at all. The tunnel practically and symbolically connected the European and Asian sides of Istanbul along its near-mile-long stretch underwater.

Saltuk loved Maiden's Tower so much he never wanted to leave. Necessity, though, dictated he not remain too long in the same place and he reluctantly made his way back to the underwater rail station with his guards once his meal was complete. Passenger traffic was light this time of the evening, leaving Saltuk and his four guards with a car all to themselves.

The train picked up speed as it whisked him back to the mainland in the tunnel beneath nearly two hundred feet of water. Then, suddenly, it shook and stopped, the stalled car rocking a bit in the moment before the lights died.

Saltuk clung to his calm, a single emergency light at the far end of the car catching his men in a faint glow. He heard a thud, glimpsed a blur of motion followed by grunts, groans, and bodies falling. Saluk started to rise to head instinctively to the nearest exit, forgetting he was in a tunnel beneath sixty meters of water. That's when he felt a strong hand clamp onto his shoulder and shove him back down.

"How was your dinner, Ismael?" said Raven Khan.

NINETY-TWO

Istanbul, Turkey

Saltuk's eyes adjusted enough to the single emergency light to find her hovering over him. "Was all this truly necessary, Raven?"

"You tell me, Ismael," she said, taking the seat next to him, the frames of his four men splayed on the floor before them. "You're the one who's been holding out."

"Paranoia doesn't suit you."

"I became paranoid too late, trusted you too long."

"What are you talking about?"

"You used me."

"I don't know what you're—"

Saltuk stopped when Raven jammed a thumb against his side, driving it between two ribs to steal his breath and send a sharp bolt of pain surging through him.

"How does that feel, Ismael? Because it only gets worse from here."

Raven pulled her thumb back and Saltuk gasped for air. "What's this about? What demon possessed you to hurt me that way?"

"You, Ismael. You're as much a devil as Black Scorpion, even worse since you used me against them, against *him*."

"You speak madness, Raven."

"So you didn't send me to Caltagirone knowing exactly what I'd find there?"

"I have no idea what you're—"

"Has that been the plan all along, from when you sent me to the *Lucretia Maru*? Get me to do your bidding, and kill Black Scorpion for you, by feeding me little bits of information at a time, making me think I was figuring it all out on my own. You're even more a cutthroat than I am." She shook her head "I should've known when we met last week."

"Known *what*?"

"The look on your face when I threatened to destroy your final original painting. All that anger and rage. But it wasn't really aimed at me, was it? It was aimed at the man who'd bled your collection dry. Tell me, is that why you decided to move against him, was that the reason?"

"Move against *Black Scorpion*?" Saltuk shot back, trying to sound shocked. "You've truly gone mad, Raven. What kind of fool do you take me for?" He laughed, the gesture sounding forced. "I might as well slit my wrists or cut my own throat to save Black Scorpion the trouble."

"And that's where I came in, wasn't it?"

Saltuk shook his head, looking genuinely hurt. "So you take me for a monster, too . . . We're family, Raven, *family*."

"You have no family, any more than Talu did. He adopted me out of guilt, ended up creating just the kind of mindless machine he needed. And you picked up right where he left off."

"Raven—"

"You knew there was no copper on that ship, Ismael, the *Lucretia Maru*. You knew what she was carrying and you sent me on board knowing I'd find it and how I'd react, because you knew the truth of my past, where this all started for me."

This time Saltuk remained silent.

"And then you sent me to Caltagirone," Raven resumed. "The farm where I was born and I barely managed to survive when my parents were murdered, knowing what it would do to me, what it would *unleash* in me."

"No, you made me tell you, you *forced* me. I only gave you what you wanted."

"Just like it was Talu who brought me to the orphanage after he orphaned me. The gunmen at the farm the day of the massacre were his. Do I need to go on?"

"No," Saltuk said, the word barely audible.

"The leader of Black Scorpion was there that day. He was the triggerman. I know that now. Did you? Did you rely on me finding out to give me even more reason to hate him and want him dead?" Raven shook her head again. "And I took the bait and walked right into your trap."

Saltuk just looked at her.

"You pitted me against a monster. And if I brought him down there'd be a void, wouldn't there?"

"Please, Raven. That wasn't my cargo, *our* cargo, on board the *Lucretia Maru*. It was *Black Scorpion*'s. And as long as they're calling the shots, our association with them leaves us incredibly vulnerable. If they go down, we go down, too. Everything we've built, the entire organization Talu built, would be finished. None of what I did changes the fact that Black Scorpion had to be dealt with once and for all and you were the only one who could do it."

"Then why not simply tell me all that and ask for my help? Why all the lies and tricks?"

Raven could see Saltuk scowl even through the train car's half light. "Because I couldn't take the chance you'd say no. You're relentless, like a force of nature."

"You should've at least tried, Ismael. You owed me that much."

Saltuk started to reach out to touch her, then pulled his hand back. "How do you tell someone a truth they've been denying all their life?"

"I couldn't deny something I never knew."

"Really, Raven?" Saltuk said, shaking his head slowly. "Those dreams you've been having for as long as you can remember, the effect seeing the contents of that cargo hold had on you . . . How was I to frame such emotions into words? How was I to tell you how Talu found you cowering beneath your mother's corpse, covered in her blood? It had to come from you, Raven, from *inside* you. I may have pointed the way, gave you the map, but you got there all on your own."

Raven shivered. "Tell me, Ismael, did you arrange for some pestilence to spread through the victims? Did you make sure I'd see a young girl hugging her dead mother just as I was left to do?"

"I knew you'd see *something*, enough to move you to the kind of action my words never would have."

"So I take out Black Scorpion the man, but his organization is still out there. Then what? Someone else moves in, someone else takes over." Raven stopped and held her stare upon him, watching him try to hide the guilt but also the affirmation in his eyes. "What then, Ismael?"

"You overestimate me, Raven."

"No, Ismael, I *underestimated* you. You know their network better than anyone. All the nooks, all the crannies, where all the cells are based because that's how the money comes in. You know things about Dracu nobody else does; you've been his proxy for a long time."

Saltuk shook his head, looking genuinely miffed. "Haven't I always taken care of you?"

"Only because it suited your interests. But I'm going to let you make amends for that and all the lies." Raven stopped and let her gaze go flat as polished steel. "You're going to tell me everything you know; the locations of Black Scorpion's cells, where it's headquartered all across the world, its leadership, and the government officials the organization holds in its pocket everywhere."

"Even if I could . . ."

"We both know you can, Ismael. Get the information

I need together. Immediately. If I show up somewhere like this again, I'll be the last sight you ever see."

"Black Scorpion's destruction will serve far more powerful interests than me. I'm not alone in this, you need to know that."

Raven narrowed her gaze on him. "No, you're not. Now you're working for me."

NINETY-THREE

Lake Las Vegas, Nevada

"We need to prep for the hearing," Naomi repeated.

"Can't you see I'm busy?" Michael asked her from the floor, where he was tussling with Nero.

"You always do that when you're stressed out."

"Do what?"

"Play with that overgrown house cat. Maybe it's because you hope he bites you."

Michael sat up, continuing to stroke Nero after the panther laid his head on his lap. "More like because I've already been bitten."

"The hearing's in two days. We need to go in there loaded for bear, not big cat."

Nero purred loudly at that.

"And we will," Michael said, trying to sound more confident than he was. "Challenges are nothing new for us, Naomi. And right now the threat Black Scorpion poses is worse than anything Kern and his commission can come up with. It's not just my future that's at stake here anymore."

"You're talking about Dracu? What's he after, Michael?"

"At the farm, he told me I was missing the point, but that I'd see it soon enough; the whole world would. Four years ago, Raven rescued a German scientist for him from a Russian gulag. A man named Niels Taupmann. I looked him up on the flight home. At the time of his purported death in a plane crash that killed over a hundred passengers in Russia, Taupmann was the world's foremost IT authority on data encryption to ward off cyberattacks."

"Data encryption," Naomi repeated, not bothering to hide her shock at what Michael had just said. "Remember what I told you about the start-up technology company that had cornered the market with its Guardian chip?"

"Sure."

"The company's called Sentinel Technologies. Care to guess whose fund basically owns it?"

"Aldridge Sterling."

"You guessed it."

"So, let's assume for the sake of argument that the Guardian chip is Taupmann's creation," Michael continued. "You know what you're suggesting?"

"That Sterling, one of the richest men in the world, and Vladimir Dracu, one of the most dangerous criminals alive, are somehow connected."

"Don't forget we know for a fact Sterling's been scooping up all our available bonds now trading at their lowest level ever. And considering the fact that his fund never covered casino investments, that can't be a coincidence."

"And it leads straight to Commissioner Kern," Naomi concluded. "All the more reason to be ready for whatever he has to throw at us at the hearing."

"Hell, it wouldn't surprise me if Dracu shows up as a witness and Kern allows him to testify."

NINETY-FOUR

Michael and Scarlett lay in bed, enjoying the darkness that seemed to make the world much smaller, Nero nestled between them taking the covers in his mouth every time either of them stopped petting him.

"He doesn't scare you," Michael noted.

"He would have a week ago," she said, shifting around to better face him. "We need whatever's left of Josephus's manuscript back."

"It doesn't matter now."

"Yes, Michael, it does." She stopped stroking Nero and swallowed hard. "Because I need to *know*."

"Know what?"

"The truth."

"We know plenty already."

"But not enough. I'm talking about the price those who've possessed the medallion have paid."

"What's the difference?"

Nero took the bedcovers in his mouth and began gnawing at them until Scarlett resumed petting him. "It comes with a curse as well as a blessing. I think the Roman order Caesar dispatched uncovered the fact that it works only for those worthy to possess it."

"Worthy? What would a frail, frightened little boy be worthy of?"

"Fate, Michael. You've been chosen for some reason by a higher power, some cosmic force. Call it God, call it whatever you want. I can't believe I'm actually saying that, but it's what I believe. What the Romans blamed for a storm, a pestilence, or a famine. Or celebrated for delivering a great

victory or a bounty. I've been all over the world these past
five years searching for a truth that now scares the hell out
of me."

"Why?"

"Because of the price you may have to pay for what comes
with it, the price *I* may have to pay," Scarlett added, turning away.

Michael took his hand off Nero long enough to turn her
back toward him, meeting his gaze. "Haven't I saved your
life twice already? Wouldn't you call that fate, too?"

"Yes, and that's the point. Because we're tempting it, *I'm*
tempting it by being close to you. There's no place for me
in this, no place for anything that comes between you and
that relic. That's why it must be worn against the skin, close
to the heart. You see the point?"

"No, I don't. I can have it both ways. Nothing's going to
come between us," he said, and kissed her as Nero started
tearing at the bedcovers with his teeth.

They let him, holding each other as best they could with
the big cat between them. Michael felt Scarlett trembling
and eased her slightly away.

"What is it?" he asked, still holding her at the shoulders.
"What is it you're not telling me?"

Scarlett cleared her throat, looked away briefly. "Oh, I
have a gift for you," she said instead of answering.

She reached under the bed and came up with a beautifully wrapped box, handing it to Michael, who sat up to take
it. Nero watched curiously as he tore it open like a boy on
Christmas morning, extracting an assemblage of stitched-
together, elegant but very strong dark leather that looked
like a combination of a harness and a holster. He held it up
and noticed a webbed pocket on its left-hand side.

"I fitted it to the exact specifications of your relic, something to hold it without worry of it being lost or torn free."

Michael looped his arm through it, much like a shoulder

holster. The slot tailored for the medallion rested directly over his heart and he squeezed his gold relic snugly into place.

"A perfect fit," he noted, stretching his arms.

"So you'll always think of me when you're wearing it," Scarlett said, and Michael kissed her again.

He broke the embrace only when his phone buzzed with an incoming text. He snatched the Galaxy off his night table and saw the text was from Alexander.

I FOUND HIM.

NINETY-FIVE

LAS VEGAS, NEVADA

"Members only," the big thug said, blocking Alexander's route to an unmarked slab of a steel door.

"How do I join?" Alexander asked, through the dim light.

"You can't, friend."

"Wrong answer," Alexander said and unleashed a quick flurry of blows that dropped the big man to the pavement.

Alexander dragged the man with him through the steel door, finding himself at the top of a stairway that spiraled downward under dim light shed only by translucent bulbs recessed into the wall at each step. He stripped the man of his gun, bound his hands with plastic cuffs, and used a kerchief as a gag. It would likely take several minutes to find him, by which time Alexander would be gone with the man he'd come for in tow.

Michael sat in front of the camera that had been set up in his home office with him seated before the bookshelves, the door closed so Nero couldn't wander in as his live interview with CNN was transpiring. He couldn't see the host who would be posing the questions, could only hear her thanks to an earpiece wedged into his ear and connected to a power pack clipped to his belt.

"We go live in five," he heard through the earpiece, "four, three, two, one . . ."

It had been Naomi who'd ordered Seven Sins security personnel to find the man responsible for Amanda Johansen's disappearance. They'd employed facial recognition software of Amanda as featured in an Elysium program through all the security cameras placed around the Seven Sins. Ultimately, the best they could do was a single shot of Amanda getting into a Cadillac sedan. The face of the man accompanying her was obscured, but his license plate wasn't: IPLEASUREU. And a call to a contact at the Las Vegas police had identified the owner as one Victor Argos who, according to police, was known to regularly frequent a certain underground strip club on Industrial Road. Running parallel to the Strip, that road held virtually all of the city's X-rated nightlife, including a high-end lounge called the Pleasure Dome that catered almost exclusively to a foreign and high-roller clientele.

It was what transpired in the private club located adjacent to the Pleasure Dome, accessible through a secret entrance that led to an underground level, though, that interested Alexander most. And he descended the stairs into the artificially cool air scented by hidden misters struck by the odd sensation he was entering hell itself.

A big Asian stepped out when he neared the bottom, unleashing a flurry of martial arts strikes and kicks. Alexander stepped back, working his body from side to side to avoid the blows that whistled past close enough to rustle his hair. Then he darted inside a more desperate blow, wedged a thumb into the man's eye and used his other arm to force the man backward into a wall padded softly in black.

"One chance," he said, free hand lodged strategically against the man's throat and larynx. "Victor Argos. Where can I find him?"

The man started to struggle. Alexander pressed just a bit harder.

"I exert any more pressure, you'll hear a crack and you'll never speak again. So one last time, where can I find Victor Argos?"

The big Asian man's eyes tilted sideways, a single quivering hand rising to point in the same direction toward a door at the end of the hall.

"Now that wasn't so hard, was it?" Alexander said, pressing just hard enough to shut off the man's air so he'd pass out.

"Mr. Tiranno, what do you have to say about the allegations that led to you being barred from your own casino earlier today?"

"You mean, besides the fact that they're baseless?" Michael said, meaning every word of it as he pictured this going live out to millions of homes on television, the Internet and, later, YouTube. "As you know, Barbara, such absurd allegations are nothing new. I've had them lodged against me ever since I got started in Vegas. And now that someone never accepted into this exclusive club operated by a select few is prepared to expand here and abroad, they've resurfaced."

"Are you saying the other casino owners are jealous?"

"No, I'm saying competition is very real and cutthroat in Las Vegas and that these allegations are completely false."

Alexander waited for the man to slump down the wall before proceeding through a twisted take on Dante's nine circles of hell. Literally, because that's how many doors the hall held, sloped slightly downward. The light mist providing an artificially fragrant scent collected in a thin cloud just below the black drop ceiling. Music of the techno variety blared from unseen speakers, tuned low to provide ambient background noise until the first door Alexander approached was thrust open, allowing louder riffs to emerge with a hulking shape.

The man, garbed in black as all the others were, was carrying a serving tray he quickly shed to the floor in favor of the pistol wedged in his belt.

"Hey!" he started.

And stopped. Hesitating not for a moment, Alexander barreled into him, slamming a knee into his groin and then the same knee into his face when the man doubled over. Alexander felt his nose mash on impact, his cheekbones seeming to buckle as he let out a wheezing sound like air fleeing a balloon.

Alerted by the sound of glass breaking from the discarded tray, another pair of lineman-size figures rushed Alexander out of the darkness, seeming to rise out of the floor.

"Stop!" one of the men said, both freeing their pistols.

Alexander kept going, spilling their legs out from under them and shattering their knees with vicious kicks before they could fire their own pistols, continuing on without breaking stride as he collected their fallen weapons and left them screaming in his wake.

"Mr. Tiranno," the voice of the host chimed in his ear, "the matter of this employee of the Seven Sins Elysium show who was found murdered in Turkey has also surfaced."

"A true tragedy."

"Did you know her?"

"I know and care about all of my employees, for their loyalty and devotion. I can't tell you I remember Amanda Johansen personally, but I can tell you I won't rest until the person who harmed her is brought to justice."

"So what do you have to say about an investigation conducted by Interpol into your possible culpability in her death?"

"Did you ask Interpol about that?" Michael challenged, fighting to retain his composure, imagining Naomi's voice inside his head.

"We inquired and never heard back."

"That's because there is no investigation, never was. It was a rogue agent who spurred all this."

"And that would be Edward Devereaux, the man who died in your casino during last week's blackout in Las Vegas, isn't that right?"

More of the doors along the hall were opening now, customers peeking out from inside whatever fantasies they'd paid exorbitant fees to bring to life. Alexander glimpsed enough to curdle the contents of his stomach, evidence of depravity of the sort everyone hears about but wants to believe could never happen.

Alexander continued on toward the door at the end of the hall.

"Actually," Michael corrected, "the unfortunate victim's real name was Faustin. He had registered in the hotel under an alias."

"Why would he do that?"

"I can't even begin to speculate."

"So you're saying this man's charges have no basis in fact, that you are totally innocent and the victim of harassment."

"The only real victim here is Amanda Johansen," Michael said. "But, yes, I'm totally innocent."

Alexander kicked in the door, finding Victor Argos pressed against the far wall, holding a pistol against a naked girl's head.

"Really, Victor? How badly do you want to die?" Alexander asked him.

Argos dropped the pistol.

"Mr. Tiranno, what would you like to tell the millions of visitors who patronize your casino every year?"

"The same thing I'm telling you, Barbara. That I'm cooperating fully with law enforcement and using all means at my disposal to assist them in their efforts. Nobody wants the real guilty parties here found more than I do."

"In order to clear your name, right?"

Michael leaned in toward the camera, cracking the slightest of smiles in a brazen show of confidence and self-assurance. "Tell me, Barbara, do I look like a guilty man to you?"

NINETY-SIX

LAKE LAS VEGAS, NEVADA

The man hung from the balcony off which Michael fed his big cats, supported only by rope that was more like clothesline and seemed to be weakening by the moment. The cats gathered beneath him, growling and pacing, occasionally rising up on their haunches in anticipation of a meal.

A living one potentially tonight, adding to their excitement.

"Victor Argos," Michael said, reading from the man's wallet as Alexander looked on. "I'm going to assume that's not your real name, but it'll do for now."

"I'll scream!" he cried out, between desperate heaves of breath.

"Go ahead. Roma Vetus is too isolated for anyone to hear and then you'd leave me no choice but to ring the dinner bell," Michael said, holding up an end of the rope that featured a knot that was all holding the man in place.

"You'll never get away with this!"

"Get away with it? I think the city of Las Vegas will name another road after me for getting rid of a man involved with a human trafficking ring in the city."

"Don't be so sure," Argos said, trying for a smirk that never came.

"And why's that?"

"Let's just say several city officials know all about what's going on, *high-ranking* city officials."

"And I'll deal with them in good time. Right now, you're the one on my menu."

"Fuck you! You think I'm nobody? You think I haven't got the right people in this town behind me? You think I don't have the kind of powerful friends who won't eat you for lunch?"

"Right now, the only person in danger of being eaten is you, Victor. And I'm not worried about these powerful friends of yours. In fact, I'd like to meet them and introduce them to my big cats, too."

"Pull me up! Pull me up!"

A low guttural growl sounded and Michael swung to see Nero standing just behind him, his black hindquarters turned sideways so Argos could see him, too. "Let's start with the most simple and obvious. You're the one who kidnapped Amanda Johansen, yes?"

Argos swallowed hard, tried to still the trembling of his lips.

"I asked you a question, Victor," Michael said. "I'm going to assume you know who I am, my reputation."

Argos nodded. He had the look of a fake playboy, a caricature more than a man. No part of him looked real, not his skin, his hair, his teeth, not even his eyes. A character created for a specific purpose.

Michael showed him the rope. "If I let you go now, we'll dispose of what little remains will be left over. My cats haven't eaten since yesterday so right now you look like breakfast, lunch, and dinner all rolled into one. They'll have to subpoena my big cats to find your DNA in their stomachs which will probably be shitted out by dawn. Amanda Johansen worked for me, Victor. That means I was responsible for her well-being. And when you fucked her, you fucked me, too. You can see why I have no patience for your silence. So let's make this simple: Answer the question or, first, I'll give my cats a taste of your blood and then I'll feed you to them."

"Yes!" the man yelped suddenly, eyes fixed downward.

"Yes *what*?"

"Yes, I arranged the woman's kidnapping."

"Good. Then we're getting somewhere."

"She was taken to the Middle East like all the others."

Michael stiffened at that. "How many others?"

"Two dozen over the past year."

"Two per month."

"Those were just mine. There are other men like me operating in town."

"Because this is the perfect city out of which to operate, isn't it, Victor? So many beautiful women coming and going, traveling from somewhere else to get here. No one knows them and it takes time for them to be missed."

Argos managed a nod. "I made a mistake choosing a resident, someone who lived here, someone who . . ."

"Worked for me?" Michael finished when the man's voice tailed off. "Yes, I believe we can safely say you made a very bad choice there." He exchanged a quick glance with Alexander. "And you took all these women for Black Scorpion, right?"

Argos looked genuinely confused. "Who?"

Michael exchanged a longer look with Alexander. "Who do you work for, Victor?"

No response.

Michael let the rope slide down just a bit farther.

"No, wait! You're right, I work for an international human trafficking syndicate. It doesn't have a name. Just phone numbers and e-mail addresses that change constantly. When I deliver a girl, money gets deposited into an account. That's the procedure. It's all I know."

"What about other cities?"

Argos looked befuddled. "I don't know what goes on in other cities. I keep to my business. You think I want to fuck with these people?"

"Right now, you're fucking with me."

Michael loosened the knot, giving more slack to the rope so Argos's feet jerked down a foot lower, just out of reach of the big cats when they leaped, starting to work themselves into a frenzy. Then Alexander came forward and dumped a tray of raw meat blood juice from their last feeding all over Argos.

"You want to rethink your last answer, Victor?"

"I'm telling you the truth!"

Michael leaned over the railing to better regard Argos, who'd crimped his legs up as high as he could. He noticed a lion tearing one of the man's shoes apart on the lawn below.

"I believe you, Victor, and I also believe they'd never trust a lowlife like you with anything important. I should've known this would be a waste of time, leaving you in no position to tell me what I need to know to destroy the organization you're working for. Good thing you mentioned those high-ranking Las Vegas officials, because their names are going to keep you alive. You're going to tell the authorities everything you know, how the process of selection and kidnapping goes. You're going to confirm the existence of an international organization that runs it all, an organization you're beholden to and are probably almost as frightened of as you are of me. Almost."

And that's when Michael's phone rang.

"Hello?"

"It's Raven, Brother."

NINETY-SEVEN

LAS VEGAS, NEVADA

Michael was leaning casually against his Lamborghini directly outside the entrance to the Mandalay Bay valet the next morning, when Special Agent Del Slocumb emerged from inside.

"Enjoy your stuffed French toast, Agent? I hear Raffles makes the best in the business."

Slocumb stiffened, his cocoa-colored skin seeming to pale briefly as his gaze flitted from side to side, as if expecting Michael wouldn't be alone.

"It's just you and me," Michael told him. "I would've invited you out to breakfast, but since I've been barred from my place of business, I don't know when my next paycheck's coming."

"What do you want, Tiranno?"

Michael dangled the Lamgorghini's keys. "Let's go for a ride."

"Excuse me?"

"It's time we had a talk, you and me."

Slocumb stiffened again. "I'm afraid I can't—"

"It's in your best interests. And . . ." Michael tossed him the keys, Slocumb snatching them cleanly out of the air. ". . . you can drive."

Slocumb drove slowly and clumsily at first, having trouble getting used to having the paddle shifters on the steering wheel.

"That's why you want to have your hands in the ten and two positions, instead of the nine and three," Michael instructed. "Remember, there's no clutch. You only need one foot to drive, just like an automatic transmission. But keep your left foot on the rest to maintain your balance at high speeds. Welcome aboard the Tyrant Class model, the only one currently in existence. Isn't that right, Angel?" he said, words aimed at the touch screen that controlled virtually everything in the car.

"Yes, Michael, it is," a sultry female voice returned.

"Say hello to Agent Slocumb, Angel."

"Hello, asshole."

"Angel," Michael scoffed playfully, "you should be ashamed of yourself."

"I couldn't help it, Michael."

"Very funny," Slocumb snickered, still trying to familiarize himself with the controls. He adjusted his hands and Michael watched his fingers tighten, looking uncomfortable. "How fast can this thing actually go?"

"Two hundred miles per hour, give or take. I've driven the track at those speeds but the same principles with this baby apply when it comes to braking for a corner on regular roads. What you want to do, Agent, is brake hard initially and then pull off gradually, rather then depressing the pedal slowly. If the strength of the brake was on a scale from one to ten, with ten being the strongest, you want to start at ten and get to three before you even start to turn the steering wheel."

"Wow," Slocumb said, trying just that at the next street.

"See, we both love a great ride. We both appreciate what true power can yield."

Slocumb seemed too focused on the road to respond.

"I think you're as ambitious as I am, Agent, in your own way. I think you latched on to me to further your career and now you can't let go even though the weight of this is bringing you down. What if I could give you something bigger, something that would make you famous in the annals of law enforcement? I'm talking book deals, talk shows. Naomi told me you and she met at the Mob Museum. Well, you listen to what I have to say and you'll end up with your own exhibit, bigger than Estes Kefauver or Elliot Ness ever dreamed of being. I'll really miss our friendly little chats once you get promoted to Special Agent in Charge of a big office, maybe even an assistant director in Washington."

Slocumb continued to keep his gaze fixed forward out the windshield, never even turning Michael's way. "I need to advise you that anything you say to me can and will be used against you in a court of law."

Michael rolled his eyes. "Save the speech for true criminals, Agent. We're just having a friendly conversation." He pointed ahead of them. "Take that ramp up there for the freeway and open her up a bit. Speed limit's seventy-five, Agent, but I don't suppose I need to remind you of that."

Slocumb eased onto the ramp accessing the freeway. The Lamborghini rumbled on, straining a bit like a thorough-bred being held back down the stretch. Welcoming the burst of acceleration that followed Slocumb's entry into the climbing lane as he merged with traffic by flying past all of it in an effortless burst.

"Two words," Michael said, once Slocumb was neatly settled in the right lane doing sixty, the Lamborghini bucking as if begging for more. "Black Scorpion."

Slocumb looked his way briefly, a combination of recognition and disbelief flashing in his eyes. "Nasty bastards from what I've heard. But you might as well have said 'boogeyman.' And it's out of my jurisdiction anyway. They don't operate in the U.S."

"Wrong again, Agent. It was the boogeyman who kidnapped Amanda Johansen. The man who arranged it all is waiting to have a talk with you and anyone else you want to bring in. Not too many, since you don't want somebody else getting the credit for the bust that will allow you to write your own ticket. This man will confirm everything I'm saying is true. He can't wait to talk to you."

"How's that exactly?"

"Let's just say he found God and wants to clear his conscience. And you don't have to just take his word for it, Agent, because it turns out the chief of the Las Vegas police department is on the boogeyman's payroll, among other officials I'm sure you'll want to have a friendly little conversation with."

Slocumb looked across the seat again, warily, as if expecting Michael to go on and hoping he wouldn't. "Say I was interested."

"What if I had a list of where Black Scorpion's largest cells were headquartered across the United States, as well as Europe, the Middle East, South America, Asia, Russia, and beyond?" Michael told him, thinking of his conversation with Raven Khan the previous night. "Imagine being celebrated as the hero who brought down the world's largest criminal organization, now operating freely right here in the homeland. Who better to coordinate the international effort to take them down than the FBI? You are the FBI, aren't you?"

Slocumb's eyes narrowed. "Which begs the question, how do you know all this?"

"Amanda Johansen worked for me. Enough said?"

"No, not even close."

"Then pull the car over and get out. Angel will call you a cab. Won't you, Angel?"

"Dialing now, Michael."

"Hold on," Slocumb blared toward the screen.

"Yes, asshole."

He snickered again but didn't pull over. "If you're wrong, or setting me up, I'll bury you, Tiranno."

"If I'm wrong, Agent, I'll give you the shovel."

NINETY-EIGHT

HOIA-BACIU FOREST, ROMANIA

Vladimir Dracu felt the scorpion venom pulsing through his veins, mixing with his blood to fight back the disease that otherwise would have consumed him long ago. He had ordered Armura to remain outside his quarters in the mountain fortress so he might be alone with his thoughts.

Right now, the indescribable agony slowly ebbed to be replaced by a soothing warmth indicative of the venom laying waste to the pestilence that was turning his body against itself. Feeling the euphoria beginning to take hold, Dracu studied his priceless collection of paintings. No matter how many times he looked at them, he always saw something he'd never noticed before. Yet they never changed, remaining forever frozen in time just as he felt the venom did for him. His appearance had remained the same for twenty years now, the scorpion venom seemingly having stopped aging in its tracks along with the disease that would still ultimately kill him.

But who knew when now, who knew anything like that for sure? The venom could halt the process, though do nothing to reverse the ravaging effects the disease had already produced. Often he'd watched his veins grow flush with dark color after a sting, knowing that the pain was soon to follow and would remain until the color receded. Maybe someday it wouldn't recede. Maybe someday it would cling to his veins and mark his final undoing before the wretched disease could finish its work.

Or maybe there was something out there that could prolong, even assure, his survival indefinitely. Something currently in the possession of his half brother.

He looked up and suddenly, amid the euphoria seizing him, the paintings spread about the walls didn't look as they normally did, the light striking them differently for some reason in that moment. Light changed everything, light controlled what you could see and couldn't see. Light could reveal incipient beauty or ugliness and sometimes, depending on one's perspective, they were one in the same.

But Dracu had learned long ago light was something that could not be controlled with near the same effectiveness as darkness. Darkness bred fear and fear made people predictable, reducing lives to their most base form. So he had come to embrace darkness, to master its exploitation and simplicity. As a child, light had neither brought his father to him, nor saved his mother, nor kept him from a life of unspeakable pain, both physical and psychological. Light had not stopped him from becoming a victim.

So Dracu had turned to darkness. When he killed his first love, when he murdered his own father, when he came back to Romania after the fall of communism to build Black Scorpion, when he returned to the farm that should've been his home to confront Michael Tiranno. There was no point in trying to find light amid the darkness; much better to turn that light dark.

And thus control it.

He wondered if his half brother understood the true purpose behind the plan that had begun when he rescued Niels Taupmann from the gulag. But Michael Tiranno wouldn't, *couldn't*, because he lived in the light and like virtually all men was blind amid the darkness. He'd never be able to conceive of Dracu's true intentions because to do so intrinsically meant understanding the depths of depravity from which he had risen. His half brother considered himself a victim, too, forever scarred by witnessing the massacre of his family at Dracu's very hands. But that experience had hardly been enough to turn him away from the light, because Michael Tiranno chose to battle the tides, swimming upstream into that light instead of joining the smooth currents of darkness.

Because the relic was his. For now.

And in just over twenty-four hours Dracu would not enter the light so much as drag the darkness with him over it. An eclipse of his making was coming and he couldn't wait for that magical moment when darkness at last swallowed the light, literally as well as figuratively.

He found himself studying a landscape draped almost entirely in shadows, a painting Niels Taupmann had drawn for him of a single farmer working in fields ahead of an approaching storm.

"There's something you need to see in this," the old man had said proudly, upon presenting the painting to him.

"What might that be, Professor?"

The old man had gone back to sucking on a marijuana blunt. "I don't know."

Today, though, Dracu looked at the landscape and grasped the message Taupmann had instinctively fashioned. The farmer could no more avoid the storm building overhead in the painting, than Michael Tiranno could avoid the one about to consume him. But it wasn't enough for Dracu to imagine the fall of the Tyrant any more than it was to imagine the farmer being swept away by the winds and torrents.

"A man with your vision? You are a great artist, my friend, on a different canvas of your own choosing."

More of Taupmann's words, Dracu finally able to understand the old man's message: He needed to be *there*, inside the painting drawn by his own hand featuring a storm of equal savagery. He needed to witness the ravaging of Michael Tiranno's world firsthand, not while standing back as he was to this landscape. Because he was the artist and this was all happening based on his own notion of what the world's shape should be and where he should fit within it.

And then, for the first time in all the times he'd studied Taupmann's painting, Dracu realized the farmer's gaze was tilted toward the sky and the source of his own coming destruction. Just as Michael Tiranno needed to see the source of his to realize the fury about to consume him and swallow all he had built.

Not from here, Dracu thought, feeling the scorpion venom spread the pleasure through his veins, *not from my old home.*

From my next one.

Where he would reclaim not only his destiny, but also the means to achieve it.

NINETY-NINE

SARDINIA

Aldridge Sterling positioned his father's wheelchair so the old man could follow the action unfolding on a half dozen monitors dangling from the ceiling at the back of his glass-top desk.

"How does it feel, Father?" he asked, standing over his father's form, inert save for the drool dribbling from his mouth. "How does it feel watching the son you despised becoming rich beyond anything you can possibly conceive?"

Sterling moved in front of his father, stopping short this time of sponging up the old man's drool. He seemed to be viewing only the screen directly over him, eyes fixed forward as always, perhaps attracted by the motion of color the way an animal might. But Sterling wanted his father to *see* it all. He remained convinced that at some rudimentary level inside his mind, Senator Harold Sterling could indeed grasp the implied message and was being tortured by the reality of his son's ultimate triumph even now. Aldridge Sterling would never know for sure, but the mere possibility of his father's comprehension intensified the excitement and satisfaction that continued to unfold before him.

Sterling manually positioned his father's head to face the first of the six screens, each split into two separate scrolls of ever-changing numbers. "That's Hong Kong and Tokyo." He moved his father's head again. "London and Nassau." A third time. "Kuala Lampur and Moscow." A fourth. "Saigon and Seoul." His father seemed to resist the firth turn, but Sterling persisted and felt something crackle in the old man's skeletal neck. "Caracas and Lagos." And one final, effortless turn. "Lichtenstein and Panama City. All offices of Sterling Capital Partners, Father. Currency is traded in pairs, the price of each set in terms of the other. What you're watching is a hundred billion dollars being pumped into currency markets through my offices across the world. Shorting the American dollar means betting on these other native currencies to hold or increase their value as the dollar declines steeply and sharply. The difference becomes the profit. And would you like to hear how much that profit is?"

The drool was dribbling down onto Harold Sterling's bib now.

"That's right, father. Your son is on the verge of becoming one of the richest men in the world, maybe the richest. And you know the best of it? History will remember my name long after yours is forgotten. What was that, Father?" Sterling asked, leaning over. "At a loss for words, are you? Speechless over what I've been able achieve with no help from you. You know why? Let me show you." He eased his father's wheelchair closer to the screens. "Because I'm a fucking genius. The son you disowned doing something no man has ever done before. And the only thing you gave me was your fucking DNA and you can take that back, too, along with everything else you took away."

Sterling stopped and angled his father's head so the old man's unfeeling eyes met his. "Witness your legacy, Father.

"Me," Sterling finished.

ONE HUNDRED

VADJA, ROMANIA

Alexander rendezvoused with Raven Khan in the village of Vadja, where the same municipal building where she'd met the town elders initially became their staging ground for a planned attack on Black Scorpion. Those same elders had agreed to facilitate their needs, no longer trusting the authorities and believing Alexander and Raven, along with whoever was backing them, were the only ones who could get their children back.

Michael promised to supply any and all resources they required for men and equipment, no matter the cost, to be channeled through secret, untraceable offshore accounts. A fund he'd established after the terrorist attack on Vegas five years earlier in case a new enemy surfaced. And whatever was needed from that fund would go to the GS-Ultra group with which Paddy was associated. Alexander had then immediately reached out to his most trusted and expert contacts, relying on Paddy to add a dozen or more special operators to the number he was able to gather, along with all the equipment and ordnance required. Raven, meanwhile, summoned the best of the criminal cutthroats she used for her most elaborate operations: Killers first and foremost, all veterans of military units, who in this case would be receiving exorbitant fees for the risks associated with their efforts. Still a bargain, given that they'd be going up against an extremely well-fortified target defended by somewhere between a hundred and two hundred men, by all indications, who were all trained killers.

The problem remained finding Black Scorpion's headquarters. It could be located anywhere in the sprawling Black Forest, maybe underground or even under one of the myriad of lakes, for all Raven or Alexander knew. And without a firm location inside an endless forest of lore, they could not plan an attack, never mind mount one no matter the troops and ordnance Michael's resources afforded them.

Though hardly experienced in confrontations of this scale, Raven knew they'd have to stage their attack from multiple positions at once. But there were hostages, the young women and children of Vadja, to consider first and foremost in her mind, her task being to rescue them while

Alexander and his men laid waste to what was certain to be a well-defended fortress. Kill Vladimir Dracu and, if at all possible, recover an ancient manuscript of great importance to her brother.

"There's something you need to know, big man," Raven said. "Dracu has a bodyguard the villagers say is as big as a tree and just as strong."

"All moot if we can't find where he's hiding," Alexander said, as he continued to study standard satellite photographs and imagery of the area to no avail.

A knock fell on the door ahead of a woman with snow-white hair entering with a very old man in tow. She supported him every step of the way, like a human cane.

"You promised you would bring back our young women and children," the woman said to Raven, not even acknowledging Alexander's presence.

"I know. And I will."

"You promise on your life?"

"Yes," Raven said, nodding.

"My grandchildren are among them," the woman said solemnly, turning toward the hobbled old man Raven realized was plagued by tremors. "This is their great-grandfather. He has something he wishes to show you."

With his daughter's help, the old man moved toward the wall papered with schematics, maps, and satellite images of the Hoia-Baciu Forest. He spotted a mountainous section, approached the satellite image, and managed to circle one mountain in particular with a pen he'd snatched from a nearby table. He began to jabber away in Romanian, his tremors making his words slur into one another.

"He says he worked as a structural engineer for the Soviets here during the Cold War because he knew the land better than anyone," his daughter translated for them into English, "where best to hide their nuclear missile silos. He says those silos are scattered in the area he just circled, contained beneath a man-made lake the Soviets built to disguise their presence. Apparently one of the primary command and control bunkers for the Soviet nuclear arsenal based in Eastern Europe was built inside a huge cave system located within the mountain this lake surrounds, accessible by a system of tunnels that link the silos. There is a river that flows over the top of the mountain, feeding the lake and a waterfall."

"You're saying this bunker is inside *the mountain*?" Alexander interrupted.

"My father is saying that, yes," the woman confirmed.

She stopped and listened to the old man continuing his tale, stammering through some of the words and stopping only when his breath finally deserted him.

"He says the waterfall is a doorway. He says he was working for the Soviets when they built the entrance to the bunker directly behind that waterfall, made to look like part of the mountain itself. He says that's where you may find Black Scorpion."

"If that's the place, I'll return," Raven promised, her gaze fixed on the circled area along with Alexander's, "with your children in tow."

"Not if we don't get a better idea of what we're going to be facing inside this bunker, if it's really the place we're looking for," Alexander said, unclasping the satellite phone from his belt and dialing Paddy's number.

"Miss me already, mate?"

"Looks like I need something else. Where are you?"

A knock fell on the door and one of the gypsies yanked it open.

Paddy stood there, speaking into the satellite phone he was still holding. "Right here, you bloody wanker."

ONE HUNDRED ONE

"Mr. Tiranno," said Commissioner Kern of the Nevada Gaming Control Board, taking on the chore of swearing Michael in himself today, "please raise your right hand. Do you solemnly swear to tell the truth, the whole truth, and nothing but the truth, so help you God?"

"I do," said Michael, waiting for Kern to be seated before taking his own.

He stole a glance toward the hearing chamber's rear as the crowd noise dropped to a murmur and silenced altogether, spotting FBI special agent Del Slocumb seated in the very back. Slocumb nodded. Michael nodded back, having just heard the news about the chief of the Las Vegas police department being taken into custody by federal authorities. He was about to turn away when he spotted the same small man he recalled from the previous week's hearing, with the awful comb-over wearing the same rumpled suit from the last time. He was holding a Mont Blanc pen again that looked out of place in his hand.

"Mr. Tiranno, this hearing has been called to further determine your fitness to hold a gaming license, entitling you to the privilege of operating a casino in this state," Kern began, the words droning from memory. "I am required to inform you that while you are under oath, you are still protected by your Fifth Amendment rights against self-incrimination."

"I have nothing to hide, Mr. Chairman," Michael responded, feeling Naomi tense alongside him. "I have every intention of answering each and every question posed to me."

"I'm glad to hear that, Mr. Tiranno, because the bonds of Tyrant Global, King Midas World, and the Seven Sins Resort are plummeting even as we sit here."

"That will change soon, Mr. Chairman, not quite as we sit here, but soon enough."

"Refreshing news, since new information has come to this committee between hearings in the wake of your recent travels and a death at your hotel that further complicates your standing." Kern leaned forward, pushing the microphone ahead of him and looking like a poker player who'd just drawn a full house. "Would you care to explain?"

Michael eased the microphone before him. "I had business to attend to in London."

"London?"

"I believe that's what I said."

"You spent three days in London. That is your statement."

"It is, Mr. Chairman, and I'm prepared to present my hotel bills and restaurant receipts through my stay. I was in the city to meet with a number of investment bankers representing European money to help rectify the current financial situation you referenced that escalated in the aftermath of the recent blackout and tragic death at my casino. You'll be happy to hear I sufficiently reassured them."

"Indeed, Mr. Tiranno, and this committee will give all due notice to these bills and receipts, although something more evidentiary would be of far more use in helping to prove your case."

"I wasn't aware I had a case to prove. But, since you asked . . ."

With that, Naomi rose and approached the dais, handing an eight by ten photograph up to Kern. "This is a picture of Mr. Tiranno and his girlfriend, Scarlett Swan, taken by paparazzi while they were exiting a restaurant in London," she informed the committee, reassured that Michael's strategy to have her "arrange" just such a photo opportunity after landing in London from Caltagirone had proven fortuitous indeed. So, too, on his instructions she had arranged a pair of actual meetings for him with bankers scheduled around the meal, further establishing the validity of his alibi. "Another picture, snapped by paparazzi, appeared in several London gossip rags," she continued. "And I can also present to this committee evidentiary materials attesting to meetings held while Mr. Tiranno was in the city."

"That won't be necessary at this time," Kern said, taking his glasses off and putting them back on, as if to stall for time.

MUMBAI, INDIA

Prakash Singh, captain of the elite commando team attached to the Indian Police Service in Mumbai, waited until he was certain all his men were in position before giving the signal. To avoid suspicion, they'd been gathering for upward of an hour in the innocuous disguises of street vendors, beggars, and street cleaners charged with making this the most beautiful city in the world.

All were now in place before the majestic Greek Revival building secured behind a high security fence. Locals had long assumed its palatial confines set against the Arabian Sea held a prestigious school for girls. The security, even the helipad perched on the roof, was understandable since the city had been on edge ever since a small band of men had terrorized it just a few years before. Singh's rapid response team of commandos had been formed in the wake of that, ready to deploy at a moment's notice with training received at the hands of the American Special Forces under their belt, one of whom he thought he recognized while his men were gearing up back at the operation's staging ground.

Singh had never given the girl's school a single thought

until today, had asked that his orders be repeated to make sure he'd heard right.

A coordinated international attack, the rules of engagement that of war instead of a typical police action, a target as dangerous as any terrorist or Pakistani offensive.

Black Scorpion.

Even now, Singh could barely believe it himself. His father, a former director general of police, had dismissed the organization's existence as a myth, an old wives' tale concocted to excuse police failures at bringing down ordinary criminal gangs cloaked in a fantasy of evil. Singh himself had always suspected otherwise, even though he couldn't prove it, and now his suspicions had been justified.

He checked his watch, a gift from his father, and began the mental countdown in his head. He had twelve men with him because any more would've been certain to arouse suspicion from whoever was watching from inside the building. Once Singh's forces secured the perimeter, Indian Army troops were prepared to storm the compound with armored vehicles from the front and helicopter gunships from the sea at the rear. All it would take was his signal at the proper time.

Singh waited for his father's watch to reach the moment of his attack, watching the second hand draw out the final minute.

"Go!" he ordered his men finally.

And a half hour later, the American Special Forces operator Singh thought he'd recognized earlier in the day lifted a phone from his forward observation post. "Mumbai is down," was all he said.

"I remind you you're under oath, Mr. Tiranno," Kern resumed. "Tell me, sir, have you been to Italy in the past week?"

"No."

"What about Sicily?"

"No, again."

"It is your contention, then, that you flew to London and remained there for the entire time you were away from Las Vegas."

"It is," Michael told him, "as I've already indicated. And if you require additional photographs . . ."

"I'm sure you could provide them." Kern looked put off for a moment, before quickly regaining his composure. "Mr. Tiranno, you disrespect this committee the same way you disrespect this city and this country," he resumed, voice growing louder and almost shrill through the microphone. "I believe you are a dangerous man who spits in the face of laws and any authority that seeks to challenge him. I believe you're a bully of the worst kind, one who doesn't mind or care who he leaves crushed in his wake, a man who's left a trail of blood that rivals any left by the infamous gangsters who formed the original scourge of this city.

"Because that's what I believe you are, Mr. Tiranno: A scourge, even though I may not be able to prove it. A symbol of excess and non-accountability who should name a bulldozer after his company instead of a car, a phone, or a jet. Would you like me to continue?"

"Please do," Michael told him calmly.

THAILAND

The Thai Army had closed all the main roads leading into Khao Sok National Park before the attack began. Waves of troops getting as close to the dense jungle as the trucks could bring them before climbing off and proceeding on foot. Their target was a sprawling camp pinpointed by satellite reconnaissance after intelligence furnished by the American government marked the camp's general location amid overgrowth of giant parasitic flowers. Those flowers had earned their name and reputation from sapping the life out of the vines to which they were attached in order to thrive.

Whoever was occupying the camp had done much the same thing to the jungle itself, dirtying it with landmines, trip wires, and other crude security systems. That alone was enough for Colonel Nyu, the attack's leader and an ardent believer in his country's beauty, to despise his targets. He would lead the attack from the front, vicious and relentless enough to distract the camp's soldiers from a second wave that would descend on the enemy from its rear flank where a waterfall spilled water into a luscious green lagoon. It had taken that phalanx of his troops more time to get into position than expected, making Nyu fear he might not be able to stage his attack at the apportioned time. But then the snipers he'd staged along the tree line reported in, telling him just what he needed to hear.

"I have twelve targets in my sector."

"Eight in mine."

"Ten in the northeast."

"Sixteen on the southwest flank."

Nyu pictured the sights as the snipers rotated their scopes, zeroing their soon-to-be targets once the attack commenced. Just then his second-in-command lowered a walkie-talkie from his lips and nodded, indication that his troops staging by the waterfall were now in place.

"We move on my signal," Nyu said into his walkie-talkie. "Spare no one and burn all the drugs."

Just within earshot, an American in civilian clothes moved to a shady space and raised a satellite phone to his ear in a callused hand. "Thailand is underway."

ONE HUNDRED TWO

CARSON CITY, NEVADA

"We may not have firm proof of criminality on your part, Mr. Tiranno," Kern resumed, "but the old saying that where there's smoke, there's fire has never been more true than in this case. Unless we are to pass all these allegations and suspicions off to coincidence, it stands to reason that you are a dangerous man who has no place operating a casino in the city of Las Vegas or the state of Nevada, or anywhere else for that matter."

Michael pretended to be flipping through pages.

"Do you have a response, Mr. Tiranno?"

"I'm sorry, Mr. Chairman, I was searching through your rule book for the section on innuendo and rumor. Apparently, this edition left out the fact that either can be grounds for the revocation of a gaming license."

Kern rapped his gavel on the desk before him, when the crowd responded to Michael's statement with a smattering of applause.

"Mr. Chairman," Michael said, seizing the moment, "may I make a brief statement?"

"So long as it's relevant to these proceedings."

"It addresses one of your primary concerns, specifically the Forbidden City."

"More excuses and explanations, Mr. Tiranno?"

"No, quite the opposite," Michael replied, speaking as much to the crowd squeezed into the hearing chamber behind him as Kern, "I'm happy to report that the Forbidden City will officially open in three months time."

Now it was Kern who leaned forward, looking more dismayed than surprised. "And what happened to the tour we were promised?"

"I'm prepared to schedule it at your convenience, as early as tomorrow, and have brought in some of the Forbidden City's primary props to provide you as full an experience as possible."

"Props, Mr. Tiranno?"

"I'm afraid I can't elaborate further," Michael said, smiling. "That would ruin the surprise."

"So as long as you don't expect these props to turn this committee's attention away from the recent death that forced you to close your so-called Daring Sea suites. This legendary vision of yours is killing people, isn't it? And let's not that forget that it further weakened your financial position and is certain to cause even more untold losses, only adding to your exposure in the marketplace and making your company a prime target for takeover. Especially given your increasingly weak liquid position."

"That's about to change. We're expecting a cash infusion in the coming days."

"Please be specific."

"All I can say at this time is that a substantial investment fund is about to put all its strength behind my company."

Kern's spine straightened, his bluster returning. "This committee will not accept such vague assurances."

Naomi stole a glance toward Michael and watched him nod ever so slightly. "In that case," she said, sliding the microphone before her, "I have a few questions for you, if you don't mind, Mr. Chairman."

BEIJING, CHINA

The gunfight began ferociously but quickly grew sporadic before fading altogether as the Chinese Ministry of Public

Security forces overwhelmed the building's meager defenses. Of course, security around this abandoned factory,
located in a decrepit slum Chinese and Beijing officials
referred to as an "inner-city village," was understandably
light given that the proper officials had been paid off.

That had not stopped the waves of trucks and troops from
descending on the area and bulldozing their way into the
factory where tons and tons of weapons were held for planned
shipment all over the world. The factory functioned as a kind
of clearinghouse, a fulfillment center from which orders
were packaged to extremist, paramilitary and criminal organizations on every continent.

Colonel Yan Ling, his blue police uniform encased in
body armor, entered to find the last of the surviving guards
being rounded up and the bodies of those guards killed in
the gunfight hastily covered with sheets his men had brought
along for just that task. Around him, stacked on shelves that
stretched the entire three-story height to the ceiling, was an
assortment of military grade ordnance far beyond even that
of the MPS supply depots. Light and heavy weapons alike,
in addition to a lifetime's supply of ammunition for all of
them, explosive devices, hand grenades, state-of-the-art
shoulder-held rocket launchers, even some smaller artillery
pieces.

Ling stood stiffly, having seen enough to end his inspection here, unable to calculate the potential cost to human life
held within this abandoned factory.

"Captain," he called to his second-in-command, "you
have your orders."

"Destroy the building and leave nothing behind."

Ling nodded and turned to the "official" from the American embassy who'd accompanied him inside in the raid's
aftermath. "I imagine the results please you?"

"Very much," the man said.

He lifted a phone from his pocket and stepped aside,

dialing a number that would be answered without benefit of a ring.

"China is down," he reported.

"That is highly irregular, Ms. Burns," Kern said, tapping the frame of his reading glasses against the table.

"Humor me, sir, if you don't mind. But I'd recommend we move to a closed session."

"Why?" Kern smirked. "Mr. Tiranno may have plenty to hide, but I don't."

"Then you won't mind explaining this picture," Naomi told him, as a photograph suddenly claimed the screen dangling behind the commission members, picturing Kern greeting a man on an airport tarmac before a private jet.

"Not at all. The man's name is Aldridge Sterling. I was meeting him as a courtesy when Mr. Sterling came to explore expanding his considerable interests into gaming here in Nevada."

"Came here?"

"Yes."

"But this picture was taken at a Long Island airport where Mr. Sterling flew you in on his private jet to enjoy a weekend at his mansion in the Hamptons last summer."

A quiet murmur sifted through the crowd.

"That wasn't for pleasure," Kern tried to insist, putting his glasses back on and taking them off again. "It was more a trip to ascertain the true boundaries of Mr. Sterling's intention to invest heavily in our state's gaming industry."

"Then I assume you reported this trip and meeting to the proper ethics officials."

Kern stiffened, just enough to show his discomfort. "This hearing is not about me, Ms. Burns."

"Then perhaps it should be. Would you like to explain, for the record, your relationship with Aldridge Sterling?"

"That's irrelevant to the purpose of this hearing."

"Is it, Mr. Kern? In spite of the fact that this is the same Aldridge Sterling who's been buying up King Midas World and Tyrant Global bonds at less than fifty cents on the dollar after the recent ordeal at the Seven Sins and the publicity stemming from last week's hearing before this board. Wouldn't you call that a bit coincidental?"

"Not at all."

"What about this?"

Naomi touched the proper icon on her phone app that functioned as a remote control. Instantly the picture of Kern and Sterling together was replaced by six pages arranged side-by-side in two rows across the wide screen.

"These are recent brokerage statements showing a position with Sterling Capital Partners, modest by Sterling Capital's usual standards but still amounting to over five hundred and eighty thousand dollars. Recognize them, Mr. Kern?"

"I can't say I do."

"You should, because the brokerage account numbers linked back to a woman with the same name as your wife."

Kern didn't turn around to look. "Since when is making a wise investment a crime?"

"When it's a potential ethics violation definitely worthy of an investigation. Why else would you hide it by having your wife use her maiden name? At the very least," Naomi continued over the murmur that had intensified through the crowded chamber, "you cannot expect to keep overseeing this particular investigation as a fair and impartial arbiter. Unless you'd like to further explain your relationship with Aldridge Sterling and your association with his attempt to buy the Seven Sins on the cheap."

"This insolence has gone far enough," Kern said. He slammed his gavel down on the desktop and started to rise. "And this hearing is adjourned."

"Mr. Chairman!" Naomi shouted loud enough to freeze Kern in his tracks. "Before we formally adjourn, I respectfully request that Mr. Tiranno's gaming license and access to his own properties be restored. Otherwise, you leave me no choice but to seek an injunction in—"

"Mr. Tiranno," Kern blared without the microphone, interrupting her, "provisional access is hereby granted to you for the Seven Sins property until such time that this commission can reach a final resolution." He rapped the gavel again. "We are adjourned."

At that, members of the press gathered in the chamber stormed the dais, surrounding Kern before he could exit and battering him with questions. Michael actually had to dodge a pair of television reporters when he stepped into the aisle himself, looking up toward the back row where FBI special agent Del Slocumb was just pocketing his phone. He nodded Michael's way, smiling almost imperceptibly. The man with the Mont Blanc pen, though, was gone and Michael thought he recognized him from his ridiculous comb-over exiting the chamber just as his Samsung Galaxy buzzed with an incoming text from Scarlett.

WATCHING YOU ON TV RIGHT NOW.

Michael turned toward the camera following him and smiled.

ONE HUNDRED THREE

VADJA, ROMANIA

"My god, it's incredible," Raven said, shaking her head while continuing to study the thermal imagery of the mountain the old man had indicated, courtesy of a satellite feed arranged by GS-Ultra.

"Looks like the old man was right," Alexander nodded, his eyes flashing like the lights of a computer.

"Not bad, eh, mate?" Paddy asked Alexander.

"How much you say this is costing my boss again?"

The big Brit winked. "I didn't."

"My God," Raven said, continuing to focus on the prints papering the walls, "these big patches of red show the largest concentration of men, right?"

"The bigger blips are more likely machines," Paddy explained, "but you're right as rain for the most part. Thing looks to be a dozen stories high and you can even see from the scoring where Black Scorpion added the top seven or eight levels."

"And this must be the Soviet command and control bunker," Alexander noted, pointing to what looked to be an underground level where the heat signatures recorded by the satellite imagery were pink, instead of red.

"But what do you make of this, mate?" Paddy asked him, gesturing toward what looked to several more heat signatures also underground, but above and to the right of the command and control bunker.

"Where I expect to find Black Scorpion himself once we're in," Alexander told him. "Exactly where his private quarters should be given the schematics."

"Then it's a good thing I'm coming along to take charge of the rest of the men and make sure we get the door open for the babe here."

"Babe?" Raven raised.

"Spoken with the utmost respect, my lady," Paddy said, feigning a bow.

"Speaking of which," started Alexander, "you're a bit long in the tooth for a mission like this, Sergeant-Major, don't you think?"

"Bollocks, mate! Why should you young blokes have all the fun? Experience is what it's gonna take to pull this off and I got that coming out my arse. And know what else I got? Enough arthritis to tell the weather better than any damn weatherman, and right now my knees say there's a bloody storm brewing for tonight that'll make for ideal cover."

"He's right," Raven told Alexander, checking the latest weather forecast on her phone.

"Lucky for us, then."

"And we'll need plenty of it, mate," Paddy added, "to take down all these bastards."

ONE HUNDRED FOUR

LAS VEGAS, NEVADA

"Del Slocumb?" Naomi repeated, having trouble believing his role in what was transpiring all over the world, as Black Scorpion's cells were being taken down in a series of near-simultaneous strikes.

"With a little help, actually a lot of help, from Homeland Security," Michael told her. "Homeland handled the bulk of the international coordination in conjunction, I'm guessing, with the CIA. But Slocumb was smart, and ambitious, enough to make the call to them himself once the chief of the Las Vegas police confirmed Victor Argos's story. I'm sure that pissed off his superiors no end but he was actually following protocol. Homeland saw it as a national security issue and pushed the red button all over the world."

"How many sites was this coordinated effort able to hit?"

"A dozen at last count, with many more reports yet to come in," Michael said, as the Tyrant Class Gulfstream streaked toward McCarran. "But those are just the primary sites, and they don't include the strikes stateside which are being kept under tight seal, including Las Vegas itself. Thanks to the intelligence provided by Raven Khan, there are hundreds of others that need to be dealt with fast, before those cells have a chance to close up shop once word of the international effort gets out. Our advantage right now is the disparate cells have no knowledge of each other to prevent one from giving up another."

"Meaning we're using one of Black Scorpion's greatest strengths against them. And the cells that are alerted will end up on the run, flushed into the light. You're destroying Black Scorpion, Michael."

"I haven't destroyed anything, not so long as my half brother is still out there."

"There's something else. It's about Hans Wolff," Naomi continued, handing Michael her phone after jogging the screen to an e-mail that had come in during the hearing. "Prepare yourself, because you're not going to believe this. . . ."

And he hadn't, just one more incredible piece of information piled atop all the others in the past week.

Stepping through the entrance to the Seven Sins felt like the first time for Michael, bringing him back not to the gala opening but to the official completion of construction when he entered the lobby alone without fanfare or paparazzi. The smell of fresh granite, polish, lacquer, wood, wax, and cleaning solvent had dominated the air. Only a portion of the electricity had been switched on, so the lobby was lit only by the meager spill of work lights leaving the bulk of it bathed in shadows. But that didn't stop Michael from seeing *everything*, all the fruits of his labor realized. He had to pinch himself to make sure he wasn't still dreaming, since it had been his dreams that had brought him to that moment.

That's what he felt like now, a mere forty-eight hours

after being barred from entering his own property. No one seemed to notice Michael through all the bustle and activity in the lobby. Just the way he liked it, since it gave him the opportunity to see the Seven Sins as others saw it, appreciating the spectacle and magic of it all the more along with the vision that had spawned both. Even though his goals now stretched far beyond this property and the city, the resort would always form the foundation on which everything else was built, would always be home. That explained why being barred from entry two days earlier angered him so much. He'd already lost one home.

He wasn't going to lose another.

Michael realized he hadn't called Scarlett yet with the news. He pulled out his phone, wondering where she might be on the property. According to the time displayed, and assuming all had gone according to plan, the attack launched on Black Scorpion by Alexander and Raven would be commencing any moment.

More guests brushed past him, the Seven Sins returning to the life he knew and loved. That's when Michael spotted the figure of the rumpled man with the bad comb-over he recognized from both Gaming Control Board hearings. The man was seated within the lobby's Peccato Bar Lounge, checking his phone and seeming to pay Michael no heed whatsoever, until he looked up and their eyes met.

The man's showed no spark of recognition, showed nothing at all before returning his gaze to his phone. But something about his gaze left Michael unsettled enough to start toward him. Searching for the nearest plainclothes members of the Seven Sins security force, in the same moment the explosion sounded outside on the Strip.

ONE HUNDRED FIVE

Alexander watched his men strapping on their parachutes aboard the Lockheed L-100 Hercules aircraft, a civilian version of the special-ops-favored C-130 and available thanks to the blank check Michael had provided GS-Ultra. It would be flying under the false designation of a commercial airliner to avoid detection or scrutiny. That meant they'd have to make a HALO jump from around twenty-five thousand feet, the altitude typical in this airspace. All the men hired for the mission were trained in high altitude low opening jumps, well used to completing the initial portion in free fall while breathing oxygen from a small tank.

Alexander could feel the chop in the night air as soon as the jump bay opened, already wearing his wet suit over his combat garb. They would be dropping straight into the night and storm while on oxygen for several minutes until low enough to deploy their chutes, through the cloud cover and into the manmade lake that enclosed the mountain fortress of Black Scorpion.

Dropping straight into the teeth of the storm left Alexander feeling virtually weightless in the grasp of what felt like a tornado's funnel cloud that whipped him about in all directions. He and the others managed to shed their oxygen masks and get their chutes opened at the proper time, resulting in a mad jockeying to stay on course. Alexander found himself holding his breath along with everyone else until the lake came up faster than expected, the dark waters feeling like concrete that collapsed beneath him on impact.

He went under into the total blackness, almost twenty feet down before he began the swim back to the surface, fighting against the sensation of decompression the free fall on oxygen had left on his brain. He shed his chute and readied his scuba gear, while inventorying his troops. One of Paddy's operators had died of a broken neck on impact with the water and one of Alexander's shattered his ankle, splitting the bone through the skin. Alexander helped him shed his chute and equipment and then left the man to reach shore on his own.

Alexander felt the chill of the lake waters through his wet suit as he led the remaining twenty-two men slowly to the bottom fifty feet down. Unlike traditionally formed lakes, this unusually large manmade one had a uniform bottom that might as well have been a swimming pool's. Alexander shined his underwater flashlight ahead in search of one of the hatches accessing the tunnel system that ran under the lakebed and linked the former nuclear silos together. He believed he'd swam over three of those silos already, noticeable for the darker patches of lake floor and slight depressions that came with the settling of their camouflaged structures.

Alexander spotted one of the tunnel access hatches just after passing the third depression. He positioned himself properly and started twisting on the wheel, fearing the years may have seen it welded shut or, at the very least, rusty and stuck from disuse. The Soviets, though, built such facilities intending them to last forever and, sure enough, the wheel turned easily after some initial resistance, then opened with a *sssssssssssssss* into an underwater airlock that maintained a constant pressure to prevent flooding.

Alexander and Paddy lowered themselves into the tunnel first, the last man to reach the ladder closing and sealing the hatch behind him. The men all stripped off their wet suits, shed their scuba equipment, and geared up for the next phase of the mission. Alexander had laid it out for them as best he could with only an old man's memory and thermal satellite imagery taken from a hundred thousand feet up in the sky to go by. The bulk of the men would accompany Paddy up into the complex, leaving him to make his way to the underground living quarters contained amid rock and shale.

Where he hoped to find Vladimir Dracu himself.

And along the way they would mine the tunnel with a bevy of shaped charges that, when added to the explosive force of identical charges placed within the complex, would rupture the structure's integrity and bring it down, flooding it from both above and below. Nothing could be left to chance.

"Raven," Alexander said, into the microphone extension of his lightweight tactical headset, "do you copy?"

"Loud and clear, big man. What's the word?"

"In the tunnel and heading toward the complex now. Stand by. Move into staging position and wait for my call."

Raven and her ten-man crew had moved up to a hidden position off the narrow trail within clear view of the waterfall, when something rustled the brush nearby. She and her men tensed, going utterly still and silent as a Black Scorpion sentry appeared out of the darkness. He was lighting a cigarette and had his assault rifle slung uselessly behind his shoulder.

Raven snapped a single fist into the air to hold her men back, then extracted a knife from her belt and slid out in the guard's wake. She pounced on him from behind and drove the blade into his heart between his ribs, felt him stiffen without so much as a sound or breath. She covered his mouth with a gloved hand just to make sure as she lowered him to the ground and dragged him to the cover of some thicker brush.

There were likely more guards lurking about and Raven

chose three men to accompany her in a sweep to locate them to eliminate the risk of being spotted and have their presence betrayed. The sweep brought her closer to the mountain itself for a look-see, to use Alexander's term, which left her doubting the old man's tales back in Vadja of some secret entrance to the cave system here beyond the waterfall. As far as she could tell, this was a mountain face and nothing more.

She clung to the hope she was wrong, and that the old man's memory was right. Otherwise, she and her men would have no chance to free the young women and children who'd been stolen from the village, certain then to join the tens of thousands of others who'd preceded them into human trafficking at the hands of Black Scorpion.

Raven wanted Vladimir Dracu dead more than she'd wanted anything in her life. He was the demon, quite literally it seemed now, who haunted her dreams and left her own youth shrouded in anguish and misery, the man behind the bullets that had shattered her life as a mere toddler. He had robbed her of her childhood and left her sentenced to the dark criminal underworld where there could be no trust, devotion, hope.

Or love.

And it all made sense now, her own twisted fate coming full circle. Her mother had died protecting her, just as she would die, if necessary, to save the children held hostage inside this fortress.

But she wasn't going anywhere unless her brother's man, Alexander, breached the entrance to the fortress behind the waterfall for her. Not used to relying on others left her cringing with an unfamiliar sense of dependence. Regardless of this man's reputed prowess, he would need to pull off the impossible just to enter the complex contained within a mountain, never mind beat back the forces concentrated inside.

Raven had begun to fear Alexander's part of the mission had been an abject failure, when his voice finally crackled in her headset again.

"We're in," said Alexander. "Get your men ready to move."

The pressurized tunnel ended at a flat rock wall before a ladder and hatch identical to the one they'd used to access it a half mile back. This time the wheel refused to give at all and Alexander summoned one of Paddy's demolitions specialists up the rungs to join him. The man didn't need to ask what was required, just set the proper small charge at the proper joint and backed off with Alexander before detonating it.

The blast sound was more like a cough, enough to rattle the hatch upward and open their route into Black Scorpion's fortress up a narrow chute. It had a single ladder climbing through the darkness and Alexander went first, popping yet another hatch open on a sub-level he didn't recognize from the thermal imaging. But he found his bearings quickly, identifying the steel door on the left to lead to the command and control bunker and the one on the right down a hall to what he felt certain were Vladimir Dracu's living quarters.

As such, he expected that hall to be heavily defended. Not surprisingly, the windowless heavy steel door was locked from the inside, meaning it too would have to be blown, and this time Alexander himself readied the charge from his pack.

"Leave me two men," he said to Paddy. "The ground floor is yours."

Paddy winked at him, beaming like a kid on Christmas morning as he adjusted his headset microphone closer to his lips. "Don't do a bloody thing, mate, till I do it first."

Paddy led his team up a ladder to yet another hatch that, according to his sense of the fortress's structure, led onto the ground floor it was his job to secure. He drilled a small hole in the hatch itself and poked an eye-line device through that was no thicker than a straw. Rotating it provided a 360-degree view to his eye pressed against the bottom half and what he saw wasn't good.

Eight men occupying what looked like an expansive concrete and steel space packed with vehicles. He'd been smelling oil, gasoline, and tire rubber for a few moments and now understood why. The entrance to the mountain he needed to breach was very well defended, the size and scope of the complex surprising him. Hearing it had been constructed within a mountain cave had him picturing something more contained. He was thinking submarine and what he got was an aircraft carrier, but he'd come prepared.

Paddy had learned long ago that nothing beat distraction when it came to overcoming superior numbers and positioning, at least initially. At this point, there was no way he could get his people into position without taking significant casualties and forfeiting the surprise of his team's presence earlier than planned.

Paddy slid the eye-line device out from the hatch and replaced it with a tubular extension rigged to a small tank he removed from his pack containing a simple compound that stunk to holy hell once it mixed with air. Something like the overflow from a septic system, only much worse, and easy enough to take the guards' minds off anything but its source. Make them so sick to their stomachs, they'd want to puke.

Distraction.

Paddy turned the small spigot on the tank and heard the initial hiss of the noxious gas escaping above.

"You read me, mate?" he called to Alexander through his throat mic.

"Loud and clear."

"Shite's about to hit the fan."

He signaled his men to pull back down the ladder a bit, ready a mere minute later when the access wheel to the hatch begun to turn above him. Paddy could hear one of the guards retching and coughing from the odor as he started to hoist it open, flooding the chamber with light.

"Evening, mate," Paddy greeted him, and then opened fire.

Alexander triggered the charge he'd set himself as soon as he heard the gunfire clanging above. He and the two commandos with him backed off and covered their ears, assault weapons dangling at their chests in the ready position. His own M-4 carbine came equipped with an M203 40mm grenade launcher attached beneath its barrel, the additional handling weight well worth the extra firepower it provided.

Poooooofffff!

The latch disappeared in a flash and the door blew open behind a surge of smoke. His men were through the door just as Alexander spotted the red laser line amid the smoke.

"No!" he cried out an instant too late, just as the wall-mounted mines blew a blanket of shrapnel outward that ripped the men apart before they could even scream.

Alexander dove into the smoke, through what was left of the shredded bodies and beneath the bursts of gunfire coming from the other end of the hall. Three shooters, he figured, as he steadied his M4 and fired on full auto in a sweeping motion aimed at the muzzle flashes that had erupted through the smoke-riddled darkness.

He heard cries, screams, enough to tell him he'd felled all three gunmen. Back on his feet and sliding down the hall in the next instant, spotting the trio of bodies lying in a heap halfway down the iron hall. He fired one grenade from his launcher and then a second straight for the door.

The explosions seemed to merge, the flame burst and smoke clearing to reveal a jagged chasm blown in the now charred, smoking steel. Alexander picked up his pace, fresh magazine jammed home and fresh 40mm grenade chambered. Drawing closer to the lair, he thought he heard classical music playing somewhere, expecting movement to flash within, more targets making themselves known to defend their leader.

But he reached the breach recording neither; he was beginning to feel something was awry, even before he surged inside, rifle rotating and ready.

No more guards. No more defenses.

"Shit," Alexander muttered to himself.

Vladimir Dracu's lair was empty.

ONE HUNDRED SIX

LAS VEGAS, NEVADA

Michael felt the lobby's marble floor seem to quake beneath him. He could see smoke and flames climbing down the Strip through the Seven Sins glass façade that had shattered from the percussion and blown inward, flying shards of glass wounding a number of guests who were already being tended to by a combination of other guests and Seven Sins security personnel. He grabbed one of those plainclothes security men as he surged forward.

"Was it a bomb?" Michael asked the man, whose nametag identified him as JACOB, as shrieking, panicked visitors stormed the lobby from the valet area.

"I don't know, sir," Jacob told him, after a moment of shock over whom he was addressing. "Reports are all over the place," he continued, touching his earpiece. "Just got one that said it was the gas station on Paradise Road."

Police and rescue sirens had just begun to sound, when Michael felt the next series of explosions through what felt like vibrations at his very core. Jacob instinctively shoved Michael behind him to protect against any further pieces of glass and debris falling from the ceiling. Michael felt dust showering him and looked up to see the lobby's crystal chandelier breaking free of its bonds, in the next moment spotting a child and father standing directly beneath it.

He lit out toward them, shoving both out of harm's way, and shielding them an instant before the chandelier exploded on impact with the marble floor. The sound alone fed the panic, guests charging about desperately in all directions, crying and screaming.

An all too familiar scene.

"Mr. Tiranno!" Jacob called, catching up to him.

"Go," Michael ordered. "Help the people who need it."

More patrons shuffled past him to see whatever had befallen the Strip, indicators, no doubt, that Las Vegas was under attack again.

But by whom?

The answer came in the next moment when his phone beeped with an incoming text. Michael wedged it close to his eyes in a thinning pocket of smoke and saw SCARLETT light up, a single message displayed on his Samsung Galaxy.

THE FORBIDDEN CITY, MICHELE. COME ALONE OR SHE DIES. TAKE YOUR PRIVATE ELEVATOR.

And Michael rushed across the lobby.

ONE HUNDRED SEVEN

Paddy's initial burst had taken out three guards clustered over the apparent origins of the stench, his bullets pouring out of the hatch once they'd raised it open. He went through the breach first, tumbling to the floor to a fusillade of fire from the five remaining guards who'd reacted faster than he'd expected.

Combat had been his life for long enough to recognize men for whom it wasn't. He'd come to think of them as "rookies," soldiers used to bullying their way and seldom, if ever, facing the kind of professional resistance, much less attack, he was prepared to provide. But the lack of a gap in the Black Scorpion soldiers' response told him they were as professional in ability as they were fearsome in reputation. That meant this wasn't going to be easy, which in Paddy's mind meant it was going to be more fun.

He rolled upon hitting the floor, firing on motion more than shape, his initial bursts meant to clear the way for more of his men to join him. The bursts did that and more, felling a fourth and fifth of the guards and leaving several more pinned behind vehicles, suddenly on the defensive. That meant the advantage was Paddy's for now and he had to seize it.

He figured he had maybe a minute at most before the first wave of reinforcements arrived, giving him just that to get the main entrance open for Raven Khan and her men.

"Keypad!" he yelled to the two-man team of operators responsible for breaching the main entrance for Raven Khan, identifying the means of entry for them.

And they rushed toward it under fire from the remaining

gunmen shooting from behind the cover of the vehicles parked in neat rows. In between his own shots, Paddy glimpsed his men tearing apart the keypad and running thick wires to a bypass device. But triggering the bypass tripped the system and the door remained frozen in place, forcing them to resort to explosive charges instead.

Big ones, real big ones, Paddy thought, stealing more glimpses of them wedging concentrated shaped charges into place. Reinforcements would be arriving any moment now and Paddy waved his rear phalanx on and provided cover for them to the stairwell accessing the floors above. Their mission was to secure those levels by blowing the stairwell at the third level, denying Black Scorpion's men passage downward, and then holding at the second level in case anyone got through or tried an alternate route. They didn't have the firepower to hold them forever but the strategy should hold them long enough for both Alexander and the woman to work their parts of the mission, while Paddy prepared to blow the fortress to hell once their mission was complete.

The thermal satellite imaging hadn't told him everything, but it had told him enough to identify the best structural points at which to plant explosives. The problem was once he blew the main entrance for Raven and her team to enter, all bets were off and he'd be in the kind of old-fashioned firefight he'd known for what seemed like all his life.

"Have at it, boys!" he yelled, as his men rushed for the stairwell and Paddy fired a pair of 40mm grenades from his M4 carbine to better clear the path for them.

Then he put two more into the elevator to close it off as an access point as well.

Raven counted the seconds in her head. She'd moved her men into position even with the waterfall and could do nothing more until Alexander's forces carved open the entrance beyond. She used these particular men only for the most challenging jobs when violence would almost certainly be required; like the rescue of Niels Taupmann from a Soviet gulag or, much more recently, the planned seizure of the *Lucretia Maru* at sea. Hardened criminals and cutthroats, with prices on their heads across the world, for whom violence was normally a first resort.

All of them here only because of the huge payday thanks to Michael Tiranno opening up his offshore "emergency" coffers, Raven was thinking when she heard explosions and the rattle of percussion within the mountain. The feeling was akin to the slight tremor of a jet flying low overhead, enough to tell her the battle inside had begun.

Hurry up, you damn Brit, Raven thought.

"Paddy, do you copy?" Alexander said into the microphone dangling even with his mouth.

"How's the party going down there, mate?"

"Empty."

"No shit? Having a fucking blast up here."

"Listen, Paddy, Dracu's not on the premises. Repeat, primary target is not—"

Alexander's last words were choked off by the most powerful grasp he'd ever felt closing over him from behind. He managed to twist and pull free at the last, just as he started to feel the pressure in his ribs. Whirling sideways and then back to find himself facing Armura.

"Heavy resistance on third level!" Paddy heard chiming in his ear. "Holding at stairwell to heavy fire!"

"Blow it to fuck and pull back!"

"Affirmative! We got men down, sir!"

"Blow it to double fuck then."

Paddy's men down here had just cut down the last Black Scorpion guard, providing a moment's respite in which the only firing he heard were the echoes still bouncing about his head. His men at the main entrance were slapping the final shaped charges into place and he had started to breathe just a bit easier, when the drop ceiling seemed to collapse beyond the rows of vehicles stowed between his position and the other side of the sprawling floor.

Bloody hell!

Because reinforcements spilled down through the ruptured tiles one after the other, something he cursed himself for not anticipating. He angled a wild spray upward to cut as many of them down as he could but plenty of live ones continued to pour out like ants from a nest.

Paddy skirted along the periphery of his team's return fire, into the open to catch as many enemy troops as he could in a nonstop barrage. He never felt more alive than in these moments when time froze, nothing but the staccato bursts of sound and glimpses of movement registering with him at all.

Time changed. Places changed.

But not combat, one fight exactly like the last and the next. There was the gun, his targets, and nothing else. And right now he pumped out two more 40mm grenades, turning a pair of big SUVS into flaming husks, in the same moment one of his men at the main entrance hit the signal on his detonator.

The huge blast blew a burst of rubble from the mountain into the air, forming a heavy cloud that briefly swallowed the waterfall. It cleared to reveal a chasm where the mountain face had just been, a face carved away years before to be replaced by iron and steel dressed to mesh perfectly with the rest of the mountain.

Opening the door for her.

"Move! Move! Move!" Raven ordered her men.

She led them into the lake waters that glowed greenish-black in the rain still pouring from the dark sky. They sank almost immediately up to the waist and then quickly to chest level with weapons raised overhead to keep them as dry as possible. Closer up, the waterfall's roar was much louder and the force of its spill much more intense than it seemed from the edge of the woods.

Those waters pelted Raven and her men with a pounding spray of needles as they passed under the flow. They cleared the waterfall's drenching force, the lightest of the blast-strewn rubble clinging to the surface of the lake. Raven and her men surged past it, charging through the blown entrance to the fortress with guns blazing amidst the water pouring in ahead of them.

She immediately saw the big, steely-eyed Brit named Paddy and a small group of his men struggling to hold their ground against increasing levels of resistance and advance from a much larger Black Scorpion force. The dark figures were dropping out of the ceiling from the level above, huge amounts of fire, constant barrages, exchanged back and forth. If her analysis of the satellite's thermal imaging scans were correct, the hostages she'd come to rescue were clustered somewhere at the far end of the corridor Black Scorpion's forces were currently defending. Looked to be nearly impossible to break through the front they'd established.

Nearly, Raven thought to herself, as her gaze fell on the array of vehicles lined up in neat rows between Paddy's guns and Black Scorpion's.

———

"We're under attack!" one of the monitors called out to Bemke in the control room. "We must evacuate!"

Bemke shoved him back down in the chair set before his station. "We stay here and finish our job. We wait to make sure the signal is sent."

"We're trapped down here! Are you mad?"

Bemke took his hand off the man's shoulder. "No, only a madman would act against our employer's orders. If you want to flee, be my guest."

The man didn't.

"We wait," Bemke told the monitor. "Those are our orders and that's what we do."

"And if the signal doesn't come on time, as expected?"

"Then we follow those same orders and activate the operation ourselves," Bemke said, his eyes scanning the various electronic wall maps depicting the United States, thousands of green lights about to be flashing red.

Alexander had never felt such power, such strength. No one he'd ever encountered before could rival this giant of a man for sheer brutal force, his hands like vices that had to be pried free instead of opened. Every time those hands managed to close on him, Alexander felt something spasm and start to give. Knowing there was no time or space to waste trying to free the assault rifle he'd swept behind him or even the pistol snapped into his hip holster, Alexander went for his knife instead, a much easier motion to conceal until he thrust it outward from the cover of his own body.

Armura grabbed hold of the blade, closing a hand around it, just before it plunged into his stomach. Alexander saw the blood, *smelled* the blood, but squeezing his hand around the sharp edge seemed to have no effect on the giant. He didn't even flinch, an utter stranger to the kind of pain he should've been feeling now.

Armura gained the upper hand long enough to slam Alexander into one side of the wall and then the other. He'd never felt so light, so helpless under the bigger man's incredible strength, struck by the illusion that Armura was actually two different men sewn together thanks to the mask that covered one side of his face.

The giant discarded Alexander's blade from his bloodied hand, the two men continuing to grapple about what looked like an art gallery fashioned amid old, heavy furniture. Little space existed for them to move, the blows of each either parried or absorbed by the other.

Alexander felt each of the giant's like a sledgehammer pounding his flesh and one blow he took on the fleshy part of his shoulder numbed his arm all the way to his fingers. His M4 carbine remained slung behind him, within reach but not without the risk of opening himself to the kind of single blow from a man this strong that could incapacitate him on its own.

Alexander ducked under Armura's next blow and seized the brief advantage that gave him to go for the Beretta holstered low on his hip, managing to free it when the giant slammed into him, pinning the weapon in place as they crashed through a heavy door into what felt like a fetid jungle. Alexander felt his shoulders smash into some kind of terrarium, followed by a matching one and then a third. His pistol went flying, clattering to the tile floor while the giant moved in for the kill.

But Alexander had learned to always carry two knives. He managed to free his second, a Gerber MK2, and plunged it deep into Armura's midsection once and then again, feeling it cut through cartilage and scrape against rib bone.

The hulk of a shape stiffened before him, but showed no pain, not even a grimace or a wince, no signs of slowing whatsoever. Alexander had started to plunge the blade in a third time when Armura wrenched his wrist and jerked the blade out. Alexander heard it first clatter and then flit across the floor, freeing Armura to capture him in a grasp that felt like steel clamps tightening on his ribs.

He tumbled to the floor with the giant atop him, his assault rifle pinned beneath him against the floor. Blood was everywhere, soaking Alexander and widening in a pool through which the army of scorpions skittered.

ONE HUNDRED EIGHT

LAS VEGAS, NEVADA

Dracu was standing in the middle of the Forbidden City atrium, holding a gun to Scarlett's head, when Michael emerged from his private glass elevator. Her nose was bloodied and looked swollen. One of her eyes was half-closed. More blood dribbled from one side of her mouth.

"Put your hands in the air," Dracu ordered.

Michael obliged and started forward.

"That's far enough, Michele," his half brother continued when they were thirty feet apart.

Michael held his gaze on Scarlett. Her hands had been bound behind her in the chair Dracu had placed her, but the barely perceptible jostling of her shoulders told him she was working to free herself.

Their eyes met again, Michael seeing the resolve and belief in him displayed. She tried not to appear scared, trying to make herself look strong and resilient.

"You're just in time," Dracu said, grinning. "The real show's about to start."

And, as if on cue, another blast sounded, more like a loud *pop* that Michael recognized as a main transformer blowing. An instant later, all the lights in the Forbidden City and virtually all the Strip beyond flickered and died. The Forbidden City's emergency lighting snapped on from the fixtures' wall mounts not far from the security cameras that were still off-line, barely touching either Dracu or Scarlett in its reach.

"After what you and your warrior did at the *Securitate* building," Dracu told him, "forgive me for not taking chances."

"I don't blame you," Michael said, leaving his hands poised above him. "You're real good at beating up women, Vlad. Children, too. I've always wondered what it feels like when a coward like you meets his match."

"Like the lucky coward who hid in the barn while I killed his family? You should know, my brother."

Michael watched Scarlett stiffen. Dracu must have as well.

"Wait," Dracu continued, "she doesn't *know*, does she? What have you told her about your past, Michele? Does she know you were born a peasant? Does she know I did you the greatest favor anyone ever could by murdering the family that would've otherwise held you down? Did you explain our relationship, that we're half brothers?"

"We don't have a relationship and you're not my brother."

"I'm talking about blood."

"So am I."

Michael felt something churn inside him, up here in what he envisioned as the crown jewel of the Seven Sins property—literally, since it occupied the top three floors of the complex stretching from one side all the way across to the other. The three-story atrium in which they stood was an architectural model of form and function; authentic wrought iron holding up glass on all sides that finished with a dome on top. That dome was enclosed by a custom-sewn tarpaulin to shield it from both the elements and prying eyes, except on a single side where workers completing a section had neglected to replace the tarp. Even the most spying eye peering inward, though, would have trouble determining exactly what the Forbidden City was to be.

Just the way Michael wanted it, until the very moment it opened. At that point the world would be treated to a beautifully balanced mix of retail, relaxation, gaming, entertainment, and two hundred high-end, glass-walled suites that could be booked for extended durations at exorbitant prices.

All themed around a jungle environment, including the "Tiger" suites built to offer guests the opportunity to effectively live in the wild with the majestic animals. Only a foot of glass would separate those guests from the most accurate re-creation of the tigers' native habitat ever fashioned. The finish work remained to be completed, the structure little more than a raw shell. No furniture had been brought in yet, nor was there any signage for the vast array of shops, stores, and restaurants that encircled the atrium, accessible by elegant reproductions of rope-style bridges that climbed upward to the second story and the third.

Had it been daytime, however, anyone up here would've been treated to a re-creation of the golden plains beyond the glass at the Forbidden City's rear. A sunny glade of tall, swaying pampas grass gave way to a lazy river shifting in man-made winds through the section Michael himself had named the Valley of Thunder. Clumps of giant bamboo dotted the river's edge where the tigers would soon be seen lapping up water.

"Us sharing the same blood isn't something I'm proud of," Michael said, seeing the shock still showing in Scarlett's eyes.

"Why, when we have so much in common? Our father made me the monster that I am and I made you into the Tyrant you are that day you escaped death. You might even say you owe me more than you owe anyone else on Earth."

"Then let the girl go, so we can discuss the terms further."

"The time for negotiation is long past, Michele. You might say what's about to happen, what I'm about to do, is the ultimate hostile takeover. See how well I speak your language?"

"Sorry, I don't speak crazy, deviant, or murderer."

"Deviant? It is the curse of all great men to be ostracized, isolated. You should look in the mirror and count your friends, those you can truly trust. Something else we have in common."

"We have *nothing* in common. Now let the woman go so we can finish this, just the two of us."

"We need a witness to our arrangement."

"What arrangement is that, Vlad?"

"The one I'm about to force upon you."

Michael could see Scarlett's shoulders shifting ever so slightly, evidence she was continuing to work to free her bound hands. "What happened to your veil?" he asked Dracu.

"You convinced me to shed it. See, I'm learning from you."

"I was wrong. You should put it back on to remind yourself how ugly you are on the inside," Michael told him, holding Vlad's dark eyes with his own to keep him from looking up at the hands he still held overhead.

Dracu's expression didn't change. "Be careful, Michele."

"I guess you haven't heard the news, Vlad," Michael told his half brother. "All of Black Scorpion's primary cells have been or will soon be hit across the globe. Human trafficking, drugs, gun-running—all of it. You're out of business."

Dracu smiled, holding up a cell phone in his free hand. "All the more reason to cement the business we have between us and solidify my new life in your world."

"Don't tell me. You touch a key and a signal gets sent, through Romania, to all those Guardian chips I heard about."

Dracu's eyes widened. "I'm impressed."

"I'm not. What's it going to be this time? Las Vegas again?"

"I'm far more ambitious than that, Little Brother: The whole United States. America goes dark, back to the stone age where it belongs until I see fit to turn the switch back on." Dracu grinned again. "You're forgetting something else, aren't you, Michele?"

Michael realized he was. "Aldridge Sterling . . . Buying up my company's bonds, shorting gaming stocks, doing everything he can to make my casino default on its debt and take me out of the picture."

"You're finally getting it," Dracu said, grinning again. "And, you mean, *my* casino, don't you?"

Michael felt something sink in his stomach.

"Surprise! This won't be your casino very much longer. Once the lights come back on, I'll own it. Black Scorpion the man is a myth and he's about to disappear, only to resurface again just as Michele Nunziato did as Michael Tiranno. So you did me a favor by taking out Black Scorpion's cells around the world and eliminating any possible connection to me in the process. I made you from a peasant and now I'm going to send you back to being one. Everything you have, everything you own, will be mine soon."

"Sterling shorting the dollar," Michael started, working it all out for himself, "betting on economic collapse. The lights come back on after he's bought up everything on the cheap, after the dollar crashes, and the two of you are left sitting on a mountain of cash. . . ."

"Yes, but I don't care about a mountain of cash. It's all of this I really want," he said, gazing about the Forbidden City dramatically. "I'm killing your dream, turning the light of your world to darkness. Don't you see? We're trading places, you with nothing and me with everything. Just as it should have been all along."

Michael grasped it all now, both the madness and genius in Vladimir Dracu's plan. He wasn't out to destroy his half brother so much as replace him, his entire plan all about seizing what he felt was rightfully his. Dracu wouldn't actually *own* the property, of course; that role would be filled by investors beholden to Aldridge Sterling. But the casino would be his all the same, even if the management company brought in to operate it never knew.

"Ah, I see you've figured it all out." Dracu's grin held on his expression, stretched from ear to ear, his attention rooted entirely, obsessively, on Michael just as it had in Caltagirone. "Your efforts only destroyed who I was, not who I'm about to become. And nobody knows who Black Scorpion really is, do they? You want to know why I hide my face? Now you do. When the light returns, Little Brother, I can be anyone I want to be and nobody will know any different. And I believe the show I've arranged for you is just about to continue." Dracu turned toward the exposed glass on the side of the atrium overlooking the Strip. "Behold, my brother."

A series of flame bursts indicating fresh explosions could be seen both close by and in the distance behind heavy, insulated glass. But then the glass on that side of the building facing the rear of the property shattered from the blistering percussions, opening the Forbidden City up to the night to reveal a chorus of car horns, vague shouts and screams and, finally, an endless cascade of sirens.

"Your world's on fire, my brother," Dracu resumed, "in return for what you did to mine. But I'm pressed for time, so I can offer you a trade," he added, his eyes wide and glistening. "The relic in exchange for your love." He shook his head almost whimsically. "How can you resist such an offer, a true romantic like yourself? Therein lies your weakness, Little Brother. You feel too much. You think you crave power, but what you really crave is love. That's why you'll make the trade, because you can live without the relic, but you can't live with yourself if you let your love die."

"You're wasting your time, Vlad," Michael told him, feeling the warm night air blowing in through the now open side of the Forbidden City. The sirens and car alarms continued to wail, the fires from the blasts set by Black Scorpion dotting the night beyond through the darkness.

"About your feelings for this woman?"

"About the relic. It can't help you. Whatever power it has doesn't come from just possessing it. You don't choose the relic; the relic chooses you."

"Sure, whatever you say, Little Brother, but I'll take my chances. Your relic for your woman. Otherwise, I'll kill her right in front of you, so you can know the kind of loss I've lived with all my life." Dracu's hand twitched ever so slightly, ready to pull the trigger. "Get ready to say good-bye to her. But, first, say good-bye to your world."

Vlad returned his gaze to his cell phone, ready to press a button on the touch screen, when Michael hurled the knife he'd tucked up his sleeve forward. Vlad twisted at the last moment, the blade still grazing his shoulder enough to send his cell phone flying.

ONE HUNDRED NINE

HOIA-BACIU FOREST, ROMANIA

For Raven, it was all about the hostages—everything. She struggled with her hearing, the staccato bursts of gunfire seeming to come from everywhere at once. And now the lake waters were surging in through the entrance, blown out in jagged fashion and exposing the fortress to the torrents.

She had six men left by the time she reached a big black SUV parked at the head of the pack. Raven climbed in behind the driver's seat, her remaining men firing even as they joined her inside and continuing to spray fire through the vehicle's open doors. She was ready to hot-wire the car when she found the key already in the ignition and just turned.

The powerful engine roared to her life and Raven wasted no time in screeching into reverse, shoving the vehicles behind her SUV aside before she spun it around in a whir of grinding rubber to face Black Scorpion's gunmen. They opened up on her, her men literally dangling out the windows to better return their fire as the view through the windshield disappeared before a blur of pockmarked glass.

Bulletproof! Raven realized, finding the confidence to give the SUV more gas, plowing through anything and anyone it encountered.

She sped past the Black Scorpion gunmen still firing on her and twisted the vehicle onto a wide hall where more troops were rushing to join their fellows in reinforcing the fortress's first level. She was down to four men now and all were clacking off a constant cacophony of fire that held the enemy at bay well enough for her to continue barreling along.

Finally, her tires bore the brunt of a fusillade that spun the SUV to a halt at a break in the maze-like hall bending both straight and to the left. Climbing out with her own assault rifle at the ready, Raven reframed the thermal satellite imagery in her mind, convinced the hostages were being held somewhere to the left. Just three of her own men remained, and they all accompanied her in the mad dash through the waters that had begun to collect this far down as well.

But how to find the hostages' exact position?

That's when Raven glimpsed a parade of rats scurry past her, absurdly feeling a burst of instinct-bred fear. But where were they coming from?

Food, she thought. *They'd congregate in areas where there was the most food to be had.*

As in that part of the fortress where the hostages were being held.

Straight ahead.

The lake waters continued to rush in through the breached entrance, halfway up the height of the SUVs' big tires as the firefight raged on. Thanks to the reinforcements who'd dropped through the ceiling, Black Scorpion maintained the advantage over Paddy's forces that were down to six now with dwindling ammo to boot.

Paddy glimpsed two of those placing shaped charges at key points of the structure's ground floor meant to undermine its integrity once the explosive wave was triggered. Then a blast sounded from above, followed by another and then a third.

"Second Squad, report!" he called into his mic between firing bursts from his assault rifle.

"They're blasting through our debris field!" the squad leader's report came back in a hollow echo bred by the confines of the stairwell from which he was making his stand.

"Gotta hold 'em for me, mate!"

"I can buy you another three minutes, sir!"

"Make it five, you bloody wanker, or I'll shoot you myself!"

"Five, sir, that's a roger!"

He'd had just clicked off when one of the two men planting shaped charges fell to a barrage of bullets that sent his pack skittering across the floor in Paddy's direction. Paddy had never been much for explosives himself, preferring bullets to bombs, but knew an opportunity when he saw one.

Wasting no time, he flashed the hand signal to his remaining troops to give cover and then darted out for the pack, diving to the floor to scoop it free of the rising waters.

The floor had been built with a slight upward grade, steep enough for Raven to feel in her thighs, as she sloshed through the water up to her ankles now. Gunfire erupted behind her, one of the three men left accompanying Raven shot down immediately while the other two returned fire.

"Go!" one of them cried out and Raven knew she had no choice but to do so, continuing to follow the last of the line of fleeing rats to a break in the hallway.

Raven swung right at the head, certain the hostages, her very purpose for being here, must be close. Before her, though, was nothing but wall, this hall a dead end. And she could hear the ratcheting of more gunfire, recognizing the steady clacking from Kalashnikov-style assault rifles with which she was familiar. Her last surviving men would be overwhelmed before long, leaving nothing between Raven and the coming charge of enemy gunmen.

But the rats couldn't be wrong.

That thought left her looking at the walls again, before turning her eyes upward for the ceiling. She spotted a grooved rectangular outline up there consistent with a pull-down ladder of the kind normally used to access attics. Smelling her own sweat and feeling it beginning to soak through the Nomex gloves Alexander had provided, Raven leaped up and felt her hand close inside a deeper groove that gave behind her momentum. The folding ladder attached to the floor above dropped effortlessly, and she scrambled up the rungs and yanked the ladder back upward into what felt like hell itself.

As the gunfire and blasts continued to sound above the control room, portions of the battle visible on several of the screens monitoring the fortress above, chief engineer Bemke watched the LED wall clock freeze at 00.00 without the signal having been received from Black Scorpion's leader. He moved to his own keyboard, located on a raised dais in the front of the floor along with a half dozen technicians who'd be responsible for monitoring the effects of the United States being shut down.

Before Bemke, the control room was aglow in the lights flashing on the dozens of screens, focusing on the largest congestions of targets and highest areas of population densities. Different regions of America, different cities with separate monitoring screens for the largest twenty, different targets all highlighted and soon to be followed in real time as the Guardian chip spread its magic from coast to coast, shutting the country down. From sea to shining sea, Bemke thought, unsure if he had the words right.

The responsibility to trigger the plan was his now, and he had to do it fast, while there was still time to escape the battle raging in the levels above.

The freed scorpions seemed everywhere, the floor theirs as Alexander twisted his head and shoulders to the right to deny the giant the grip his thumbs sought on his neck. Otherwise, the man's incredible strength would have crushed his throat, even with one of his hands mangled from grasping the knife blade. That gave Alexander the opportunity to tense his neck muscles, fighting to buy the time he needed as thumbs like steel bolts continued to press home. He had already sucked in as much breath as he could hold, pretending to flail at Armura's rigid form desperately the way a normal man would.

But Alexander was not a normal man, his focus rooted

entirely on the Beretta pistol just out of his reach to the right, amid the sea of scorpions clacking across the floor.

Paddy used the water, *disappeared* into the water. Held his breath as he dragged the explosive pack with him from one SUV chassis to the next. These shaped charges, fortunately, were waterproof, as were the detonators he'd wedged into place in each charge after affixing them beneath the engines, as opposed to the gas tanks themselves, to make better use of the fumes as an accelerant. He might not have been an expert on explosives, but he knew the effects of a dozen vehicles erupting in conjunction with the other strategically placed shaped charges. The nature of explosives was to multiply the effect on a geometric level as the blast radius found additional fuel to feed itself and expand. And who knew what latent gases might have been collecting here over the years to further increase the effects of the blast?

A much bigger boom in other words.

"Sir!" he heard in his earpiece the next time he popped up for air, while gunfire continued to echo and clang around him.

"You still owe me a minute, mate!" he told his squadron leader above, more heavy fire reaching his ears.

"Not much more than that before they're through and heading your way!"

"You done good, son. Hold as long as you can, then you and your men pull back to my twenty."

"Just me and one other now, but we roger that."

"Alexander," he called again into his mic. "Where the hell are ya, mate?"

Raven drew up the ladder and slid the lock over the closed hatch. She found herself on a long narrow floor with heavy doors on either side. Old-fashioned, low-tech cells barred from the outside and outfitted with a grate around eye level.

She heard whispers and whimpers as she started moving along them. The guards assigned here must have rushed to join the battle, and she found the cells holding the young women and children halfway down. Thirty-six hostages in total, as it turned out, crowded into four separate cubicles. Twenty-eight boys and girls not more than early teens and eight young women between that age and around twenty.

Raven drew them out of their cells, arranged them in a double line with the oldest of the young women bringing up the rear. Just about to get moving when a torrent of fire blew the hatch holding the fold-down ladder into shards and splinters that showered the air.

Armura kept pressing his hands attached to arms the size of fire hydrants into Alexander's throat, Alexander's oxygen-deprived brain starting to make him feel light-headed. Alexander felt the blood from Armura's knife wounds soaking both of them with little if any effect on his strength. But his grasp finally slackened just enough for Alexander to latch on to his Beretta. He pressed it against Armura's midsection, fired and kept firing.

He felt the bullets literally lift the giant off him, back to his feet where he staggered backward with his torso marred by widening pools of red to go with the damage done by the knife wounds Alexander had inflicted. Armura ground himself to a halt. The giant's eyes had started to dim when he retrained his attention toward Alexander, ready to pounce again when Alexander yanked his assault rifle free, steadied its grenade launcher on Armura . . .

And fired.

The shell thumped into Armura and exploded with a force great enough to launch him airborne and spill him to the floor, blown in half with his upper and lower bodies skewing in different directions.

Taking no chances, Alexander climbed back to his feet, wobbling a bit as he approached the huge downed form, *forms*, cautiously, leading with the barrel of his M4. But the giant's one exposed eye was locked open and sightless, both halves of his body still smoking from the heat generated by the blast.

"It's about fucking time," Alexander said out loud.

Bemke finished keying in the sequence, finger poised over the Execute key when it froze in place, seemingly on its own. The responsibility he would bear for the cataclysm to follow meant nothing to him, not when measured against failing to execute his orders from the man in the black veil.

Bemke pressed Execute.

In that very moment the command center was plunged into darkness broken almost immediately by the bright spill of emergency lighting, more than enough to illuminate a crazed old man wearing a bathrobe standing over a hissing and smoking section of the mainframe holding an empty water bottle in his hand.

The man Bemke knew as "the Professor," designer of all that lay before him, fixed his eyes on the digital wall maps depicting the United States instead of Russia as were displayed whenever he was down here to coax him into lending his genius to the plan.

Niels Taupmann saluted and began to sing.

"Oh say can you see, by the dawn's early light . . ."

With Vlad Dracu nowhere to be found, Alexander busied himself with a rapid search for the manuscript Scarlett Swan had described for him back in Vegas.

"Alexander!" he heard Paddy call in his earpiece.

"Finishing up down here right now," he replied instantly.

"Well, mate, whatever you're doing, do it fast."

"Give me a clock."

"Three minutes, give or take, and be prepared to swim."

Alexander clicked off, then resumed speaking again. "Three minutes, Raven."

No response.

"Raven?"

Still nothing.

Alexander was about to give up the search for the ancient pages to focus on finding her, when he spotted a sealed glass case resting amid several shelves containing other artifacts of history. He slid the ammo pack from his shoulder and eased the case inside it into the space vacated by all the magazines he'd spent.

Raven had heard Alexander's voice in her ear but was too busy with the rescued hostages to respond. She led them to the far end of the prison hall to find not another door or hatch, but some kind of chute accessible through a square cutout in the wall. The stench told her it must be part of a crude sewer system built into this otherwise high-tech facility typical of the Soviets. And that meant it would offer a direct route to freedom; unless, of course, it had been bricked or cemented over.

With time ticking down, though, she had no other choice and began hoisting the children of Vadja through the hole, starting with the youngest. She followed inside after pushing the last through, sliding downward into a stagnant, lime- and stench-riddled, dark pool of water where the bunker's drained sewage collected. The hostages, soaked in grime and muck, were already helping each other from the pool placed at the cave's lowest point outside the bunker's rear inside the mountain.

Raven collected her bearings quickly, realizing that circling around the massive structure would take them back to the breached front of the cave wall and escape. Already hustling her charges forward, when the wall of water surging into the cave slammed into her.

ONE HUNDRED TEN

LAS VEGAS, NEVADA

Dracu managed to maintain grasp of his pistol, re-steadying it on Michael in a shaky hand, when Scarlett launched herself backward. Her chair seemed to actually rise into the air, an illusion fostered by the force of her smacking into Dracu.

Instead of continuing to right his aim, he slammed the pistol across the side of her skull, toppling the chair over to the floor with enough force to shatter the wood. Michael had burst into motion by that point, recalling the lesson that hesitation killed more men than bullets. He didn't hesitate, not at all, and was on Dracu just as his half brother was again righting the pistol on him.

Bang!

At such close range, the gun's percussion alone made Michael think he'd been shot. But he hadn't and continued to battle Dracu for control of the weapon, while beneath him a badly dazed Scarlett struggled to free herself from the remaining bonds of the chair.

Michael and Dracu continued to whirl about, past unfinished sections of the Forbidden City still mired in exposed wires lacking protective panels. This as more shots jerked from the Beretta's barrel to skewer the walls and ceiling. Dracu jerked the pistol hard to regain control of it, Michael feeling the shoulder injured in his fight with Durado Segura wrenched again, his whole arm starting to go numb and weak.

Even in those moments, Michael's mind raced with the madness of Dracu's plan. He and Aldridge Sterling flipping a switch, only to turn it back on after they'd made their money and their mark. And when that moment came, their power and control would be solidified to a degree certain to avoid retribution or retaliation. Vladimir Dracu was a shadow, a specter. With Michael out of the way, who would even know his true identity, much less his singular goal of claiming what he believed to be rightfully his: The Seven Sins and all Michael had created and built, including his multitude of successful ventures across all spectrums and industries.

Vlad would conquer Las Vegas without a gaming license and, just like the Mafia in the sixties and seventies, he'd be nowhere and be everywhere at the same time. Above all else, though, Vlad wanted the relic. The very object he considered mandatory to obtain power and success and the reason why, he must've believed, Michael had been able to rise from a peasant in Sicily to a billionaire tycoon in America.

Michael spotted Scarlett crawling away from the broken chair, stripping the rest of her rope bonds free. Going for Dracu's cell phone.

The next three shots flew sideways, kicking up sparks when at least one of them bore through a nest of exposed wires and circuits. Another shell expended before Michael realized lights powered by the hotel's emergency generators were flashing everywhere, the system overloading and triggering portions of the atrium floor sliding open to the sublevel below, a holding area.

Where the tigers had already been brought into their habitat, the one part of the Forbidden City that was completely finished.

The animals surged up through the openings provided two at a time, tethered to posts mounted below by thin but incredibly strong ballistic-nylon chains. Michael could see the tigers whipped into a frenzy by their sudden relative freedom, loud shots and energy swirling through the air. They surged about, a few rushing toward him and Vlad only to be yanked back by their tethers at the last moment.

One of the tigers swiped Dracu's phone away, just as Scarlett was about to grasp it. But she had the sense to lie totally still, even when the tiger roared with its teeth bared before lurching to join the other animals as they kept lunging for Michael and Vlad.

Seeing and smelling the ferocity of their struggle seemed to activate some primal instinct in the beasts' minds, increasing their level of aggression. They began circling, pawing the floor furiously, poised to attack had it not been for the limits their tethers placed upon them.

Their struggle took Michael and Vlad into the range of the tigers' tethers, and one of the big cats leaped for Dracu. The man known better known as Black Scorpion gave up trying to right his pistol on Michael and, instead, fired two shots into the animal when it was airborne, before Michael finally knocked the Beretta from his grasp, fresh pain exploding in his shoulder from the effort. The animal fell short of Dracu, hitting the floor dead and whipping the other tigers into an even worse frenzy. They started forward, hunched low in attack mode, only their tethers stopping them as Michael and Dracu drifted out of range again.

With no gun to battle for control over, Michael and Vlad wheeled across the floor, Michael fighting to angle for Scarlett while Dracu continued to maneuver toward the fallen cell phone. They wheeled in and around the tigers snapping and clawing as they tested the absolute limits of their bonds. Michael thought he had a clear path to Scarlett, but his injured shoulder betrayed him again and Vlad tripped him up before he could reach her.

Michael felt the animals clawing the air before him as he rose, spotting Dracu reaching down for the cell phone when a tiger lashed a paw at him, inadvertently swiping the phone away. That forced Dracu to backpedal, clearing a path to him for Michael.

Michael slammed into him hard, both men crashing to the floor, then swiftly regaining their feet and seeming to twirl dance-like across the floor. Michael managed a sidelong glance toward Scarlett who was moving for the phone again, before a pair of tigers caught the motion and lunged toward her. Michael's breath seized up as she managed to roll out of range just in time, barely escaping their attack.

His divided attention, though, gave Dracu the opening he needed to pound Michael's groin with a knee. A twist at the last instant spared him the brunt of the impact, but robbed him of his balance enough for Dracu's next blow to launch him off his feet. Crashing hard to the floor and sliding through the piles of glass he felt scratching at his skin through his clothes.

Recovering his senses, though, found Michael in easy reach of Dracu's phone. He took it in his grasp and smashed it upon the floor, then smashed it a second time, a third, and then a fourth, until nothing recognizable of the device remained.

"Michael!"

He swung at Scarlett's raspy cry to find her in Dracu's grasp, bent over the railing sixty stories over the Daring Sea on the back side of the resort opened up to the night beyond the shattered glass. His half brother grinning madly as he prepared to drop her from the top of the Forbidden City.

ONE HUNDRED ELEVEN

Water was pooling along the access hall to Vlad Dracu's private lair and starting to climb. It surged down the tube accessing the first level and Alexander had to hold his breath, fighting against its torrents as he climbed.

He pushed himself out under four feet of rising water and burst upward to add his fire to the ratcheting shells of what was left of Paddy's team. Just three men, maybe four, by the look and sound of things when a big hand clamped down on his shoulder.

Alexander swung and found himself locked with Paddy's ice blue eyes, the grin stretched across his face belying the wounds he'd suffered in his shoulder and leg.

"I hate the bloody water, mate. Might never go for a swim again."

"We ready to rain hell?"

Paddy flashed the detonator he'd taped to his palm "Just say the word."

"You're gonna need to go for one more swim first."

Alexander twisted to resume firing at the remaining forces of Black Scorpion, pushing backward through the climbing waters when Paddy latched a quivery hand onto his shoulder.

"We lost a lot of good blokes today, mate."

"Then let's make sure it was worth it," Alexander followed, when a stairwell door burst open to allow a fresh surge of Black Scorpion forces to pour through into the waters.

He pumped one 40mm grenade out and then a second, his last, before the first had even exploded. The near twin blasts blew the door off its hinges, crushing whoever was behind it even as they left a thick enough debris field to block that route to anything but a few stray shots of errant fire. Return fire from Black Scorpion's forces continued to rage, and Alexander moved to help Paddy through the waters that had reached their necks, backpedaling as he held his M4 over the flow until it clicked empty and he tossed it aside.

They were almost to the breach now, the first light of dawn visible beyond through a clearing sky when both spotted an old man wearing a drenched bathrobe standing directly before them with one hand clamped to his forehead in the position of a salute. The other looked to be holding what looked and smelled like a marijuana blunt.

"Reporting for duty!" the old man said, saluting as the water climbed past his chest.

Bemke watched his technicians working feverishly to get the mainframe up and running again. Finally, the lights in the command center snapped back on, the steady whir of machines following immediately.

Wasting no further time, Bemke rushed back atop the dias to reboot his computer and reinitiate the activation sequence. His fingers flew across the keyboard, watching his screen return to life, ready to press the Execute key to complete his orders.

Raven managed to herd her charges into a tight cluster with the oldest, teenage girls mostly, on the outside to help the younger ones, the youngest of whom were already held in their arms. Raven scooped up a pair of six- or seven-year-olds who were floundering and about to panic, struggling against the waters rising through the exposed cave's diameter.

Dawn broke beyond it across a sky that had cleared during the course of the battle. Somehow the light reassured her and she pushed herself on with children hoisted over both shoulders.

If she felt the rising sun upon her, she was safe.

The simplicity of that notion was enough to speed her on, legs churning against the current and feeling the force of the tight cluster of former captives pressing forward behind her. If she stopped, they'd stop, a constant reminder of the very purpose that had drawn her here and in which she couldn't fail, simply couldn't. Every time she started to weaken or doubt, she thought of being soaked in her own mother's blood thanks to the very man who'd taken these children hostage.

Before she knew it, the spill and roar of the waterfall was upon her and Raven felt her legs sink into the waters of the manmade lake.

Alexander could see no trace of Raven or any of the hostages as he helped Paddy and the old man across the waters of the mountain lake that glowed green beneath the rising sun. That old man could only be the scientist she had reported rescuing years before from a Russian gulag, the man responsible for devising Black Scorpion's plot against America who might well prove to be a treasure trove of information.

And who knew what else?

Alexander pushed the old man atop the opposite shore and then dragged Paddy along with him the rest of the way.

"Time to rain hell . . . mate," he said, and watched Paddy depress the detonator he'd taped to his palm.

Raven had gotten her rescued charges several hundred feet into the woods, safe from the blast zone, when she felt a rumble beneath her feet. Then the ground began to actually tremble. She heard any number of explosions muffled by the mountain itself, too far away and under too much cover to spot anything but a dark char cloud that must have burst through the breached entrance.

She felt strangely at peace, having done for these children what no one could had ever done, or could do, for her. Adnan Talu had rescued her from the massacre to which he was party, giving her a life more out of guilt than anything. But Raven had saved these young women and children to give them *back* their lives so they might never know the kind of pain and heartache that had rippled through her youth and clung to her still as an adult. The world had too many victims.

Now it would have thirty-six less.

Alexander had just reached the relative safety of the tree line with the old man and Paddy in tow when the initial series of explosions shook the ground with the fury of an earthquake, the illusion of the mountain itself shaking cast when he turned that way. A dense cloud of ash and smoke burst outward through the blown entrance, continuing to thicken and spread, huge cascades of water blown in all directions under the collective force of the blasts and resulting shock wave.

"Raven," he said into what was left of his microphone.

"Heading toward the rendezvous point now and have collected a few of the Brit's men on the way. Two—no, three."

"That'll please him no end," Alexander said, stealing a glance at a still grimacing Paddy. "Get the vehicles ready to travel. We won't be long."

Bemke had been literally counting down the seconds until the Execute command was ready when he heard the rumbling overhead. He had lived through earthquakes, some fairly large in scope, and the feeling of this was akin to that. The floor beneath him trembled and the keyboard and monitor atop his desk began to shake, actually lifting up and down before he clamped a hand down to hold them in place.

That's when he felt the first trickle of drops, drizzle-like, that could've simply been condensation dripping from the natural stone walls. But the drops quickly grew larger, and Bemke looked up to see water starting to stream down through the ceiling, finding gaps and spaces where none should have existed. Then he looked down and saw the stone floor cracking, water bubbling up through the fissures before beginning to surge through everywhere, as if someone had opened a million spigots at once.

Suddenly he felt his whole body shaking along with everything else in the command center. He maintained the presence of mind to still stretch a finger down toward the Execute key, almost there when the fortified ceiling ruptured and an endless blanket of water swallowed the world around him.

ONE HUNDRED TWELVE

Las Vegas, Nevada

"Complete the trade, Little Brother!" Dracu raged, still holding Scarlett over the railing. "Your woman for your relic! Come on, I don't have all night!"

Michael watched him push her further over from twenty feet away, too far to mount a charge or do anything before Vlad released his hold and let her go. The darkness broken only by the spill of emergency lights left both of them in the shadows lit by the splash of flames rising off the Strip.

"You want love, you can have it! I want power, I want *life*, I want *the relic*!" Dracu cried out in a rage, so intense it drew a roar from the tigers straining the limits of their tethers. "That's why it was never truly yours to possess. You're not worthy of its power. You're no Caesar! You're weak, predictable, so much less than I'd thought you'd be. You disappoint me, Michele, just as you must have disappointed our father; a weak, frightened, deceitful soul back then, just as you are now. A victim yet again. You can learn something from me, you truly can. I'll never be a victim again. I'd rather die."

Thoughts flooded through Michael's mind; clashing, colliding, contradicting each other. All lived out in a moment's time that defined everything that had become his life and his fate.

"Choose, Little Brother!" Dracu taunted. "Choose!"

Michael climbed back to his feet, conscious of the tethered tigers snapping at him, ignoring them even though they were dangerously close. He started across the floor toward Dracu, meeting Scarlett's fearful gaze, trying to reassure her as he reached down toward his shirt.

"No, Michael," he saw her mouth in the flickering light of the flames beyond. *"No . . ."*

"I've chosen," he said to Vlad Dracu, anyway.

Michael tore open the buttons on his shirt, exposing the harness Scarlett had given him so he might always wear the relic over his heart. Hesitating no longer, he reached toward the slot tailored to the relic's precise specifications. But it seemed to resist his efforts and it took all Michael's strength to finally pluck it free. Taking the medallion in his grasp, ready to give it to his half brother.

Before he could hand it over, though, Scarlett reached up with a single hand and dug her nails deep into Vlad's face, raking downward across his cheek and splitting his paper-thin flesh in four neat lines.

Dracu's hands lurched upward in reflex and pain, Scarlett released from his grasp in the process. She dropped, clawing for the rail but missing and just managing to latch a single hand onto the ledge to which the rail was fastened. Michael rushed to her, slamming an elbow into the face of a still shocked Vlad and then hurling him to the floor, pocketing his medallion in the process.

Michael pressed his torso against the railing with hand stretched over the steel, reaching down toward Scarlett who was groping desperately for the ledge with her free hand to join the other there. But the wind this high up had caught her, shifting her legs about and keeping her from finding a second handhold.

Michael canted his own body over as far as it would go, fingers dangling just short of her. "Reach up! Take my hand!"

Her free hand clutched at the air above her, flailing for purchase. "I . . . can't."

"You can! Trust me!"

She continued struggling to lift her second hand, the one in place on the ledge starting to slip.

"It's over, my brother," Michael heard from behind him.

He stole a glance that way, saw Vlad rising from the floor not far from where Michael had smashed his phone to pieces. His half brother raised his pistol in a trembling hand, as blood dripped from the four neat gashes forged down his cheek all the way to the floor.

"Help me!" Michael said to him. "I'll give you anything you want, *everything*, just help me!"

"I already did, Little Brother, years ago when I birthed the Tyrant in you. But it wasn't enough, so I win," Vlad said, with surprising calm. "You don't have to give me anything. It's already mine."

Spoken an instant before the largest of the tigers pounced on him from behind. Having somehow broken free of its

tether, it took Vlad down with claws and teeth already digging in, spraying a thick curtain of blood into the air.

Michael turned away, back toward Scarlett. Starting to
lower his body over the rail, risking his balance to expand
his reach to her. Hearing that rail creak and then feeling the
concrete mounts start to give under the additional strain of
his weight, as he started to lower a second hand to join the
first, until his shoulder balked at the effort and he gasped
in pain.

"No, Michael, don't!"

"I'm nothing without you!"

"You'll die!"

"I won't. Just grab my hand!"

Her eyes fastened on his, the life draining out of them,
as he felt himself almost slipping with his hand still out-
stretched, nearly to her.

"Take my hand!"

"I can't!"

"You can!"

Scarlett gritted her teeth and finally got her free hand
stretching up in line with Michael's. Grazing his fingers
when she slipped just enough to make him lurch farther
downward to grab hold of her hand in a quivery grasp.

"I've got you, I've got you, goddamnit!"

But his final lunge had been too much for the railing to
take. The first of the rivets bolting it to the concrete burst
free with the force of gunshots, further weakening the rail
that was now wobbling under his weight.

"I've got you, baby," he still said. "Just hang on tight and
give me your second hand. Come on, you can do it."

Scarlett looked up, her legs swaying in the wind beneath
her. "Michael . . ." Spoken on an empty wisp of air that
barely reached him, as she watched the rail start to cant over
the edge just moments away from tearing free altogether.

"We can do this!" Michael insisted.

"We'll both die."

"No! I can do this, I can save you! You've got to let me save you!"

"No, Michael," she said, tears rolling down her cheeks now.

"Give me your other hand!"

"I can't."

"You can!"

"I won't, I won't let both of us die. Let go, Michael. Please."

"No!"

"Let go. For both of us."

"Give me your hand or I'll come down there and get it!"

Scarlett looked up at him, their stares meeting as she eased her first hand from the ledge. Her expression the emptiest of any he'd ever seen when she pulled her second hand from his grasp.

The moment froze in Michael's mind, seen hazily through a dreamlike cloud, a sight too horrible to bear. Scarlett seemed to hang in the air for a brief moment, their gazes meeting and holding again, before the night swallowed her and her shrinking shape dropped into the flame splattered night below.

After pulling himself back up over the teetering rail, Michael didn't turn away from the sight below, not right away. He continued to stare downward, as if hoping Scarlett might magically reappear. What just happened wasn't real, *couldn't* be real, any more than the memories of the massacre of his family at his half brother's hands all those years ago.

Michael finally backed off, still reluctant to turn away as if that would acknowledge the awful reality he refused to accept. The stairwell door burst open ahead of a flood of

Seven Sins security personnel and animal handlers armed with tranquilizer guns they fired in a continuous stream at the still tethered tigers. The big one who'd broken loose, now soaked in Vladimir Dracu's blood, charged them and was met by a fusillade of actual bullets fired by the security guards.

After the animal was down, they rushed toward Michael with guns still drawn.

"Mr. Tiranno?"

Michael continued to gaze out into the night, toward nothing.

"It's okay, Mr. Tiranno," the guard said, stretching a tentative hand out to take Michael's shoulder, while other guards tended to Vlad. "We've got everything under control. It's over."

Michael winced and finally turned from the night. "No, it isn't."

PART SEVEN

AFTER

Without victory there is no survival.

Winston Churchill

ONE HUNDRED THIRTEEN

INDIANA

Michael stood in the back of the cortege, the mourners crowded around Scarlett Swan's grave site beneath a sea of black umbrellas to shield them from the drizzle of rain. Michael stood in the open, well back, not even feeling the drops soak his hair and clothes. Alexander had left him to himself, lurking somewhere close, but out of sight to provide the space Michael needed.

It was my fault.

He didn't shirk from his responsibility, mourning not just Scarlett but the fact that he'd failed to heed her warning their final time together.

"We're tempting it, I'm tempting it by being close to you. There's no place for me in this, no place for anything that comes between you and that relic. That's why it must be worn against the skin, close to the heart."

So she'd made him the harness and now he would indeed think of her every time it held the relic safely in place, as it was now. Michael had promised to keep her safe, too, to protect her, to make sure nothing ever came between them. And now he had failed, lied, and Scarlett had paid the ultimate price for that. He should have listened to her warning and sent her away, to someplace safe far away from him. Her suspicions and fears had been proven right, but they'd been spoken with a kind of grim acceptance, as if Scarlett knew there was nothing Michael could've done to change anything.

Because of fate, the fate he was destined to fulfill.

Michael felt the outline of the relic's gold beneath his shirt. He loved and hated it at the same time. Loved it for the destiny he now understood and accepted, hated it for the price that destiny had brought with it.

At the grave site, Michael heard the priest reading from the Bible, something about finding meaning and purpose in death. That's what he needed to do here to make Scarlett's death mean something. Not just to ease his own guilt, but to justify her faith in him and do everything he could to make a difference in the world.

"Haven't I saved your life twice already?"

But he couldn't save it a third time, any more than his father could return to his first true love in Romania. He was the Tyrant now and forever, a tyrant for good. His vast resources and power all focused toward the singular purpose of honoring Scarlett's memory and sacrifice. And no one would, or could, stop him. Not Vladimir Dracu, Max Price, or anyone else. Because he was the Tyrant, reborn into something entirely different than conjured by his dreams or his nightmares.

"One might say being a knight in Armani armor is bad for business," Naomi had said to him barely a week ago, that felt more like a lifetime.

And so that was what he would be. A Tyrant Knight.

"Michael," he thought he heard Scarlett call, expecting to see her when he twisted around.

But no one was there.

"Mr. Tiranno?"

Michael swung back, not realizing the funeral service had ended, the participants scattering across the cemetery lawn. A middle-age couple stood before him holding hands, their eyes red with too many tears already shed.

"We're Scarlett's parents," the woman said, squeezing her husband's hand tighter. "She told us so much about you. She loved you very much."

Michael swallowed hard, nodded. "Thank you," was all he could say.

Scarlett's father reached inside his suit pocket and came out with a Seven Sins stationery envelope. "She said if . . . anything ever happened to her to give you this."

Michael reached out to take it, for a brief moment holding the envelope in unison before Scarlett's father let it go.

"I'm glad we got this chance to meet," Michael told them both. "I loved her, too. Very much."

Michael waited until he was back in the car with Alexander to open the letter. It had started to rain harder and drops dappled the windshield, quickly closing off sight of the outside world as Michael unfolded the page of Seven Sins stationery contained in the envelope.

Michael:
If you're reading this, it means something bad has
happened. I know what you must be feeling, but
always remember what we both know about fate now.
You should feel no guilt or sadness, at least not for
long, because whatever's happened was as inevitable
as you coming to possess the relic to begin with. And
that's what this note is about, to share something I
never knew how to say before. But it's something you
need to know, no matter how hard it may be to
believe. The molecular chemists who analyzed the
relic weren't just unable to establish its chronological

origins, they found something that makes no sense . . .
or too much. They found something organic, *Michael.*
Your relic is alive.

She signed it "Love always," Michael reading that final salutation while grasping the medallion beneath his shirt, as the tears began spilling from his eyes.

ONE HUNDRED FOURTEEN

SARDINIA

Aldridge Sterling returned to his yacht aboard the launch. He'd spent most of the day making arrangements meant to forever erase his connection to Black Scorpion. Vladimir Dracu was reportedly dead, Black Scorpion's cells being eradicated across the globe.

Everything going according to plan.

Sterling shorting the U.S. dollar hadn't paid off, but the profits he'd made in gaming stocks that had plummeted after the explosions throughout Las Vegas more than made up for it. But even that told only part of the story, a small part. The strategic fall of Black Scorpion's forces across the world had left him with a vast sum of invested capital, distributed among hundreds of offshore accounts, he no longer had to share or account for. A multibillion dollar fortune that was now his free and clear, and with no record for the authorities to trace.

Also according to plan.

Climbing back upon the *Big Whale*, Sterling found himself exhausted and craved no more than a scotch followed by a long, restful sleep next to the green-eyed beauty, his final link to Black Scorpion. He'd have to get rid of her, unfortunately, a small price to pay given the rewards he was reaping.

Too tired to notice his guards were nowhere in evidence, Sterling entered his stateroom to find the girl sitting up on the bed to which he'd left her tied when he departed that morning. But she was no longer bound to the headboard and someone had placed his father's wheelchair at the foot of the bed. The old man's eyes were fixed emptily forward as always—not aimed at him, Sterling thought, aimed . . . somewhere else, toward a darkened corner of the stateroom toward which Sterling turned as well.

"Nice to finally meet you, Aldridge," greeted Michael Tiranno.

Sterling twisted around to look for his guards.

"Don't bother. They're currently unavailable," Michael told him.

Sterling saw the pistol Michael was holding by his side. "You come here to kill me?"

"That depends on whether you're in a cooperative mood or not," he said, raising the gun. "This is just to keep you from doing something else stupid. I'm here to get your signature on a piece of paper," Michael continued, removing it from his pocket and flipping the page open. "To officially transfer all Tyrant Global's bonds held by Sterling Capital Partners to an entity in the Caymans called Legion Seven Investments. We created paper that justifies the transfer as payment of debt your company had off the books. I'm sure this won't pose any problem, given the thousands of offshore accounts you control and that rogue client list you maintain worldwide."

"Have you lost your fucking mind?" Sterling said, stopping

just short of a laugh at Michael's demands. "Because you're asking me to give you seven hundred and fifty million dollars."

"A great deal, if it keeps you alive."

Michael walked over and extended the document to Sterling, who snatched it from his grasp angrily.

"And what if I don't sign?"

"You will."

"What, you think I'm a wimp, that I'm gonna let the first asshole with a gun steal money I worked my ass off to make? Thing is, you don't scare me the way you scare everybody else. Fucking tyrant," Sterling added, shaking his head with disdain. "You think I'm another Max Price? He was small-time, just like you."

"I have a secret to share with you, Aldridge."

"Hey, if you want to threaten me with exposure, go ahead. You won't find a paper trail linking me to a single illicit dealing, not a one."

"Well, the United States government officials behind the takedown of Black Scorpion's cells across the world might beg to differ. I think they'd be very interested to hear all about your connection to the organization, how the richest man in America truly built his fortune. But this particular secret concerns someone else," Michael said, aiming his gaze at the wheelchair-bound form of Harold Sterling. Then he looked toward the girl he'd untied on the bed. "Alexander's waiting for you on deck."

Terrified, she covered her naked form with a sheet and shuffled past him from the stateroom.

"There's something you need to see," Michael resumed to Sterling once she was gone, extracting a photograph from his pocket.

Sterling snatched it from his grasp, regarding it diffidently. "A picture of my father from twenty years ago, the day he retired from the United States Senate. So what?"

"Actually, it's not."

"Not what?"

"Harold Sterling. It's a picture of another man, the man your father really is. A man named Hans Wolff, one of the most notorious Nazis ever."

"Flip it over," Michael instructed, and Sterling did to find a black-and-white photograph on the back. "That's Wolff as a young man when he was a captain in the SS. My people had it aged to see what might have become of him after he disappeared. Imagine my surprise."

The picture Naomi had received during the Gaming Control Board Hearing slipped from Sterling's hand and fluttered to the stateroom floor. He opened his mouth to speak, but no words emerged, so Michael moved to the inert figure of his father and crouched to look the old man in the eyes.

"I have something for you, too," Michael said to Harold Sterling, sliding the SS ring he'd also recovered from his father's footlocker onto the old man's finger. "For old times' sake."

The ring flopped in place, just skeletal bone remaining where there had once been thick flesh.

"Want to hear a story, Aldridge?" Michael continued. "My father and yours had their own run-in back in the late fifties in Romania. My father was there in the guise of a Jew named Davide Schapira, was in the business of making assholes pay then . . ." Michael stopped, eyes boring into Sterling. ". . . just like I am now."

Sterling swallowed hard, his gaze drifting toward the man in the wheelchair again.

"Your father stole the identity of one of the many Jews he murdered in the camps he operated for the SS. The fortune he brought with him to America came from money and jewelry those Jews tried to buy their lives with. He was a monster, just like you and Dracu, only a different kind. And he still has the scar my father noted in his journal," Michael said, pointing to the small, jagged piece of mottled flesh just to the right of the old man's chin.

Aldridge Sterling remained silent, staring at his father as if seeing him for the first time.

"Either you sign that document," Michael continued, as he stood back upright, "or the world finds out the truth about your father and family name. I imagine Jewish and German authorities will take whatever measures they need to freeze your assets until an investigation as to their original source is conducted."

"My father disowned me, Tiranno," Sterling blurted out. "That's public knowledge."

"Then I'm sure you'll be able to prove it. Last investigation like this took six years to complete. And what do you think the Israelis might do? They believe in fruit of the poisoned tree, Aldridge. That means they take you down, too, and they're not nearly as pleasant to deal with as I am."

Sterling stood there, seeming to study him. "Vladimir Dracu was right about you. I guess I shouldn't be surprised you were the one who finally took Black Scorpion down. I tried to tell him to give it up, to let his obsession with you and that relic of yours go."

"You mean this?" Michael said, reaching under his shirt to pry the medallion free of the harness Scarlett had given him and holding it up for Sterling to see. "I guess you could say more of Vladimir Dracu got bitten off than he could chew."

In that moment, Harold Sterling's empty eyes sprang suddenly to life at the sight of the relic. His mouth opened in a gasp, a trembling hand reaching out for it.

"What?" Sterling drawled from across the room, his voice

barely audible, shocked by his father showing any life at all, never mind this much.

Michael looked down at the old man groping for his relic with still widening eyes and felt a chill slide up his spine. Remembering tales of how Hans Wolff had been searching for mystical artifacts in Romania, remembering tales of a powerful American who hired modern-day pirates to retrieve the same relic from his father years later.

Hans Wolff . . . Harold Sterling . . .

"It was *you*," Michael said, in shock out loud to the father, shaking his head through the chill that had overtaken him. "You're the one, you got my family killed. It all makes sense now. . . ." Then, to the son as his shock slowly ebbed, "Your father wanted my relic, first as Hans Wolff and later as Harold Sterling. But he didn't get it either of those times and he's not going to get it now."

Sterling opened his mouth to speak but no words emerged from him either.

Michael looked back down at his father. "You never realized Davide Schapira and Vito Nunziato were the same man, did you?" He replaced the relic over his heart and raised his pistol again. "Sign the document, Aldridge, or I may forget I'm just an entrepreneur."

Sterling moved behind his desk, reading the page quickly before scrawling his signature at the bottom and tossing it into the air. It fluttered briefly, then settled on the floor between them. Michael scooped it up and stuck it back in his pocket.

"You wanted to invest in my companies, Aldridge. Well, at least you got your wish. And you got off cheap," Michael said, looking from son to father. "Just like him."

"You call that cheap?"

"Until he gets to hell, you bet I do. This ends here, as far as you and I are concerned."

Michael started for the door, wishing Sterling would pull a gun, a knife—anything.

Instead he resumed speaking. "How do I know that? How do I know I can trust you?"

"We both know the answer to that," Michael told him. "I'm sure Vladimir Dracu told you the truth about me, too. We both have our secrets to bare, secrets that can destroy us. But I'm out of debt, thanks to you, and you've got all of Black Scorpion's money, thanks to me." Now it was Michael who smiled. "Not a bad deal, all things considered."

Michael stepped off the launch back onto a dock at Porto Cervo. He walked before Alexander up toward the pier where music emanated from a dockside bar filled with a smattering of high-end patrons that included a young woman and older man seated next to each other at the bar, hardly an unusual sight.

He never looked toward Raven Khan nor Ismael Saltuk, just kept walking when the huge blast sounded a half-mile offshore. Patrons lurched to their feet in disbelief, drenched briefly in the orange glow of a yacht exploding, as Michael continued on.

ONE HUNDRED FIFTEEN

VADJA, ROMANIA

Michael led the girl along the dirt road from the spot where he'd parked his rented Land Rover. It was late afternoon and, thanks to Raven Khan, children played about nearby and in the distance without fear. Halfway to the police post that was manned again, a couple with two younger children in tow rushed out to greet the missing daughter they'd feared was gone forever when she didn't return with the rest.

"What if they come back?" the girl's mother asked him, fear lacing her voice and her eyes.

"They won't be coming back, none of them. Ever."

He left the family to themselves and started back toward Alexander and the Land Rover, when the girl caught up and hugged him tightly.

"Thank you," she sobbed, in English. "Thank you for everything."

"I never asked you your name," Michael said, realizing, as he eased her away.

"It's Stefania," she said.

ONE HUNDRED SIXTEEN

LAS VEGAS, NEVADA

Naomi stood across from Michael's desk in his bubble glass office at the bottom of the Daring Sea, pocketing her phone.

"Our chief financial officer has confirmed that as of to-day forty-five percent of the Seven Sins bond debt is now officially held by Legion Seven Investments. Aldridge Sterling's contribution, finally, has been properly allocated."

His and his father's deaths at sea was the subject of a huge investigation by Italian authorities. Initial reports blamed the explosion on a propane leak, but that hardly dissuaded investigators given the number of enemies Sterling had made over the years who had reason to want him dead. Robert Kern, meanwhile, had resigned as chairman of the Gaming Control Board and was the subject of an investigation himself by the Nevada Commission on Ethics, the watchdog of public employees. The manuscript Scarlett had found, and Alexander recovered from Black Scorpion's fortress, meanwhile, was stored in its sealed container inside Michael's personal safe. Eventually, he'd bring someone in who could finish the job she'd started by completing the translation, to find the remaining secrets of his relic's origins. Michael touched his chest, reassured by its presence over his heart.

"What about Vlad?" he asked Naomi.

"He's still in a coma, not expected to recover."

"Don't be so sure about that," Michael warned.

His assistant buzzed him from upstairs. "There's someone here to see you, Mr. Tiranno. He won't give his name, but says he has information you need to hear immediately."

Michael looked toward Alexander. "If he won't give his name . . ."

"He says he's here about Scarlett Swan."

"Send him down," Michael said.

Alexander positioned himself strategically before the elevator leading down from the offices located just off the lobby, jacket unbuttoned to allow for easy draw of his pistol.

"What now?" Naomi muttered, shaking her head.

Michael rose from behind his desk, watching the glass elevator open moments later to reveal a small man with a bad comb-over wearing a rumpled suit. All that was missing was the Mont Blanc pen Michael recalled him twirling on both occasions he'd spotted him in the rear of the Gaming Control Board chamber and then again in Peccato Bar Lounge, just before the explosions set by Black Scorpion had gone off on the Strip.

The man emerged from the elevator with his hands in the air, passing through the reception area and entering Michael's private office.

"Thank you for seeing me, Mr. Tiranno," he greeted, nodding toward Alexander.

"Who the fuck *are* you?" Michael demanded.

"You'll find my identification in my inside jacket pocket. Please excuse me for not wanting to make any sudden moves by reaching for it on my own."

Alexander slid toward the little man and extracted the ID wallet from his pocket. His eyes widened as he regarded it and then passed it across the desk to Michael.

Michael's eyes widened, too. "Is this some kind of joke?"

"Not at all, far from it."

"You said you were here about Scarlett."

"And I am. To help ensure that she didn't die in vain." The man slid his ID back into his pocket. "We've been watching you since your escapades . . ." Here the man's voice tailed off as his gaze hardened slightly. ". . . and your crimes . . . captured our attention, along with that mysterious relic of yours."

"What do you think you know?"

"We know *everything*. You see, we've been following you for quite a while, but decided to wait until the proper time to make contact. That time, I'm afraid, has come."